the
Lost
and
FOUND

ISBN 979-8-9911671-5-4
Cover Design by Jena Brignola

To my dad (I miss you so much), for being my true north and not allowing me to stay lost. And to my husband, William, for being my rock and my best friend, and for being the one who inspired Josiah's hands.

Grief, in all its many forms, is a tortuously beautiful beast, changing one fully from the inside out when permitted to come to fruition.

-E.L. Irwin

Author's Note

D ear Reader,

A little over ten years ago, I wrote the first edition of this story, and it was published by Blue Tulip Publishing. At that time, my dad was dying of cancer. Well, he was being killed by cancer treatment, but that's another matter I won't get into here. Needless to say, he passed away, and I grieved. That was one of the hardest times in my life, more so even than the abuse I experienced as a child. Though I miss him tremendously, I'm at peace now, knowing my Savior carries me. Still, grief was definitely a present part of *this* particular writing journey. As mentioned above, I was an abused child. Both physically and verbally. In addition, over twenty years ago now, I found myself unwed and pregnant, and certain options were presented to me. Options I was unwilling to take, regardless of my fears and uncertainties. Going forward, please know that while this book IS clean (no to low swears and little violence) and closed door (no sexually explicit content), it does address certain topics you *may* find triggering. I do not get graphic, however, the subjects of grief and depression are experienced by the FMC, as is the topic of rape, child abuse, sexual assault, self-defense, and abortion. Regardless, the message I desire above all to convey here is hope. This is a romance, a love story in every sense of the word. And I'd like you to fall in love with it. Because Crimson and Josiah have a story to tell and it's a beautiful one.

Contents

Chapter 1
The End

*C*rimson Sage

Snapping into consciousness, my heart pounded as I tried to ascertain what had awoken me. My younger brother brother, Ethan, muttered under his breath, then continued snoring softly in my ear. With his head resting on my shoulder, his breath lightly fanning my face brought the minty scent of the gum he liked to chew, and I figured this is what had alerted me. In my mind's eye, I saw my best friend Grace as she'd met me that afternoon at the pool. Trying to talk me into going out with her and her boyfriend Tanner and his best friend, Sawyer. I could still smell the chlorine and feel the damp and heat on my skin. Ethan snorted softly, mumbling again, the sound bringing me further awake. Blinking in the dimly lit cabin of the airplane, I tried to remember where I was. How I'd gotten here. Trembling, my brain struggled trying to discern *then* from *now* as one thought chased another.

The events from nearly three weeks ago replayed in my head—a horrifying drama with no end. I fought the tears once more and won, even as the sound of the knock on my front door echoed loudly in my head. I'd been disoriented that night, having fallen asleep on the couch, watching some late-night sitcom, waiting for my parents to come home from their date. Dad had always told me to never answer the door when we were home alone. I'd known where he'd kept his gun, and as I'd sat there on the couch, waiting to see what would happen next, I wondered if I'd need to get it or call the police. I'd been holding the phone in my hand, so when it suddenly rang, I'd nearly dropped it. Hesitantly I'd answered, then the dispatch lady instructed me to open the door for the officers.

My hands shook now as I recalled the kind, pitying looks in their eyes as the uniformed officials told me my parents were dead. Clenching my jaw, I breathed slowly through my nose, even as my eyes pricked.

Too painful. Too soon.

Don't think about this now.

Carefully, so as not to wake my brother, I checked my watch for the time. It was just after three in the morning. We should be landing in Boise in about an hour. Then there was the five-hour drive to the ranch.

It had been a long day. A long few weeks. My body was present, but my mind was somewhere in my past trying to catch up, unsure if I even wanted to. Too much had happened. Too much and too fast. And too painful. I don't know how I was expected to pick up all these broken pieces and live again. I'd have to try, though. For Ethan. He was all I had left.

More emotions than I could possibly handle rampaged through me. Fear; I didn't know what the future held, what I'd do. Pain; I longed for my parents. To hear Dad's sure, strong voice talk me down. For Mom to wrap me in her arms, in a hug only she could give. Anger; I was so angry at the person who'd done this. Who'd torn my entire world apart through one careless and selfish act. Frustration with myself; I was overwhelmed and drowning. It felt like the weight of the world rested squarely on my shoulders. And I wasn't strong enough to lift it.

Right now, I was simply trying to not be decimated by its weight. It was so heavy, though. *I* was so heavy and didn't know how much longer I could hold out. Some unnamed force pushed me onward, telling me I needed to keep trying.

But I didn't know *how*. How did I keep going? How could I survive this? Rebuild this shattered and fractured life? How could I be expected to function when everything about me and my past had shifted and realigned so drastically? How did I *live* when my life was at an end?

I glanced at the man sitting to Ethan's left. He was asleep. His big hands gripped his worn, black Bible—he'd been holding it pretty much since I'd met him three weeks ago. When I'd learned he was my maternal grandfather. Though, I couldn't call him that. No, to me, he was Billy Newell. A man—a family relation—I'd never even known existed. Not until my world had fallen apart.

And now he had custody of Ethan. Being twenty, I was on my own. Still, he'd offered me a place on his ranch, too. And for that I was relieved, I really was.

In addition to processing the deaths of our parents, I'd suddenly found myself faced with the idea of raising Ethan by myself. Both Mom and Dad had been only children. My dad's parents had died when I was young, and Mom's, at least I'd assumed so, had died before I was born. So, when I'd been informed by Social Services that my next-of-kin had been notified, and my maternal grandfather was on his way from Idaho to claim guardianship of my brother, I was both shocked and relieved. Shocked because I'd never even known he'd existed and relieved that I wouldn't have to shoulder this one burden alone. So for Ethan, because of Ethan, I was on this plane, leaving my home, my friends in Virginia to go live on this ranch in some podunk town in Idaho.

Too much.

Too soon.

Too painful.

Billy stirred, turning in my direction, catching my eye. "You all right?" His voice was quiet, gravelly.

A tiny part of me looked for Mom in his features. "Fine." My breath shook, and like a coward, I shut my eyes, turning away, feigning going back to sleep. Somehow, I'd been able to achieve a sense of numbness. If I didn't bother to look too closely, if I kept feelings, thoughts, and emotions locked tightly inside, I found I was able to function to some extent. Not living, but somehow still functioning. This was the best I could do, the most I could hope for right now.

Billy's quiet sigh triggered a tremor of guilt. He'd been everything that was kind and patient with us, with me, since he'd arrived. Whatever his history with Mom had been, he seemed to hold no animosity toward me or Ethan. Mentally, I rolled my shoulders, attempting to ease the guilt, but after a moment or two opened my eyes to apologize. Billy's eyes were now closed. A reprieve.

Eventually I fell asleep but found no rest in it. Nightmares were a constant companion when I couldn't consciously control my thoughts. I was grateful when Ethan shook me awake. Blinking slowly, I sat up and looked around. The lights were on in the cabin and the flight attendants were instructing everyone to prepare for landing.

Billy had hired someone to handle my parents' estate for us. Whatever monies were allotted from insurance payoffs and the sale of the estate would be deposited in special bank accounts for my brother and me. Ethan and I took the things that were dear—the things that held memory and sentiment—and Billy shipped them to his ranch ahead of us. Today we each had a carry-on and one checked bag.

Dully, I wondered how we'd be getting to his ranch, if we would be taking a cab. Seemed like a huge expense if we were. Maybe he'd left a vehicle in the long-term parking.

Approaching the baggage claim, a trickle of awareness broke through my numb shield. Shivers skated over my skin, neither hot, nor cold. It wasn't *fear*, just a sudden sense of awareness. Acute and unwanted. Desperately needing that numbness back, with my pulse thudding loudly in my ears, I let my gaze flicker around, trying to determine the source of my tension. It wasn't a difficult task. He was tall, standing straight, shoulders back, feet firmly planted, arms crossed over a muscled chest. His presence alone seemed a challenge thrown down, like he was daring anyone to be stupid enough to come near. Those around him seemed to pick up on the threat, giving him a wide berth.

This newfound perception seemed to sharpen the closer we drew to him. And we did seem to be moving in his direction. Didn't Billy see the way the others avoided him? Couldn't he tell? Looking at Billy, I saw his gaze was leveled in the man's direction, so maybe he did see. Regardless, we continued towards him. My gaze flickered to the man now, and as our eyes met, awareness slammed into me, going from a trickle to a tidal wave in a heartbeat. Of their own accord, my feet stopped, even as my breath came faster. In high school, we'd watched a documentary about the reintroduction of wolves to Yellowstone. One wolf, the alpha, had been captured in frame. He'd stood tall, breeze lightly lifting his ruff, unconcerned, with such a look of intensity in his gaze as he'd surveyed his domain. The people moving in the baggage claim area skirted this man the same way the pack had deferred to that alpha. Suddenly, as cognizance rolled over me again, panic clawed deep, urging escape as the man studied me with an almost predatory focus. Trembling, I held still, the desire to become invisible and numb again, an almost visceral need.

Despite my body's powerful and unwelcome acknowledgement of him, despite the surge of adrenaline now coursing through my veins, I leveled my gaze to the floor, unwilling to meet his stare a moment longer. Though, from the corner of my eye, I kept him in my sight, noting his short-cropped, dark ginger hair. The tattoos that covered his arms and neck, the piercing in his right eyebrow and both ears. Wary, and nearly short of breath, desperation to be away from his scrutiny gnawed at me like an animal on a bone.

Billy had spoken about the ranch, that it was a group home for troubled boys. A place for them to be safe and reinvent themselves. He'd named it The Lost and Found and had given both Ethan and I an informational pamphlet on it. Emblazoned across the front were the words *Tough Love @ The Lost and Found*. Inside, it talked about the ranch, what its goals and purposes were, that it grew and harvested alfalfa and apples—Ethan had whispered that knowledge to me, as I'd had zero inclination to read up on it. In addition, Billy'd rattled off a list of names that were associated with the ranch, but that had been more than I'd been capable of processing, so retained practically none of it. Though, I did recall he ran it with a couple partners. One of whom was the local sheriff, who was apparently called Red. As I surreptitiously studied the tattooed, dangerous looking man waiting beside the carousel, I figured this *wasn't* Red. My next guess would have been Bentley. At least, I think that was the other name Billy had mentioned. Billy said Bentley was in his late-thirties and was the second partner he had. Bentley worked with the school district, doing both teaching and coaching. Somehow this wasn't how I'd pictured him in my head, but as Billy walked right up to the man and shook his hand, I figured this must be him.

Billy and the tattooed man spoke for a couple minutes, and despite the surge in adrenaline I'd felt earlier, my mind, thankfully, was soon reeling once more in exhaustion. It was a little like being under water, or behind a thick wall of glass; I was aware conversations were taking place —I knew people were talking—but none of it registered. Blissfully, sound had been muted once more, and for that, I was grateful. Like a small child with their security blanket, I pulled that numbness back around me, preparing to settle in once more. Despite that, my mind still registered Ethan shaking hands with the stranger, saying words I didn't catch. Far back in the recesses of my mind, I knew I should be more involved, but my security blanket was fast becoming a weighted blanket, threatening to send me into oblivion on my feet.

As I blinked through my exhaustion, little jolts of electricity shot darts into my body, bringing that sense of awareness once more. The man's gaze, heavy, like a physical touch, kept sending those unwanted shockwaves through me—I needed my body to be just as numb as my mind.

With effort, I kept my eyes on the bags that were now moving slowly on the carousel, doing my best to ignore *him*. Spotting mine and Ethan's bags, I reached for them, but a large, tattooed, and work-hardened hand plucked them up before I could. The dark, ginger-haired man set the bags down, extended the handles, and lifted the carry-on from my shoulder without speaking. He set it on top of my rolling case. *Fine. Whatever.* He wants to carry them that bad, he can have at it—I wouldn't fight him. I didn't have the energy for any of it.

The man led the way out to a newer dark blue four-door pickup. Clicking the remote, he unlocked it, then began loading our luggage into the bed. Billy opened the back passenger door for Ethan and me, then climbed into the front passenger seat, leaving the ginger-haired man to drive—guess Billy was as tired as we were. Ethan climbed inside the cab, sitting directly behind Billy and shut the door behind himself, leaving me to walk around to the driver's side. For a moment, I simply stared at the door and my reflection on the glass, feeling defeated. Gathering whatever dregs of fortitude remained, I moved around to the other side of the pickup.

Exhaustion had taken its toll physically, causing me to stumble over the curb. Before I could right myself, or even process that I was falling, firm, warm hands caught me. They gripped my waist, long fingers nearly wrapping around me, making my breath catch at his nearness. His touch had my eyes snapping up. Dark, vivid blue stared down with gentle intensity, making me shiver.

After a moment, once he'd ascertained I wasn't about to eat the pavement, he stepped back, giving me room. Keeping one hand lightly at my elbow, he opened my door, helped me up into the truck, then closed it gently behind me. His blue eyes caught mine in the rearview once he had the truck on the road and I decided I'd had enough of their piercing, searching quality. Ripping my gaze from his, I stared blindly out my window. Five hours later, I woke as my head bounced against the glass I'd been fogging in my sleep. Somehow, miraculously, I hadn't dreamed at all.

We bumped along a dirt drive, dust pluming behind us. A large, rectangular, two-story ranch house stood in front of us. The truck stopped just to the right of the large wrap-around porch. As my gaze moved over the structure, the screen door opened and an elderly, heavyset woman stepped out. Her concerned gaze traveled over us as she wiped her hands on the white apron she wore—the cook or housekeeper I assumed. Avoiding her stare, I took in the barn set behind the house and the various pieces of farm equipment lying about, when my door opened and *he* was there, hand extended, ready to help me down.

Stupidly, I stared at it for a moment, unsure what to do. He must have thought I was pretty slow, because he reached up and lifted me down. Once again, the heat in his hands penetrated, reaching deeper than I wanted. Before I was able to process his actions and my reaction to them, he was moving towards the bed to gather our luggage. The woman stepped forward, drawing my attention, wrapping me in her embrace. "Oh, my dears. Poor things. C'mon in. I'm Sally; Red's sister; I do the cooking and the laundry here. Red and I live just down the end of the drive there." She nodded in the direction we'd just come from. "I'll show you to your rooms."

Sally led us inside, past a large, open room with an enormous rock fireplace and a couple couches, then up the stairs and to the right. She pointed out a bathroom, Billy's room, and Ethan's room which was right next to Billy's. Mine was at the very end of the hall, up a short flight of stairs. The floors in my room were plywood, the walls bare sheetrock, the ceiling bare wood. An antique-looking four-poster bed stood against the wall, framed on either side by tall windows looking out towards the back of the house. Obviously, my room was still under construction and had been hastily prepared. Boxes were piled inside—the ones we'd sent on ahead.

"I picked out bedding, not sure what your taste was. Just wanted you to have somewhere to lay your head." Sally wrung her hands, seemingly feeling awkward about the state of the room. "Billy wanted you to have your own bathroom and some privacy. Away from the other boys, you see." She pointed to a door off to my right. Stepping inside, I noted a small, tiled shower, a toilet, and a vanity with a single sink. It could have been worse, I supposed, and Billy had had very little time to prepare. I wondered who'd done the work and tried not to think about my bathroom back home, with its large shower and more counter and cabinet space than I'd needed.

"Thanks." My voice was rough from disuse. Exhaling, I nodded then turned away, taking in the green, floral sheets and brown checked quilt. She left me to settle in; said breakfast would be ready in an hour or so. Again, I simply nodded. Ethan squeezed my hand as he left my room, shutting the door behind himself. My gaze moved around the room again, snagging on the window, noting that somehow, the mountains seemed closer, almost looming.

I stared at them, feeling so tiny, so minuscule next to their magnitude. Movement below caught my eye and glancing down I saw our driver from this morning walking towards the barn. The sun caught his ginger hair setting it on fire, and I wondered again what his name was—he didn't seem like a *Bentley* to me. Ginger, I guess I'd call him for now, until I knew. I guessed he was somewhere in his mid-to-late twenties, and watching him, my subconscious became aware of the almost animal quality to his movements. He seemed so assured of himself. Full of confidence. Not arrogance, or ego. Nothing like that; just confidence. I envied him.

My mouth trembled. I didn't have any confidence, being nothing more than a broken shell of who I'd been before. With so much pain inside, I was drowning in it. My head and heart were dark. Stark. Unhealthy. I recognized that but couldn't shift the course I was on. Truth was, I was exhausted, and sometimes I just wanted to let the fatigue take me, let it drag me under, right to the bottom, where I could just let go.

Josiah

Josiah adjusted his grip on the steering wheel and glanced to his right. Billy was asleep, exhaustion evident on his face. Reaching for the mirror, Josiah checked the backseat occupants. The boy, Ethan, was asleep; his head tipped back, mouth slightly ajar. Josiah adjusted the mirror again. Crimson was also asleep. His blue eyes took her in, ghosting lightly over her features. She was beautiful. Fragile. Like even the slightest breeze might shatter her.

Josiah knew pain, was well-familiar with it. And recognized hers, wondering if she was even aware of its depths. She was drowning in it. She wasn't dealing with it, though. Was only hiding from it. Josiah knew from experience that you had to take the good with the bad. Learn to accept both. Crimson would have to face her pain if she ever wanted to truly live again. Aware that sometimes people in pain refused to try, refused to face it, just gave up, letting the despair take them, Josiah decided he wouldn't allow Crimson to do that. He'd watch her, monitor and give her space and time; but if she was still avoiding, still hiding, he knew he'd have to make his move.

Crimson Sage

Standing in the center of my room, thoughts rattled around in my brain as I tried to make sense of them. What I'd thought had been immutable truths in my life, were now turned around. Everything about me was suddenly called into question. For my whole life, my name had been Crimson Sage Smyth. I'm twenty years old and was born in Winchester, Virginia. I'd never looked at my birth certificate before. Mom had always kept those documents. I hadn't needed it yet. I mean, I must have seen it at some point but couldn't recall any occasion.

My mind thrashed within my skull, trying to come to terms with these new truths I was learning. Scattered across my bed were papers. Documents that Billy had given to me that had been kept in a safety deposit box. When he'd gone to close out my parents' accounts at the bank, they were given to him. And he in turn gave them to me.

My birth certificate lists my name as Crimson Sage *New Towne*. New-Towne. Not Smyth. Dad, the man who'd given us the last name Smyth, the man I'd always thought of as *my* dad, was not. At least not by birth. He was my dad in every way except by blood.

Because I had been created in an act of violence.

With those papers strewn across my bed was a letter from my mother, explaining everything. Or, at least attempting to. My vision blurred as I considered her revelation. Approximately twenty-one years ago, Mom had been raped here in Idaho. Her rapist had never been caught. After she'd found out she was pregnant, she'd been counseled to have an abortion, to just have me killed and her nightmare ended. Mom had refused, stating that in rape, her choices had been taken away by someone with more power and strength than she'd been able to fight. She said she couldn't take the choices away from the life growing inside her, believing I was just as much a victim as she had been. Just as she'd had zero choices in her rape, I'd had none in my conception. That was why I'd never known of my grandfather. Her dad, Billy, had encouraged her to have me terminated, to end the pregnancy. When again she refused, he'd advised her to give me up for adoption.

Sharp pain rocketed through me as these thoughts revolved in my head. Walking back to the bed, I climbed up, leaning against the headboard. A large manila envelope, stuffed full, snagged my attention where it lay amid the papers. Inside, it contained letters Mom had written to Ethan and me explaining all the things she'd been unable to speak. It was in reading her letters I'd learned about my creation. Mom wrote that, at first, she'd intended to give me up for adoption. Then, she'd felt me move for the first time. She said she just *knew* then she was meant to keep me. She met Dad when I'd been two months old. They fell in love and never looked back. She said he'd loved me from the first moment he'd held me in his arms. Swallowing the lump that threatened to choke me, I banged the back of my head against the headboard and stifled a groan. This was more than physical pain. It went deeper, dug cruelly beneath the skin, settling into my bones, burning into my soul.

Anger and pain vied for dominance as I tried to sort through it all. Why? *Why* had she never told me any of this? Why had I been left to find out like this? That my entire life and history had been built upon half-truths and assumptions. I had so many questions and there was no one left to answer them. Mom had written the first letter before I was born. She'd written hundreds of them since then and had numbered each one. The first couple were the hardest. My heart was sick and I was so angry I hadn't been able to finish, and there were so many left to go.

Looking at all the letters, blinking through tears I refused to shed, I considered my feelings of weakness. Of fear. I'd never been particularly brave. But I'd never felt this weak, this fragile before either. I hated it but had no idea how to change any of it.

Mom wrote that she'd chosen my name with care, with thought. My name had *meant* something to her. Crimson, for the color of her love for me—she'd been determined to love me, even when everyone else expected her to hate me. Sage, because it soothed her. NewTowne was the last name she'd chosen for us when she'd had her name legally changed. She'd left Idaho, pregnant with me, and moved to Virginia; new state, new name, a new start. All this she'd written in the third letter. My hand shook as I picked it up, my vision blurring again.

I'd never known *any* of this.

My life had been perfect. My parents had been picture perfect—thoughtful, considerate, available. Not push-overs, they were our parents first, friends second. I'd been on the swim team at school, had friends, went on dates. My friends and boyfriends had always been welcomed in my home. My life had been complete. And now it was over.

My perfect world had ended the night the police knocked on our door to tell Ethan and me our parents had died—some woman, texting, had crossed the center line and hit them head-on; they'd died instantly.

What was left of me had died when I read those letters. I was adrift, nothing mooring me, lost in a sea of confusion and pain. I'd simply been pretending for Ethan's sake. Only for Ethan.

My head began to pound; I couldn't think about this any longer. Sliding down, I turned on my side, wrapped my arms around one of the pillows and let the exhaustion I'd been fighting claim me.

When I woke, someone was knocking on my door. "Sage?" Ethan called quietly, hesitantly.

"Come in." I croaked.

Ethan opened the door and stepped inside. His grey eyes sought mine; I read the concern in them. "You all right?"

"Yeah." I tried to infuse some life into my voice but felt I came up short. "Just tired."

"You've been sleeping all day."

I glanced around the room, noticing the difference in the shadows. "Just tired," I said again.

"You want dinner?"

"Not hungry."

"Billy was hoping you'd come down...hang out with us."

"I'll catch you all later. Still...tired; and my head is pounding, Kid." I called him the nickname he'd had since his first birthday. We'd been studying American History in school and had just finished a lesson on the Old West—I'd called him *Kid* after Billy the Kid.

"Okay. I'll tell him."

I nodded, glad he wasn't pushing this. "How about you? You all right?"

"Yeah. Sad; I try not to think about it."

I offered a tired grin. "Me too."

"I miss them," Ethan whispered.

"So do I, Kid."

"Billy's pretty cool, though. He's been showing me pictures of Mom, when *she* was a kid. She looks like you. He's got pictures of us, too. All over the house. Kinda crazy we never knew about him, and he knows so much about us."

"Yeah; it's crazy," I agreed. And because I didn't want to talk about this anymore, said, "I might shower, go back to bed."

"You're not sick?" The Kid sounded anxious now.

"Nah, just...just tired. I'm all right. Promise."

"Okay." He inhaled shakily. "I love you."

"Love you, too."

I waited about five minutes after Ethan left before gathering my bathroom supplies and quickly slipping into the shower. I was back in bed about twenty minutes later. Someone had left a tray of food on the dresser, but I couldn't eat. I rolled away from the door to face the windows, then watched the sun set. And drifted off to sleep.

Chapter 2
Still Breathing

*J*osiah

How quickly things changed. Josiah clearly remembered stepping from the shower that morning a few weeks ago, entirely unaware his whole world was about to take an abrupt and unseen turn. He'd grabbed his towel and had quickly dried off before securing it around his waist. The coffee had called to him; that rich, warm, inviting aroma... That morning, he'd stepped into the main room of his loft apartment, making his way to the kitchen cabinet for a mug, and quickly filling it.

Josiah had carried his coffee to the large window overlooking the mountains, watching as the sun slowly made its way over the treeline. Looking down, he'd spied a buck and three doe as they'd scampered into the trees. Tipping his head back, he'd finished his first cup and contemplated a second. Setting it down, he'd quickly gathered his shorts and jeans, pulling them on before making for the kitchen again. Passing the coffee table, he glimpsed the photo lying there and paused, then had picked it up, his dark blue eyes roving over the platinum blonde.

She was at the beach, standing in surf up to her thighs, splashing water at someone off camera. The sun touched her skin, turning it golden, making her hair almost seem white. She wasn't looking at the camera, but off to her right, sort of over her shoulder. He could tell she was fit, could see the muscle tone. Her frame was slender, almost petite. Her grey and hot pink swimsuit was modestly cut, and she wore some sort of cover up item in a lighter shade of grey. The material had slipped off her shoulder, leaving several enticing inches exposed—it was a lovely shoulder, he'd reflected. She was smiling, laughing really. It was her smile that had first caught Josiah's eye.

There was such happiness on her face that when Josiah had seen the photo on Billy's desk last year, he'd picked it up without hesitation and had simply stared at her. Josiah had felt the warmth trickle through him, quickening his nerves, his muscles, his heart, his head. Her happiness somehow made him happy. Without being aware of it, a smile had begun to tug at the corners of his mouth. When Billy had offered to give it to him, Josiah had been a little surprised, a little unsure. He looked to the older man in question.

"She's my granddaughter, Crimson Sage. You've probably seen her photos around the house."

Of course, Josiah recognized her. Billy had numerous pictures of her and her brother around his big ranch house. Though, he'd never caught her name until now. He held the photo out to Billy, intending to return it. "She's cute; seems nice."

"Keep it," Billy told him, some knowing look flashing in his eyes.

Josiah had taken the photo back to his apartment and set it on his coffee table; not a day had gone by since that he didn't pause for a moment and smile with her.

A sharp knock at his door had brought Josiah out of his reminiscing that morning. He'd set the photo down and walked to his door. Opening it he'd found Kelly, one of the younger boys at the ranch. "Billy needs you! Something's happened," Kelly wheezed as soon as the door had opened. Josiah figured he must have run all the way from the big house. He left the door open and turned to his dresser. "He at the house?"

"Yeah; his office."

Quickly Josiah pulled on a T-shirt, then slid his feet into his boots, not bothering with socks or laces. He'd tried imagining what the emergency was. Had one of the boys gone missing? Was there a fight? Was someone hurt? He'd followed Kelly back down the stairs, then they'd sprinted to the big house, Josiah easily passing the younger boy.

He'd found Billy seated behind his desk, looking as if he'd just slumped there. The older man's face had been pale, his breathing shallow and hitched—he'd held his head in trembling hands. Josiah'd pulled up when he saw him; shock registering in his body. Had Billy had a heart attack? A stroke? Did Josiah need to call an ambulance? He didn't know what he'd do if something happened to the old man.

"Billy?" he'd asked; his voice raw with concern.

Billy had raised his head, looking at Josiah with pain-filled eyes. "She's gone; she's gone," he'd whispered brokenly.

Josiah leaned over the desk, unsure what to do for the older man. "Who's gone, Billy?"

"My Theresa," he'd said through trembling lips. "My Terri is gone. Killed. I got a phone call."

"Your daughter?" Josiah had scrambled to process the information, to know how to best help. "When did you get the phone call? From whom?"

"Just now." Billy had swallowed hard, wiping his eyes. Tried to calm himself. "Got a call from Social Services in Virginia. Terri...and her husband...were both killed in a car accident. About a week ago. They'd had to track me down to notify me."

Josiah instantly thought of Billy's granddaughter, knowing her smile would be shattered now. A part of him broke just at the thought. "What of the kids?" *What of Crimson?* From the first, though Billy seemed to refer to his granddaughter as Sage, Josiah, at least in his mind, had called her Crimson. Liking the uniqueness of the name, the way it formed around his tongue, he wondered at its meaning.

"I need to head out there. Take custody of Ethan. I'll need to bring them here. Sage and Ethan. She'll have nowhere else to go."

"When are you leaving?" He'd breathed a silent sigh of relief. The kids were safe. *She* was alive.

"I need to call and make the arrangements. So much to do. Call Red for me, will ya? Let him know I need to leave. I'll be gone a couple weeks, I'm sure. Can you hold things down here?"

"You know I can."

Billy had nodded, agreeing. "The upper room. I'll leave you my card, get whatever you need. I think Sage'll have to move in there. There's just nowhere else to put a girl here. It doesn't have to be perfect, just make sure it's livable and secure. Maybe Ethan can bunk with me until I can figure out what to do with him."

"How old is he?" Josiah couldn't remember.

"Fifteen."

"Bunk him with Kelly. He's the best of them. It'll be tight in that room, but they'll get along fine."

"That'll work," Billy nodded numbly.

Billy had left the following morning, and Josiah had worked tirelessly getting the room ready. Billy had planned to turn the large open area into a game room eventually but simply hadn't gotten around to it in the last couple of years. They'd worked on it here and there, getting the plumbing for the small bathroom done, installing the toilet and the sink, laying the plywood down, getting the sheetrock up. Lately it had been used for storage. Josiah cleaned everything out, installed a shower, finished the wiring, and got everything nailed off. He'd found an old four-poster bed at an antique and used furniture dealer in town. Later they'd paint and install flooring, but for now it'd have to work.

Almost two weeks to the day, Josiah got the message from Billy letting him know when to expect them, what flight they'd be coming in on. Billy described Crimson as broken and distant. Ethan seemed lost and a little scared, but had warmed to him, accepting him fairly easily. Billy wasn't sure what he was going to do about Crimson. She just seemed shattered and entirely closed off.

Crimson Sage

I'd been here at The Lost and Found ranch for four days—most of which I'd spent in my room, away from everyone. Both Billy and Ethan seemed determined to want to talk about everything that had happened. Each time I'd tried to venture from my room they were there. Asking how I was doing. If I needed to talk. Like talking somehow made it all better. I couldn't talk. Not yet. I wasn't ready. I was still trying to process feelings and fears. There was no way I could put any of that into words yet.

The morning after I'd arrived, I'd gone downstairs in search of coffee and food. My face was everywhere. Ethan hadn't exaggerated. Billy did have lots of pictures of us all over the house. It was disconcerting at the very least, uncomfortable at best.

Following the smell of coffee and the soft rumble of voices, I'd entered the kitchen. And immediately regretted my decision. A hush fell over the room. Glancing up, I'd noticed every eye had turned towards me. Sally was beside the sink, scrubbing out a pan; she'd smiled warmly in my direction. Billy sat at the head of the table; a welcoming smile spreading across his face. Ethan grinned encouragingly and nodded towards the coffee pot. *Ginger* stood by a door leading directly outside. *He* didn't smile. His gaze was the strongest however, the one that affected me the most. The one that kept messing with my ability to remain numb. Sparking something unwanted inside me.

Heat flooded my cheeks from all the attention, from *his* attention. Then Sally wrapped her thick arm around my shoulder, gently squeezing. "You hungry, dear?"

"Coffee. Please," I whispered, keeping my eyes on the floor as I stepped out of her embrace, moving to the coffee pot. Only problem? I had to pass *Ginger* to get there. Doing my best to ignore the tremor that rolled through me, the eyes that were still on me, feigning indifference, I lifted the pot, then stopped.

I needed a cup and didn't know where to look for one.

Dang it.

For a moment I considered just setting the pot back down and quickly leaving the room. Before I could put that plan into motion a mug appeared in front of me. I recognized the tats on *his* muscular forearms. "Thank you," I managed quietly.

"Mmhm," he replied just as softly, then turned away from me and spoke louder. "You guys need to get moving; your bus will be here in ten minutes."

For an instant longer, the room was silent, then sound erupted as chairs were pushed back, shoes stomped, dishes clattered, and the back door slammed. I stayed motionless until the room was cleared, then slowly, carefully poured the coffee and turned around. Only Billy, Sally and Ethan remained.

"Ethan will start school next week. Figured there's no sense in him starting now; it'll give him some time to adjust." Billy explained, I think just trying to make conversation.

"Okay."

"Sit down; you didn't eat at all yesterday—can't have you wasting away." Sally slid a plate of eggs and bacon over to an empty chair across from Ethan. I ate in silence, keeping my eyes down.

"I know things are going to take some getting used to...just know I'm always here to talk...if you need to," Billy stated kindly. It *was* kind, what he said; I just wasn't ready to talk yet. Standing, I carried my plate to the sink, "I'm still tired," I whispered. "I'll see you later."

Escaping back to my room, I closed the door firmly behind me. Connecting to Billy seemed impossible. He may have been my mom's dad, but he was a stranger to me. And he may know a lot about *me*, but I didn't know *anything* about him. I was uncomfortable, I wasn't *ready*. And to be honest I had no idea *when* I'd be ready.

I chose a book from several I'd packed and sat in the padded rocking chair by the window. Pulling the curtains back, I looked out, noticing a glimmer in the distance, behind the barn, and figured it was a pond or lake of some kind. I heard a door slam, then saw Ethan run across the yard, two dogs running with him. He headed for a large pine tree with a tire swing. One of the dogs brought him a ball and he spent some time throwing it for them. He did normal things. Kid things, and I was grateful.

The sun made slow progress across the floor and the walls. I lay on my back now, staring up at the wooden beams above me, the book forgotten in my lap. I'd tried reading to keep my mind occupied, but the story had been unable to claim my full attention. I felt like I was standing in raging waters at the top of a waterfall. The current so strong, I couldn't move away from it. I was unable to halt time and stay still. Forces beyond my control were moving me forward against my will; in vain I kept trying to at least slow my progress, but the edge continued to move ever closer.

Frustration had me jumping up, pacing my room. I walked from the windows overlooking the front of the house, to the ones facing west where I could see the barn, to the ones looking towards the back of the ranch, where I could see the body of water I'd spotted earlier.

Occasionally, I'd catch a glimpse of *Ginger* as he moved around the ranch, working with a horse, talking to Ethan, moving hay. Once or twice, he'd glance toward my window.

That was how I'd spent the first four days here at The Lost and Found. I'd sneak out for something to eat or drink, but otherwise I'd avoided leaving my room, avoided contact with those living here—avoided *him*. I hated my self-imposed cage, but it was necessary. I didn't want to deal with Billy right now; he just wanted to talk about the past. Ethan just wanted to talk about Billy.

I'd finally caught *Ginger's* name yesterday—Josiah, not Bentley. I'd heard some of the boys talking to him and thought Josiah suited him so much better than *Ginger* had. *Josiah* was tougher. Stronger. I avoided him the most. He bothered me. Always looking, watching me. His constant attention got under my skin, sparking things I'd prefer were left dormant.

When Ethan and I had been packing our things, back home in Virginia, I'd come across an unopened bottle of Vodka and one of red wine in the back of the pantry. In a spur of the moment decision, I'd secretly packed them carefully in my things that were being shipped to Idaho. My second night here, I'd opened one—the Vodka. My tongue swirled the clear liquid in my mouth, feeling its smooth texture, savoring it. Not having a cup, I'd sipped straight from the bottle, tipping it back about three times before I'd begun to feel its effects. It was my first taste of hard liquor and though it had a gentle bite and basically no flavor to speak of, I found it gave me a blessedly numb feeling that granted sleep.

I'd been considering sneaking out at night to see what exactly that body of water was—I missed the water, missed swimming. And I needed to do something. Continuing to drink my pain away was not healthy. A distant, deeply buried part of me was thankful I was at least able to grasp that concept. Problem was, I didn't feel I had any other options. I took special care to make sure I didn't smell of alcohol when I left my room, but I was always on edge, worried someone might pick up on it.

Once or twice, I'd done crunches and pushups; trying to work myself into an exhausted state like I used to get from swimming, but it wasn't the same. Not at all. This morning, I hoped after the boys left for school, Josiah might take himself off somewhere and I'd be able to make my escape. At least for an hour or so. If I didn't get out and *do* something, work off some of this nervous energy, find oblivion from the constant turmoil of my thoughts, I'd end up drinking the entire bottle dry and maybe even open the other one as well.

As I stood at the window, watching the boys finish up chores before leaving for school, I heard steps outside my door. Tensing, I waited for whoever it was to knock, or call out, preparing to rebuff them.

The person didn't knock, however. No, he just opened the door and walked right in.

My head whipped around, furious words dying on my lips as I took Josiah in. He had a commanding presence that I both noticed and resented. And I noted he was tall, taller than Billy, taller than I'd remembered. And well-muscled. His skin was tanned, darker than I'd ever seen on a red-head. Above his deep blue eyes sat thick brows; the right one was pierced with a small, dark metal hoop.

His gaze was trained right on me, pinning me to the spot. My breath hitched a little in my throat. "Crimson." His voice was even, smooth, like water. "It's time you left your room. Are you walking or will I be carrying you?" As soft and soothing as his voice was, there was a firmness there as well.

"My name is Sage, and *you* can get out." Years ago, I'd decided to go by my middle name, as my first tended to require an explanation, or invite comment. Hearing his voice pronounce it, however, sent a warm tremor through me, riling me further. "Now."

"Carrying you is fine by me, Crimson." The firmness had hardened.

"It's *Sage*, and don't you lay a hand on me." I crossed my arms, intent on looking fierce and intimidating. Josiah must not have noticed because without hesitation, he stepped toe to toe with me. Strong hands gripped, then lifted and tossed me over his shoulder. Before I was completely aware of what was happening, I was being carried down the stairs and out the back door, past the curious stares and open mouths of the ranch boys, my brother, and Billy.

Once the shock of his actions wore off, I battled him in earnest. My attempts were useless. Literally *useless*. He was immovable. Unyielding. Inflexible. My will matched his, but his strength far exceeded mine. Suddenly, I found myself flying through the air, then cold water rushed over me, shocking me into absolute awareness. Spluttering in rage, I broke the surface of the pond—it was a pond and deeper than I'd expected. Josiah silently watched from the shore. His head cocked to the side as his hands fisted, coming to rest at his hips. "Billy said you were a swimmer, I guess he was right." His voice was steady, calm.

Words, rational thought, were beyond me. I was furious, far beyond furious, so simply screamed my frustration at him. The sound ripped from my throat was that of a wild, wounded animal. I screamed until I had nothing left and my fury turned to tears. Tears choked, becoming sobs that wracked my body. Exhausted, I moved sluggishly through the water, unfettered emotion still shaking me. Finding purchase in the mud, I clawed and crawled, dragging myself along. By the time I reached dry ground I was trembling from sheer fatigue. Entirely drained, raw, and parched. Like every single part of me had been spilled out and I was an empty husk. Face down I dropped, my arms simply giving out.

After a moment, Josiah sat beside me. He waited quietly for a few minutes, allowing me to get my breath back.

"Well." His voice carried a rough edge, and yet, somehow was still gentle. "Now you know you're alive. You can learn to get back on your feet, learn to live again, or...just crawl back into the water and end it all. Choice is yours."

I hated him for saying that. *How dare he?* I hated that I had to make a choice. I hated that my parents were gone, and no one had given me the choice to keep them. Josiah got to his feet. His big, warm hand settled lightly on my head, the touch at once both comforting and fleeting. Letting me know he was there and I wasn't alone. And then he walked away without a backward glance. Panic snarled inside me at his sudden absence, then anger came, cold as ice, at his leaving, just like *they* had left and I rolled my head to the side, away from him. The sun reflected off the water, and part of me wanted to crawl back to it, let life be over, let the pain be over. Yet, a part of me wanted to live, needed to live; I simply didn't know how. I didn't know how to put the jagged pieces of me back together again—I was worse than Humpty Dumpty.

Vaguely, I heard raised and heated voices. Ethan was trying to come to me; Josiah kept him away. "She needs to do this on her own, now. Let her be, Ethan. You can't live for her," he told my brother. The voices faded away. I closed my eyes and just felt the sun. Discovered its warmth and let myself rest in it. I'm not sure how long I lay there. An hour? Two? Longer? Suddenly a flash of heat shot through me, melting the ice; I wanted to live, to prove to Josiah I could.

So, I did.

I got up. On shaking limbs, I stumbled to the house, ignoring the look from my brother as I made my way to my room. There, I grabbed a clean change of clothes and showered. Washing the mud and grime away. My numbness had been shattered in that pond. I wasn't sure what remained, but curiously, I felt a spark and wondered at it. Afterwards, I found Josiah behind the barn, unloading hay. I watched him for a moment, figuring out the rhythm in his activity, his purpose, then without a word, climbed onto the trailer and began unloading hay alongside him. He never said anything to me. Simply worked and sweated beside him.

Josiah

Josiah had begun to worry about Crimson, wondering how far down the hole of pain and depression she'd fallen when he hadn't seen her outside her room for several days. Every so often as he worked around the ranch, he'd glance up at her window, hoping for at least a glimpse of her. He'd seen her a couple times, standing there, looking down at the life taking place all around her. She'd seemed more ghost-like than human, so still and pale.

Crimson had come downstairs the morning after they'd arrived looking lost, frightened, and ready to crumble. All eyes had turned towards her, making her noticeably uncomfortable. Josiah had watched as she'd hesitated on the threshold, uncertain, until Ethan had caught her eye and indicated the coffee pot. Josiah had studied her as she carefully moved around the table, then past him. Maybe it was selfish, but he'd willed her to look at him, to acknowledge him, but she'd kept her eyes glued to the floor. He'd simply needed to know she was going to be all right.

Then she'd needed the mug for her coffee and hadn't known where to look for one. Josiah came to her rescue, handing her one before her discomfort increased. He'd seen the slight slump in her shoulders as the silence in the room behind her had lengthened, seen the relief and the lessening of the tension as the boys quickly, noisily filed out of the room. He'd followed them to make sure they all got to the bus. By the time he'd returned, she'd escaped back to her room.

Crimson's eyes bothered him. The brown color was as beautiful as always, but now they were haunted, pained; the warmth had gone out of them. Shadows stained the skin beneath them, indicating stress and a lack of sleep. Billy told him she hadn't responded to any of his efforts to reach out to her. Billy had also told him about Crimson's and her mother's pasts. Josiah could see it in her eyes—she felt like she was dead inside. She wanted to simply escape the pain. But Josiah knew from experience that you couldn't deny pain and still welcome life. You had to take both together, face both together. He decided to give her one more day. If she hadn't come downstairs by tomorrow morning he was going up after her.

Josiah stood now at the back door, staring through the screen, in the direction of the pond. He'd been standing there for nearly three hours. Crimson was still on the ground; she hadn't moved from where she'd dropped earlier. He'd second-guessed himself about every ten minutes. Torn between his desire to comfort and protect her and knowing she needed to make this decision on her own—he couldn't make it for her.

Josiah had had to force himself to stay put, willing Crimson to get up. Willing her to fight. He'd almost lost his resolve when he'd arrived at her room this morning. Almost. He'd seen her pain, seen how filled with anger and anguish she was. But he'd seen something else, too. A spark, a flare. She'd attempted to stand up to him. There weren't very many people, even grown men, tough men, who'd have had the guts to do that. It was that spark, that fire that moved him, made him solidify his intentions and see them through.

Several times now Billy had come into the kitchen, opened his mouth as if to speak, only to close it again, sigh and shake his head, before walking back out. Ethan, Josiah knew, was seated behind him at the table; waiting to see what would happen. Josiah knew he was walking on thin ice with Billy, but so far, the old man hadn't snapped. So far, he'd been willing to let Josiah see this through, seemed willing to wait and see what happened.

Movement near the pond caught his attention. Josiah straightened, narrowing his gaze. He watched as Crimson got to her feet. She faced the pond for a moment or two, and Josiah tensed, ready to spring into action. When she turned and began walking toward the house, he let out a relieved breath he hadn't even been aware he'd been holding. He watched her a couple seconds longer, then turned around; Ethan caught his eye and Josiah nodded. Not wanting her to know he'd been watching, Josiah headed out the front and made his way to the barn. Crimson had chosen to fight—she'd chosen life.

Crimson Sage

We worked for the rest of the day, unloading the trailer and restacking the hay in the barn, feeding the animals. When we heard voices, the other, older boys coming home from school, he placed the broom on the hook, and said, "We'll call it a day now."

Josiah held the barn door and waited for me to place my broom beside his. I hadn't realized I'd been so out of breath, had become so out of shape, but in the silence, my panting became painfully obvious. My muscles quivered like Jello as I fought to remain upright. Dusting my clothes off, which was a useless endeavor considering how wet they were with perspiration, I shuffled past him, avoiding his gaze. Daring him to comment, yet fearful he would in the same breath. Feeling as if one word from him might bowl me over.

Not looking back, I didn't stop until I was in my room. My bed sat there, tempting me to rest. Instead, I ignored it long enough to grab another change of clothes and shower. After I was clean again, I collapsed on top of my bed and was asleep before I knew it. For the first time in weeks I slept without dreams, without nightmares. And I hadn't needed the Vodka to accomplish it.

The next morning found me up early, before the sun. I beat everyone, except Sally, to the kitchen. The coffee was ready though and for that I was grateful. I grabbed a cup and mumbled a good morning. She had banana muffins coming out of the oven, so I snagged one of those as well, thanked her, and quickly left before anyone else arrived. I was already waiting at the barn when Josiah walked in. If I was going to succeed in my attempts to live, I needed to stay busy. The other boys eyed me speculatively as they began filtering into the barn. A couple made whispered comments, some rude, some condescending, some curious. I ignored them all, waiting for instruction from Josiah. His only comment was to say I'd be working with him that day.

We mucked stalls. It was dirty, smelly work. Exhausting, but somehow satisfying. Removing the old, dirty bedding and replacing it with clean, fresh stuff. My back and hands ached, but it felt good at the same time. *I* felt good. Lingering anger seemed to be exorcised from my system with the physical labor I put myself through. Josiah remained silent for the most part, seemingly content to allow me to work through my emotions. With one small exception. As I was spreading fresh straw in the last stall, he shifted his stance from where he'd been silently watching. "Get rid of that liquor. You don't need it, and it's not permitted on the ranch."

Wondering how he knew I had it, I opened my mouth to ask, but he moved farther into the stall, leaned closer still, and took a slow, deep breath. "I can smell it on you," his voice rumbled in my ear, his proximity causing a warm shiver to run over me. "And I know what to look for. Just get rid of it. Tonight." His tone brooked no argument.

I hated to give it up. Yeah, the physical labor seemed to be helping, but what if it stopped? What if I needed it again? Eventually this exhaustion would wear off as I continued to become stronger. What would I do then? Was *I* strong enough? I stared at Josiah, trying to determine just how serious he was, if I thought he'd force my compliance. After a minute or two I decided it wasn't worth the argument and nodded in silent agreement. Josiah's blue eyes sparked, and his lips lifted, causing flutters in my stomach. Quickly, I turned away before he could notice. Finishing up that stall, I told him I was heading in. Strength was not something I was feeling; not yet at least, and what Josiah didn't know wouldn't hurt him. Fine, I'd stay away from the drink, but I'd keep it just in case.

A man, mid to late thirties, with a receding hairline and glasses was just stepping out of an older Jeep Wrangler as I approached the house. He was dressed in tan chinos, a blue button-up shirt, and a brown and blue striped sweater vest. Sort of like an older GQ nerd. "You must be Sage." His voice and manner were friendly. "I'm Bentley, one of your granddad's partners, and...I knew your mom. Sorry to hear what happened."

Swallowing the sudden lump in my throat and wishing I didn't still smell like a horse barn in need of cleaning, I shook his offered hand. "Nice to meet you." He smiled, but I could see the words building up in his mouth. Words of sympathy or maybe reminiscing. Words I definitely didn't want to hang around and experience, so made a hasty escape. "I'm in need of a shower—I'm sure I'll see you around." Quickly, I made it past him and breathed a sigh of relief when he made no move to stop me. No way was I interested in talking about mom, or really much of anything right now. Yes, I was getting stronger but didn't want to push it.

Once again, I'd sought my bed early and slept through the night. Surprising, considering my meeting with Bentley—I'd thought I'd have had more nightmares after he told me he'd known Mom.

The sun was just coloring the sky in shades of peach and pink as I arrived at the barn. Beating Josiah again, I might add. There was a coolness in the air I hadn't noticed before. A stillness. Peaceful. Inhaling, I drug that crisp, clean air in, noting the Juniper and wildflowers. I continued my slow, deep breaths, knowing the heat of the day would soon be upon us.

Josiah arrived shortly after. He nodded in what I assumed was good morning, then pointed out several tools, a bucket with nails, another with a hammer, a claw-looking thing, something that looked like giant nail clippers, some wire ties, and various other items, instructing me to load them in the beat-up Chevy parked in front of the barn. While I was gathering and loading everything, he grabbed a couple spools of wire, several metal posts, and a couple pairs of gloves. Some of the ranch boys had shown up while we worked, I'm sure to get instructions on their work for the day. As Josiah spoke with them, I climbed into the passenger side of the cab to wait for him and closed the door.

A minute later he opened my door and told me to slide over. To the driver's seat. I stared at him for a second, my heart sprinting away as anxiety grew. "This is a stick."

"It is," he agreed.

"I can't drive a stick."

"You'll learn."

"I...I don't know how."

"Scoot." Josiah unlatched my seatbelt and gave a gentle push in the direction of the steering wheel, his hand a blazing brand on my thigh. "You're learning right now." My heart was in my throat as I maneuvered around the stick and tried to calm myself.

"That peddle to the far left is your clutch. You'll use your left foot to work that one. Your right foot will handle the others like normal. With your left foot, push the clutch in, hold it down, keep it down, and with your right foot on the brake, turn the key until the engine starts."

With a trembling hand I did as he said, and the truck roared to life. "Good." He nodded as he closed his door. "Now keep that clutch down and use your right hand to move the gearshift into first; that's the top left position."

Again, I did what he said, my heart thumping so loudly in my ears, I was sure he could hear it. "Now, what you'll do is take your foot off the brake. Gently give it some gas, letting your engine rev a bit, keep your RPMs above an idle, and slowly release the clutch, feeling as it grips the gear and moves us forward."

He made it sound so simple. And, maybe it was, but I was still a mess and couldn't seem to force myself to follow through. My muscles had locked in panic. *I don't think I can do this.* Josiah waited a moment or two and then nudged my shoulder. "Whenever you're ready."

His hand at my shoulder seemed to have unlocked my body, so I swallowed, then took a deep breath, and walked myself through his instructions in my head as I attempted to do as he'd said. The truck lurched forward, then died. Embarrassment flared and I blew my breath out in a rush, but Josiah was patient. "You released the clutch a little too fast. Slower next time. Now go ahead and restart it." Shaking out my hands, I went through the motions again and this time the truck caught, and we ambled slowly forward. Josiah pointed to the worn track that led behind the barn towards the back of the property. He told me how to shift into second and when I'd hit third and we were moving along at a nice even pace he said, "Crimson?"

"Yeah?" I breathed, focusing on the dirt road in front of us.

"You're driving a stick." I heard the gentle smugness in his voice and felt my lip lift in acknowledgement. That day we repaired a section of fence, re-stretching the barbwire and re-nailing several sagging areas. A few pieces had broken beams, so we got them repaired, then cleared brush and trash that had become tangled in the wire.

By the time we returned to the ranch house, the other boys were back from school. Several of the older ones loitered around the barn, watching us, watching me. One attempted to get my attention, shooting me a flirty grin. He was big, built like a linebacker with dark blond hair cut short, almost military style. Josiah snorted under his breath as he shook his head and climbed out.

As I helped Josiah unload the truck, each of us making trips back and forth to the barn, the blond boy made his way over, checking me out as he approached. His scrutiny made me uneasy, so I ignored him, hoping he'd get the message. I was lifting a bucket from the bed when a voice just behind me said, "Here, let me."

Up close, I noted his eyes were grey, and he was not as tall as Josiah. Not as wild or untamed. "I've got it, thanks."

Ignoring me, he carefully pulled the bucket from my grasp, and rather than fight him over it, I let him. "I'm Mike."

"Sage." I nodded as I reached for more gear.

He chuckled quietly. "What kinda name is that? Sage?"

Josiah returned then, sparing me from answering, as he stepped between us. "We've got this, Mike. Go ahead and get started on the afternoon feeding."

Mike shrugged stiff shoulders trying to act nonchalant. "All right. Suit yourself. See you around...Sage."

Josiah watched as he walked away, his jaw tight with tension. He grumbled something under his breath before turning back to me. "You did good today."

"Thanks." A part of me warmed to hear that praise. *Needing* to hear it, to feel good about myself, even if I wasn't quite ready to admit it yet. "I guess I'll see you tomorrow...?"

"Tomorrow," he agreed.

That was how it started. Josiah assigned my duties to whatever he was doing. Anything from fixing fences, to shoeing horses, to bucking hay, to painting, to pulling weeds, to cleaning out irrigation canals. He never offered me an explanation as to why he kept me with him, and I didn't ask. I assumed it was so he could make sure I didn't shirk my duties or transgress back into my numb and depressed state.

Ethan starting school again helped me keep track of my days at least. Following his schedule helped me know what day it was, and for this I was grateful. It was something. Another sign of life on my part. His first day at his new school, I drove him in. He seemed fine; not nervous at all. *I* was the nervous one. Worried if he would fit in, if he'd have any friends. If he'd get bullied. Thankfully Kelly and Ethan had hit it off well, and I knew Kelly would keep an eye on him, glad they had already become such close friends. Not having to worry over him left me ample time on my hands. Time to contemplate, to consider someone else. Namely Josiah. Who I just couldn't seem to get off my brain. There were so many things about him that were still a mystery to me. Things, a part of me argued, that should remain a mystery if I truly wanted to stay in my safe little cocoon. But that was the thing, wasn't it? Did I truly want that still? I'd made the choice to live, and doing so had effectively killed the numbness. At times, if felt like I was almost stuck in limbo. No longer numb, but entirely unsure where to go and what to do. Still, life rose up demanding my attention.

Josiah seemed to have a way of refusing to be ignored. No matter how hard I tried, I just couldn't seem to help myself where he was concerned. I'd been wondering about him. A lot. Way more than was necessary. As best I could tell he was some kind of foreman and guidance counselor on the ranch. The boys came to him each day for their chores, and he assigned their duties; he was also the one who checked up on the job, making sure it was done correctly. On the weekends there was even more work than during the week. And yet, the boys seemed to respect him. Several times I caught the light of admiration in their gazes as they watched him. Ethan, too. It was the way he spoke with them, the way he treated them. Not once had I seen or heard anything harsh from him towards the boys. Even the ones who were older and on their way out. Josiah showed them a measure of respect and in turn, they respected him back.

One Saturday I finished cleaning the chicken coop that I'd been assigned and went in search of Josiah to find out what else he had for me. The rest of the boys were in the apple orchards, picking, and he'd gone to check on them. My eyes found Josiah quickly, and as I got closer, one of the younger boys, Ryan I think his name was, gave a shrill whistle. Josiah looked over his shoulder in my direction, then turned to the boys and hollered, "Girl on deck; shirts on."

The temperature had been hovering around the mid-nineties today and the boys had taken their shirts off. I felt a blush stain my cheeks at their collective groaning complaint. I stopped where I was and stared at Josiah, wanting him to come to me. He tossed the bucket he'd been filling and headed in my direction. "Hey, it's hot." I motioned to the boys. "They don't have to do that."

"They do, actually." He nodded. "It isn't too early for them to start learning to be respectful."

"Whatever." I blew out a breath, not wanting to earn the boys' anger. "What else do you want me to do?"

"You got that coop done?"

"Yeah."

"All right, I was just heading back to check on you anyway; I'll have you help me change the pipes today." Josiah turned to look over his shoulder and said, "Mike, Adam, you two are in charge; I want this row finished, then you're done for the day."

My eyes drifted to the boys he was talking to, and as we started to walk away, they began peeling their shirts off again. Mike caught my eye, giving me sly grin as he pulled his shirt off, flexing as he did. Passively, I noted he was well-built; nothing like Josiah's rugged frame, but with his dark blond hair and linebacker build, I could tell he'd be popular with the girls in school. Turning, I quickly caught up with Josiah, who'd been several paces in front of me, the blond boy forgotten almost instantly.

One day, about three weeks later, I realized I needed to go into town and get a few items. It was Saturday, so all the boys were home from school. I ate with everyone in the kitchen now and mentioned it to Billy over lunch. "Well, lemme see how the rest of today goes, then maybe I can run you in this evening."

"I'll take her," Josiah spoke quietly. "The rest of my day is cleared."

Billy nodded and after a moment I did too. I was hesitant because a part of me was thrilled to spend time with Josiah, but another part of me kept silently reminding myself that I should keep my distance or at least keep him at a distance. Hard to do when we were constantly together.

We left an hour later. Salmon, Idaho isn't that big, but it was beautiful. The blue sky overhead ringed by rugged mountains with a couple clouds moving sluggishly in the distance made for a lovely view. Josiah took me to the Saveway where I was able to get what I needed; then he took us through the Burger King, and we got milkshakes. He stopped near a small creek on the side of the road on our way out of town and we sat out in the sunshine to enjoy our frozen beverages.

"Thank you." I told him as I sipped at the last bit of frozen chocolate cream.

"Let me know when you need to come back." Josiah stood and collected our trash before placing it in a bag in the back seat of his car. As he did, I looked the metal frame over, mainly trying to keep my eyes off him. Something that seemed increasingly difficult to do. The car had nice curves and lines, though it needed a paint job. Someone had primed and buffed it, getting it ready for that paint.

"What're your plans for it?" I nodded at the car.

"When I can afford it, I plan to do a dark blue metal flake with two white racing stripes. White leather seats."

"Nice." Honestly, I didn't know much of anything about cars. But dark blue is a pretty color, and white racing stripes and leather seats sounded cool.

"Do you know what kind of car this is?" A grin curled his mouth and those vivid blue eyes flashed at me. Heat rose and swirled before settling in my stomach, sort of the way you'll see a flock of starlings take flight, moving in sequence, then land again.

"The mustang on the front sort of gives it away." I nodded at the emblem.

"What year is it?"

"That, I don't know."

"It's a '65 Shelby GT."

I smiled. "Okay." *Like I knew what that was.*

Josiah laughed, correctly reading my thoughts. "When I came to the ranch, I had a poster of one. It was the only thing I brought with me. Five years ago, Billy found this one at an auction; it needed a lot of work. He bought it and brought it home. I've been paying him off for it, and for work I've had done to it, or did myself."

I didn't know what to say to all that. It was becoming obvious that Billy had made long strides towards repairing whatever mistakes he'd made in the past. While aware, I didn't know how to respond to it all. He hadn't offended *me* way back when, though his falling out with Mom had been on account of me. So, it seemed like a wrong was there, or at least one that had to be addressed. Again, I just wasn't sure how or what to do. Did he need forgiveness? Was he seeking it from me? Mom had written that he'd asked for forgiveness, and she'd given it. Why would he need it from me as well?

"He'd like to buy you a car." Josiah stated, seemingly out of the blue.

"Why do you say that?" I looked over at him, trying to determine if he was serious.

"He said so. Billy asked me to feel you out...see what your tastes are." Josiah rubbed at the ring in his brow as he snickered to himself, as if hiding some secret meaning in his words.

Staring at him, my mind ran through possible meanings and scenarios to his words yet somehow came up empty. "He doesn't have to do that."

"I'm sure he knows that. He'd like to do it for you all the same."

"Well," I shook my head, exasperation growing. This was way more than I wanted to deal with. "I really haven't given it any thought."

"You should. I'll help you."

"Help me how?"

Again, Josiah snorted quietly, some hidden thought flying through his eyes, too fast for me to read. After a lengthy moment he said, "I'll help you...find yourself."

Under my breath, I said, "Find myself." If only it were that easy. "Thanks, I guess."

"Doesn't have to be today."

"Well, good; because right now I've got nothin'." My gaze shifted off into the distance, absently noting the clouds gathered around the mountain peaks, before turning back to him. "I had a cute little Bug back home, but we sold that before we came out here."

"I wouldn't have pictured you as a VW person."

"It was *cute*." I defended my little car. "And it got good gas mileage."

"I'm sure it did," he chuckled.

"Either way, I'll need to think about a job. An income. I can't just stay here, with no plan, no employment."

"I doubt Billy'd kick you to the curb." He moved to the driver's door.

"No, he probably wouldn't." I opened the passenger door. "But regardless, I can't just freeload here."

Josiah snorted under his breath, then asked, "You any good at math?"

"I'm decent. Why?" What does he have in mind? I studied him over the roof of the car.

"Billy was thinking of hiring a tutor for a few of the boys; you might fill that role. I know Bentley said he thought it'd be a good idea."

"I don't know...what kind of tutoring? What kind of math? I'm not a brainiac or anything."

He leaned his frame against the car, resting folded arms on the roof. "Most of those boys are behind in school; they just need someone to assist with understanding their schoolwork and helping with homework."

I blew out a breath. "I'll think about it. I guess it'll depend on which boys need help. I don't think they really like me."

Josiah stood upright, rubbing his head in a mild show of agitation, chuckling darkly under his breath. "Actually, I think they all like you a little too much."

I snorted. "Right."

"I *am* right; trust me." We got back in the car, then, remaining quiet for the drive back, both of us seemingly lost in our own thoughts.

I wondered how the tutoring might work. If it would feel weird being employed for Billy. How much time would it take each day? How many boys would I be working with? Those were questions I'd want answered before making a firm decision.

Chapter 3
Breaking Through

Crimson Sage

Despite multiple admonishments to myself, any time spent with Josiah seemed to feed the need and desire to spend more time with him. Lately at night, even after a full day's work, when I should have been exhausted, I was so keyed up, so full of nervous energy, I'd do a small workout. Pushups, some sit-ups, lunges. Anything to get my mind to relax and stop contemplating that ginger-haired man. Tonight, it seemed, was no different. Energy still zipped through me. I dug around in my purse for my phone—music would help right now. Pulling it from my bag, I hesitated. I hadn't turned it on in well over a month. Back then, I'd received so many texts and calls from friends pouring their sympathies out, that I couldn't take it, so had turned the phone off.

Gracie filled my thoughts now; she must be so angry with me. I hoped she was able to understand I'd been lost, so lost and had truly needed space. Space to process, and find myself, and deal with this loss on my own. I still didn't know how to tell her what I'd learned about my history. With trepidation, I plugged my phone in and turned it on. For a moment it was silent, then the messages began pouring in. Over fifty by the time it was all said and done.

More than thirty were from Gracie. They started out concerned, cautious. Sympathetic. After a while, I detected the hurt and anger in her voice. The frustration. Sighing, I tried not to take her angry words to heart as I sent her a response. Basically, I apologized, telling her where I was, how I was doing, that I missed her, that I hoped she understood and could forgive me. By the time I was finished with the text I was finally mentally exhausted enough to sleep, so simply laid down and turned the lamp off.

It took twenty-four hours for Gracie to text back. At first it was a complete rant. She was furious and rightfully so. Her response came back in five separate and long texts. The last one read, "I understand, forgive you, and love you, too."

Grinning at that, I sat in the older ranch pickup, waiting for Ethan to get out of school. Glancing at the time, I decided to call her.

"'lo," Her voice sounded a little garbled. Almost smeared.

"Grace?"

Her responding shriek had me jerking the phone from my ear. Blinking a couple times, I cautiously put it to my ear again. "*Sage*? Sage, is that you?"

"Hey." My throat threatened to close at the sound of her voice. Breathing through it, I said, "Sorry I've been MIA."

"Yeah, well. If you were closer, I'd kick your butt. As it is...I love and miss you."

"Miss you, too." From the background came heavy breathing and a growling sort of sound, followed by another garbled noise. "Uh, what are you doing?"

"I was making out with Tanner, but I *told him he needs to put it on hold*."

I chuckled as she emphasized each word to both Tanner and me. "Thanks for that. I can let you go, if you need to go."

I heard Tanner say, *Good idea*, just as she said, "Don't be an idiot. I haven't talked to you in months. Tan-man can take a chill-pill and give me some time with you, or Tan-man can get his cute tush out of my house."

That made me laugh. "Tell Tanner I said sorry."

"He's fine. How are *you*? Any better?"

"I'm getting there. It's hard."

"I know. Well, I mean I don't know, but I understand. I can't imagine... You sound good, though. Better than I expected, honestly. Any cute guys there?"

"I don't really get out much." Josiah flashed in my mind, but I wasn't up for sharing that with her. Especially as I wasn't sure what I felt about him yet.

"Well Sawyer has asked about you a few times."

Oddly, Sawyer held no interest for me, so I said, "Well, tell him I said *hey*."

"Hmmm...."

"What?"

"That wasn't the response I was hoping for."

"What do you mean?"

"Either you're still *very* depressed or...you're interested in someone else."

I'd somehow forgotten how astute Grace could be. Hoping to throw her off the trail, I tried playing it cool. Neither topic was one I wanted to divulge in. "It's hard, Grace. I'm dealing as best I can."

"Okay." I wasn't sure I'd convinced her, but she seemed agreeable to moving on for now. "How's Ethan?"

"He's doing good. Better than I am, that's for sure. He's made a couple friends here; I'm at his school now waiting for him to get out."

"Oh good; I'm glad to hear he's doing all right. Give the Kid a hug from me and tell him I love him. So, what are you driving now? Anything cool?"

"No, I'm in one of the ranch trucks. An older Chevy, and let me tell you, it's a beater. Nothing cool about it, but Josiah's going to help me figure out what kind of car I should get." *Wait! No! Stupid, stupid, stupid!* Cringing, I waited for her response.

Grace instantly jumped on my slip of the tongue. "Josiah? Josiah *who*?"

Crap. Making my tone dismissive, hoping against hope she'd drop it, I said, "Oh, he works on the ranch. For Billy."

"Your voice changed when you said his name," she mused aloud.

"No, it didn't."

"And now you're defensive about it."

"No, I'm not."

"That's fine. You don't have to tell me about him. Yet. I can wait until you're ready to talk about *Josiah*."

Gritting my teeth at my blunder, I rolled my eyes. Thankfully the school bell rang then, giving me an excuse to get going. "Hey, the Kid's out, so I gotta run. Talk to you later."

"Later." I hung up quickly before she could decide to ask me again about Josiah. I'd have to be on my guard for a while, be careful not to slip any more. Agitated, I tapped my fingers against the steering wheel, eyes trained on the doors of the school.

On the drive home Ethan told me all about his day, his teachers, the classes, the drama. I laughed a little as he relayed those details. Some things never changed, I reflected. The names might be different, but the drama never changed.

Josiah

Josiah watched Crimson, the way she moved. She was getting stronger. Her eyes were warming, like melted honey. Her skin was glowing again. He could still see the pain, but she wasn't drowning in it any longer. Today she wore a black tank and worn blue jeans. He watched her shoulders flex and move as she pulled the rake through the corral dirt. He had a strong desire to touch and taste those shoulders. See if her skin was as soft as it looked. They were cleaning river rock out of the soil so the horses wouldn't be injured when being ridden. He'd taken a wheelbarrow full of rock out behind the barn where they were dumping it, and as he got closer to her, he couldn't help the heat that flared in him at her proximity.

Even covered in sweat and dirt, Crimson was beautiful. The dirt couldn't dim her beauty. He was so proud of her, of how far she'd come in the last few weeks. From that first day, when she'd made the decision to live, he'd watched as she'd gone from zombie, to living and breathing, and now she was blooming, opening like some rare flower. Josiah took pride in the knowledge that he'd had a part in her progress, that he'd been instrumental in her breakthrough. There was still so much that she needed to face, to address. Her shoulders, those lovely inviting shoulders, were still heavy with her emotional burden.

Josiah could only imagine the extent of it. He knew pain, was quite familiar with it. He knew betrayal and he knew fear. But he also knew that each person responded to that kind of pain in his own way, that Crimson would have to find the courage to face and defeat hers all on her own. He'd gladly take it from her, but Crimson would have to offer it first.

He thought back to the day she woke up, when she'd suddenly appeared at his side, after he'd dumped her in the pond; he'd decided then to keep his mouth shut, not wanting to spook her. Not when she'd just made the decision to return to life. He remembered thinking she was short, so tiny compared to him. Too tiny for the work she was attempting. Yet, she had worked hard. She'd worked out her anger and fear that day, never saying a word, just sweated and strained alongside him. Josiah had been so proud of her; but he'd kept his smile hidden, that pride hidden.

He recalled the bitter, tangy scent of alcohol on her as she'd moved passed him. It was a familiar scent he'd never thought to find at the L&F. It brought back memories he'd preferred dead and buried. He thought maybe he'd made a mistake, but Crimson had already moved on toward the house and he didn't have the heart to call her back. She'd been darn near exhaustion that first day and he knew she needed rest. He'd have to wait and see how things progressed.

That was how things continued for the next three weeks. Crimson continued to pull her weight, throwing herself into whatever task Josiah had set for them. She never balked at anything, always put in a solid effort. He couldn't have been prouder of her. And she was blossoming. The healthy glow was back in her eyes and skin. She smiled more now. She was still alive, and she was beginning to thrive again.

He'd noticed her eyes on him several times in the last couple of weeks as they'd worked together but had never commented on it. Josiah had wondered, though. Her reactions reminded him of how girls responded to him in town. He knew he got looks. Some were bold, others more reserved. All of them were curious. Wondering what it would be like having a guy like him. One known to be dangerous. The guy with the ink. The one no one messed with. Crimson didn't strike him as that kind of girl. Still, Josiah recognized an interested look when he saw one. It was the same look he was trying desperately to keep off his own face when he was around her.

After a minute or two of Josiah watching her, Crimson stopped, straightened, and stretched her shoulders, then looked over said shoulder to locate him. Their eyes met and he saw that enticing flash of heat flair in hers before she looked away. He shook his head, trying to get his thoughts right. Crimson was his boss's granddaughter, and Josiah didn't know how Billy'd feel about the two of them becoming an item. She licked her lips, just a nervous gesture, not intended to be seductive, but Josiah felt the shock clear down to his toes. Forcefully, he reminded himself again that he needed to watch it. Billy might have issues. Josiah knew this, but he couldn't help the desire Crimson stirred in him—he was only human after all.

She'd blushed again when she saw it, that heat, and he wondered if she knew she was playing with fire. Josiah watched as she turned her honey brown eyes away; she had a look of deep contemplation on her face now and he wondered what was going through her head right then. Was she uncomfortable with him? Was she bothered by his attraction to her? He didn't think so. Was she planning to talk to Billy about it? Josiah decided he'd have to tell Billy, man to man. Honestly. He hoped Billy would at least be open and not opposed to the idea. He hoped...

Josiah moved fast. We'd only spoken yesterday about the *idea* of me *possibly* giving a few of the ranch boys some math tutoring. But here he was telling Billy we'd talked. And now I was snorting coffee into my hand at the breakfast table because he'd caught me off guard. Again. Ethan pounded my back in brotherly fashion as I wiped my chin and shot an exasperated look at Josiah. Billy ignored my dripping coffee and scratched his chin in speculation. "Your mother said you were good in math."

"Yeah, but I'm not a wiz or anything." I needed him to understand what I was saying here. "I mean, I can hold my own, I guess, but I'm not like a genius or anything."

"Well, I'd intended to hire someone; there are four boys Bentley figures need some help in math. I suppose, if you're willing, we'll give it a shot. Ryan and Jack, Kelly and Dean, you were who we'd originally thought of. Anyone else think they're gonna need some tutoring?" All eight boys, ranging in ages from twelve to seventeen, raised their hands indicating they did. My eyebrows shot up in surprise. That anyone would *want* tutoring was beyond me, but that even the older boys, like Mike, who would graduate the program and high school this year, seemed interested was even more surprising.

Josiah caught my eye, and his comment yesterday, that he thought the boys liked me just fine, came to mind. I couldn't keep the color from my cheeks. In near panic, I looked to him for help, eyes pleading.

"Let's give Ryan, Jack, Kelly, and Dean a go first. They could probably use the most help. Then we'll go from there." Josiah suggested, and I quickly nodded in agreement. Billy felt that was a good idea and suggested we begin the following week. Those four boys would meet with me right after school and I'd help them as best I could. Billy said he'd call their teacher and let her know our intent and see if she could give me a better idea about where they were, what they needed help with the most.

After breakfast, Billy pulled me aside before I took off with Josiah for the day's work. "Are you doing all right, Sage?"

Josiah was the only one who called me Crimson. I didn't know why that was and I hadn't bothered to ask him. It's what he'd called me right from the start. I glanced at Billy, to where he stood, leaning against the fence rail, and shrugged. "I'm fine."

"You're settling in?"

"Yeah."

"You know you don't have to work...it's not required for you to stay here—you know that, right?"

I nodded. "I need the work, Billy. Need to stay busy."

"All right; just don't think you have to. You're family," he paused for a moment then continued. "I was planning to pay a tutor about twenty an hour. That sound fair?"

"Sure." I nodded again. *Twenty an hour?* That was more than I'd expected.

"Per student." Billy stated. I looked over at him and he nodded seriously, "I mean it. If you can help them, it'll be money well spent."

It looked like he meant to reach out, maybe to touch my shoulder, and I panicked. Quickly, I turned out of his reach, my shoulders tingling, anticipating his touch, "Thanks, Billy. I'd better catch up to Josiah. See what he has in store for me today. See ya." I'd tried not to see the look in Billy's eye as I'd turned away from him, but I had. The hurt was there, but I didn't know what else I could do about it. I wasn't ready for physical affection yet. I was barely handling the verbal stuff. Billy couldn't have known how I was barely holding things together inside. How I was so terrified that if I gave in just a tiny bit, all that hurt, all that pain, all that raw emotion would come pouring out. I knew he couldn't have known that, but I didn't know how to tell him that either.

These last few weeks, working with Josiah, I'd begun to live again. But I wouldn't go so far as to say I was alive. Yes, my brain was functioning, there was breath in my lungs, and I was able to respond to most of what went on around me. But emotionally I was still shattered. I didn't know who I was any longer.

For all my life I'd been Crimson Sage Smyth; daughter of Terri and Dean, sister to Ethan. I'd known who I was, and who and what I'd wanted to become. Mom and I had had this dream of me becoming a nurse maybe or getting into sports medicine. Now, I just didn't know. That dream no longer seemed to be mine. It was like it had died with my parents.

Sometimes it made me angry, thinking about them. Why hadn't my parents told me the truth about who I was? The truth about where I'd come from. I'd continued reading Mom's letters. Some were just random thoughts she'd had that day, noting some sweet little thing she'd caught me doing or saying. Those were the letters that read more like a journal or diary. Then there'd be the ones that talked about something from her past. Mom wrote about her friends, her boyfriend Jon, her dad. She'd describe these people, almost like she wanted me to know them. I just couldn't figure out why. Why would Mom want me to know them? It seemed for every question I'd ask, another question would arise, making me just that much more confused.

So, as I wasn't sure about my past, I wasn't sure about my future; and I sure as heck didn't know how to respond to Billy, even though I could tell he was longing for a closeness between us. I just didn't feel I had anything concrete to offer him right now. Nothing substantial. So, I'd continue to hold him at bay and hold myself together.

Josiah, however, was a solid rock through all this. Putting my unwanted attraction aside, he made me feel safe. He never pushed beyond what I was capable of giving. He seemed to read my boundary lines rather well. And, for that, I was grateful. To myself, in the quiet recesses of my mind, I'd been able to acknowledge my growing attraction for him. I pondered that attraction at length and likened it to how a cat might respond to catnip. Or the way gasoline responded to a lit match. It was like I had no control over these feelings. They were compulsive. I had to respond.

These feelings for him didn't seem to have an on or off switch either. They simply were. And each day they grew. Not being around him didn't seem to help, didn't seem to lessen them any. Every so often I'd catch a look from him that said he was feeling the same things. And that just made me more confused. He had to see that I had nothing to offer him. That I wasn't a whole person any longer. I'd been fractured down to the very core of who I was. And even though he'd forced me to face life again, I didn't know if I'd ever find the essence of *me* again. That left the question of, what did he want? What did Josiah see when he looked at me?

These were all good and valid questions. Problem was, I was way too timid to ever ask them. Way too shattered to be that bold or confident. I told myself I'd just have to wait and let Josiah make the first move—if he intended to move at all.

Chapter 4
Picking Up Strays

Crimson Sage

I told Josiah I needed to go to town again, reminding myself I'd need to do something about getting my own vehicle soon. Ethan overheard and asked to come along. Josiah told him he could, but to check with Billy first. Billy not only agreed but said, "Let's all go. Give Sally a break. Get a burger." The other boys shouted their enthusiasm for this idea and before I knew it everyone was going.

I swallowed any consternation I was feeling as it sunk in that instead of the nice, quiet, and quick trip to town to pick up a couple things I'd been anticipating, I'd now be getting a loud, boisterous, testosterone-fueled lengthy visit. *Oh, well.* At least the boys were happy, and I couldn't fault them for their excitement.

Billy had an old school bus he'd painted blue with the ranch name in white on the side of it. Everyone piled on, excited conversations taking place all around me. I took a seat a couple rows behind Billy, who was driving. Ethan sat behind me and Josiah sat across the aisle from him. Ethan immediately began chatting with Kelly; he was such a happy kid. You could see his smile from a mile away and couldn't help but smile back.

I felt someone looking at me, felt the weight of it. I assumed it was Josiah and glanced over in his direction, anticipating his dark blue eyes. *He* wasn't looking at me. He was staring at something behind me. Turning to see what it was, my eyes collided with those of Mike. It was his gaze I'd felt. When he'd caught my eye he very deliberately winked. Blinking at his audacious flirting, I turned away, uncomfortable and embarrassed by his attention. Josiah's focus was zeroed in on Mike. "Watch your manners, Mike." His voice was low-pitched, but we all heard the warning in it.

Mike scoffed. "I ain't doing nothing." His tone indicated an unspoken *yet*.

"Mike." Josiah's tone somehow became lethal, commanding. Turning back around, I caught the flash of anger in Mike's eyes, as he jerked his gaze from me to Josiah. "Whatever," he grumbled after a moment, seeming to back down, before looking out the window. Josiah watched for a moment longer, making sure that was the end of it, then turned back to me. His face was void of expression now. Closed off. After a moment, he pulled his gaze away, glancing over the rest of the bus, which had become quiet during the exchange, then turned to his own window.

Facing front again, I tried to keep the heat from my face but Billy was watching from the rearview mirror. His eyes moved from me, to Josiah, to Mike and back again. Shifting my gaze out the window, I did my best to avoid all of them.

Billy pulled into the Saveway parking lot and parked. "I see Red just down the street, boys. Don't do anything stupid and get the sheriff ticked off at you. Meet back here in an hour and we'll eat. Here's ten dollars for each of you. You younger fellas stick together. You older ones *behave*."

Billy said he was going to grab a coffee and find a bench to keep an eye on the one main street in town. Ethan and Kelly wanted to go to the pet store, and I wanted to find the library before it closed. Pretty quickly everyone took off in their own directions. I didn't see where Josiah went, mainly because I was doing my best *not* to notice. I'd been noticing him far too much for my piece of mind. And I was very much afraid he was becoming aware of it.

The library was found easily enough and then I spent about fifteen minutes in bliss as I perused the rows and rows of books. I'd just settled on the floor with a stack of them I wanted to give a closer look to when Ethan darted in, followed quickly by Kelly. "Sage!" he cried breathlessly. "Please say yes. Please!"

"They're so cute and *free*!" Kelly chimed in.

"Whoa. Wait. First off, pipe down; you're in a library. Second, what are you talking about?"

"A *puppy*. There's a girl giving them away down the street. Please?"

"A puppy? But, Ethan, Billy already has two dogs. Have you asked him?"

"He said to ask you."

Great. "Are you going to take care of it? Puppies are a lot of work."

"Yes! I promise. I'll do whatever you ask me to."

"You'll keep your grades up?"

"Promise. Please?"

Standing, I put three books back and took three with me to check out. Ten minutes later, Ethan was dragging me down the road to where a girl about fifteen years old or so sat beside a box full of wiggling tan and grey fluff balls. She smiled at our approach. "I hear you have puppies," I smiled back.

"Yes ma'am. Five."

I bent, looking into the box. The puppies seemed to be a mixed breed. Part Australian Shepherd maybe, part who-knows-what. They were cute though. Really cute. Ethan had picked one up. It was a merled blue and brown color. Had one white paw and the ears stood partly up. The puppy had one blue eye, the other one golden brown. Ethan was laughing as the puppy affectionately licked all over his face.

"I take it you like that one?"

"Isn't she beautiful?" Ethan asked through puppy breath.

Reaching over, I scratched at her ears. "She is. Have you picked a name?"

"Daisy," he replied instantly, rubbing his nose into her coat, snuggling her close.

"All right." I relented on a long-suffering sigh. "But *you* have to take care of her."

"I will. I swear."

"Well, let's go get her food and other supplies you'll need." We thanked the young girl, whose name turned out to be Maggie and then with Ethan carrying Daisy and Kelly skipping along beside them, we walked back to the bus. Billy chuckled as we approached him. "I wondered what your answer would be."

"Ethan swears he'll take care of her."

"He will. I'll see to it he does. He's taken a responsibility for the pup; he's going to follow through now. Right, Ethan?"

"Right."

I set my books next to Billy on the bench. "I'm going to take Ethan inside to get some supplies he'll need."

"Here," Billy said as he handed me a hundred-dollar bill. "This should cover most of it." I hesitated—I had money—Billy didn't have to pay for everything like we were children. "I know you can probably pay yourself; I just want to be able to do something for the kid." Taking a deep breath, I nodded, accepting his gift.

Grabbing a cart on the way inside, we picked out a few puppy toys, a couple bowls, a collar, and a leash. I was just bending to pick up the large bag of food, when I heard a voice at my shoulder. "I got it."

I jumped a little, but Josiah grabbed the bag and quickly, *easily* tossed it over his shoulder. I remembered all too well how that felt. How easily he'd done the same with me. I was blushing again when Josiah caught my eye. His grin told me he remembered as well. "You caught me off-guard."

"Which time?" he grinned.

"Both times," I grumbled.

"I know." He shrugged the bag on his shoulder. "Is this it?"

"Yeah, that's it."

After I'd paid for everything and we were heading out to the bus, Ethan asked if I wanted to hold Daisy. Carefully, taking hold of her, I held her close for a moment, letting him and Kelly carry the bags.

The other boys gathered around when they saw the puppy. Excited voices expressing awe over her, each wanting a chance to pet or hold her.

A big arm came over my shoulder, brushing firmly across Daisy's back. "I see we're picking up another stray." Turning, I found Mike standing right behind me, looking at me, not the puppy. "Soft. Cute, too. Bet she enjoys a good petting."

I stepped back, uncomfortable with the tone of his voice and the innuendo in his words. Josiah moved back to my side, his presence comforting. Mike shot me a sly grin before moving to the bus. Leaning nonchalantly against it, thumbs in his belt loops, he kept his gaze on me. Josiah followed his movements with jaw clenched tight.

"All right," Billy said. "Everyone here and accounted for? Ethan, you should take her for a potty break before we get going. Load up!"

We ate in the bus on the way home, and as we pulled back into the ranch drive, Cullen, one of the older boys, asked Billy if we could have a bonfire. The others joined in the plea and soon a large blaze was roaring in the rock-rimmed pit behind the house. I'd gone inside to put my purse away and when I came back out, stopped for a moment, unsure as to where to sit. There was only one seat available, so it shouldn't have been that difficult. Problem was, the open seat was right between Josiah and Ethan. My brother was fine; I'd have chosen to sit by him regardless; it was sitting beside Josiah that gave me pause.

I'd been trying to ignore the stares, ignore the way his voice, his scent, his touch, had been prodding at me. I'd thought if I'd kept him at a distance, I could ignore all he was making me *feel*. Josiah was having none of it. And the more I responded to him, the more I was around him, the harder it was to remain closed off, the harder it became to fight this attraction I didn't want to deal with.

For a brief moment, I debated if I shouldn't just move quietly back inside, and I'd nearly turned, slipping away, when Ethan spotted me. "Sage! Come on, I saved you a seat."

Fighting the urge to roll my eyes, I silently sighed and focused on the open seat. Not the person sitting next to it. Careful not to trip over anyone, I found my way to the log chair and quietly sat down. The fire was hot, scorching. It took me a minute or two to realize that the fire wasn't what was heating me so thoroughly. Certainly, I felt the heat from the flames, but my backside was just as warm as the front side. In fact, I'd say my right side, the side not closest to my brother, was the hottest.

I'd been staring into the flames when a bag of marshmallows suddenly landed in my lap. I looked up, searching the faces around me. Mike grinned and, on the surface, it was friendly, maybe too friendly, overtly so, but there was something in his eye, some look that bothered me. Not wanting to appear rude, I just nodded in thanks.

From beside me, Josiah's hand tightened into a fist, the movement drawing my gaze. He had big hands; wide, blunt-tipped fingers, the nails trimmed short. I stared at those hands, noting the way the tendons and veins stood out. The coarse hair sprinkled across the backs and the callouses on the wide palms. Ethan jolted me out of my mental wandering when he handed me a stick to roast the marshmallow on. I grinned at him, thankful for the distraction. No need to remember the way those big hands had felt on me. The strength. The heat of them. Nope, didn't need to remember that at all.

Adding two marshmallows to my stick, I leaned forward, holding them above the fire for a moment, just letting them brown, before sticking them directly in the flame to finish them off. Ethan grinned, turning to Kelly. "Told ya. She always burns them."

"They're not burned." I disagreed. "They're perfect."

Ethan snorted. "Uh, that's burned."

"It's how I like them. You cook yours your way; I'll cook mine my way."

Billy let the boys stay up for another hour, before sending them to bed. "Make sure that's out before you head in," he reminded Josiah. I started to get up, to follow everyone inside, but Billy told me to sit back and relax. Unsure how to convey that I didn't want to be left alone with Josiah, that I didn't trust myself to be alone with him, I swallowed my words and leaned back in my seat, burying my hands in my pockets.

Fifteen minutes later the lights went out and silence fell over the big house. Outside, crickets sang as the breeze danced through the trees and grass, rustling leaves and lifting my hair. I tucked a wayward strand behind my ear and took a deep breath, enjoying the quiet, the smell of the wood, Josiah. *I should stop right there.*

Josiah wasn't like any boy I'd met before. He had something distinctly wild and untamed about him. I was used to proper jock-boys who at least pretended to follow the rules. The kind I used to be able to maneuver with a look or a promise I never intended to keep. The kind that would never make a move I didn't want. I very much feared Josiah was not that kind of boy. And really, he wasn't a boy at all. He was a man. And maybe therein lay the danger. I didn't know what to expect from him. And I found myself wanting to know him better, know more about him. Which was stupid.

Josiah should have come with a warning label, or at the very least a theme song. *Bad to the Bone* worked well here. Maybe it was the piercings in his brow and his ears, maybe it was the tattoos on his arms, his neck, and I suspected his back as well, but he put off distinct 'bad boy' vibes. Still reminding me of a lone wolf, unpredictable and feral. A part of me, one that grew and came alive more each day, was secretly hoping to discover the truth of the matter. He *was* dangerous and yet I still felt safe with him. This was a different sort of danger. Stronger and much more potent.

As I'd contemplated the man beside me and my growing awareness of him, tension had begun to build. To the point that I felt tense. Tight. Trying to ease that tension I shrugged my shoulders carefully and rotated my neck around. In doing so my eyes collided with Josiah's blue ones, and I froze. "Be careful of Mike."

That brought me up short. "What?"

"He's got his eye on you, and I don't like the look in it. Just be careful."

"Oh-kay. Thanks. He's not really my type or anything. Little young, too. But I'll keep that in mind."

"You do that. I'll be talking to Billy and Bentley about it. They should be aware. And whether he's your type or not isn't the issue. He's dangerous and you need to be cautious around him. Don't give him any green lights. At all."

My heart rate kicked up. "Okay. I'll watch out."

"Don't allow yourself to be alone with him either."

After a moment I asked, "If he's that bad why does Billy keep him here?"

"Mike has this one option, this one chance. He screws this up and he's heading to prison. Billy's trying to give him every opportunity to turn himself around." I didn't know what to say to that, how to respond, so said nothing. Why would Billy do that? What drove him? Was it the past still? I couldn't wrap my head around any of it. "You about ready?" Josiah asked sometime later.

"For what?" Lost in thought, still trying to understand Billy, I'd been inside my head, unaware of how much time had passed.

"To turn in? Or do you want to stay here for a while longer?" Even though I knew I should go in, and was getting too used to him, too comfortable with him, I simply remained silent, staring into his blue eyes, and let my worries fade into the background. Seemingly recognizing my unspoken request, Josiah nodded his head, relaxing back into his seat. We sat in silence; each lost in our thoughts until the fire died down. Josiah stood then. He held his hand out, a silent offer. When I placed mine in his, noting again just how big, how strong and warm those hands were, he pulled me to my feet. "See you in the morning?"

"In the morning," I agreed. Quiet as a ghost, I made it up to my room but couldn't seem to settle. My muscles jumped, jittery from Josiah's touch. Checking the time, I saw it was just after midnight. Music didn't sound good. Nor even a book. My eyes flitted around my room, seeking a distraction from this constant influx of electrical charges Josiah sparked in me; they landed on the manila envelope. The one with Mom's letters. Taking a deep breath, I retrieved it and retreated to my bed. This wasn't quite the distraction I'd been searching for, but it would do. I closed my eyes for a moment before I began to read.

Josiah

Growing up in the system and being familiar with how the hierarchy and the almost pack-like mentality of the group-home was fostered, how it festered within the ranks of the boys, Josiah had learned early on that if you wanted to survive, if you wanted to be left alone, you had to be an Alpha—you had to learn to fight. Being an Alpha didn't necessarily mean having your own pack, though there had been those who'd followed his lead. It meant that the others had learned to leave him alone or suffer the consequences. Josiah hated violence, but used it when necessary with fierce determination and precision. After graduating from the system, then being offered the honest-to-God job at the Ranch, an opportunity he'd never imagined receiving, not with his history, he'd made the decision to remove the Alpha mantle. Now he was a lone wolf. Still dangerous, still someone to be left alone; and now he stood alone.

Mike, seventeen, with a linebacker's burly build and inbred aggression had been in the foster system since he was ten. He'd come to the L&F when he was fifteen, having been bounced around the state to various group homes and foster care for one reason or another until he and two seventeen-year-old accomplices were charged with armed robbery. The older boys were sent to prison; he was given the option of going to the L&F, or Juvie. Mike chose the L&F, where he, no doubt, bided his time, just waiting until he was eighteen and free of the state. Some, when faced with adversity become stronger, some crumble; some are driven to success, some think the world owes them and will do everything to make sure the world pays up. And then there was Mike.

Growing up on the streets, having the upbringing that Josiah had, he'd learned fast how to read people. And how to correctly anticipate them. And Mike, Josiah knew, wanted to be Alpha. It was there in the young blond man's eyes, the way he looked on everything with either contempt or greed.

The way those grey eyes studied Josiah, it was evident Mike wanted to be the big man on the block and have people fear and respect him the way they did Josiah. It wasn't hero-worship that Josiah saw in Mike's eyes. No, there was nothing respectful in his gaze. But Mike wasn't quite there yet, wasn't ready to take on the tall redhead, but Josiah knew it was in his mind to see it accomplished all the same.

Having gravitated towards the rougher elements of life, Mike would have heard all the urban legends about Josiah. And Mike wasn't the first, nor would he be the last to feel the need to challenge Josiah. Still, Josiah could see the younger man was working up the nerve. Knew he'd eventually get around to questioning whether Josiah was all talk, or just a legend. If he could put up. Craving the fear and respect Josiah was given wherever he went, no matter who he was with, Mike would hate leaving that question unanswered.

From experience, Josiah knew bullies like Mike tended to harbor a deep-seated fear, lashing out at anyone they perceived as a threat. Much like a cornered snake. But Josiah knew how to stomp a snake and wasn't concerned about this particular one. Wasn't concerned about him at all, with one exception.

When Mike saw Crimson, something seemed to have shifted in the younger man. Sure, like the other boys, he'd seen her pictures at the Ranch, knew she was the old man's granddaughter. But the lust Josiah witnessed in his gaze, the way those cold eyes settled on Crimson, had Josiah's hackles raised. It had him gnashing his teeth, wanting to eliminate any and all perceived threats to her. To guys like Mike, she was no more than a picture in a magazine. Something to assuage their desires. Josiah wondered which Mike wanted more. To best Josiah, or to have Crimson.

Currently, he seemed to focus his desire on Crimson. Always watching her. Stalking her. Trying to get her to respond to his attention. Josiah knew Mike had a reputation at school. That girls seemed to throw themselves at him. This would feed his ego. But only for so long. Eventually, Mike would want more. So far, the blond man had remained on the periphery, content to watch. But that wouldn't last. Josiah could read him like a book and knew the confrontation between them was coming.

His gut reaction was to take the punk out, make an example of him. End it hard and fast. But Josiah was also distinctly aware the repercussions were so much bigger now. He'd have to stay alert and try heading off any attempts Mike made towards Crimson, try discouraging him. Josiah hoped that Mike would wise up, decide not to buck the system, and leave Crimson alone. That was one of the reasons he'd kept Crimson with him, assigned her duties to himself. Josiah wondered how long Mike was willing to wait before he tried for more.

Josiah had watched her carefully these last several weeks as Crimson came alive again. The pain was still there, but it was no longer the all-consuming beast it had been when she'd first arrived. He thought maybe she was beginning to respond to him as well, that she was noticing him as a man. Josiah tried holding himself in check, keeping his desire for her under wraps. She made it difficult, unknowingly testing him as they worked together. And those times he'd catch her honey eyes moving slowly across his body... His stomach clenched as he recalled the heat that had slammed into him. The heat that coursed through him now. The way his mouth dried out, how his blood would pound. And then, like now, he'd remind himself she wasn't ready yet.

Knowing now was the time to talk with Billy, Josiah knocked on the office door. Billy was seated behind his desk, working through the never-ending mountains of paperwork he had to fill out on each boy. The progress reports, school reports, medical and performance evaluations; the list went on and on. At the sound of Josiah's knock, Billy looked up. "Got a minute?" Josiah asked, leaning against the door frame.

"Sure; c'mon in. What's on your mind?"

Josiah sat in one of the chairs in front of Billy's desk. He rubbed his head in a show of mild agitation, then leaned forward, resting his forearms on his knees. Taking a deep breath, he looked Billy right in the eye. "Crimson."

"What about her?" Billy set down his pen and leaned back in his seat.

"I like her, Billy," his voice was low, quiet. "And I don't want there to be any hard feelings between us about her."

Billy crossed his arms over his chest, silently studying Josiah, contemplation clearly written on his face. Josiah waited, allowing the older man to gather his thoughts, knowing Billy liked him, respected him even. He knew Billy would take into consideration that Josiah had come to talk with him, man to man. Billy would respect that.

"All right." Billy finally said. "She's an adult and I won't attempt to tell her what to do—I won't make that mistake again." He scratched at his chin thoughtfully. "But you be careful. You be cautious with her."

Josiah nodded. "I am. I'm not rushing anything. She's still trying to find herself. I just wanted you to know I plan on being the one to help her."

"Fair enough." Billy knocked his knuckles against the desk surface in a show things were settled.

"There's another thing."

"And that is...?" Billy's gaze sharpened.

"Mike."

"What about him?" Dread rang in Billy's voice.

"He's zeroed in on her, and his focus isn't the healthy kind."

"You think she's in danger?" Billy leaned forward now, no doubt his mind in a whir, wondering what to do with this problem.

"I think he's unpredictable and it's possible."

After a moment, he blew out a breath. "This is his last chance, Josiah. I'd hate to take that opportunity away from him without any proof."

"You can't save them all, Billy," he said softly. "And I'd hate for her to get hurt."

"I don't want her hurt either. We'll have to be more careful. More vigilant. I'll let Red and Bentley know. You continue as you have, keep her with you as much as possible. Mike'll be gone by June. That's about ten months away."

Josiah nodded, promising to keep an eye on the situation. He also promised Billy that he'd keep him apprised of any changes. He hoped, for

Billy's sake, that things would work out all right. That Mike would toe the line. But he didn't trust the seventeen-year-old, and he could see it coming. A confrontation with Mike was looming on the horizon but now was not the time. Josiah would have to be extra vigilant and on his guard. And when the time came, he'd be ready.

Chapter 5
A Darn Good Reason

*C*rimson Sage

As I made my way to the barn in search of Josiah one morning, I came to a stop in the middle of the yard, mildly shocked to realize how much time had gone by. It sure hadn't seemed like I'd been here for two months, and yet, as I did the numbers in my head, that was exactly how long we'd been here. Ethan had adapted so much better than I had. He and Billy were close, and I was glad of that. Glad they had that connection. Billy continued his efforts with me, but I remained hesitant of him, unsure. Maybe it was because we'd just met, but I couldn't seem to let those walls drop, effectively keeping Billy on the periphery of my emotions and trust.

I found myself looking to Josiah for guidance, however. Which sorta shot my whole, *"We've just met and that's why I don't trust him"* philosophy regarding Billy all to heck. I'd actually known Billy longer. And yet, it was Josiah I looked to. Josiah I trusted. And this in spite of the fact I'd been firmly and repeatedly telling myself I couldn't afford to let him in or let him come close. To allow him to draw close meant danger; it meant I could be hurt again. Not the same kind of hurt as losing my parents or finding out the truth about my past, but painful all the same. Devastating even. There wouldn't be any pieces left to pick up, because for whatever reason, I knew Josiah would pack a big, crushing, annihilating hurt if something ever went wrong between us. And I couldn't afford that. For Ethan's sake.

Ethan had an early release today. He rode the bus now, with the other boys from the ranch. I'd wanted to continue driving him, but he'd said he wanted to ride with his friends. So, I'd taken a deep breath and let him. Glancing toward the driveway, I grinned when I spied Daisy lying in the shade of the fence; her gaze focused toward the road, waiting for Ethan to come home. Daisy was another that Ethan had bonded with, and Josiah as well. Ethan seemed to look up to him. Copied him. Almost hero worshiped him. But then again, a lot of the boys did, except for maybe Mike and Adam, who, though they never really challenged Josiah, still had looks of contempt on their faces whenever he or Billy were around.

I nearly mentioned it to Josiah several times, but he didn't seem the kind to be unaware as he always seemed to notice *everything*. And he didn't take crap from anyone. No, they all seemed to give him room. Unsafe to everyone but me. Unless you were referring to my libido. Then he was plenty hazardous. I wasn't the only one who noticed that aspect of him either. Everywhere we went he exuded this completely confident, almost alpha mentality. Men treated him with respect, or he stared them down until they did. Women were intrigued by him; I saw the longing looks they gave him, the jealous looks they gave me. And I really couldn't blame them.

Shaking my head as I spotted him loading that lumber we'd bought last week into the bed of the old Chevy, I moved in his direction. It looked like we were fixing fence again today. And he looked hotter than I had any right to notice. His shirt was already clinging to his tall frame. Sweat glistened on his arms and neck. He acknowledged me with a nod as I approached. "Grab that bucket of nails and the hammer, will ya?"

Swallowing, I ripped my mind off that broad back, those biceps, those lips as they formed words. Turning quickly away, I grabbed the two buckets he'd indicated and carried them to the truck, keeping my eyes firmly on the ground. Anywhere but at him. Josiah held his hands out for the buckets. I set one down at my feet and used both hands to lift the other up to him. He took it with one hand, squatted down to make it easier for me to lift the other to him and then stood with both, like it was easy. Like they weighed nothing. I marveled at his blatant strength and tried to calm my pulse.

Spying the keys on the tailgate, I quickly grabbed those and moved to the driver's door. "I'm driving." I needed to keep my mind focused and was hopeful driving would offer that relief. Josiah didn't say anything, just climbed into the passenger seat. Despite the fact he'd been sweating, he smelled good. Mouthwatering, really. "Where to?"

"We're on the road today. Head north."

I did as instructed, and after about fifteen minutes he told me to pull over. About forty feet of what looked to be recently broken fencing sat before us. Like someone had plowed through it. In a car, or truck. Like they'd wrecked. The ground was torn up, big gouges in the grass and soil. My throat tightened and I fought to keep my emotions in check. "When did this happen?" My voice sounded low and little hoarse to my own ears, and I hoped he wouldn't notice it.

Josiah scratched his chin, thoughtfully. "About two weeks ago I guess."

"Why are we just fixing it now?" Two weeks seemed a long time to let this go. I knew we'd kept the horses up close to the house for the last couple of weeks and I was guessing this was the reason, I just didn't know why we hadn't dealt with it sooner.

"Billy thought it'd be too soon; I told him I thought you'd be fine. You're strong."

My gaze flew to him, but Josiah was already stepping out of the truck. He said *I* was strong. I didn't feel strong, though. I felt weak as a newborn kitten. I know I'd come a long way, but still. Any courage I'd managed to exude came directly from Josiah, and I wondered how he couldn't see that. After a moment, I followed him, and we got to work.

I tried to keep my focus on the work we were actually doing—fixing fence—and not the reason behind it. We worked steadily for about two hours. Both of us sweating now. We'd stopped once for water, then kept at it. Today it seemed harder than ever for me to keep my mind off Josiah. To not see him as a man. Maybe because he was an easy distraction from the evidence of the car wreck we were fixing, because looking to him when I felt threatened had become habit. And maybe it was because Grace had asked me several times about him now, ever since my slip to her a few weeks back. And due to her pestering, I'd given her a pretty decent description of him and her response had been, "Whoa. He sounds *hot*. Like really hot. I need a pic."

"No! I am *not* taking a picture of him. How would I explain that?"

"Are you kidding? Do it when he's not looking. *Duh*."

"I can't."

"And why ever not?"

"Because he'll see."

"He won't if you do it when he's not looking." The *duh* in her voice was disgustingly evident.

"He's always looking, though."

I mentally shook my head for telling her that. Grace immediately dived in, wanting to know more. Claiming he must like me. I'd told her I had to go. And I hadn't answered her texts since Monday. This morning she'd sent one that said, "Fine. You win. I'm crying Uncle. Don't send me a pic. Why would I need to know exactly what your hottie boss-man looks like? It's not like we're best buds or anything." I'd chuckled then sent her a picture of Josiah from a distance, as he walked away. Even if she enlarged it, she'd never be able to tell a whole lot about him. Her reply had been a photo of her dog's poop.

Josiah was using the post-hole digger, and I was standing by with said post, waiting to drop it in the hole. I watched his muscles bunch and flex, almost mesmerized by their movements.

"What's up?" Josiah asked suddenly, never stopping his work.

Jerking, I felt heat that had nothing to do with the sun flood my face. "Nothing," I rasped, then cleared my throat.

"You've been staring a hole in my back for the last ten minutes. You got something to say, just say it." Actually, I'd been staring at him for closer to twenty minutes but didn't feel the need to voice that correction. I wracked my brain for something to say, some explanation to offer for why I'd been staring at him. Other than the truth, which was that despite my best efforts,

I was extremely attracted to him. Darting a glance around, my eyes settled on the broken posts we'd pulled out and suddenly I found myself talking about my parents. How they'd died. What I'd learned in Mom's diary.

Josiah listened silently, just let me get it all out. Every painful detail. He was quiet for several minutes once I was done. We'd finished digging all the holes by the time my tale was complete, and I waited for him to look at me in horror, in pity. He didn't. He just continued working, instructing me how to hold the wire, how to keep it taut so he could nail it off. No judgement, no commentary. He simply accepted those parts of me and seemingly moved on. Relief was sweet on my tongue, sending a cool, almost refreshing rush through me. I exhaled and felt lighter, freer.

My heart lodged tightly in my throat, however, when I began to lose my grip on the wire. It began slipping in my hands; I couldn't hold it and a gasp slipped from my clenched teeth, expecting the sharp barbs to slice into me as the wire uncoiled. Suddenly Josiah was behind me, one arm on either side, caging me in, anchoring me as he gripped the wire, preventing it from slipping further. His front pressed to my back as he shifted his grip on the wire. Pulling it. Tightening it. His breath fanned my neck, my hair as his thighs pressed firmly against mine.

Briefly, I forgot what we were doing. Completely lost in each sensation he conjured. Letting them register in my body and my head. Josiah was quiet for a moment, then he breathed nearly against my skin in rough voice. "Tighten that down some Crimson; or we're gonna have a serious problem here." Goosebumps erupted along my skin, and I wanted to lean back into his warmth and strength. *What?* What was he saying? Josiah shifted again, nudging my arm with his shoulder. The one I needed to use to tighten the wire that was slipping. *Oh, yeah, right. The wire.*

Snapping out of the spell he'd put me under, I took a firmer grip on the wire. "Got it." I sounded out of breath, because I was. He'd stolen it all. Josiah loosened his hold, checking to see if I really had it, before moving to swiftly get the wire nailed down. Once done, he turned without a word to the truck, then lifted the small ice chest down to the ground. He opened it and tossed me a bottle of water.

We both drank deeply, heavily, not stopping until we'd finished our bottle. Shooting me a contemplative look, he said, "Lunch."

We found a spot under a scrubby pine, and sat to eat in silence. I kept my eyes off of him, though, I could have sworn I felt his gaze a time or two. I was nearly finished with my sandwich when he said, "It's gotta be a good feeling...knowing someone wanted you despite the pain they experienced on your behalf. No one ever wanted me until Billy came along," he paused, taking a drink of water, then continued. "I hated everyone. Especially my parents. They never wanted me, did what they could to get rid of me, and when Billy told me he'd wanted me, I'd called him a liar."

This was one of the first times Josiah had told me anything about himself. I knew he'd gone through the program. Had graduated from it. But I hadn't known what brought him here. I looked around taking in everything as far as I could see. I could just glimpse the top of the house through the trees. As I let my eyes trail along the fencing, down the drive, down the road to where we worked it occurred to me that Billy might have done all this, gone so far out of his way, to help those who needed help because he'd been unable to help his own daughter. "It must be because he'd turned his back on Mom," I told him, indicating the ranch around us. "I think he was trying to make amends, do the right thing."

"He was. And is. You need to forgive him. He loved your mom and thought he was doing the right thing at the time."

I didn't want to talk about me anymore. "What are you, his lawyer?" My tone was sharp, but I couldn't seem to help it.

"An observer. He wants you, too, Crimson."

"Why do you call me that? Why not Sage like everyone else?"

He was quiet for a moment. "It's a beautiful name. Unique." He shrugged. "Besides, I like saying it. Does it bother you?" I shook my head now, unsure why I'd even brought it up. I loved the way he said my name.

His gaze sharpened now. "He loves you, you know. Billy. He really does love you."

I knew I was the one who'd begun this conversation—I'd spilled my guts, shared my awful past with him—but I no longer wanted to talk about Billy or my past. I looked away, then right back at him. Josiah's eyes were still on me. Those piercing blue eyes. I abruptly changed the subject, needing to be on firmer ground, "What are your tattoos anyway?"

Josiah's gaze was heavy on me, intently fixed, then he suddenly grinned. "Are you trying to get me to take my shirt off?"

Yes, please. "*No!* I...I just wondered is all. Keep your clothes on."

Josiah chuckled darkly, a knowing look on his face, then swiftly stood, towering over me, and in one smooth motion, removed his shirt. Fascinated, I simply stared. He was more beautiful, more wild, more untamed than I'd imagined. My eyes roved slowly over him, his chest, his arms, his shoulders. He was well-muscled; not bodybuilder hard, where everything looked direct and intentional, proportionate. Josiah was an artful display of a working man's roughened and toughened body. Cut. Chiseled. Rugged. Beautiful.

Centered on each pectoral plane, a sun was tattooed in shades of black and yellow. The center of each sun had some sort of design in it—I couldn't tell what it was until I got to my feet. Josiah held still, unmoving, even as my fingertips lightly grazed his skin. My stomach tightened as I realized the center of each sun was a scar. My gaze flickered up to his in question.

"Courtesy of my mother; for my fifth birthday. I'd asked for a cake with candles. She burned me instead."

My throat tightened as I swallowed back nausea and steadied my breath. His arms and his neck drew my attention, and as my gaze shifted, Josiah turned around, allowing me easier viewing. Wings. Big leathery-looking wings were inked in intricate detail across his back and shoulders. Beginning on both sides of his spine, the tattoo was extremely detailed in shades of black and gray and blue. The wings had hooks. Claws? I'm not sure what they're called, but those claws curled up the back of his neck and around to just under his ears. At the points just over his shoulder blades were two more burn marks; these ones were bigger, more defined. The tattoo artist had done an amazing job of incorporating the scars into their work. Gently, I trailed one fingertip along the wings, up his neck, down to the scars, his skin pebbling as I went.

Josiah glanced over his shoulder; his eyes sparking with some inner turmoil and heat. "Those were from Dad. He wanted to get me something, too."

"That's sick." The lump in my throat forced a raspy whisper. How could anyone do that to their own child?

"Billy helped me get the ink done when I turned eighteen, to mark myself over their ugliness with something of my own choosing."

"I'm so sorry." I wanted to weep for him. Words were not possible to express this level of evil. But just as I wouldn't want anyone's pity over my circumstances, I knew he wouldn't either. So, I swallowed my tears and emotion, not letting them out.

"I told you, it's gotta be nice to know you're wanted. I was born to both my parents—who never cared a crap about me. The state had to take me away from them. A stranger took me in. You were born to a mom who loved you and wanted you. You had a dad who felt the same. Circumstances took that away from you. And I know it's hard, but I learned to live, to survive. You will, too."

"It's...*so* hard." My eyes drifted over the muscles under that ink. Marveling at the blatant strength displayed there. Marveling at the strength of his character and determination. Josiah waited a moment, then turned to face me. Now my eyes were staring at his chest, heat building, rising.

"I know." His voice had a gravelly quality to it now. Rough, but still comforting, gentle. "Giving up is easier. But giving up is for cowards. You're not a coward, Crimson. You're a fighter—you just never knew it before."

I knew the answer to this, but asked anyway, "Are you a fighter?"

"I learned to be."

I inhaled, catching traces of his musky scent. "Will you teach me?"

"I will."

"Thank you."

"You're welcome." I heard the grin in his voice.

There was something else I needed to know, and it felt like I was on a cliff, on the edge of a huge drop and right now I couldn't even see the bottom. I couldn't know the bottom, or what it looked like until I asked the question now burning inside me. "Why, Josiah? Why are you helping me? Why did you wake me up and make me choose?"

He inhaled slow and deep, then exhaled the same. "Because you needed to know you were still alive. Because I saw something in you I recognized." He paused then continued. "Because if you didn't wake up, I'd never be able to do this." He stepped closer, our bodies a whisper apart; my eyes focused on the suns on his chest. His hands slid along my skin, up to my shoulders, trailed up my neck, to my jaw, my mouth. There, he dragged a slow thumb along my lips, almost smearing them, before gently grasping my face and lowering his mouth to mine. His lips were firm and hot as they met mine over and over again. Tender touches, the pressure increasing with each gentle pass as his mouth possessed mine effortlessly. His hands moved around to the back of my head, wove themselves through my hair, gripping me, holding me.

Whoa. I was definitely alive. In this moment I was *glad* I was alive. My world, my awareness, my focus narrowed to him. His mouth on mine. The feel, the taste, the texture of him. I kissed him back, letting my hands travel over his shoulders to feel his strength. Josiah gave that strength to me, freely. He enveloped me in it, surrounded me with it. And I completely trusted him. Several slow, delicious minutes later he pulled back, lifting his head until he could meet my eyes. After a moment, he pressed his lips to my forehead with an unsteady breath. His heart raced in his chest, pounding alongside mine.

Closing my eyes, I simply breathed him in, then after a moment, said, "That's...that's a pretty good reason to be alive."

Josiah's chuckle rumbled in my ear as he stepped back. "I've been waiting a while to do that."

"I'm glad you finally did."

"Me too." He chuckled again. "Fair warning; I plan on doing that often."

"Duly noted," I breathed.

"Good." He smiled as he kissed my lips gently, then said," Let's finish this up, get back to the house."

Josiah

Billy had worried about Crimson, if she'd be able to do this job, if it'd be too much for her. Josiah had reassured the older man she'd be fine. The wreck had been cleared away; the only evidence of it was the broken fence-line and torn up ground. Crimson had come such a long way, and Josiah felt she was strong enough to handle it. Chase McFee, one of the locals from Salmon who'd graduated the same year as Josiah, had, after a night of drinking, attempted to drive himself home. He'd lost control of his little Honda and had torn through the fence; thankfully no one else was injured in the accident. Dazed, he'd been able to climb out of the car, and after several minutes had made his way down to Red's house, crying, where he'd confessed the whole thing. Chase was arrested; Red called Billy to let him know. He also arranged to have the wreckage towed away. Billy told him he'd take care of the fence.

Normally fixing the fence was a job for Josiah. As the ranch foreman, it was his duty to take care of those types of things. But Billy knew Crimson worked with Josiah, so he'd asked him to put it off for a while. When two weeks had passed, Josiah told Billy he intended to get that fence fixed.

"You sure she's ready?" Billy had questioned. He could hear the concern in the man's voice.

"She's ready." Josiah reassured him. "Crimson can handle this."

"Maybe she needs more time...."

"She's ready, Billy."

Billy had reluctantly agreed, but admonished Josiah to play it by ear. So, he'd watched Crimson carefully as they'd pulled up to the crash site. She'd seemed a little distracted that morning, and he'd noticed her face had been a little flushed. Josiah had caught her looking at him several times and wondered what was going through her mind. Now, as she took in the torn and broken fence, her brown eyes widened and for a moment the blood drained from her face. She asked what had happened, her voice low, and a little raw with emotion.

Josiah wanted her to relax, so he'd stayed calm, nonchalant—this was just another duty to perform, no need to worry, no excitement here. He scratched his chin, casual-like and told her it had happened a couple weeks back. Immediately, Crimson snapped her focus from the broken fence to the reason behind allowing it to remain unfixed for so long. She knew that wasn't normal. After he explained Billy's reasoning, Josiah gave her a much-needed dose of confidence. He told her he thought she was strong enough to handle it. Then he quickly stepped out of the truck, leaving her no choice but to follow him.

As they worked, Josiah could feel her eyes on him like a physical touch. Like her small, gentle fingers were grazing over his back, his neck, his shoulders. Tension was building and he felt explosive. He tried working off that extra energy through the job he was performing. But he could still feel her eyes on him. He wanted his hands on her. He just didn't know if she was ready yet. Yes, Crimson had made great strides. She was no longer the walking dead. She was alive. But was she alive enough to handle him? That he didn't know yet, so he'd have to rein it in and wait.

Finally, when Josiah couldn't take the tension any longer, when he'd been contemplating throwing down the post-hole digger, pushing her up against that truck, and taking her mouth with his, he suddenly asked her,

"What's up?" If he was going to control himself, she was going to need to redirect her thoughts, or at least her eyes.

And then suddenly she was telling him everything. All her pain, all her fears, all her worries. Josiah already knew the gist of what she was sharing with him from Billy, but he was relieved she was now able to articulate her own feelings in all this.

Josiah let her talk. He didn't interrupt or question; he simply let her get it all out. As she talked, he continued working, the only comments he made were instructions for the work they were doing. And, after she'd finished talking, he saw her shoulders lift as that burden left her. Then after a few more minutes, she'd sagged again, no doubt anticipating his reaction, his horror at the truth of her life. And, while Crimson's past was a painful and confusing one, it wasn't the worst he'd heard or experienced. So, he'd just kept working.

When the wire had begun slipping through her grip, Josiah moved swiftly to assist her. He'd seen people cut up pretty badly from a snapped line as it rebounded. He took a firm hold of it, one arm on either side of her, and suddenly there she was, her sweet little body pressed up against him. The feel of her against his chest, his arms were nearly around her...it felt so danged right. She *belonged* there. And he never wanted to let her go. As he inhaled, her lemon, vanilla, and sunshine scent twisted his gut in need and desire. And then she'd begun to relax into him, to accept him. He could see the flutter of her eyelids, hear the catch in her breath, feel the softening in her stance.

Josiah knew if they didn't pull it together right then, he'd be lost. He'd had to gently nudge her arm to get a reaction out of her. It was like she'd just melted and melded into him.

Josiah was both relieved and frustrated at the loss of her in his arms. Nailing that wire nailed down as quickly as possible, he found himself in desperate need of ice water. In the form of a shower preferably, but he'd have to settle for the water bottles sitting in the small ice chest. He tossed one to Crimson and they both took a moment to collect themselves. Josiah decided he wasn't ready to get back to work, not just yet, not when he might find a need to put his hands on her again. He knew he needed to distract his mind, get it off Crimson and her body. Because he could still feel her pressed against him and it was driving him insane. He reflected on what she'd shared with him, reminding himself she was still hurting. And then, because she'd been so open with him, he decided to let her in, let her see a little of his own personal, hellish past.

Josiah knew Crimson tended to steer away from anything having to do with Billy. He could see she was still uncomfortable around him but also knew that Billy desperately loved her and regretted his actions in the past. So, he'd told Crimson about Billy, how Billy'd helped him, how Billy had saved him. And as he spoke, he watched the walls come back up. Crimson tried making light of the situation, tried to shift the focus from her and Billy, and their lack of relationship. In doing so, she'd inadvertently brought the conversation right back to Josiah and herself.

When she'd asked about his tattoos, Josiah had grinned, knowing he was cornered. Her diversion slapped his desire for her right back in his face. He kept his gaze focused on Crimson. Maybe it was time she was made perfectly aware of his feelings, made to face her attraction to him. She'd read his intent pretty accurately. And she'd responded. He'd seen it in her eyes; seen it in the blush staining her cheeks. The raw, male animal in him surged to its feet, growling in anticipation.

He'd watched then as Crimson devoured him with her eyes. Every place her gaze landed was like a physical touch. Everywhere her eyes landed he burned. And then as she'd moved closer, barely a breath separating them, and had lightly touched his chest...he'd barely been able to hold himself in check. What he wanted to do was loose the beast. Pull her into him and wrap his arms around her. To take her mouth and make it his. Instead, he'd held himself absolutely and perfectly still. When her eyes caught his, he saw the questions in them.

He'd explained about his mother and saw the horror, the sickness in Crimson's eyes. He also saw the flash of anger. That fury sparked something inside him. She was protective of him. And that somehow gave Josiah peace. He'd turned around, letting her see his back. It was a beautiful work of art. Dragon wings were tattooed there in intricate detail. He'd picked a dragon because the flame that was meant to break him had only made him stronger. Dragons were not conquered by fire; it was their weapon, their defense.

When she'd finally asked him why...why was he helping her? Why had he made her wake up and choose? Josiah knew then where his answer was going. That he was going to kiss this woman in front of him. So, as he'd told her his reasons, he'd stepped closer, brushing against her enough to feel her slight tremor. He'd traced his hands gently across her shoulders, those shoulders that drove him crazy, reveling in the softness under his palms, feeling the smoothness of her skin, savoring it. He'd trailed those hands up her neck, acknowledging just how small she truly was. Traced her jaw, ran his thumbs over her lips, priming them just a little before he took them.

Then, he'd moved his hands into her hair, weaved his long fingers through that soft platinum thickness, and fisted them there, holding tight, but not too tight. He wouldn't hurt her, and hoped and prayed she wouldn't be frightened, that she would accept his advances, because he honestly wasn't sure how he was going to pull it back if she said to stop. When his mouth, finally touched hers, tasted hers, he'd thought he'd died. Words couldn't express how sweet, how addicting she was, so hesitant and willing. Trusting. He'd felt that trust like a physical touch and refused to do any damage to it. He'd clamped down tightly on his desire, forcing himself to release her mouth, pulling back. Then he'd gently placed a tender kiss on her forehead, all while he'd been on fire inside. Desire was a hungry, voracious beast, and he desperately wanted to loose the animal. Instead, they'd quickly finished the work, before heading back to the ranch. Now that he'd tasted her mouth, he'd have to watch himself more carefully, knowing he'd only want more. So much more.

Chapter 6
Alpha and Dangerous

*C*rimson Sage

By the time we'd arrived back at the house, Ethan was already home, playing outside with Daisy. We sat in the truck for a moment, just watching them. "Josiah?" I asked after a moment.

"Yeah?" His thumb tracked slowly over the back of my hand.

"Are we going to tell anyone...about us?"

"That depends." He faced me now. "Did you not want to?"

"I'd like to keep this private, for the time being. Ethan is just finding himself here and I don't want to supply him with any distractions." Now, I turned towards him. "Is that okay?"

"It's okay." He dipped his chin. "I'm not sneaking around though. I won't be made to feel like we're doing something wrong. Because we're not."

"No, I didn't mean that." I shook my head. "I just don't want to confuse him. And what about Billy? What do you think he's going to say?"

"I'm pretty sure Billy already has a pretty good idea of how I feel about you."

"He does?"

"I've done my best to keep everything under wraps, mainly because you weren't ready, but Crimson? I've had my eye on you long before you arrived here."

"I don't understand."

"We'll talk about it later." He tucked a wayward strand of hair behind my ear, lingering as he did. "Just know that Billy shouldn't be a problem and we'll keep things under the radar for the time being, so as not to confuse Ethan, but if it comes up or out, then I'm going to be straight with him."

"Thanks."

"Seeing as how we have an audience right now, I won't kiss you. We'll have a bonfire tonight, and I'll figure something out, because I definitely want to be kissing you again. Soon." I blushed, then nodded.

Ethan ran up and threw his arms around me as I stepped from the truck. "Hey, Sis."

"Hey, Kid. School okay? You have homework?"

"Just a little."

"I'm going to catch a shower, then you boys meet me at the table so we can get it done."

"Ah, c'mon!" He whined. "It's Friday! I have all weekend to get things done."

"Well, you'll do it now and then have all weekend left to enjoy your free time." Ethan grumbled good-naturedly, then ran to tell the other boys. They were all waiting for me when I came back to the kitchen about thirty minutes later. This was our second week working together and already I'd had a note from their teachers letting me know how well they were doing. We worked on math, going over basic algebra. I told them to not look at it like math, but rather like they were detectives and each problem was like a crime scene that offered so many clues that would allow them to solve it. This seemed to help, because they embraced it rather than fighting it. It certainly made tutoring them easier.

After dinner we gathered outside for the bonfire. Billy let them stay up an extra hour due to how well they were all doing in school. I listened to the conversations taking place around me, taking in how well these kids were doing. Josiah had told me that most of them had stories similar to his; abusive parents, negligent parents, no parents at all. My heart healed a little, softened a little towards Billy as I realized where his heart lay. He really did love these boys and desperately wanted them to succeed, and to be a positive difference in their lives.

At ten he called it a night, having them turn in. Josiah stayed me with a light touch to my wrist. Settling back in my seat, I waved Ethan off and said goodnight to Billy. It bothered me a little to see how he reacted to that. To know that my distance had hurt him. Tonight was the first time I'd said it *to* him; usually I just responded, never initiating. Maybe this too was healing inside me.

Josiah and I silently watched as the lights in the house were turned out one by one and it became dark and quiet. The fire had burned low, so Josiah added another log. Soon the flames were rising again, snapping, and crackling in the pit. He sat back down beside me, scooting his chair a little closer, then reached for my hand, simply holding it, slowly rubbing my palm with his thumb. We sat that way for roughly an hour, not speaking, just enjoying the fire, the night, and each other's company. When the flames were once again down to embers, Josiah squeezed my hand gently before releasing me.

I watched as he doused the ashes with the hose, putting the fire completely out. A three-quarter moon crept just above the tree line, so we weren't in complete darkness. He held his hand out and swiftly pulled me to my feet and against him. There his arms wrapped around me as his mouth found mine. He growled a little, just a gentle rumble in his chest. Still, I heard it, felt it. And thrilled at the sound.

Josiah wasn't like any boy I'd ever kissed or known before. He didn't allow me to set the tone or the pace. He was entirely in charge yet wasn't forceful. I never felt like I was out of my element, or that I couldn't stop things if I felt the need to. He was simply confident, knowing what he was doing. Knowing what he wanted from me. He seemed to know what I wanted him to do. When to draw the line and back off. When to bring on the heat.

He nibbled my mouth, lightly tasting, brushing his lips across mine. His hands moved slowly up my back, holding me to him, burying themselves in my hair. He ran his fingers through the strands, letting it slither through his grasp. Now he cupped my face, ran his thumb over my lower lip, touched my tongue, and kissed me again.

I was dazed. Dazed and fluid. Feeling like I would just slip into a puddle on the ground. My eyes wouldn't focus; my heart was pounding out a heavy, steady rhythm. I swallowed and he gently kissed me again. Josiah stepped back, taking my hands in his, kissing my knuckles. "You'd better go inside. Get some sleep. I'll see you in the morning."

Exhaling a shaky breath, I nodded then leaned up on tiptoe and kissed his jaw. "Goodnight, Josiah." He watched me as I entered the house, nodding at me to go on. I locked the door, then made my way carefully through the darkened house, had just begun climbing the stairs, when I was startled by a noise from above me. Gasping, I looked up. Mike stood silently in the shadows, taking up most of the stairway, leaving me little room to get by. "Mike! *Jeez.* You scared the snot out of me!" I whispered, clutching at my throat, willing my heart to calm. He didn't say anything. Just stood there. A shiver tiptoed down my spine.

"I was thirsty," he finally said. "Real thirsty."

"Well, okay. I'll see you in the morning I guess." He didn't move, didn't give me room to get passed him. As he stood now, I'd practically have to rub against him to get by. "Excuse me." I looked him in the eye, letting my wishes be known. His mouth tilted up as he shuffled minutely to the side. Only by tightly hugging the wall was I able to make it by without touching him. I could feel his eyes on me, on my body and quickly climbed the steps to get away from him. I'd just reached the top when he said, "Sweet dreams, Sage."

Josiah slowly inhaled, the sound whispering in my ear, causing delicious shivers up and down my spine. My breath caught a little in my throat, and

I tried to calm myself. It was a useless endeavor because his hands were slowly sliding up and down my thighs. His mouth lingered at my shoulder where he'd lowered the collar of my shirt, leaving it bare. He seemed to love this place, and I loved what he did there. Out behind the barn, Josiah had created a small, private patio area for himself; he'd leveled the ground and paved it in large flat stones he'd dug up around the ranch. He'd formed a small fire pit and built rustic log benches and lounge chairs that were grouped around it. We were seated on one. Or Josiah was seated on one; I was seated on him.

It was just after eight in the evening. The boys had already gone in for the night, and Josiah had texted asking me to come over. He met me at the backdoor, and we'd walked over, hand in hand. I'd never been to his room above the barn. Had never been out back here with him before either. Yesterday he'd surprised me with red roses. I'd never had a boy do romantic things like that before. Especially without the expectation of some sort of payment. A touch. A kiss. Josiah wasn't like that. Even now, with me on his lap. His hands traveling my thighs, my back. His mouth on my neck, my shoulders, my lips. He'd never once attempted to grope me. He was careful to skirt those areas, those private areas. He never made me feel those parts of my body were his intention or goal. More, like he respected me and wasn't going to trespass. I appreciated that. There was no pressure in his touch. Just pleasure.

He turned me, pulled me back against his chest, my back towards him. His arms wrapped around me. Threading his hands with mine, he lifted them up together, watching the way the firelight played on our skin. We sat quietly for a while. Every now and then he'd kiss my neck or graze me with his teeth. I was content to stay right here all night if possible, except my bladder, which had been mildly complaining about the amount of coffee I'd consumed earlier, was now screaming madly. I tried shifting my position, but nothing helped, and I could no longer ignore it.

"I have to get going." I told him reluctantly.

"It's early still, barely after nine." He nipped my shoulder. "Stay for a while. At least until ten."

"At least let me run back to the house for a minute."

"For what?"

I blew out my breath. "I need to use the bathroom."

Josiah laughed quietly. "I don't use the bushes out back, ya know. You can use mine."

"Oh. I just...you've never...I've never been up to your loft before."

"Come on." He stood, me still in his arms, then set me on my feet, before taking my hand and leading me to the stairs. I asked about the fire. "We won't be inside that long. Too risky."

"Risky?"

"Much too risky." The heat in his gaze and weight in his words had me blushing as he reached for his door.

Josiah's loft was open and spacious. A small kitchenette area, with a short bar and two bar stools that served as a table sat to left side of the back wall. He had a couch covered in some kind of Navajo print and a coffee table with several books scattered on it. In one corner stood a TV. On the opposite side of the room was his bed. A large, uncovered window stood between the bed and the couch. The moon rose above the trees, lighting the space, giving everything a cool tone. In vain, I tried not to stare at his bed but couldn't help the way my eyes kept being drawn back to it. "The bathroom is right through that door."

Josiah had to say my name to get me to notice where he was pointing, what he was saying. My eyes had been glued to his bed, and I just hadn't heard him. To the right of the bed was a door. This is where he was pointing. Blushing, I shook my head and quickly walked towards his bathroom.

When I came out Josiah was leaning against the counter, his back to the sink; his eyes on me. He held a glass of water, then after a moment, his eyes still glued to mine, he downed the rest of it before setting it on the counter beside him. He grinned a little and I shivered at the animal-like quality of it. "I figured it was safer over here, but we should get back outside. Quickly."

Nodding, I looked down to avoid any tripping hazards, and my eyes strayed to the coffee table and something on it caught my eye. Sticking out from under one of the books was the bottom portion of a photo. I recognized it. It was a picture of me, taken about a year ago. I'd been standing in my front yard, goofing off for the camera. Dad had taken the picture. I was in a body builder pose, my arms curled up, flexing to show my biceps. I was laughing.

I held it in my hands for a minute as tears pricked my eyes. I looked to Josiah. How had he gotten it?

"I'd asked Billy if I could have it. Never thinking I'd actually meet you." He shrugged. "I have another one, too; you're at the beach. Billy gave them to me—last year."

"But, why? Why do you have it?" I was at a loss, my emotions in turmoil, confused by his possible reasons.

"Your smile." He shrugged again. "So much joy in that simple smile. Looking at it made me happy, peaceful. I just wanted a little of it, to keep and hold that happiness here. It made me feel a little less lonely."

I stared at him. Josiah was never weak. He was never needful. He was so strong, so self-contained, self-assured. I was having a hard time picturing him needing a picture to make him feel better. He approached me, gently grasped my hand, threaded his fingers with mine, our palms rubbing enticingly together. The abrasiveness of his skin against the softness of mine. "Yes, Crimson. I needed that sunshine. *Needed* it. I still need it." He pulled me against him, rested my head against his chest, ran his hands over my hair. Kissed the top of my head. I heard the way his heartbeat picked up, the way it throbbed in his chest, echoing mine. His breathing sounded a little rougher.

"We need to go back outside." He rumbled softly, yet firmly in my ear. "Now." I set the picture down and let him lead me downstairs. The fire had burned low by the time we returned. Josiah still held my hand; I moved aside to allow him to close the barn door and suddenly found myself pressed against the side of the barn. His mouth moved over mine, his hips held me in place, as his hands were in my hair, then moved down and around my back, squeezing gently, tightly. Josiah's mouth left mine to travel down my neck, to focus on his favorite spot, that sensitive juncture where my neck and shoulder connected. He kissed, then lightly bit me, holding on for a moment causing a thrill to rock through me before letting me go. He pressed his lips against my forehead then pulled back after a moment. "I'd wondered how dangerous it would be, having you in my place."

"And?" I was entirely out of breath.

He kissed my jaw, my neck, my mouth again. "Very dangerous. Too dangerous. We should probably forego the remainder of the fire. I'm hot enough as it is and I don't want to forget my limits." I grinned, liking that I could affect him that way. That I wasn't the only one having a hard time with this attraction. He kissed me again, nipping at my lip. "Good lord, you need to go back to the house... I'd walk you back, but we may not make it." Josiah gently pushed me away from him, shaking his head.

"Goodnight," I whispered, turning towards the house.

"Text me when you get to your room." His dark gaze smoldered, and I quickly turned away.

I'd nearly reached the patio when I heard a sound behind me. Thinking Josiah had changed his mind, unable to help himself, I chuckled, turning back around. "I thought you said it was too dangerous?"

My heart lodged in my throat as Mike stepped from the shadows. "Oh, it's dangerous all right. He left you all primed and ready. Guess I'll have to take care of business for him, seeing as he's not man enough." I barely had a chance to respond, before he reached for me, then suddenly he was gone, and I was stumbling backward.

Landing on my butt, I heard a deep thud, then Mike cursing loudly. Blinking, I saw Josiah standing over him, fists tight. "Touch her again and I'll kill you," he growled menacingly.

Mike climbed slowly to his feet, wiped the blood from his lip, and looked at Josiah with hard, hateful eyes. "Yeah? What's she to you?"

"Get your sorry butt in the house, and up to your room, or I'll be waking Billy. You're already breaking protocol just being outside."

"I didn't even touch her. And you hit me. I can file charges against you."

"Go ahead. Let's call Billy now and you can file a formal complaint."

Mike chuckled darkly. "I got time. I'm going." He turned to me, letting his eyes travel down my body, hesitating on my chest. "When you get tired of him, you come and see me."

Josiah swore low as he stepped forward, anger in every line of his body. Mike beat a hasty retreat, tossing another grin over his shoulder as he entered the house, closing the door behind himself. Josiah quickly turned and helped me to my feet. My body shook as I trembled, and Josiah wrapped his arms around me, holding me tight.

"Are you all right? I should've killed him. Answer me, Crimson. If he hurt you, I *will* kill him." Josiah's voice was harsh with emotion, and I felt the tears spill over my cheeks.

"I'm...I'm not hurt." I tried to draw a deep breath but couldn't seem to get it past the lump in my throat. Josiah lifted me, cradling me against his chest and began walking back toward the barn. "You're staying with me tonight. I don't trust that bastard. Billy's going to hear about this. I want him gone. You'll be safer with me; I'll sleep on the couch."

Josiah

Josiah watched her sleep. Crimson lay on her side, knees curled toward her stomach, her hands fisted. Her hair was thrown out over his pillow. One foot peeked out from under his blanket. Her breathing was slow, settled, and deep. He could smell her. Lemon and sunshine and vanilla. He hadn't been able to sleep. First, he'd lain awake, intensely aware of her just a few feet away. Then, to distract himself from that knowledge, he'd thought back to earlier when Mike had made his move.

Fury twisted his gut, tightened his jaw, anger throbbed in his veins. Silently he'd stood, moving away from the couch, and into his little kitchen. After getting a quick drink of water, he'd lowered himself to the floor and did several sets of pushups, hoping to work off some of that fury. When that didn't work, he slipped from his loft, making his way down to the barn where he had a weight bench and barbells.

For two hours he worked out, sweating away his anger and frustration. Periodically, he'd step to the barn door and look out towards the house. His eyes would connect with the second story window that housed Mike, and the fury would rage through him again. Finally, he returned to his apartment, locked the door after himself, then headed for the shower. He stood in the bathroom doorway, wrapped in his towel, warring with himself. Wanting her, wanting to end Mike. Blowing out a breath, he let his eyes travel over Crimson's slim form. Mind in a whirl, he dried himself off and then headed back to the couch, knowing he needed rest.

He doubted he'd sleep much tonight. Regardless of the workout he'd had, he was still a live wire. Crimson was just feet away and his body fully recognized that. He wanted her. Bad. But Josiah wasn't a selfish jerk. She wasn't ready. Especially after what had happened tonight. He'd have to wait and just be patient.

First thing in the morning he planned to discuss what happened with Billy. The old man needed to know what Mike had done. Josiah settled back into the corner of the couch; his eyes stayed on Crimson. He'd watch over her, keep her safe. He inhaled and her lemony scent assailed him again, making his mouth water. It was going to be a long night.

Crimson Sage

All things considered, I didn't expect to sleep well at all, but I was a little surprised when I rolled over and the sun was shining brightly through the large window. Josiah was seated on the couch. Coffee mug in hand. His eyes were on me. They were so filled with varying emotions I didn't know which one to address first. Amusement, most-likely at my messy hair. Anger, still left over from last night. Desire; I was in his bed, after all. Caution; he was being careful with me. Possession; again, I was in his bed. "Good morning," I whispered. "Did you sleep at all?"

"Some. You?"

"Surprisingly I slept pretty well. Your bed is soft. It smells like you." Josiah took a slow, deep breath at that and then let it out just as slowly. He shook his head a little. Cautiously I continued, "I was thinking...I don't want to tell Billy. It would break his heart to know about this. You threatened Mike; I'm sure he'll stay away now."

"Crimson...I think we should tell him. I'm obligated to tell him. Mike attacked you."

"Really, he didn't; he made innuendos, but you stopped him before he actually did anything. Let's just let things be for now. I promise I'll be careful around him."

"I think this is a mistake. I'm not okay with this."

"Please?" Josiah looked hard at me for a moment and then nodded, his lips in a tight line. I knew he didn't like what I was asking, and I understood his reasons, and a small part of me even agreed with him, but I still didn't want to deal with this right now. It was too much on top of everything else. Josiah made me promise to let him know immediately if Mike tried anything. I readily agreed, relieved he was allowing me to keep last night between us.

Josiah

When Crimson opened her honey eyes in the morning, Josiah was still seated on the couch. He'd risen to get some coffee, but otherwise had stayed in place, just watching her. He'd imagined being in that bed with her all night long, telling himself he had to wait. Wait until she was ready. When Crimson told him she didn't want to tell Billy about what had happened, Josiah cautioned himself to remain calm. He tried talking her into it, but he could see she was determined in her thinking. Crimson promised she'd be extremely careful around Mike and would tell Josiah if he so much as winked at her.

Josiah agreed to her request, but not happily. He didn't know how he was going to keep his hands off Mike. He didn't know how he was going to keep his hands off Crimson. He decided he'd just have to be that much more vigilant. For Crimson's sake Josiah hoped Mike would leave her alone. Unfortunately, he was certain Mike would only understand the language of the Pack. The street mentality, the violence...that was the only thing the younger man would listen to.

Chapter 7
Beauty and the Beast

rimson Sage

For nearly two weeks Mike stayed away from me. I'd catch him looking, but that was pretty much it. Ignoring him seemed my best course of action. Once or twice, he would position himself in a spot where I'd either have to squeeze past him or go out of my way to avoid him. Those times were nerve-wracking because he was always careful to do it when Josiah and Billy weren't around to see.

One afternoon, I needed to run into town, figuring I'd swing by to see if Ethan wanted to ride home with me. If I timed it correctly, I should be there just as he was getting out of school. I got the things I'd come for and quickly returned to the truck. I had my keys out and checked the time on my cell phone, not wanting to be late, when, as I reached for the handle, out of nowhere a hand gripped my arm and spun me around. My back was pressed against the door, the handle digging painfully into my back, as Mike leaned into me from the front. "Now I got you alone, we need to get some things straight."

"Get away from me." My voice was nowhere near as cold and firm as I'd tried to make it.

He chuckled darkly, a finger tapping my nose. "Not just yet. I kinda like this."

"I'll tell Josiah."

He tightened his grip on my arm, leaning closer, tobacco-scented breath skated along my neck, bringing nausea. He chuckled again as he skimmed his nose along my jawline. "You do that. Your saintly boyfriend already has a rap sheet; bet ya didn't know that, did ya? He gets one more infraction for assault and he's facing hard time. And I'd let him beat me, just to see him locked away."

My eyes darted around, desperately hoping someone would see us and come to my aid. One man, he looked to be around forty or so, had paused beside his car, watching us. Mike winked at him, kissed my cheek, and said, "I'll see you tonight, Babe. Love you and remember what I said."

He walked away, and tremors shook my body as I fought to keep the panic at bay. The man who'd been watching us, had shrugged then driven off. Still shaking, I climbed into the truck, locking my doors behind me. I couldn't move, couldn't think. Fear eddied in my middle, blurring my vision. Then I remembered Ethan and quickly started the truck, revving the engine as I took off down the road. Glancing at my cellphone again, I knew I was too late—Ethan would have left on the bus already. Still, I drove to the school anyway, just to make sure. The buses were already gone. Tears kept forming in my eyes, but I refused to let them fall. I needed to get myself under control and figure out what to do.

My first reaction was to tell Josiah, but I truly believed he would kill Mike and then it would be my fault if he went to prison. My next choice would be to go to Billy, but that would be telling Josiah in a roundabout way. I couldn't risk that either. I could call the police, but again, same outcome. Josiah would learn of it and hunt down Mike. No, what I had to do was pull myself together and learn to stand on my own two feet and protect those I cared about. Maybe I could learn self-defense and get some pepper spray or something.

Josiah

Crimson seemed off. Like maybe she had something on her mind, or something was bothering her. Josiah wanted her to open up about whatever it was but wouldn't press her on it. He'd be ready when she did finally turn to him. Whether she needed a shoulder, an ear, or advice, he'd be ready.

He wanted to do something for her, something she'd never expect. Something that would blow her mind. As he watched her work beside him, something he found himself doing quite frequently, and saw the sweat trickle slowly down her neck, he watched as she wiped it away, rolled her shoulders, and continued painting. She looked hot. Not just attractive, not that kind of hot, but warm, like she could use a swim to cool off. His blue eyes flicked to the pond, then up to the house. *No privacy here.*

If he managed to keep the boys away from the pond, they'd be in the upstairs windows with binoculars. A flash of inspiration had him telling Crimson he'd be right back. Josiah turned away, jogged back to the barn, and headed up to his loft. He grabbed a couple bottles of water from his small fridge. After setting those on the counter, he dialed his phone. "Jake," he said when the call was answered. "Hey, buddy, I need that favor. Can you leave me your key for the pool?"

"The pool?" Jake asked. "You going swimming?"

"Yep."

"Why not just use the pond?"

"Not enough privacy."

"What do you need privacy for?" Jake chuckled.

"It's more of a date, than leisure time."

"You don't say," Jake chuckled again, clearly enjoying this conversation. "Anyone I know?"

"Not likely. Just leave the key under that potted plant by the side door. I'll make sure things are locked up nice and tight when I leave."

"All right. It's just you and your date; right? No secret wild party going on?"

"Nah, man. It's just me and her. Promise."

"All right. I'll make it happen. Have fun."

"Thanks." Josiah checked the time before sliding the phone back in his pocket—it was just before three right now. The public pool closed at five during the weekdays. Josiah made his way back to where Crimson was still painting and handed her a bottle of water. They painted for another hour and a half, getting over half of the fence completed. Crimson straightened up and stretched. They'd finished the front side and just the back remained. Josiah slipped up behind her, sliding his hands around her waist, pulling her back against him.

He nuzzled her ear. "I want you. Away from prying eyes. Let me take you out tonight." He loved the little catch in her breath at his touch, loved the color that stained her cheeks, too. Crimson smiled as she turned in his arms and asked when. "Now. Let's call it a day. We'll get cleaned up, head to town in about an hour. How's that sound?"

"Sounds good, but where are we going?"

"Can't tell you, but make sure you bring a bathing suit." Her look of confusion had him grinning, but she agreed. Managing to keep the satisfaction off his face, Josiah saw her back to the house before running up to his loft and jumping in the shower.

Crimson Sage

I was careful, so very careful, not to give any indication that I was unnerved by Mike, or that he had gotten to me, or that anything at all had taken place. It was a constant battle not to alert Josiah that anything was wrong. But Mike's threat kept playing on repeat in my head, making it difficult to focus. So, I'd held the words inside, determined not to give Mike the satisfaction of knowing he'd unnerved me. That night, after he'd cornered me at my truck, once everyone had gone to bed, I'd searched online for local self-defense classes, anything I thought might help me deal with this situation on my own. Unfortunately, all I saw were martial arts/exercise classes, and that wasn't what I was looking for.

Days later, I began to wonder if there was some way I could approach Josiah, convince him to teach me some things, without letting on the reason why. I'd have to do it in such a way that he wouldn't suspect anything and yet still be willing to teach me anyway.

"You hungry?" Josiah asked once we were on the road. He'd told Billy he was taking me to town for dinner and a coke and that we'd be back late and not to wait up. Billy had only chuckled and said to be safe. "We could eat first if you want."

"I'm game for whatever."

Josiah chuckled wickedly, sending a thrill through my middle. "Careful now." That had me grinning. He took my hand in his as we drove down the highway, then through town. He seemed to be in no hurry, just taking his time, shifting with our hands entwined. After several minutes he pulled to the side of the road, behind a big warehouse. "Do you trust me?" A gleam of excitement sparked in his blues eyes, and I couldn't stop myself from agreeing. Those eyes of his might be the death of me. Reaching into the glove box, he pulled out a faded blue bandana. Cocking an eyebrow, I looked from him to the bandana. "*Trust* me." His voice was smooth, like cool water over rocks. Grumbling under my breath, I allowed him to blindfold me. "No peeking," he warned.

We drove for only a couple more minutes, then he parked, and turned the car off. "Hold on a sec; just wait here." He was out of the car, the door slamming behind him. I wondered what he was doing and was just thinking of peeking when he opened my door and took my hand, helping me out. It was a little disorienting, not being able to see where I was going, but we slowly walked forward with him guiding me. A door opened, then I was hit with a sudden gush of warm, wet, chlorine-scented air. I knew that smell; my lip trembled.

Josiah walked me forward a few steps before bringing me to a stop. Gently, he untied the bandana, pulling it off. My gaze took in the large indoor pool and my breath caught.

"Surprise." Josiah wrapped his arms around me from the back.

Craning my head around, I looked up at him, a little awed and thoroughly touched at his thoughtfulness. "How?"

"A friend owed me a favor; I called it in." He checked his watch. "We have it for the next three hours. Just us. Just you, me, and the water." Josiah showed me where the locker rooms were, and I quickly changed into my suit. As fast as I was, he still beat me back out to the water. He stood near the edge, his gaze on the ladies' locker room, watching for me. Slowly I made my way to him, letting his eyes move over me. His look wasn't like Mike's; Josiah never made me feel dirty and in need of a shower. No, his vivid blue eyes worshiped me.

My eyes were busy, too. Josiah wore a pair of grey trunks. His legs were lighter than his chest and neck—a working man's tan. They may have been lighter, but they were every bit as muscled as the rest of him, and they were covered in dark red hair. As I looked up at him, I suddenly found myself feeling a little frisky. Just a couple steps away, I launched myself at him, taking us both into the water. I was gratified to hear his startled yelp as the water closed over us. We both reached the surface at the same time. An evil grin spread across his face, but before he could reach me, I kicked hard, diving deep. Josiah tried to catch me but soon seemed to give up and headed for the side, content to watch me swim.

This was heaven. My body remembered exactly what to do, like I'd never left. After several laps though, the burn in my muscles let my absence from the pool be known. Pushing myself, I did another five laps, before finally stopping, entirely out of breath. Josiah sat near the ladder, on the side of the pool, feet in the water, just watching me. Sluggishly, I swam for him, feeling my work out. "Josiah...I...*thank you.*" My breath came embarrassingly loud, practically panting. "I can't thank you enough. I forgot how much I missed this."

"You're welcome." His voice was velvet-coated steel as he checked his watch. "I was glad to do it."

"I know I'm out of shape...but we haven't been here for three hours yet?"

He shook his head. "About forty minutes now. We've got time yet. Unless you're getting hungry?"

Treading water in front of him, I chuckled. "Oh, I'm feeling it; I could eat a horse."

"Glad there're no horses around, then." He stood, then leaned over the ladder, offering a hand to help pull me up. My limbs felt like wet noodles as I climbed the rungs and was grateful for his assistance. He pulled me to him and reached for my mouth. "Crimson?" he said between kisses.

"Yeah?" I whispered back.

"There's just one more thing..."

"What's that?" I breathed, my head now swimming in that desire he so easily sparked.

"Well...this—" His arms clamped around me like steel bands as he launched us back into the water, eliciting a strangled scream from my throat. This time, Josiah's laughter echoed across the water as I breached the surface again. Intent on dunking him, I ignored my exhaustion, moving toward him. The fire in his eyes caught me as I neared him, slowing my approach. Capturing one of my hands, he slowly pulled me through the water, our bodies sliding together. Firm, warm hands settled on my waist, pulling me closer still. Strong fingers splayed across my stomach, tracing the muscle there, before skimming around to my back. He moved up my spine in a slow, tantalizing motion, pausing at my shoulders. "Have I ever told you how *much* I love this spot?" His mouth moved over the skin of my left shoulder. Nipping, kissing. He growled low in his throat. "So much, Crimson."

My breath shuddered as his hands moved up my throat, cupped my neck, and dragged my mouth to his. His kiss was slow, deliberate. He made each touch, each nip, each taste seem somehow like the most intimate of touches, and yet pure and innocent at the same time.

My arms tightened around his shoulder, as I clung to him. My legs somehow ended up around him, and I felt cool concrete against my back. Breath came in short, sharp gasps as I panted, entirely lost to the sensations he evoked in me. He groaned something unintelligible against my mouth, and dimly I became aware as Josiah pulled away. Only for him to move back in as he reached for my mouth again. "We should…" he kissed my jaw. "We really should…" His teeth gripped my shoulder before dragging up to my mouth again.

Suddenly he ripped himself from me, swimming several feet away. Treading water, he kept his back to me, his shoulders tight with tension as his head tipped back. "I'm sorry." His breath was rough, causing me to shiver in longing. "Just give me a minute, okay?"

Swallowing, I considered all that had just happened, then silently made my way to the ladder. There, still shaking, I carefully pulled myself out of the water. "I'm going to shower and change." My voice was hoarse, even to my own ears.

Josiah turned and nodded, evidently not trusting himself to speak. I was in the locker room, and probably the shower before he was even out of the pool. My shower didn't take long; I was done in about fifteen minutes. Josiah was waiting for me when I came out. He seemed back in control of himself, though almost distant. Maybe reserved was the right word. In silence, he locked up, then drove us to Smokey's Burger Hut. Smokey's was a drive-in, fifties-themed joint. We found an open booth near the window and ordered our meals. When the silence stretched on, I extended my hand across the table to him. "Hey, what's going in that head of yours, huh?"

"Just thinking." He traced designs onto the tabletop with a finger, keeping his eyes down.

"About?"

"The pool. You." He inhaled, long and deep. "Whether I went too far, too fast."

Heat pooled in my middle, and I waited for him to look at me. When his deep blues eyes finally met mine, I offered a smile and extended my hand further. Josiah's hand was a solid, warm, and comfortable weight as he placed it in mine. "You didn't go too far." His eyes asked questions his mouth refused to voice. "Josiah, you didn't. Did it get...heavy? Yes, but even in all that, you never trespassed. You have no idea how much I appreciate that."

"I wanted more." His voice held a gravelly note, and an apology was there as well.

"But you didn't take it or cross lines, did you?"

Our order was delivered then—the house guacamole-bacon cheeseburger, which was to die for—saving him from answering.

We ate in silence, too hungry to continue our conversation, simply devouring the delicious food. Once we were no longer so ravenous, I sat back, enjoying the feeling of being full, sipping on the remains of my mint-chocolate shake. My eyes moved around the room, noting the responses to Josiah from those around us. There was still that unnamed respect and wariness that men showed him. Several sets of eyes were on him. All of them considering. Especially the heated, interested stares from women. Josiah seemed unaware of the attention he was receiving. Or, if he was aware, he wasn't bothered by it. In fact, he was doing his fair share of staring also. His deep blue traveled over my hair, my jawline, my collarbone. I blushed under his gaze and Josiah flashed a wolfish, knowing look my way. I wondered if he was thinking about earlier again. Just as I was getting ready to ask, someone stepped to our table.

The man wore official dress and a sheriff's badge. Remembering what Mike had said about Josiah having a rap sheet, I worried the sheriff was here to give Josiah a bad time. Instead, he stuck his hand out, greeting Josiah like they were olds friends. "How's it going, Joe?" The sheriff asked.

"I'm doing well, Red. How're things here in town?"

"Troubling." Red shifted his eyes to mine; the look in them was warm, friendly. "You'd be Billy's granddaughter. I'm, Red—Sally's brother—and your granddad's other partner."

"Sage." I nodded, gripping the hand he held out.

Soft grey eyes studied me a moment. "I knew your mother. She was one of the finest people I ever knew. You look like her."

"Yeah, I get that a lot." The lump in my throat made further conversation difficult, so I just offered what I hoped was a thankful smile.

No doubt noticing my discomfort, Josiah asked, "What's troubling, Red?"

The sheriff studied me a moment longer, then shook his head and turned to Josiah. "Had a girl attacked last night. Just walking home from the store."

"Attacked, how?"

"Attempted rape. A car came along, scared her attacker off, thank the Good Lord."

"Any suspects?"

"Not as yet."

"She able to give a description?"

He shook his head. "Just that it was a man; she thinks white."

"Who was she?"

"Maggie Tyler."

At the sound of that name, my heart jerked. Maggie: that was the name of the girl we'd got Daisy from. "Is Maggie about fifteen, blond hair?"

Red nodded, his lips pursed in thought. "You know her?"

"She's the one we got Daisy from—my brother's dog." My gaze flashed to Josiah before returning to Red. "Is she all right?"

"She will be. Obviously, she's pretty shook up. Her daddy's on the war path. Wants the animal that did this dead or behind bars."

"Can't blame him for that." Josiah took my hand in his, giving me a gentle squeeze.

Red focused on our enjoined hands, then suddenly grinned at me. "You know you've got the tiger by the tail; don't you?"

I grinned a little at that, squeezing Josiah's hand in return. "I'm not too worried; he seems tame enough."

"You've got yourself a good man; I'd hold on to him, if I were you." Red then tipped his hat and headed for the door. I wondered at the respect in his voice; it wasn't what I'd have expected from a law enforcement officer towards someone with a long rap sheet. I found it puzzling to say the least.

"You think I'm a tiger, huh?" Josiah teased, bringing my gaze back to him.

That had me blushing again. "You do come across as a little *untamed*, at times, yes."

"You still thinking about earlier?" He looked concerned now. "I am sorry for how far that went."

"I wasn't thinking about that, but now I am. And I told you, I'm *not* sorry."

The wolf was back in his eyes, causing my pulse to speed up. "Duly noted."

Blushing, again—I swear this man could melt ice with just a look—I noticed a young woman walking through the parking lot. She was young, blond, like Maggie, and a sick, twisted feeling settled in my middle. "Maggie...I can't believe what happened to her. It's so awful. I hope they catch whoever did that to her."

"What that animal attempted to do to her is awful. It's disgusting, and I hope her dad finds him first. Save the taxpayer."

I nodded. "I was just thinking..."

"About?"

"I'd like to learn some kind of self-defense. Maybe get a can of pepper spray or something."

Josiah studied me carefully for a moment, then slowly nodded. "I can teach you some things, and I'll ask Red where I can get you a can of that spray. I'd like you to postpone your trips to town unless I can go with you. At least until this is ended one way or another." So relieved that he'd readily agreed, and even though I chafed at having to be escorted to town, I willingly accepted his request. A calculating look entered Josiah's eyes as he studied me. "You won't be in any danger." I nodded, not trusting myself to speak, emotions boiling inside me. Worry for Maggie. Anxiety over the attacker. Relief that Josiah had agreed and wasn't questioning my request. "You ready? They're about to close."

"Yeah, I'm ready."

Josiah

Josiah lay in his bed, propped against the wall, cellphone in hand. He'd dropped Crimson off at the big house about thirty-five minutes ago. He'd showered, then slid on some knit shorts before climbing into bed. Lemon and vanilla wafted up from his sheets to assault his senses, tightening his muscles, and creating a deep and burning longing. A need.

He took a deep breath and growled softly. He was waiting for Crimson to text him when she was in bed. She'd told him she planned to shower again, too. Josiah had nearly run out of patience when his phone buzzed. Her message read, "I'm in bed. Thanks for tonight. I miss you."

"I'm in bed, too. And I can smell you."

"Is that a good thing?"

"It's a good thing. You're just driving me crazy is all."

"Lol; sorry."

"Don't apologize. I just wish you were here. Right next to me. Right now."

"I'm blushing."

"I'd like to see that."

"Still blushing."

"You know I'm not kidding; right? I want you. I think I made that obvious earlier."

"I know..."

She didn't respond right away, so Josiah decided to let her get some sleep. "Good night, Crimson. Sleep well."

"Good night."

Long after they'd ended their late-night texting, Josiah sat awake. Just thinking about her. About what had happened this evening. About Maggie—hoping she was all right. It made him sick to think of anything like that happening to Crimson. She'd asked him about getting pepper spray. He thought that was a good idea and liked the idea she'd at least have the option of defending herself. He'd talk to Red in the morning, determined to keep her safe.

Crimson Sage

Five days later, Josiah and I were working in the tack room, sorting out old stuff, determining what needed to be repaired or replaced, when he said, "I've got that can of pepper spray for you."

"Oh, good; thanks."

"When we stop for the afternoon, I'll run up and grab it for you."

We worked for another two hours and then called it a day—I needed to get cleaned up before the boys got home, so I'd be ready to begin their tutoring. I was very pleased with their progress. Two of them, Ryan and Kelly, had brought their grades up so much that they were now caught up with the rest of the class; and the other two weren't far behind. Extremely proud was putting it mildly.

After my shower, I grabbed a water bottle and waited on the front porch for the boys to get home. Daisy ambled over and sat beside me, her amber and blue eyes focused intently down the driveway, watching for Ethan. Five minutes later Josiah joined me, leaning against the railing beside me. He handed me the can of pepper spray, and I began to read the instructions for use, wanting to be as knowledgeable as possible. Beside me, Daisy whined loudly, and I figured the bus must have dropped the boys off. I was still reading the instructions when Josiah cursed mildly under his breath. His tone had my eyes jerking up to see him staring down the driveway. Following his gaze, it took me a moment to see the problem.

Ethan was bleeding, holding his sweatshirt to his nose. Kelly walked beside him, his hand on Ethan's back. My heart stopped for a moment, then I was running down the driveway. Daisy beat me there, her worry for Ethan evident. "What happened?" I gasped when I reached him, my hands going to his shoulders to stop him so I could look closer at him.

"Nothing; I'm fine." He shrugged out of my grip, trying to walk past me.

His brushoff shocked me, but I tried again. "Ethan, you're bleeding. *What* happened?"

"I said nothing. I'm fine." He shoved past me, continuing into the house.

Standing there I was at a loss. *What could have happened?* In something of a daze, I walked back to the house, my steps heavy. Josiah reached for my shoulder as I neared him on the bottom step, giving it a gentle squeeze. "Let me try, Crimson. I'm a guy; he might talk to me."

Nodding, I sat before my legs could give out. *Why was Ethan acting like he was mad at me? Didn't he know I was just worried about him?* I was still sitting there, my mind tied in knots over what had happened, when Josiah returned. Without a word he took my hand and led me away from the house, in the direction of the barn. I was in such a fog it didn't occur to me to protest. We were just passing the Chevy when I pulled back, bringing him to a stop. "What happened? What did he tell you?"

Josiah ignored my question, asking one of his own. "Has Mike bothered you at all since that night? Besides the looks?" His voice was hard, not accusatory, just hard. Angry. Worried.

I just stared at him. "*What*? Josiah, what happened to Ethan? Are you saying Mike did that?"

He studied my face for a moment, then he pulled out his cell phone. He held it up for me to look at. At first, I wasn't sure what I was seeing. Then as I took a closer look, really focused, I realized it was Josiah and me at the pool. Kissing. Passionately. Shocked, I looked at him. "Where did you get this?" I whispered.

"Some boys at the school were talking about you. Saying...things...about you. And me. They teased Ethan, calling you names, running you down. Ethan defended you, called them liars, and they sent him the pictures, as evidence. He attacked the boy who sent it to him. Ethan's been suspended for the rest of the week for fighting. Billy's going to the school to talk with them. We'll need to tell him, about us."

"Oh, my word," I breathed. "What did you say to him? What did Ethan say to you?"

Josiah pulled me into his arms, rested his chin on my head, rubbed my back soothingly. "I told him the truth. That I was in love with you, that I loved him. That I'd never do anything or let anything hurt you." I pulled my head back to look at him. He'd just said he loved me. *Josiah said he loved me.* He kissed my forehead, "I do. I'm in love with you. And I will protect you. I'll make sure you're safe. Ethan, too." Josiah pulled me close again, just held me for a bit. After a few minutes he chuckled under his breath. "Ethan said so long as I watch myself and treat you right, he'd let us be." He kissed my forehead. "He's sorry for how he acted and wants to see you."

Ethan was sitting at the table when we came in the back door. He stood when he saw me, and we embraced. "I'm sorry, Ethan."

"No, *I'm* sorry, Sage."

"I love you." I squeezed him tight, hating that he'd been so upset and hurt over me.

He pulled back, head down. "I got suspended. Billy said he was going to the school to talk with them tomorrow. He's taking me with him."

"I'm going, too. I want to know who took the pictures, who is spreading them around."

"We're both going." Josiah said. "I'm getting to the bottom of this one way or another. Then there'll be hell to pay."

Our meeting didn't go as well as expected. The principal, Mrs. Kenzy, was appropriately dismayed to find out about the pictures. We ended up finding out that four different boys were involved in distributing them. But they claimed they weren't the ones who took them, that they'd been sent to them by someone else. They were, of course, unable to say who that someone else was. All four of the boys were suspended for a week. Unfortunately, due to school policy, Ethan's suspension was not lifted—fighting was not tolerated, for any reason.

Ethan thought that was cool; he enjoyed his time at home. Daisy enjoyed his time home as well. He and I talked about my relationship with Josiah; I explained my reasoning for not telling him sooner. Ethan understood, just wished I didn't feel the need to protect him so much.

"You're all I have left, Kid. I love you."

"I love you, too, Sage, and you'd have Billy, too if you'd let him in."

"I guess maybe I just don't know how."

"Maybe just go talk with him. You need to tell him what's going on with you and Josiah, anyway. He's in his office. FYI."

"All right, Kid. I'll go talk with him." Ethan gave me a fist bump and a smile, then headed out the back door. After a moment, I made my way to Billy's office. He was seated behind his desk, going over some paperwork.

Knocking gently, I leaned on the door jamb. "Got a minute?"

"Sage, of course. Come in." Billy gathered the papers together, stacking them neatly, before placing them in a manila folder.

"I don't want to interrupt you."

"You're not; what can I do for you?"

"I...uh...wanted to talk to you about something...." I wasn't sure exactly how to broach the subject of me and Josiah.

"Sure; whatever you need." He indicated one of the chairs in front of his desk.

I smiled nervously as I sat, unsure how to begin. "Josiah..."

"Sage, stop." Billy held up his hands, indicating I go no further. "Look, regardless of what I think about him or you, you're both adults."

"What *do* you think of him?" I couldn't help my curiosity. Mike had said he had a rap sheet, that he was dangerous, that he'd go to jail. If that was true, how could Billy have him here?

"I think the world of him. He's a fine man. He's like a son."

"And his rap sheet?" I whispered.

"Rap sheet?" he chuckled. "He told you he had a rap sheet?"

I shook my head. "Someone...someone else did."

"They were just messing with you then. Josiah hasn't had any problems since high school. He's been a model citizen, and an able, reliable employee. I haven't told him yet, but I intend to name him as a partner on the ranch."

I sat there, stunned, my heart pounding in growing anger. *Mike had been lying.* Of course he'd been lying. He was a snake. I should've known that, should never have doubted Josiah.

"I've been aware of your attraction to each other for a while; so long as he treats you right, and your relationship doesn't interfere with the ranch, I have no qualms about the two of you. I trust him. I trust you."

"Okay. Well, thanks."

I rose to leave, but he stopped me. "Hey, hold up a sec, will ya?"

"Sure." I waited.

"Come with me." Billy led me out of the house and around to the garage. I'd never been in the garage before. It was always locked, and the windows were papered over. Billy's keys jingled as he found the right one to unlock the door. Swinging it open, he flipped a switch, and lights flickered on and off for a couple seconds before catching and staying on. In the center of the room was a vehicle of some kind, covered in a brown cloth tarp.

Billy's gaze was on the car. "I've been thinking about this for a while now. I'm not sure just why I held on to it, but I guess if you don't want it..." He pulled the tarp off and once the dust settled, I was able to see more clearly the older, white convertible. "It's a '67 Pontiac Firebird. It was your mom's."

It took a moment for the shock of his words to penetrate my mind. Then the tears began to fall. *This had been my mom's car.* Billy was giving it to me. Turning, I threw my arms around him. Billy froze a moment, then hesitantly wrapped his arms around me. He simply held me, let me cry, and awkwardly patted my back. When I'd pulled myself together some, he silently handed me a handkerchief, then opened the driver's door for me. I slid onto the seat, and an almost reverent feeling rushed through me. Turning to the garage door, he said he'd let Josiah know where I was.

Josiah

Josiah stood in the barn doorway; his dark gaze focused on the boys playing hoops in the backyard. On one boy in particular. He still didn't have any idea how Mike had done it, but he'd have bet money the punk was the one who'd taken and disbursed those pictures of Crimson and himself. Which meant that somehow, he was sneaking off the property. Josiah ground his jaw in agitation, restless. Angry. He wanted to take action, make his move, crush something. Preferably that piece of crap. They'd be tangling soon—he could feel it.

Chapter 8
Good Friends

As Josiah skidded into the garage, his eyes devouring the Firebird, I couldn't help but grin. And hiccup, emotion still holding me tight. His eyes roved quickly over the frame, taking in every little detail, as he came around to the driver's door. Finally, his gaze landed on me, saw my tears and was instantly on his knees, taking my hand in his, asking what was wrong.

Josiah's innocent question started a fresh round of crying. He pulled me up and into his arms, then sat down, me on his lap. He let me cry, let me get it out of my system; let me use his shirt to wipe my tears. After a few minutes, as I quieted down, he gently brushed the pads of his thumbs across my eyes and waited. "This was my mom's car." My voice was rough, thick with tears. "Billy just gave it to me."

He squeezed me gently. "Bit overwhelmed, huh?"

"It was just so…entirely…unexpected. And generous. Did you know he had this?"

"No; I've never been in here before. He's always kept this place locked up nice and tight."

"I don't even know how to feel about it. I mean, I'm *so* thankful. But it's painful, too, you know?"

"I do; and that's what I'm here for. I'll take the pain." He kissed my temple. "He's not trying to hurt you; you know that, right?"

"Yeah." I did know that, still it was a lot to process.

We sat quietly then as Josiah rubbed slow soothing circles on my back. After a while, I began to relax, my emotions spent and felt a spark of excitement glimmer to life inside me. *I had my mom's car.* She'd have driven this when she was my age. He'd had it all this time. As I thought about my mom, I remembered a picture she'd had. She'd kept it in the top drawer of her dresser. She'd been sitting on the hood of *this* car. Wearing denim shorts, a bikini top, hair pulled back in a ponytail. Sunglasses on. Her smile had been infectious. I remember that I'd asked her about it. Mom had looked at the picture, studied it for a moment, then brushed it off, saying it had simply been her first car, and she wasn't sure why she'd kept the picture.

"Billy give any indication if this thing runs?"

I shook my head. "He just told me what kind it was, and said it had been Mom's"

"I can take a look at it if you want. See what she'll need."

"Would you? Josiah, thank you."

"Crimson...kiss me." Josiah gently tugged my chin around, his fingers a caress on my face as his mouth met mine in a soft, tender touch. "I'd do anything for you. I hope you know that." He kissed me again, let his mouth linger over mine in an agonizingly slow dance as his grip firmed on my jaw, holding me in place, before pulling back. He ran a finger down my nose, tapped my needy lips, then held up a set of keys. "Billy told me to make sure I locked up after we're done. I'll pop the hood, see how she looks, see what I might need, then we'll get to work on her tomorrow."

"We can't tomorrow; it's Halloween."

"Right...day after then. Let's take a look. Go ahead and pop that hood."

He stood and set me on my feet, and as I was unwilling to part from him just yet, reached up and pulled his face down to mine, kissing him hard. "Thank you. For being here. For being strong."

"I'll always be here, always be strong for you."

Josiah

Josiah had been preparing the tractor, needing to get that fire barrier dug in the field, when Billy found him. Telling him that Sage needed him in the garage.

Part of his mind registered it couldn't be an emergency—Billy was too calm for that. But, still, something was going on. So, he'd raced to the garage, stepped through the open side door, his eyes landing on the car.

Wiping her tears, he'd rubbed her back, simply trying to soothe her. Crimson finally whispered that this had been her mom's car; that Billy had just given it to her. Josiah's heart swelled, going out to his girl, knowing she must be overwhelmed, emotions completely shot. So, he'd held her, would always hold her. He'd take her pain away if she'd let him. He'd bear that and more, and wondered if she knew just how far gone he was for her, how much she affected him.

Crimson Sage

Billy didn't allow the boys to go trick-or-treating, but he did take them every year to the school Halloween/Harvest party. Ethan dressed as a vampire, and I dressed as an elf from the Lord of the Rings. Josiah flat-out refused to dress up, but he did go with us. Even though he was there as co-chaperone, we managed a few quiet minutes to ourselves away from the boisterous crowd, either in a darkened corner or outside when Josiah walked around the gymnasium to make sure no one was messing around. He enjoyed my legs encased as they were in the dark, stretch material, and played with the ties on my shirt, grazing my collarbone and neck, driving me insane.

I'm sure the boys had too much candy, punch, caramel apples, and pumpkin pie, but they only got to do this once a year, so I was glad Billy took them.

Throughout the night, as I watched their activities, my mind kept going back to Mom's car, eager to get busy restoring it. Wanting to start her up, to hear her run. I was relieved when we called it a night, excited to get started. Josiah kissed me goodnight, lingering, his mouth against my forehead. "'Night, Crimson; see you in the morning." He released me, and I headed up for bed, somehow falling asleep faster than I'd ever done before.

Waking early, I was at the garage as the sun lit the sky, turning it various shades of lavender. Unlocking the door, I turned the light on and went to sit behind the wheel. Gripping it, I stared unseeing through the windshield. The seat wouldn't need to be adjusted—our legs were the same length. Everything was dusty; I'd have to do a thorough cleaning on it, inside and out. Leaning over, I opened the glove box. Several papers and pictures fell out. Quickly gathering everything, I shuffled it all back together in a neat stack and began sorting through them.

Josiah found me there about an hour later; he'd brought coffee and a toolbox. "Thought I'd find you here and doubted you'd stopped for coffee." He leaned down to kiss me as he handed me the steaming mug.

"Thank you." I smiled at him through our kiss.

"Whatcha got there?" He nodded at the papers on my lap, the passenger seat, the dash.

"I found these in the glove box. They're letters, pictures of Mom's. A couple are phone numbers, written on a napkin. I guess she was popular."

"If she looked like you then I can see that." His words had me blushing, and I shook my head.

"Look at the date on this one." I held a photo out to him. "It was taken the year before I was born." Josiah took the photo, studied it. There were three girls in it. Mom was in the center, two friends, one on either side of her. The car was parked in the background. Mom was blowing a kiss at someone.

"She was cute; but you're hotter." He handed the picture back to me, then turned to open the big garage door. "Let's get started."

Josiah worked for several hours on the Firebird. He changed the oil, the filters, spark plugs, checked all the wires for corrosion, and changed the battery. While he worked, I got Windex and leather cleaner and began cleaning the inside. I gathered all the papers, the pictures, even any leftover trash and put them aside to take in later. I wanted to ask Billy about the pictures, get names, dates, locations from him, and share them with Ethan.

I was in the back seat, wiping them down, rubbing the cleaner in, giving the red leather a shiny, healthy glow, when my cell phone rang. Suddenly OneRepublic's *I Ain't Worried* was blaring, alerting me to Gracie's call. I saw Josiah's head pop up, his eyebrows raised. "Hey, Gracie!" I grinned at him as I answered.

"You're sounding awful chipper. What's new?"

"Hold on a sec." I snapped a quick selfie of me in the car and sent it to her.

"Has that hot boy *finally* got you in the back seat of his car?"

"Dork. No, this is *my* car. He's under the hood; I'm in the back seat, cleaning."

"Too bad he wasn't under *your* hood in that back seat. That'd be something to get excited about."

"Psht. You're such a *pervert*. Listen! Get this; Billy gave me Mom's old car. From when she lived here. It was her first car, and now it's mine! Can you believe it?"

"Whoa. That's pretty awesome."

"Right?"

"Well...now the reason I called won't be all that cool. Dang."

I chuckled at her now dejected sounding voice. "What're you talking about?"

"Well...I told Mom and Dad I wanted to come see you. So, if you'd be so kind as to swing into Boise to pick me up, I'll be there on the 22nd."

"*No way!!* Are you freaking kidding me?? You're coming here? Gah!! I'm so excited. I can't wait to see you."

"Me, too. Then I can get a firsthand look at your hottie bad boy."

"How long can you stay?" I ignored her comment about Josiah.

"I gotta be back on the 30th. But I'll be there through Thanksgiving. We can make pies again, like we used to do. Can't break tradition just because you live in another world now."

I laughed at her description of Salmon. She'd looked it up online and had been dismayed it was so small. Knowing how she felt about small towns, I was beyond thrilled she was coming to visit me. I reminded myself to tell Billy about her impending visit when Josiah and I went in for lunch. Billy had no problem with it, said it'd be nice to have her.

Josiah worked extra hard to get the car ready before Grace arrived. Making sure both the tires and brakes were in good shape, knowing we'd want to do some driving around. He told me the car purred, and he couldn't wait for me to test her out.

My breath clouded the air in front of me, a fall chill making itself known, as Josiah rolled the Firebird out of the garage. Everyone gathered around, eager to see and hear when this car came to life. Billy and Ethan stood, one on either side of me, just as eager as the rest of them. Josiah handed me the keys. "It's all you now, Crimson."

Cautiously, I slid behind the wheel, closing the driver's door behind me. Josiah slid in next to me on the passenger side, and I took a deep breath as I turned the key. The Firebird rumbled to life, sputtered a little, then caught, her engine roaring loudly for a minute before idling quietly. My breath left me in a rush, and I threw my arms around Josiah. "Thank you, so much."

Billy was wiping a tear from his eye as I turned to him, offering a smile. Everyone was cheering. My heart swelled in my chest. Josiah squeezed my shoulder. "Go on, put her in gear; let's take her down the road a bit. See how she goes."

Moving the gear shift, I turned the wheel and drove the car slowly around the house and down the driveway. "We'll need to get the plates renewed, but I think you'll be set. She's a nice car, Crimson. She suits you."

"I think so, too." Tears slipped from my eyes, my heart a complicated well of emotions. "Thank you so much, again, for getting her running."

The next morning, Josiah drove me into town, and I was able to get new tabs for the car. That, along with getting my insurance squared away gave me a feeling of accomplishment. With Thanksgiving just two weeks away, the boys were all feeling anxious, eager to be out of school for break. Excitement for the looming holidays was an almost palpable thing. I was barely containing my own excitement—Gracie would be arriving in nine days. As I counted down those nine days, and my excitement grew, I realized just how much I'd been missing her.

Josiah and I left early in the morning on the 22nd, making the drive to Boise in his car; I didn't know how mine would do, and didn't want to risk breaking down, leaving Grace stranded at the airport.

We waited near the baggage claim, and I couldn't help but remember the first time I'd seen Josiah standing here. Now, he held me from behind, arms wrapped around my middle, thumbs tantalizing my stomach in slow circles. Josiah's grin, when I looked at him, held that wolfish glint as his thoughts seemed in accordance with mine, remembering that moment, too. Leaning down, angling just right, he slowly pressed his lips to mine; one hand was splayed across my stomach, his fingers gently clutching, the other moved up to cup my cheek; his thumb brushed over my lip. I was sure he'd meant it to be simple, soft, a tender reflection of his inner feelings, but as his mouth, warm and firm, moved gently over mine, I reached up and pulled his head closer, deepening the kiss. Without lifting his mouth, he turned me to face him, tugging me closer still.

"Um...excuse me..." a voice spoke over my shoulder. "Come up for air, Sage. At least to say hello." Josiah growled a little, warning the intruder to back off, but I recognized that voice, so reluctantly pulled away. Turning, I

had only a moment before Gracie jerked me into her embrace. "*Holy crap!*"
She sniffed emotionally. "I've really missed you."

After a moment, I held her at arm's length to get a better look at her,
then choked on a sob, as I pulled her right back, holding her tightly. Tears
were falling and I just couldn't seem to stop them. "Gracie, I've missed you
so much. I can't believe you're here...."

She wiped her own tears away, and grinned. "Uh-huh, sure. You'd still
be attached to lover-boy there, if I hadn't interrupted you. Security was
getting ready to call the fire department to put those flames out." She
fanned herself as she shook her head.

Laughing at that, I was able to stem the flow of tears and perform the
introductions. And as I did, a look I recognized was in her eye. From
experience, I knew she was taking his measure. She'd withhold judgment
until she'd had a chance to view us together. As much as Grace enjoyed a
cute face and a nice body, she didn't let those things blind her to any faults.
She'd want to see how he treated me, if I was happy. I didn't fault her for it;
that's what best friends were for.

We gathered her bags, and Gracie didn't travel light. In addition to her
carry-on, she had three extra bags, one of which she said was just shoes. "A
girl needs options, Sage. Just because you're out in the sticks, doesn't mean
you should stop wearing shoes."

Grinning, I just rolled my eyes and let Josiah take my hand as we headed
out to the car. Grace took the backseat, I'm sure just to be able to keep
an eye on Josiah and me. We stopped for dinner, then got on the road.
For most of the drive I sat with my back to the door, so I could talk with
Gracie better; Josiah rested his hand on my leg, as that's what he could
reach. Occasionally I'd catch him glance at her in the rearview. I could tell
he was puzzled by our friendship. Grace and I were day and night different.
I'm quiet, have a slender build; and though I have my own sense of style,
I'd never be in the same ballpark as Grace. She was loud, in both her voice
and personality. Her rich chestnut hair was cropped to her chin and was as

straight as could be. Her makeup was always perfect. Her fashion sense was generally right out of the latest magazines.

I'd puzzled about it myself a few times. Grace and I *were* different. But, somehow, we just clicked. We fit. And as I helped her lug her overpacked and heavy bags up to my room, I had to remind myself how much I loved her. It was well after midnight before we finally fell asleep. Sweet relief washed over me when Grace said she'd wait until tomorrow night before she'd make me dish on Josiah.

The next morning, we surprised everyone by making French toast. It was something Grace and I used to do when she or I spent the night, and it just seemed fitting. Besides, it was nice to give Alice some time off from kitchen duty.

Josiah came in, his eyes seeking mine before he even reached for coffee. I was a little confused by the look he gave me, as he studied my face, seemingly looking for something and was maybe relieved to find it there. Before he even went to the coffee pot, right in front of everyone, he took my face in his hands and kissed me. Thoroughly. Vaguely, I registered the catcalls, whistles, and clapping hands.

Then I heard Grace. "So...this is a thing with you? The kissing? It's like it never ends. How do you all deal with it?"

Even as I grinned, knowing she was only kidding, a look flashed in Josiah's eye. Like he was worried I might take her teasing comment to heart, like I might change my mind about him. My heart clenched—*no*. I needed him to know that would *never* happen. Squeezing his hand, I lifted it, kissing those hard knuckles of his, then shot Gracie a look as I kissed them again. "Jealous much?"

"I am." She sighed theatrically.

The look in Josiah's eyes seemed to soften; he kissed my forehead, lingering for a moment, then went to get his caffeine fix.

Josiah

Gracie was not what Josiah had been expecting. She was the opposite of Crimson in so many ways. He wondered about their friendship, how it worked out. He didn't have any close friends; he was dependent on himself alone. He found himself a little worried. What Grace's impression might be of him, what her influence might be with Crimson. Gracie looked like she came with a tall price tag. And maybe she'd look down on someone like him, think her friend could do *so* much better. Josiah wouldn't disagree with her on that point; Crimson *could* do much better, but he had no plans to encourage her in that line of thought.

On the drive home from the airport, Josiah could feel Gracie's eyes on him. She'd sat in the back seat, just watching. He didn't feel condemnation from her, or even judgment per se, but she was definitely taking note of everything. Several times, he'd caught her eyes on his hand where it rested on Crimson's thigh. The wolf in him awakened, eager to face off, to prove himself and defend what he felt was his territory. If Gracie, or anyone else for that matter, even attempted to come between the two of them, he'd unleash the animal because there was no way he'd go down without a fight.

Crimson and Gracie would have had an entire evening together, doing nothing but catching up and talking. Josiah wondered what changes, if any, the day would bring. When he entered the kitchen the following morning, his eyes sought Crimson's, searching for those changes in their pale-brown depths. Relief melted through him, like hot honey, as the only thing he found in her eyes was the same warm heat she always had for him. He was so relieved, so thankful, he forgot himself. Forgot where he was, who was watching, the boys, Billy. Needing to kiss her, now, he gently took her face in his big hands and kissed her soundly.

It was the sound of loud jeering that brought him back to reality. Blinking, he lifted his mouth from Crimson's and gave her a satisfied, wolfish grin, hoping she wouldn't be upset by his public display of affection. At Grace's teasing words, Crimson took his hand, squeezing it, then raising it to her lips. Reassuring and causing his heart to swell in affection and pride.

She still loved him. Relief still coursing through his veins, Josiah kissed her forehead, breathing in the fragrance that was Crimson, then made for the coffee pot. After breakfast, he told Crimson to take the week off while Gracie was there visiting, wanting her to have ample time with her friend.

Crimson Sage

Josiah told me I was relieved from duty while Grace was here, and for that, I was thankful. He recruited Mike and Adam to be his helpers. This relieved me in a two-fold way. I was thankful to spend that time with Grace, and it was nice not having Mike hanging around all day long, too. Gracie and I stayed in the house for the most part, baking and watching movies, reading books, or just talking. But on her third afternoon here, it began snowing lightly and she had a wild hair to go out in it. So, we bundled up and walked around the ranch for a couple hours or so as I showed her the barn, the horses, my car. I could tell that despite the fact that Salmon was remote and the ranch even more so, Grace was enjoying her stay. She took several deep breaths, relishing in the cold, fresh air.

We were standing on a small knoll; the ranch house was about a hundred yards in front of us. I'd just finished telling her all I'd learned about my past. Grace knew me so well, knew I didn't want to hash it out anymore, knew I just needed acceptance. "It's so quiet out here," she breathed.

"It takes some getting used to."

"I like it. I didn't think I would; I thought I'd feel too exposed out here, too isolated. But I don't." She was quiet for a minute. "I'm glad *you're* here. I hated it at first, hated you'd moved so far away from me. But I think this place is good for you."

"I'm glad I came, too. Glad Billy invited me."

"Glad you met Josiah." She nudged my shoulder with hers.

"Yeah, I'm glad about him, too." Grace chuckled, as though what I said was an understatement. And I guess, really, it was. I was way more than glad. I was euphoric. I was at peace. I was energized. I was alive. I was in love.

"I hear hot chocolate calling...and maybe brownies." She hugged me, kissing my cheek, then hand in hand, we headed back to the house.

Grace and I went to bed a little earlier than our normal after-midnight time, though of course, we stayed up and talked. "So...Josiah."

We were lying side by side in my full-size bed, bundled under three thick blankets. The snow was still falling, and the moon was a shadowy glow peaking in the window. The snowflakes brushed lightly against the frosted glass, layering on the windowsill as well. Turning in her direction, I waited for Grace to finish her thoughts on Josiah. My defenses sparked—I didn't want her badmouthing him and had no intention of letting her. "He's not what I expected," she admitted quietly. "Not your usual type."

"No, he's not," I agreed.

"There's something rather *untamed* about him, don't ya think?"

"There is." I agreed. It was something I'd acknowledged myself. "And I'm sure he could be very untamed if he wanted, but he's always been careful with me. He's never made me feel anything less than completely confident in him."

"You sleep with him yet?" She asked after a minute of silence.

"I haven't changed that much." I rolled my eyes silently; amazed it had taken her this long to ask.

"Still clinging to your innocence, huh? Gonna be a virgin and all when you get married?"

"That's still the plan."

"And he's cool with that?"

"We haven't talked about it."

"Say *what*? That boy? That hot *stud* who can't keep his eyes or hands off you or his tongue outta your mouth, *that* boy hasn't tried to get in your pants?"

"Grace. Please. Josiah isn't like that."

"Please." She snorted. "So, is *he* a virgin?"

"I don't know... we haven't talked about it." I leaned up to look at her. "This is something important to me—for me. I don't know how Josiah feels about it...I don't know what his beliefs are. I—" Daisy had been lying on the rug beside the bed when she suddenly jumped up, growling softly. Normally, she slept with Ethan, but Grace had asked if we could have her for the night and Ethan had graciously relented. With her focus holding steadfast on the door, her hackles raised as she lowered her head and continued growling. We watched the door for a moment, and I put my hand on Daisy's head, trying to calm her so we could listen. After a moment of silence, we distinctly heard the bottom step near my door squeak. Daisy began growling again and ran to the door.

Quickly scampering out of bed, I tiptoed over, pressing my ear against the door. I couldn't hear anything over the pounding of my pulse, so took hold of Daisy's collar, and quietly opened it. The hallway was dark and seemed empty, but I waited a moment or two, then pulled Daisy back, silently closing the door again. My heart thudded heavily in my chest; my racing pulse made me breathless and jittery. Someone had been outside my bedroom door—I didn't have any proof as to who, but I had a pretty good hunch.

"That was weird and a little spooky." Grace said after I'd climbed back in bed. "Please, tell me I'm not staying in a haunted house."

"No," I tried to assure her. "It was probably just one of the boys, getting up to get a drink of water or something." Grace didn't seem all that convinced by my explanation, but she didn't make any further comment. We soon succumbed to sleep. Daisy would alert us if anyone came back.

Thanksgiving was a beautiful affair. We ate too much food, watched too much football, and laughed and talked. I'd expected to be sad and maybe a little depressed, but I wasn't. Whether due to Gracie being here, or because of Josiah, or Billy, I just felt good. Peaceful. And I was thankful for it. I watched Ethan closely for signs of sadness, but he seemed emotionally sound. At one point during the afternoon, I was seated next to Josiah on the couch, watching the game and Ethan sat beside me, his gaze focused on the screen. A little bit of cool whip was stuck to his chin, and I couldn't help but smile. Daisy ambled over, sitting at his feet and my gaze returned to the television. Then I felt Ethan take my hand, squeezing it gently, holding it in his grasp.

Emotion had my eyes misting, and Josiah tightened his arm around my shoulder, just offering comfort. He wiped a wayward tear, then leaned over, placing a kiss just above my ear, where he inhaled slowly, a soft contented sound rumbling in his chest. My head dropped to his shoulder, and chuckling quietly, he tucked me under his chin. Where slowly the food coma began setting in. My eyes drooped and next thing I knew Gracie was shaking my knee. "You guys gonna sleep the rest of the night right there, or what?"

Josiah

Crimson was asleep, curled up on his bed. One tanned leg peeked from beneath his sheets, drawing his gaze. Her shirt had slid off one shoulder, baring it for him, sparking desire. Holding himself in place, Josiah stood there, looking down at her, studying her. The moonlight spilled in, blanketing her in its glow. Her blond hair was tangled across his pillow. He knew if he went to her, if he got any closer, he'd be able to smell her and he'd be done for.

Still, Josiah removed his shirt, silently moving towards her as he slowly knelt on the bed. Her scent ripped at him, inflaming him further as he drew closer. His mouth found her thigh, and he inhaled, drawing her into himself. Slowly he kissed her skin, moving enticingly upwards.

Crimson moaned softly in her sleep, stretching cat-like. Her golden-brown eyes flickered open and he watched as the fire began to build in them. She rolled to her back, reached for him, pulling him closer. Josiah rumbled in satisfaction as his mouth found hers...

Crimson was shaking. Pulling away from him. He blinked and his eyes opened against the glare of late afternoon sunshine. Grace was leaning over Crimson, shaking her awake.

Just a dream.

He'd just been dreaming. His dark eyes glared at Grace in irritation.

Crimson Sage

Blinking groggily, I tried to remember where I was and what day it was. Somehow, I'd slid closer to Josiah, my back against his chest; he had one arm wrapped around me, across my chest. Our hands were joined; we'd both fallen asleep. "Come on now, you love birds, we're fixing to get a snowball fight going and we need all hands on deck."

"Seriously, Gracie?" I grumbled, "I was having a really great dream."

"Yeah, well, by the look Josiah is shooting at me right now, so was he. Now get up. Go get changed, or I'll drench you in snow right where you sit."

I groaned, complaining under my breath, as I moved to comply with her request. In silence, Josiah stood and helped me to my feet. He kept one hand at my waist, to steady me as I swayed; his fingers gripped me lightly. Grace gave me the stink-eye before turning around and heading outside.

Still grumbling, I turned to the staircase, needing to grab my winter gear. Josiah permitted me to move away from him, his fingers grazed along my skin until we were at arm's length, then his hand gripped mine and gently jerked me back. His mouth found mine and he kissed me like he was drowning and I was oxygen, clung to me like I was his life raft. I sensed an almost desperation in his touch. An urgency. Josiah kissed me breathless. As suddenly as he'd begun, he ended our kiss as he breathed against my mouth, "It was a *really* good dream." The look he gave me should be illegal. All heat and sexy wickedness. His lips curled in a knowing grin and my stomach clenched as butterflies wreaked havoc there. He kissed my forehead, then released me. "I'll wait for you. Go on."

Blushing, I ran up the stairs, trying to get my pulse under control. You'd think after all this time, getting used to the way Josiah kissed me, that I'd be better at controlling my responses to him. Instead, he still managed to stun me repeatedly. And as I wriggled my snow gear on, I reflected that was not a bad thing.

We survived the snowball fight, thankfully. Because the following day, Black Friday, was Josiah's birthday. He joked it was a fitting day for him, but I was determined to get him to see himself in a better light. Less black, at least. Since I'd met him, he'd turned my life a nice glowing, golden red. He filled me with heat. With warmth. Before I met him, I hadn't thought I'd ever feel warmth again. To celebrate, I talked Billy into taking us into town for pizza and ice cream.

The Pizza Palace didn't offer one of those birthday packages where the staff come to sing the birthday song to you and you get a free slice of cake. So, I had Gracie pick up a cake at the grocery and we all sang *Happy Birthday* as loudly and as off-key as we could. The other patrons joined in, and soon we'd incorporated the entire establishment into our party. I was pretty sure that no matter what happened to us in the future, even if we didn't last, Josiah would remember this birthday with pleasure. Knowing someone went out of their way to show him he was treasured.

For Josiah's present I gave him a gift certificate to the tattoo parlor he preferred, called Grey Sky Designs—he'd been talking about getting another one. Billy gave him money towards getting his car painted, and Ethan and the other boys had pooled their resources and gave Josiah a Ford baseball cap with a Shelby on it in the same year and color that he liked. Even Grace got in the spirit and gave him a picture she'd snapped of him and me; she'd had it framed and everything.

The next day, Josiah and I took Gracie to the airport. She and I cried as she stood in line at the security checkpoint. We promised to come see her as soon as we could. Tears were still falling from my eyes even after we were on the road and heading home. Josiah held my hand, letting me cry the emotion out. "What do you say about a swim later tonight?" he asked as we pulled into the driveway.

"I could use one, that's for certain."

"I'll pick you up about eight, then?"

"Sounds perfect."

Josiah

Josiah decided he liked Grace. She was funny and interesting. And she loved Crimson very much. And Josiah thought she accepted him, approved even, and that pleased him.

Thanksgiving was...well, it was the first time Josiah had felt like he had a family to celebrate with. He'd celebrated the holiday before, here at the ranch—been included in the festivities; Billy had always made him feel welcome. But this year it was Crimson who made the difference. It wasn't just that Josiah was welcome, but that he was wanted.

Crimson made him feel needed and wanted. She was the tie that held him, the glue that bound him. And yet she acted like he was the thing she needed. He caught the looks, the need and longing in her eyes. Heard the peace and relief in her voice. Felt them in her touch. He wished she knew just how much he needed her as well.

Chapter 9
The Cravings of Life

*C*rimson Sage

Last year I'd thought my body had been made for one thing—water. Swimming was the ultimate high for me. I was like a fish in water; it was my home. And I still loved and craved it. Craved the challenge, the resistance, the way I was able to push my body past all my preconceived ideas about its limits. But, in these last several months I'd discovered another craving my body had been made for—Josiah. He brought a whole new realm of challenges, a new level of resistance, a new way to push myself, a new *home.*

My eyes searched for him as I completed my last lap. My breath was coming in shuddering gasps, some of which I was certain was due to the amount of food I'd consumed a few days ago. Josiah sat on the side of the pool, his feet in the water. Basically treading water, I eased my way to him, noting his eyes trained to mine. "How d'you feel?"

"I can definitely feel it." I dunked my head, then came back up. "I think I need to stay more active."

Josiah chuckled darkly. "I'll see what I can do to help you with that." His gaze was a heated caress, causing my pulse to speed up. He jerked his chin to the door, eyes never leaving mine. "You done? Wanna get going?"

"Yeah." I climbed out and Josiah handed me my towel. Quickly I changed, taking less than ten minutes to be back at his side.

He eyed my still-damp hair critically. "You got a hat?"

"I'll be fine," I assured him.

"Here, take mine." Josiah pulled the dark grey beanie from his head, extending it to me. It smelled like him, like his spicy shampoo, and I tried not to be obvious as I sniffed at it. His low chuckle said he'd noticed. Blushing, I quickly stuffed my hair into the hat and after he did a heated once-over, led me out to his car.

When we arrived back at the ranch, it had started to snow again. "It's only ten; you wanna come up for coffee or something?"

Pausing, I wondered what exactly he had in mind. My recent conversation with Gracie came to mind, and I couldn't help but think about her words and what she figured Josiah would want from me. Of course, he caught my slight hesitation, raising his eyebrow in silent question. "Yeah," I smiled. "That sounds good."

"You sure, you're sure?"

"Yeah; why?"

"Just...making sure."

"Okay." I chuckled. Josiah opened the door to his loft, flipping on the light as we entered.

"Make yourself comfortable." He moved to his tiny kitchen area as I walked to the center of the room and stopped. My eyes shifted between the couch and his bed. "You want something other than coffee to drink? Tea? Water?" he asked, pulling my gaze to him.

"Coffee sounds good."

Josiah turned to his silver tea kettle, filled it with ice-cold water from the tap, and turned the burner on high. When he turned around, I was still standing in the same spot. "Crimson?"

"What would you say if I told you I needed a shower?"

Josiah quietly studied me for a moment or two. I could see several thoughts racing around in his head. He rubbed at his chin with a knuckle. "I'd say, towels are in the cabinet next to the sink."

"That's it?" Did he want nothing else? I *knew* he did.

"Do you need something more?" he seemed perplexed.

"No; I mean...you don't have any other thoughts...about me showering at your place?"

"I've got plenty of thoughts about it." His voice sounded rough. "I'm trying not to think too hard on them."

"So...you won't think I'm making a play? Or think I'll want you to make a move? Or, that this is a prelude to sex?"

"Not if you don't want me to." Josiah made his way to me, his movements deliberate, his pace purposeful, his deep blue eyes never once leaving mine. When he stood before me, he lifted warm hands to my shoulders, where he kept his grip gentle, but firm. His thumbs rubbed back and forth, causing shivers to run up and down my spine. "Crimson," Such promise and assurance in his voice now. "You can *trust* me—you want to lock the door, that's fine; I won't be offended."

"Josiah, I..."

A gentle finger across my mouth halted my words. "Shhh... I want you—do not doubt that. But I see the line you've drawn, and I'm not crossing it. That's a promise."

"It's just...I'm a virgin." My eyes closed as I blurted that statement out between us.

He inhaled slow and deep, his chest expanding as he did, and I felt it when he released it again. Felt the way his body stilled, locked down for a moment, becoming immobile as he blinked down at me. "I guessed as much," he admitted after a moment, leaning forward, placing feather-light kisses along my cheekbone, across my eyes, down my nose, to my mouth. Against my neck, he made low sound. "Will you be disappointed if I'm not?"

"No." I shook my head, trembling slightly.

"Go get your shower." He stepped back. "We aren't having sex tonight. Even if you begged. So don't bother asking."

I chuckled as he nudged me toward the bathroom; the teapot was just beginning to whistle as I closed the door behind me. When I finished, Josiah was seated on the couch; he'd turned it to face the large window.

The moon was full; snow still sifted gently down. I had my hair wrapped in a towel and I'd snagged his comb from beside the sink. My coffee sat, still steaming, on the coffee table—he must have rewarmed it for me. I sat beside him. "Mind if I use your comb?"

"Not at all."

Pulling the towel from my head, I carefully brushed through the tangles. With my hair being so pale, I'd learned early on that showering after a swim was vitally important to prevent it from turning an awful shade of green.

Josiah watched me for a minute or two, his eyes just following the movements of the comb through my hair. "How was my shower?"

"Nice."

He made a noise deep in his throat. "I did my best...not to imagine you in it—I'm not perfect though." He chuckled darkly at his own weakness. "I'm afraid I'll be picturing you there from now on, clothed in steam..."

Deciding silence was the safest response, I said nothing, just continued working at those tangles. Josiah moved suddenly, climbing behind me. He took the comb from my hand and began gently working through my hair. The action was both relaxing and exhilarating at the same time. "Why?" he suddenly asked. "Why are you still a virgin? What's your reasoning?"

"Who says I have a reason? Maybe it's because no one has asked me before."

Josiah gripped my hair, gently pulling my face up to his, before lowering his mouth to mine. After a lingering moment he pulled back. "Yeah," he muttered. "I don't think so. I'm sure you've had plenty of opportunity. You've made the choice to remain innocent, and I'd like to know why."

He released my hair, and I lowered my head, staring out the window. "It's the way I was raised." I said finally. Josiah continued combing my hair, the teeth massaging my scalp, relaxing me. "My mom believed it was important. She'd been a virgin...all the way up until someone stole that from her." I only learned that last bit about her after she'd died, when I read her journal. "She'd told me, back in junior high, to respect myself, to respect and honor my future husband and the vows I intended to say to him by remaining a virgin." I sighed quietly. "I remember asking her, 'Won't he think I'm inexperienced?' I'm going to get married and not know how to please my own husband; I won't even know what I'll like; he'll be disappointed."

Josiah's hands tightened, clenching in my hair; the comb stilled for just a moment before he continued. "No man in his right mind could be disappointed in you, Crimson. I'm dead serious about that."

"You're not disappointed we won't be having sex?" Skepticism bled through in my tone, though I'd tried my best.

"Disappointed? No." In the reflection on the window, I saw him shake his head. Suddenly, he chuckled darkly, leaning down to run his mouth along my throat before gripping my hair tighter, moving it to the side, then lightly taking my nape in his teeth, and finishing with a tender kiss to that spot. "Do I *want* to have sex with you? Yes. *Oh, yes.* You bet I do—more than you can possibly imagine. Am I disappointed in you because you have standards and morals? *Heck* no."

My throat closed up, but I managed to rasp, "Thank you."

"No, Crimson, thank *you*. I wish I could offer you a similar gift, but I can't. Just know that I would if I could. And the way I look at things is, you didn't say *never*; you only said not until you're married. That's a workable, attainable goal."

Now that my hair was free of tangles and nearly dry, Josiah moved to sit beside me again, pulling me into his shoulder, and arranging a blanket over us. I snuggled into his side and sighed as I relaxed. "Would Billy be angry, do you think if I stay here, on your couch tonight?"

"Guess we'll find out. And I'll be on the couch; you'll be in my bed. I'm starting to like you there. I have a vivid imagination, and I've been remembering you there from last time. It'll be nice to have the reality for a change, at least to some extent." I smiled, so thoroughly in love with this man. We sat there for another hour as I sipped my coffee, just savoring this time with Josiah.

Josiah

Crimson is a virgin. Innocent. Pure. And he could be her first; her only, he hoped. Josiah chewed over that information for a while as he watched her sleeping form. He liked her there, in his bed. Liked it an awful lot. Absently he pulled on the small black hoop in his right eyebrow, just thinking, absorbing all she'd shared with him. A feeling was growing in his chest. A strong and powerful feeling of possession and protection.

She was in his bed. Again. And he wanted her to remain there, make it permanent. His vivid dream flashed in his mind, stirring him, teasing him without mercy. He wanted to be there with her. Even though he'd guessed, maybe deep down he'd known somehow that she was a virgin, he was still a little shocked by her admission. Not that he thought she looked impure, or anything even remotely like that; she could have been with a dozen guys and would have still looked as beautiful as she seemed to him, as wonderful and as, well, pure. It was more that he'd never met anyone over the age of fifteen who had claimed to be. It was not something he'd run into before. Especially as she responded to him with such passion.

He imagined her strength of character was immense. To stand by that self-imposed rule really took a lot of integrity and a strong will. He was impressed. Immensely impressed. And thankful. So very thankful. The world tended to snicker and chide people like that, like her, people who lived differently from them. Like somehow their standards and morals were personally offensive. And yet, she'd stood firm. Resolute. She blew him away.

He wished he had something of equal value to offer her. But he'd squandered that gift a long time ago. And there was nothing that could be done about it now. He could offer and show her respect though. He could honor her decision. Not make things more difficult for her, not make unfair demands of her. Josiah wanted something else as well. Wanted to give her something else. His innocence was long gone; he searched through his mind for something else of value he could give, aside from honor and respect. After an hour, as he continued to watch her sleep, he reached the conclusion that he could offer whatever knowledge and skills he possessed. No matter what it was, if she wanted to know it or learn about it, if he knew it and had that knowledge, he'd give it to her. Freely.

Crimson Sage

Eventually I must have fallen asleep, though I had no memory of having done so. The sun shone through the large window, lighting the room and the bed I found myself in. Rolling over, I searched for Josiah. One quick glance to the bathroom showed he wasn't there. The door was cracked, but the lights were off. The loft wasn't that big, so it didn't take long to realize he wasn't there. I checked the time; it was after nine.

Crap; I must have been really tired. Scrambling from bed, I quickly washed my face in the bathroom sink, then made his bed. I was just searching for my shoes, when I heard steps outside his door. The lock clicked and the door opened, then Josiah stepped inside, carrying two plates. "Good morning."

Suddenly shy for some odd reason, I blushed and mumbled, "Morning."

"I brought breakfast." Josiah set it on the bar in front of one of the stools. "Coffee's still hot; sit down and I'll get you some."

Doing as he asked, I watched as he moved about the tiny kitchen. After serving us both, he sat beside me, and we began to eat. "Billy say anything?"

"Yeah," he nodded between bites.

I blew out a breath. "Well?"

"He said to give you this and to tell you he installed a lock on your door, for added privacy."

"*What?*"

"Billy installed a lock on your bedroom door, for added privacy; he asked me to give you the key."

"Yeah, I heard that part. Did he say why?"

"Nope."

"Did he say anything about where I stayed last night?"

"Nope."

"Do you think he will?"

"I'm not worried about it."

"You're not?"

"No, are you?"

"I don't know. I mean...I'm an adult an all, but I'd imagine he'd have an opinion about this...and you and me."

"I'd imagine," Josiah agreed. "Look, I told you before—we've done nothing wrong; I won't act as though I have. You shouldn't either."

"Okay," I agreed; no reason to worry about it, really. "What's on the agenda today?"

"You. Me. And Trigger."

Trigger, I knew, was one of the ranch horses. I wondered what Josiah had in mind for us today that involved the horse. "Um...okay. What are we doing with him?"

"You're going to learn to ride him."

"*What*? Nuh-uh. I'm not riding that horse."

"Crimson." His voice was soft and persuasive. "You're going to learn to ride today."

"I don't *want* to learn to ride."

"That's because you never have. Once you try it; you'll love it."

"No, it's because I just don't want to ride horses."

"Are you *chicken*?"

"No." I scoffed. I so was.

"I think you are." He rubbed his jaw thoughtfully.

"I. Am. Not." I ground out.

"Prove it." He locked eyes with me.

I glared at him. How did he always manage to get me to bend to his will? He'd maneuvered me into a corner and now I was trapped. And he knew it. "Fine. Whatever. But, if I get hurt, it's all your fault."

"You won't get hurt." His assurances did little to calm my anxiety.

"So you say."

"So I know." He was confident, I'll give him that.

I rolled my eyes. "Whatever."

"I told Billy you'd be gone all day, with me."

"Look, if I'm going to play cowboy with that horse, I refuse to do it where the boys are going to see me land on my butt."

"Already taken care of. You'll ride behind me, until we get to a place I know, and you'll learn there, away from prying eyes."

At first that sounded like a good plan. Then, I wondered if that was truly a wise decision. *What if I fell off and needed medical attention?* I bit my lip and watched as his eyes followed the movement. "I like that lip the way it is, Crimson." Josiah reached out, running his thumb over said lip, before leaning in to claim my mouth with his. He kissed slow, and easy, and deep. My head whirled and I couldn't remember what I'd been worrying over. It was hard to stay focused when his mouth moved over mine, against mine like that.

"No fair," I breathed.

"Very fair. This is all I get to do. I'm going to make sure I do it well. And often. And you have a mouth that was made for kissing."

"I trust you."

"I know," he grinned. "Let's get going."

I helped him clean up our breakfast and then went to brush my teeth with a borrowed toothbrush. Josiah gave me one of his hats and a sweatshirt. Both had his scent firmly embedded in the fabric, which I loved. Finally, he handed me one of his jackets, and I figured, between his clothing and the looks he kept giving me I doubted I'd feel the frozen air at all.

Josiah must have already been to the horse barn, because when we got there, Trigger was standing outside his stall, already wearing his saddle and bridle. Josiah mounted first, then helped me up behind him. Instinctively, I wrapped my arms around him and leaned into his back. Trigger sidestepped a little nervously and I remembered hearing or reading once that horses could smell fear on people. I tried to calm myself down by breathing deeply and in doing so caught another enticing whiff of Josiah on the clothing he'd lent me. My fears eased and I was able to relax enough to enjoy the ride with him.

The snow wasn't that deep, maybe a foot or so; some areas were deeper than others. Trigger didn't seem to have any problems with it. He seemed eager for the crisp white morning, snorting and prancing around. As close as I could tell, we rode for little over an hour, following some unseen trail that only Josiah and Trigger seemed to know about. We crossed a small creek that I was sure fed into the pond back behind the ranch house. Josiah took us through a narrow canyon that ran for maybe thirty feet. It was much cooler there, in the shade of the towering rocks and cliffs. The wind was brisk as it blew over us and I couldn't help but shiver. Josiah dropped a hand to my thigh and rubbed it encouragingly. "We're almost there."

"Okay," I breathed against his shoulder.

The canyon opened into a small valley that was for the most part free of snow. Against the far wall stood the remains of an old log cabin. Most of it had caved in at some point, but it looked like someone had cleared some of the debris away and built a small fire ring. I saw wood that had been cut and stacked nearby. Josiah rode right up to the cabin, then stopped.

"I found this old place a few years back. Billy said I could check it out, see what I could find. I'll get a fire started and then we'll get busy with your lesson."

Josiah was in his element out here. As I watched him expertly start the fire with minimal effort, it occurred to me that he seemed to be in his element no matter what he was doing. I'd watched him in many varied activities from fixing fence, to automotive care, to tractor driving, to teaching me how to drive a stick, to starting a fire, and now teaching me how to ride a horse. I found myself trying to peg him, to classify him, but was coming up short.

Josiah was a puzzle. A delicious puzzle. He wasn't a cowboy—no Wranglers, no western boots or cowboy hat. Yet he was comfortable with horses and ranch life. He wasn't a farmer either, and yet he knew his way around farm equipment and crops. I carefully looked him over now as he showed me once again how to mount Trigger. Today he wore faded blue jeans that sat low on his hips. The material hugged his butt, not to the point of being indecent, maybe just to the point of being distracting. Because he looked so darn good in them. The denim was neither too tight, nor too loose. His dark, red hair was hidden under a black beanie today, and his chest and shoulders were covered in a couple layers of flannel and knit.

He was rugged. Like Gracie had said, he was untamed and wild, and I couldn't contain the shiver that traveled my body.

Josiah wasn't a jock, but he was fit enough and clean enough he could have passed for one. He wasn't punk or biker, but with the piercings, the tattoos, the moody eyes, and the muscle he could've been. Josiah, I decided, was his own class of man. His own breed: he was one of those rare men who were supremely confident in themselves, completely and thoroughly at ease in their maleness.

He caught me looking, those blue eyes sharpening. "You play dangerous, Crimson."

I drew in a deep breath and shook my head. "Not really; I was just deep in thought."

Josiah dismounted, dropped the reins, as he moved to where I'd been standing, warming by the fire, warmed by watching him. "And what were you thinking about to put such heat in your eyes?"

My breath caught. Here, again, he was completely at ease with himself as man. Completely at ease with how a woman should respond to him. Another facet to consider and solve. "Guess I was just trying to figure you out."

"And what conclusion have you reached?"

"That you're your own breed. You're not like anyone I've known before."

Josiah studied me quietly. His blue eyes strayed from mine, slowly moved down to my mouth, and focused there for a minute. Those eyes continued downward, to where my heart was now pounding in my chest, as if he had x-ray vision and could see it thundering there. His gaze flicked back up to mine. "I don't think you're ready to know me completely yet. We'll both just have to be patient. Now, let's get you on that horse, before I run out of will."

I hated admitting it, but Josiah was right. Riding a horse *was* fun. Trigger was patient, responsive, and well-behaved. Josiah was instructive and informative. It didn't take me too long to discover that riding horses had its own rhythm. At first, after I was in the saddle by myself, I felt a little unstable. Like I might slide off one way or the other. With Josiah on the ground, I had nothing to grab on to except the saddle horn, which didn't feel as reliable as Josiah had. But, after several minutes, I was able to adjust and move my body in the correct motions. We stayed in the little valley for another hour. Josiah had me saddle and unsaddle Trigger. Then we mounted again; this time he rode behind me as we headed for home.

About twenty minutes after we'd left the mouth of the canyon, we came to a clump of bare white birch trees. Josiah had his chin resting on my shoulder, his arms around me. I was maneuvering Trigger around the trees, just skirting them, when Josiah went from relaxed to rigid and alert in the span of a half a second. "Hold up."

Pulling Trigger to a stop, I swiveled around, only to have Josiah slide down, quickly moving to the trees, scanning the area. In silence, I watched, wondering what had triggered his agitation. He scouted around, his gaze on the ground as he walked down our back trail a little way, before returning to me. "Josiah, what's wrong?"

"I think someone may have followed us out here."

"Who?" I looked around, not seeing anything.

"Not sure yet." The tone of his voice belied his words. As he prepared to remount the horse, he did one more quick scan of the area, his blue eyes hard, flinty. Suddenly, my mind turned to Mike, wondering if Josiah suspected him. Though, I couldn't imagine why Mike might have followed us today. Then again, I couldn't figure out who else might have been interested in what we were doing either.

We arrived back at the ranch and in silence Josiah and I unsaddled and tended to Trigger. I gave the golden gelding an extra scoop of grain for all his efforts. A couple times on the way back, Josiah had me stop and he'd gotten down to check something out, then without a word he'd remount, and we'd be on our way again. "Hey." I nudged his shoulder with mine. We stood just inside the barn, leaning against the open door. "Everything all right?"

He turned us so we faced each other, hands lingering at my hips. "I want you to promise me something, Crimson."

"What?"

"Promise me you'll let me know if anyone here bothers you. Mike especially. You're a beautiful woman, on a ranch full of pubescent male youths and testosterone-fueled young men; things can happen. If any of the boys here is in *any* way inappropriate, whether by word or by action—I want to know about it."

"Do you suspect one of them of followed us today?"

"Those tracks I saw led back here. Someone from the ranch followed and spied on us."

"Who?" Anxiety filled my chest.

"I have my suspicions, but no proof."

"Is that why Billy installed the lock? Did you ask him to do it?"

"No," he shook his head.

I tried to decipher the look in his eyes, then the sound of the back door slamming, drew our attention. Billy stood on the patio, waving us over.

"Crap." I said weakly. Josiah chuckled, took my hand, lifted it to his lips, kissing me there as he winked, then led me to the house.

"What's up?" I asked as we got closer. His eyes looked worried or anxious about something. I wondered if we were about to get a reaming for where I'd stayed last night.

"Something happened," he began. "Ethan—" My ears stopped working as panic took hold. Not waiting for him to finish, I raced into the house, yelling for Ethan, fear tearing through me. Footsteps pounded behind me, and I could barely breathe past the lump in my throat. Spots began crowding my vision making me lightheaded and dizzy. Skidding to a stop, I reached for the wall as my eyes landed on my brother who was calmly seated on the couch. His right arm was bound tightly in a black brace and sling.

Relief had me swaying, and Josiah's strong arms encircled me, held me up, held me against him. "Ethan," I breathed. "What happened?"

When Ethan lies, his tell is avoiding eye contact. And as I looked at him, needing to know what happened, that he was all right, he looked right through me. His grey eyes focused on the space between mine, and my heart clenched tightly. "Just clumsy, I guess. Fell outside with the guys. Slipped in the snow."

Inhaling, I meant to question him, to call him out, but Josiah stopped me with a pressure to my side where his big hands were still holding me. Reluctantly, I pulled my gaze from my brother and looked up at Josiah. His deep blue eyes told me to wait, to let Ethan's explanation stand for right now. I nodded slowly, and he kissed me just above my ear. "Well, Kid," I said calmly, "next time...be careful; all right?"

Ethan sagged a little in relief, and said, "Yeah, I will; I promise." Kelly sat beside my brother and caught my eye as he nodded. Daisy sat at Ethan's feet, practically wrapped around him. No doubt picking up on the tension and fear and was on high alert. I let Josiah lead me back out to the patio where Billy was waiting. Josiah leaned against the railing, pulling me into his arms as we faced Billy.

"What happened?" Josiah asked quietly, his voice barely above a whisper.

"Kid won't say. Just that he slipped outside."

"Bullcrap," I spit out.

"That's how I figured it, too, Sage." Billy took a sip of his coffee. "I was in the kitchen, getting more coffee." He lifted his cup again. "The boys were all outside, throwing snowballs and the football around. Then, I heard raised voices; they seemed angry, but I couldn't tell who was doing the yelling. I set my cup down and was just heading back out when I heard the Kid scream. I hoofed it out to where they'd gathered out by the barn. Ethan was on the ground; Kelly was on his knees beside him—in a defensive position. The others were grouped around him.

"I asked what happened and got silence. I questioned Ethan and he said he'd slipped and fallen. I got him to the clinic. Left Alice here with the boys, to keep an eye on things; Bentley had a meeting in town. I got back only just before you two arrived."

"Someone followed us, today. I'm guessing, while Alice oversaw things, one of them slipped away and followed us—well more Crimson, than me."

"On foot?"

"Horse."

"It'd have to be one of the older boys, then."

"Figured as much." Josiah said. "Question is, *why* would one of them follow us, and does it have anything to do with what happened to the Kid?"

Josiah

Now more than ever Josiah wanted to take the fight to Mike. He spoke with Billy again about his concerns; Billy agreed dishearteningly. But he maintained that without proof or evidence they didn't have a leg to stand on with the courts. He said they'd just have to be more vigilant, keep Mike under surveillance.

Josiah decided it wouldn't hurt to make Mike aware of the added scrutiny. He found the seventeen-year-old the following day, loitering inside the barn. Josiah walked right up to him, crowded him, forcing him to step back. "You so much as think about touching her, or Ethan again, and you'll answer to me."

"You threatening me, Josiah?"

"I don't threaten, punk; I make promises. Best you learn the difference.

"I ain't scared of you, man. You know you can't touch me, and I know it, too. So back the heck off."

Mike stood tensed and ready. Josiah held his gaze, not backing down. Mike grinned and stepped casually around Josiah. He paused at the barn door and over his shoulder said, "Tell Crimson I said hello."

Chapter 10
Forgiven

*C*rimson Sage

The snow only lasted a few days; then a change in the weather brought with it warm winds that melted the ice and dried everything out. Billy said not to get too excited, this was only a lull in the weather—more cold, and snow, and ice were certainly coming. Either way, I enjoyed the break. For a week the temperatures hovered just below sixty during the day and just above freezing at night. Of course we had the wind to deal with; the speeds varying from five to ten miles per hour, on up to forty miles an hour, with gusts upwards of sixty.

Josiah grumbled about all the extra work the wind was creating for him, but I reminded him I'd be helping, so he wouldn't be alone doing that work. And besides, all that extra wood made for more bonfires. And I liked bonfires, especially with Josiah beside me to share them with.

Josiah swung the axe, embedding the head deep in the tree trunk with a loud thud. He left it there and turned to me, a wickedly exciting gleam in his eyes. I was sitting on the tailgate of the Chevy. Josiah had been chopping the wood while I loaded it in the truck. I was caught up with my part and had been waiting on him. Without taking his eyes from mine, he removed his gloves and tossed them on the ground. Stretching a little, he flexed, letting his muscles move enticingly, knowing how it affected me. My breath hitched as I watched him. Stepping closer, he moved between my legs, slid his hands up my thighs, to my hips, gripping me there. His fingers flexed firmly, then he jerked me to him.

"We don't need all that wood to make a fire." He rumbled against my mouth; his voice low and rough; his lips hot, making me shiver. Not because I was cold. I was so far from cold it wasn't even funny. How was it even possible to shiver like this when I was burning up? Josiah created his own special kind of fever in me. "Every time I look at you, every time I smell you, feel you, taste you, I'm on fire."

My hands slid up his back, feeling the smoothness of his skin, the firmness of his frame, reveling in the way he responded to my touch. Today his beanie cap was navy blue and a close match to his eyes. My hands moved up the back of his neck and I gently eased the cap off, running my fingers through his dark red hair. "You are pretty hot, Ginger."

Josiah reared back a little, eyeing me in seeming speculation, as my eyes trailed over the dark stubble on his jaw. "*Ginger*?"

I chuckled. "That's what I called you, at first, when I didn't know your name. In my head, at least."

"I see." He leaned down and kissed me again, tugging gently at my bottom lip. I felt that stubble now, an abrasive caress against my skin.

"You don't mind, do you?" I breathed.

"Not particularly."

"You don't think it sounds too feminine?"

"As long as *you* don't think I'm feminine, then I guess I'm fine with it."

"And if I did?" I teased.

Josiah gently pushed me back down on the bed of the truck. "Well, *Little Red*, I'd have to convince you real hard that I wasn't." His gaze moved over me, and I watched him as he watched me. Felt it like a physical touch as his blue eyes slid over me.

Any other guy I've known would have taken advantage of me in that position. At the very least they'd have copped a feel and groped me. Josiah never did. Not one time did he allow his hands to brush against me anywhere that might have been considered a personal and private space. I marveled that he respected me so fully. That I could trust him so completely.

"Wait." I raised up on my elbows. "*Little Red*? How do you figure that? My hair is blond—far from red."

"You're *my* Little Red. Little, because compared to me, you are. And Red, because of your name. Crimson—Red."

I'd never had a nickname before, not from a guy, at least. My parents had called me Tadpole, because of my love for water. But, never had a guy given me a nickname. I liked it. I couldn't keep the stupid grin off my face. Josiah correctly interpreted the look. "I take it you don't mind?" I shook my head silently, that stupid grin still on my face. "You like it?"

"I do."

"All right, Little Red." He kissed the tip of my nose. "Let's get this finished before you weaken my resolve further. Keeping my hands off you is fast becoming a full-time job."

We worked another couple of hours chopping and loading the wood from six trees that had fallen in the latest windstorm. It took three pickup loads to get it all moved. Josiah and I tossed the wood from the truck, and the boys stacked it in neat piles. I looked around for Ethan but didn't see him anywhere. Kelly was closest to me, so I asked him, "You seen Ethan?"

"Yeah, he's watching TV."

"He all right?"

"Seems to be," he shrugged as he reached for more wood.

I'd asked Ethan several times about his arm, just *how* he'd fallen, how it'd gotten broken, but each time he would vaguely brush aside my concern and reiterate that he'd just fallen. I stared in the direction of the front room, where I was sure he'd be sitting. Five days ago, he'd discovered Billy's collection of *The A-Team* on DVD and had been steadily moving through them. My eyebrows were drawn in concern; Josiah nudged my shoulder. "Go on in; check on him. I got this."

"Thanks." I hopped down from the truck, taking a minute in the kitchen to make sure I was calm, and not about to give away my suspicions. I stuck my head around the corner, leaning into the room. "Hey Kid. I'm making more coffee; you want some?"

Without turning looking in my direction, Ethan simply shook his head. "Nah, I'm good." Frowning in silence, I quickly finished with my coffee before joining him on the couch.

"How's the arm?"

"Fine."

"Not bothering you?"

"It itches a little."

"I hear that's normal." My eyes moved over him, trying to remain patient. Ethan's response was more silence. For a couple of minutes, I simply watched him as he watched Hannibal, B.A., Murdock, and Face bring their plan together. My eyes took in his curly, slightly shaggy, light-brown hair that was right on the cusp of needing a cut and looking adorable. Ethan's grey eyes were sharp, intuitive, and a little haunted. Absently he stroked Daisy's head where it rested in his lap. Grinning grimly, I tried to think of a way to get him to open up about what had really happened.

A furious, sick feeling had settled in my heart that he was maintaining his silence for my protection. Ethan was generally a peacemaker, not wanting trouble. That was why his getting suspended was such a big thing for me—it was just so unlike him. He could get along with most anyone. And now this thing with his arm. His vague answers, his refusal to meet my eyes, all made me doubt what he'd told me. And yet I had this gut feeling that pushing him, might put him in more danger. Ethan was obviously standing between me and someone else, trying to protect me, I was sure.

I wished there was some way I could get him to understand that I could take care of myself, and besides, I had Josiah firmly in my corner, in Ethan's corner too, for that matter. Turning back to the TV, I was content watching it with him in silence. When the current episode was over, as Ethan was skipping to the next one, I said, "Hey, Kid? You know I love you; right?" Ethan glanced in my direction and nodded. "I won't let anyone hurt you, and Josiah won't let anyone hurt me; you know that; right?"

"Yeah," he whispered.

"If you ever need something; you can always come to me, or to Josiah."

"'Kay."

"You need anything before I head back out?"

"Nah; I'm good." Ethan grinned, and I tried not to notice that the grin didn't quite reach his eyes. "I really like this show. It's pretty good."

"Yeah; it is. You take it easy. I'll see you later."

Though I worried for my brother, I tried not to dwell in that concern. I couldn't let it eat at me, stealing what peace I'd gained. Too much was at stake. Christmas was two weeks away and the tutoring was finished. I still helped the boys with their homework, but only as they needed it. I knew I was going to have to find another job. I mentioned it to Billy, and he reiterated again that it wasn't necessary. I knew he meant well, but I wanted to work. Josiah had things on the ranch handled fairly well. Really, my help wasn't needed there. I went with him mainly to have something to do and to spend time with him. I started scouring the want ads looking for any kind of employment.

Salmon was a small town, so the pickings were slim. I just figured I'd keep looking and maybe something would come up after Christmas.

Three days before school let out for the Christmas holiday it began to snow again. I was happy and annoyed at the same time. This time the snow was sticking. Standing on the porch; my hands wrapped around a steaming mug of coffee, Josiah wrapped his warm, strong arms around me. I contemplated the big, fluffy, white flakes, and sighed as he said, "You need to learn to drive in it at some point. May as well be now."

Josiah had been trying to talk me into learning to drive in the snow, and I'd been fervently praying this would be a mild winter and the need to learn to drive in snow wouldn't be necessary until next year. That maybe the little bit we'd already had would have been it. I sighed mentally, realizing that prayer wasn't being answered, at least not to my satisfaction. "Come on, Crimson. Now's the perfect time. The boys are at school, no one around to make you uncomfortable."

I groaned in response.

"You're scared." He stated quietly. I shrugged silently in answer. "Crimson, I won't let anything happen to you. I promise."

Grumbling a little more, I let him lead me down the steps and out to the Chevy. I climbed up behind the wheel and sat still for a moment, just staring glumly out the windshield. I had a sudden inspiration. "Wouldn't you rather we go up to your loft and make out? No one's around to bother us…"

Josiah studied me carefully, and I watched the heat begin to build in his gaze and thought for just a moment that I'd succeeded. "You *must* be scared." He shook his head in disappointment. "To use that sort of tactic to distract me. Any other time I'd take you up on that offer, but this is important. You need to know this."

I let my head drop forward onto the steering wheel, my shoulders sagging in defeat. Then taking a breath, I pushed in the clutch and started the engine. Driving in the snow wasn't that different from driving in any other condition, all things considered. I had to start and stop a little slower, take more time; but other than that, there really weren't too many differences.

Of course, Josiah had me practice sliding and how to correct those. I'll admit the spinouts and donuts were fun. He had me drive to town, and even though it was barely above freezing we still got our milkshakes. As I drove slowly back to the ranch, I'd been thinking and decided to share my thoughts with him. "I need to talk with Billy."

"About?"

"About…everything, really."

"Everything?" he questioned.

"Yeah." I nodded. "About my mom, me, the accident…you."

"Everything." He agreed.

"Yeah."

"You want me to be there?"

"It'd be easier having you there, but I also think it'd be best if I talked with him on my own, ya know?"

"I'm always here if you need me." He lifted my hand to kiss my knuckles, letting his mouth linger for a moment.

"I know."

My opportunity came two days later. Billy asked me to drive him to town while the boys were in school. He needed to pick up some prescriptions and he thought it'd be good practice for me. We drove the Chevy again as it was safer in the snow. We were just a few minutes from the ranch when I worked up enough courage to begin a conversation that was ripe with emotion for both Billy and me. I glanced over at the older man; he was staring out the window like he was deep in thought.

Taking a firmer grip on the steering wheel, I said, "Hey, Billy?"

"Yeah?" he glanced over in my direction.

"What happened? Between you and Mom?"

Billy took a deep breath and then let it out just as slowly. "Ignorance and pride," he sighed quietly. "I thought I was doing the right thing. I just wanted her to not hurt any more. I had nothing against you, Sage. At that time, I never really thought a whole lot about you being a baby. In my eyes, the pregnancy was just evidence of the...pain Terri'd already suffered." Billy paused again, seeming to choose his words. "I didn't know how to respond, and it tore my guts out when she said she wanted to keep the baby. I couldn't figure it out." Billy rubbed his eyes tiredly. "Nothing made sense."

"She felt I was as much a victim as she had been." I softly explained.

"I know that now. She'd written to tell me about it later on. I'd asked her to come home, but...your momma—she was a proud one. And tough. Always had been. Took after her momma. She had to be. So, it was my ignorance; I should have known better. About the pregnancy, about her feelings, her pride. I should've known better. My ignorance; her pride."

I chuckled a little. Mom had always been strong and proud. She'd stood on her own two feet and had no problem speaking her mind. "I'm not mad, Billy," I said quietly. "And if you need it, I forgive you. Really there's nothing to forgive. I don't blame you."

Billy cleared his throat and sniffed a little, nodded his head, and took another deep breath. When he spoke, his voice was quiet, barely more than a whisper. "Thank you."

"I'm not mad at you, but I've been pretty mad at her. All of this, my existence, you, my real identity...I just wish she'd told me herself. *That's* been hard. I've just been so confused."

"I can imagine. I know she'd intended telling you. She told me that. It was just hard for her to talk about. She'd only been afraid of hurting you; that was all. She'd been protecting you for so long, it was hard to know when to stop."

"Yeah; she mentioned that." I slowed the truck, letting it coast when the speed limit dropped as we neared town.

"You seem to be adjusting all right. Especially lately."

I blushed lightly. "Yeah; I am."

"Josiah. He's a fine man. That boy has come a long way, and you'd be hard pressed to find better," he stated. "Just swing into the Saveway and I'll run in. I'll be back in a moment."

Billy was only gone about fifteen minutes, but I still had plenty of time to think about all we had shared. When he climbed back into the truck, I started her up, and headed back for home. "Did you ever suspect anyone? When Mom was...?"

"At the time, to me, because she was my baby girl, *everyone* was a suspect. Terri gave as best a description as she could, but it wasn't much to go on."

"Do I...do I *look*...like anyone she knew then?" This thought had bothered me a lot. Had I been a constant reminder of her attacker?

Billy looked over. His older blue-green eyes slowly slid over my face, lighting on several features, finally he met my gaze and sighed. "You're a lot like she was. Same facial features, same frame. Your hair is lighter and your eyes...your eyes are different."

My heart skipped a beat. "You're thinking about someone; aren't you?"

Billy's jaw tightened as he ran a hand through his thinning hair. "There was a boy. He was a friend of Terri's boyfriend, Jon." He paused, eyes somewhere in the distance. "He had eyes like yours. And his hair was that same shade of pale blond."

I processed what he'd said as my heart beat a steady pace in my chest. "You think it was him?"

"I don't know; I guess it doesn't really matter much now. Terri's gone."

Thoughts flew like a tornado in my head; finally, I snatched one. "What was his name?"

Billy rubbed at his chin and blew out a soft breath. "Lance. His name was Lance McDaniels."

Josiah was waiting when we got back. With a wave to us, Billy headed inside; it seemed like there was always some form or other to fill out on one of the boys. Inspiration suddenly struck and I told Josiah I'd be right back as I ran up to my room. Mom had boxed up lots of pictures I hadn't gone through yet—I wondered if that guy, if *Lance* was in any of them. If I might recognize him. If I might recognize me in him. Grabbing the box with all the photos, I headed back to Josiah.

He arched a thick brow when he saw what I was carrying, but after studying me a heartbeat, he seemed to gather this was somehow important. Without a word, he took the box in one hand, and with me in the other, led me to his apartment. Feeling as if I'd just run a marathon, my legs nearly gave out as I sat on his couch. He placed the box on the coffee table then quietly asked, "How about some coffee?"

Biting my lip, my gaze on the box, I nodded. Not gonna lie, trepidation was settling in. What would I find? What if I *did* find a picture of Lance and he *did* look like me? And what if I didn't? What then? As my mind puzzled everything over in my head, I was vaguely aware as Josiah moved about his little kitchen. What seemed only moments later, he was sitting beside me, placing our coffee on the table near the box.

"Crimson." His hand slid over mine, disentangling my fingers from where I'd been knotting them, his voice a soft caress. "Come on, Little Red; why don't you tell me what we're looking for."

Blinking, I looked up and saw the concern, the emotion in his dark blue eyes. A calmness came over me, and I was able to breathe again. "We're looking for someone who looks like me."

Josiah studied me silently; speculation, awareness, then understanding and maybe a touch of heat sparked in his gaze. "Someone who looks like you." He didn't ask a question, he simply made a statement.

"Yeah." My voice was barely more than a whisper, and suddenly I couldn't look at him anymore. My gaze shifted back to my hands where they rested in my lap. "He'll have my color hair and eyes. His name will be Lance."

"You think he might be...?"

"Yeah."

Silence settled between us. I was afraid to look at him, to see pity, or anything like that. He waited, then after a moment or two spoke. "Crimson, look at me." When I didn't, Josiah gently took my chin in his grip and turned my face towards him. "I'm not scared, and I'll help you look. Because I don't care what we find. You are and will remain the most beautiful person in the world to me. I need you to know that." Tears pooled in my eyes, then slid down my face. Blowing out a breath, I nodded as I wiped them away. "All right; let's do this." His voice rumbled as he kissed my temple, then reached for the box, sliding it closer.

I removed the lid and set it aside. "Billy said Lance was a good friend of Mom's boyfriend, Jon. So, I figured there might be a picture of him together with them."

We went through every photo in the box. It took us over an hour. There were several photos that had Jon and Mom in them, but none with a pale-haired boy—I wondered if that was significant. There was one photo that gave me pause. Mom and Jon were standing close together; their arms around each other. They were smiling. The picture had been torn. About one-third of it was missing. In the part I had, there was a shadow of someone else standing there with them. But their image was the part that had been torn away.

I'm not sure how long I stared at that picture, only becoming aware as Josiah gently tugged it from my grasp. He set it on the coffee table, then pulled me to my feet. "You've been staring at that for close to an hour." He kissed my forehead. "C'mon, let's take a break; I've got a surprise for you."

He led me down the stairs and outside, where I was met with the most beautiful sight. The sky was lit in stunning shades of pink and coral, violet and orange. I hadn't even realized how late it had gotten. I must have missed dinner, missed Ethan getting home—that made me feel bad.

Josiah led me around to the front of the barn. Waiting in front of it was Trigger; the big gelding was hitched to a sleigh—a real, honest-to-God sleigh. Surprise stopped me in my tracks, and I turned to Josiah. "It's the perfect night." He shrugged. "Gorgeous sunset, beautiful woman at my side; it's not too cold. We've got a few thick blankets, and I packed a couple sandwiches and some hot chocolate."

Throwing my arms around him, I breathed against his neck, tasting the salty texture, inhaling him. "I don't deserve you. You're so good to me. Thank you, Josiah."

"No, thank you. And it's me who doesn't deserve you. Besides, I'm hoping this will give me some brownie points and I'll be able to steal a few kisses from you tonight."

I smiled at his teasing and let him help me into the sleigh. After we were settled and the blankets were wrapped around us, he urged Trigger on. It was by far the most romantic night of my life. My anxious thoughts were banished to the back of my mind as I reveled in my time with him. And, yes, I let Josiah steal a few kisses—several, in fact.

Josiah

Josiah sat on his couch, deep in thought. He'd already taken Crimson back to the main house; she'd texted when she was upstairs. It agitated him that she was in that house with Mike so close by. But he reasoned, she was essentially safe with Billy there. And he, himself, was always no more than a text or phone call away. After he'd put Trigger in his stall and had the sleigh back in the shed, he'd gone upstairs and showered. Now, deep in thought he sat, holding a steaming cup of coffee and that photo. The one that had held Crimson's attention for so long. Still wrapped in his towel, his chest bare and already dry, he didn't even notice the chill in the room. No, his thoughts were on that picture.

Josiah wondered if indeed the reason it was torn was because Crimson's mother hadn't wanted to see her rapist. And, if that was the case, and Crimson did resemble him, how hard must it have been for her to see him in her daughter. It was a testament to her love as a mother that she and Crimson had been so close. Maybe she never saw her rapist in her daughter. Maybe she only saw Crimson. He thought it was interesting that if Lance had been Jon's best friend there weren't more pictures of him. Or even any pictures of him at all. It made him wonder. Then again, it could have been a girl in the photo, maybe someone her mom had been friends with until that friendship ended; it was hard to tell from the shape of the shadow. It could have been anyone, and it could have been no one. Either way, and regardless, he loved *his* girl and hated seeing her upset. And, even if she did, in fact, look like the man who'd raped her mom, she was still the most beautiful and precious thing in all Creation to him. And nothing could ever change that.

Chapter 11
Mistletoe

Crimson Sage

A white Christmas seemed almost cliché, but that's what we ended up with. Everyone stayed up late on Christmas Eve watching holiday classics on television before stumbling up to our beds with sleepy eyes. In the upstairs landing, Ethan wrapped his arms around me and whispered, "Love you, Sis."

Hugging him back, I said, "Love you, too, Kid."

It felt like I'd just closed my eyes, when my phone buzzed with an incoming text. It was 12:01 and Josiah was wishing me a Merry Christmas. He told me to come to the window and look outside. Blinking the sleep from my eyes, I stumbled from bed and rubbed the frost from the glass as I peered out into the snowy night.

A glowing message, written in candlelight that spelled out the words *I love you*, waited for me in the snow. Josiah stood beside the message just below my window. In his arms he held a large bouquet of red roses. My heart swelled even as my eyes welled in tears. Josiah pointed to the back door, so I quickly dried my tears, grabbed my robe and slippers, and headed downstairs.

My fingers were all thumbs as I struggled with the lock while Josiah waited on the porch. Finally, I had it open and seconds later was in his arms. Josiah held me tightly. "Merry Christmas, Little Red."

Hiccupping through happy tears, I kissed him and whispered, "I love you. And Merry Christmas back."

"Think Billy would mind if you stayed over?" That idea had so much potential. Raising my head, I took in the look on his face, the heat in his blue eyes, trying to gage his intentions. He kissed my nose, then nuzzled my neck before breathing against my cheek, "I promise your virtue is safe with me. I'd just like to spend this time with you. In a few hours this house will be full of noise." His voice took on a deeper cadence. "I'd like you to myself for a little while."

The gritty rumble of his words had me shivering as they slid over me, and I looked down at my outfit. "I'm not really dressed...."

"Yeah..." he groaned into my hair. "I was trying not to notice that." Stepping back, he looked me over, heat trailed where his eyes landed. "Look, run up and grab something to wear for tomorrow. I'll wait. Don't worry about changing now. Just hurry. I have another surprise for you."

Quickly and silently, I ran back up the stairs and grabbed a change of clothes, then turned out my light and locked my door behind me. I carried everything back to Josiah, planning to slip my boots on down there so I wouldn't wake anyone up clomping down the steps. Before I could put the boots on, Josiah swung me into his arms. "You hold that; I'll hold you."

"You can't carry me all the way to the barn!" My whisper-shout echoed on the porch. "I'm too heavy!"

"Please." Josiah lifted me closer to his chest, holding me tightly as he stepped off the porch and into the snow. "Soaking wet you're about as heavy as a feather. Besides, I like you here."

"Should we blow those candles out?"

"Nah, they'll be fine. Took me forever to light them; besides there's nothing to burn out here."

Josiah wasn't even breathing hard when we reached the barn. I thought he'd set me down, allow me to climb the steps to his loft myself, but he didn't. He carried me all the way to the top. When we reached his door, he stopped. "Okay, now you need to close your eyes."

"You have a thing with my eyes." I teased, as I closed them. "You're always asking me to cover them."

The door opened and Josiah shifted as he carried me in, kicking the door shut behind us. He took a few steps forward, and I pictured his room, guessing he'd stopped near the middle. He kissed my temple, lingering for a moment before nuzzling along my neck and ear. "All right, you can look."

My eyes opened and then my breath caught audibly in my throat. A warm glow surrounded us—candles of varying sizes and colors lit the room in a soft glow. Roses sat on the bar, adding a subtle fragrance. But it was the mistletoe that caught me—I couldn't count them all. What had to be hundreds of sprigs were hung all over the ceiling of his little apartment. I don't think there was much room for me to stand where I wouldn't be under it. The corner of my mouth lifted as I took them all in.

Josiah really was like a dream come true and I hoped I never woke up. He was tough, rugged, strong, and physical enough to set my body on fire. He was capable and confident. Compassionate and thoughtful. He was safe and trustworthy and he knew how to stoke the fire inside me. And he was romantic. *So* very romantic. I didn't know what I'd done to deserve him, couldn't fathom what he saw in me. I'd been such a broken mess, and yet he'd treated me like a rare gem, like I was priceless and worth something. Even when I felt I'd nothing to give him, nothing to offer, he gave to me until I overflowed and was able to reciprocate. I never wanted to let him go, just wanted to stay here with him forever.

He must have recognized whatever look was on my face, because Josiah didn't hesitate. His movements were purposeful as he set the pace, allowing my feet to slide to the floor. Strong, warm hands skimmed my waist and hips, before moving upward, caressing the column of my throat, angling me for better access. He took my mouth easily, with such intent in his touch. Slow. Deep. Tasting and nibbling. Effortlessly stoking that fire.

We were both breathing heavily when he finally pulled back, those blue eyes searching mine. Suddenly, he grinned and whispered, "Surprise."

Chuckling, I leaned up to kiss him again. Soft feather kisses along his jaw. Down his throat. Josiah held still now, letting me be in control. I could spend eternity just kissing this man. He smelled so good. Pine and musk and man. He tasted even better. I wanted, *needed,* to be closer, and made a sound of frustration as I strained upwards. Because even standing on my toes he was still so much taller than me. Sensing my irritation at our height difference, he chuckled softly, then gripped me and lifted. My sleepover clothes dropped to the floor as Josiah moved, our mouths still entangled, carrying me forward.

Suddenly he stopped again and raised his head. Indecision was on his face now as he looked around. Torn between heading for his bed, a delightful and dangerous option, or playing it safe and choosing the couch. Not to say that the couch didn't hold its own set of dangers, but when compared to Josiah's bed and the heat already burning between us, the couch was definitely the lesser of two evils.

Josiah caught my eye and grinned again. He took a deep breath, settling himself, bringing himself under control, then he lowered his head to mine, resting his forehead against mine. "You may kill me," he grumbled good-naturedly.

"Same." My breath was all shaky. Sighing, and evidently resolved to behave, Josiah set me down. As my feet touched the floor, I felt a little off balance, the room spinning slightly. Holding his hands tightly, I kept my head buried against his chest until I felt better, then glanced up, the ceiling catching my eye, and laughed quietly.

"What?" His thumbs traced circles on my arms.

"I was just thinking that for both our sakes I should find a safe zone, but by the looks of things there isn't one."

"You're safe with me, Crimson." He nuzzled my ear again, bringing goosebumps. "I didn't bring you here to seduce you."

"I know." I placed a hand on his arm, loving the strength under my palm, the heat, him. "But I also know it's hard on you. I mean, it's hard on me, so I can only imagine how hard this is for you."

"Maybe we should stop using that word, huh?" His comment had me blushing, and I buried my face in his chest again. Chuckling, Josiah took my hand. "Come on." He led me to the couch, and we sank into the cushions.

Lacing our fingers together, his thumb rubbed the back of my hand in slow, soothing motions. "I just want to sit here with you and enjoy the evening. We'll go to the big house in a few hours and celebrate Christmas, but this, this here, this is our time." Snuggling into his warm shoulder, my eyes blinked heavily, and I was surprised I could even be tired right now. Moments ago, my every nerve ending was firing in pure excitement. Now, I was so relaxed I couldn't seem to keep my eyes open. Josiah must have noticed because he squeezed me gently, as his lips brushed my temple, and his voice rumbled in my ear. "Go to sleep, Crimson. I've got you."

"No," I yawned as I tried to battle the pull of exhaustion. "I'm good."

Josiah chuckled, just a soft whisper against my skin. "Hold on." He stood, moving around the room, blowing out the majority of the candles, leaving just one lit. He grabbed a blanket from the bed and rejoined me on the couch. With his arms wrapped around me, his heartbeat strong, steady, and comforting in my ear, it didn't take long for sleep to claim me.

Josiah

Crimson smelled good. Lemon, vanilla, and sunshine—even in the middle of winter. Her warm body was pressed against him. Enticing. Comforting. Driving him completely insane. Josiah wanted her like he wanted his next breath. Such an intense need. But he'd wait for her, for the right time, the right place, the right reasons.

Shifting carefully, easing Crimson closer to him, he settled more fully into the cushions. Shifting still more, he molded her body to fit the length of his. He didn't trespass. No, he wouldn't do that, but he couldn't help imagining when she'd say yes and truly be his. Heart, body, and soul.

Of their own volition, his lips skimmed her temple, then the inside of her wrist as he entwined her hand with his, lifting it to his mouth. Crimson mumbled under her breath, said his name, then, *I love you* in an exhale and snuggled closer still, wrapping herself around him. At the sound of her voice, Josiah froze, trying to determine if she was still sleeping. When her breathing once again evened out, he relaxed and let sleep claim him.

Crimson Sage

Josiah woke me slowly, tenderly. He kissed along my fingertips, trailed teeth over my knuckles, my palm, nipping as he went. He inhaled the scent at my wrist, softly groaning, then continued upwards, pausing at my elbow, my shoulder. There, Josiah lingered, spending considerable time. "Have I expressed properly just *how* much I love this. Spot. Right. Here." He punctuated each word with a kiss, before moving on again. This time to my neck, then my mouth. "Good morning, beautiful," he breathed against my lips.

Enjoyable being woken in this way. Sleepily, I grinned up at him as I stretched and moaned. "Good morning," I whispered back as I reached up and touched his face.

"Merry Christmas." He turned his head and kissed my palm. "Again."

I giggled. "Merry Christmas. What time is it?"

"Almost seven."

"What time will everyone be awake up at the house?"

"They usually get the ball rolling fairly early. In fact, I'm sure they're already up, just getting their coffee and breakfast. I didn't know if you wanted to shower or not...."

"Are you saying I stink?" I teased.

"You smell like you always do." Josiah buried his face against my neck, kissing along my collarbone. "Edible. Like lemon and sunshine and *desire*." Pulling back, he looked me over through half-lidded eyes, then he made a low sound as he shook his head. "But we need to get over there, so I'll stop right here." Rising swiftly, he pulled me to my feet. "Go on, get ready; I'll wait."

Grabbing my clothes from his bed—Josiah must have picked them up from the floor while I was sleeping—I headed for the bathroom. Deciding not to shower after all, I simply washed up and brushed my teeth. I dressed in record time, just adding some mascara and lip balm to complete my look. Glancing in the mirror, I wasn't super impressed but figured it would have to do.

Josiah waited, leaning against his little bar. After doing a slow, once-over, he took my hand, and we headed to the big house. Most of the occupants were seated around the table when we stepped through the backdoor. I tried to ignore the knowing and questioning looks but couldn't seem to keep the blush from staining my cheeks. Josiah grabbed a couple mugs and filled them. We sat together at the table and when I looked up Billy caught my eye. "Merry Christmas," he grinned.

"Merry Christmas." I replied, then feeling like an explanation was needed, said, "Josiah...woke me...a little earlier this morning than the rest of you."

"MmmHmm." Was his response as he sipped his coffee. "I wasn't asking. We all saw the message in the snow." He looked to Josiah. "Nice touch, by the way."

"I thought so." Josiah grinned.

Ethan passed a plate of pancakes down to us, a grin on his face. I quickly glanced around the table before dropping my eyes. Most of the looks were friendly. Mike's was anything but. Hostility broiled there and fear slithered down my spine. Subconsciously, I slid a little closer to Josiah, needing the comfort he gave so freely. Sensing my tension, Josiah took my balled fist where it rested on my thigh, smoothing my fingers out. He kissed my temple, lingering for a moment. Then he lifted his eyes, letting his gaze touch everyone in the room, pausing on Mike. The look he gave sent a clear message. If anyone crossed his line in the sand, they'd answer to him.

We finished breakfast, then everyone crowded into the great room. Mountains of presents surrounded the tree, making the large room seem smaller. Boys were perched on all available surfaces, including the floor. Josiah and I found a spot together on one of the oversized chairs near the far corner, away from the tree. He sat on the chair; I sat on his lap. Billy read us the Nativity story, then led us in singing a few carols, before we began to pass the presents out. Then we began the long process of opening all the gifts. Billy had it down to some semblance of order. We started with the four youngest, they opened their gifts first, then we went on to the next four youngest and so on.

I watched as each boy unwrapped his presents, saw the light in their eyes, the happy smiles on their faces. Billy, Red and Sally, and Bentley had all chipped in to get them gifts. Some of the boys' families had sent gifts as well. I was impressed with the personal attention given to each of them, based upon their needs and wants. Soon there were mounds and mounds of discarded wrapping paper piled around the room. And as each boy began to use and explore whatever gift they'd received, the volume in the room increased.

While I sat, basking in the glow and the euphoria around me, just taking it all in, Josiah handed me a small box wrapped in muted silver paper with a deep red bow. Turning, I looked back at him. Blue eyes met mine. "Merry Christmas, Crimson."

My heart fluttered as I carefully pulled off the bow and then, trying not to tear the paper, unwrapped the gift. I stared at the small black box for a moment feeling warmth flood through me. Inhaling, I lifted the lid. Nestled inside, on a bed of gold velvet were a pair of garnet earrings. They were hoops and reminded me of something Victorian or maybe bohemian in their design. Lightly I touched them, a smile lifting the corner of my mouth as I turned to Josiah. "Thank you; they're beautiful. I love them."

Josiah helped me put them on, then leaned back to get a better view. "What do you think?" I asked.

"I think I love you," he replied.

I smiled, "I think I love you back," then handed him a large black and grey striped gift bag. I turned a little on his lap so I could watch him open it. Josiah removed the tissue paper, then pulled out a deep blue sweater and a beanie in a similar shade. "It reminded me of your eyes."

Gently, he lifted me from his lap as he stood to try the sweater on. Thoroughly infatuated, I watched as he lifted his arms to pull his sweatshirt off. Several enticing inches of exposed abdomen were displayed before he lowered his arms again, and caught me looking, flashing me a wolfish grin. "Like what you see, Little Red?"

I nodded, eyes still on him. The sweater really did look amazing. Complimenting his physique and those eyes.

Dragging me to him, he growled against my mouth. "Thank you; I love it. But you keep looking at me like that and we're going to have a serious problem."

Chuckling, that came out *way* too breathlessly, I said, "There's more; keep looking." Josiah gave me an exasperated look, then dug further into the bag. He pulled out a bottle of cologne—one that I thought would smell amazing on him—and another small box that held a new pair of hoops for his ears. These were a deep metallic blue.

"This is too much." He shook his head. "You shouldn't have done this."

"Yes, I should; you're worth it."

We settled on the chair again and he pulled me closer. "I think you're worth it too, so don't get mad, but I kinda got you something else." Then he reached down beside the chair and lifted another, bigger box wrapped the same way as the first. I hesitated, giving him a teasingly hard look. "Go on," Josiah encouraged. "Open it."

Even though we were surrounded, everyone was so enthralled in their own gifts, we enjoyed the illusion of privacy. This time I quickly pulled the paper off, then laughed quietly as I gazed into the box. Evidently Josiah and I had been on the same wavelength when shopping for each other. We both chuckled as I lifted the soft sweater with its matching scarf and beanie from the box. The sweater was slate grey, and the scarf and beanie were burgundy and slate grey striped. He'd also got me a bottle of perfume, bringing another smile to my face.

"I've been imagining you in this scent," he rumbled low so only I could hear. "You should go try your sweater on."

Running up to my room, I quickly changed; the new sweater was as soft as cashmere and felt like a warm hug as the material slid over my skin. It fit like a glove—I was impressed—he'd done a great job. Josiah had the perfume bottle waiting when I returned. Taking my wrists one at a time, he sprayed the fragrance there. Thumbs rubbed enticingly over the area, infusing heat and longing with each stroke. With eyes closed, he lifted them, bringing them to his face, where he inhaled with a soft, rumbling sound and placed a kiss on each wrist. He opened his eyes, kissed my nose, then lowered my hands as he stepped back with what seemed a satisfied look on his face.

For the ranch boys, I'd given Billy money to get them each a five-dollar gift card to the Java Shack—a local coffee shop. When I'd stepped back into the room, they'd all yelled a collective thank you to me. Their appreciation almost didn't register in the onslaught of Josiah's most recent actions. But after a moment, the expectant silence behind us had me turning with a blush to smile to the room at large, enduring their chuckles and whistles. Evidently, our privacy hadn't been so private after all.

Ethan gave me a big hug, thanking me for the A-Team t-shirt and iTunes gift card I'd given him. Apparently, Josiah and I had been on the same page with more than our gifts to each other, because he'd bought Ethan a sweatshirt with Mr. T on it that said, "I pity the fool!"

"These are awesome; where did you find them?" Ethan asked as he tried on one of his new shirts.

"Amazon." We said in unison, then laughed.

"Seriously?" Ethan laughed. "Thanks again, guys; I really love my shirts."

Billy came over next, wanting to thank Ethan and me for the John Wayne print we'd given him. "It'll look great in my office." Then I thanked him for the books he'd given from my ever expanding to be read list.

It didn't take too long to clean up the mountains of wrapping paper and ribbon from the living room floor. Everyone pitched in, hauling bags to the dumpster. There was an almost tangible atmosphere of peace, and love, and happiness in the air. Josiah and I stood on the back porch watching the younger ranch boys as they frolicked and played in the snow. Daisy ran around, barking and leaping, chasing after Ethan and Kelly. I turned into Josiah's chest, sliding my arms around him, loving the feel of him. The warmth, the firmness of his frame, the way he always welcomed me. My lips pressed against his neck, enjoying the way his pulse leaped, the way he smelled. "Thank you. For everything. You made today beautiful."

"You make every day beautiful." He rested his chin on my head as he pulled me closer.

Josiah

Josiah sat on the wooden steps of the back porch and watched as Crimson, Ethan and the other boys worked hard to build a snowman. After all the wrapping paper had been cleaned up and the great-room was looking more normal, Sally set the table for Christmas dinner—it was more lunch than dinner, really. She'd cooked and carved a ham. There were fresh-baked rolls, sliced cheeses, and mouthwatering sides. Everyone ate more than they should and decided to work off some steam by building the traditional ranch snowman.

The boys build one every year, and apparently last year's model had stood nearly six feet tall—Crimson was determined to top that. Right now, there was more snow on them than on the man they were attempting to erect. Josiah laughed quietly as Kelly and Ethan, in the process of bringing more buckets of snow to where Crimson was working, suddenly tripped, and the bucket of snow, somehow, haphazardly landed on her.

She wiped the snow from her face and hair, then gave her brother a loving, yet murderous look, before launching herself at him.

"It was an accident!" Ethan laughed as he tried fighting her off.

"Sure it was, you little twerp," Crimson growled smearing snow into Ethan's hair and down his jacket. The siblings continued their good-natured ruckus, until Josiah finally made his way over. The other boys had been standing around, unsure just how to help their fallen comrade. After all she was a girl, and just *where* did you touch a girl that wouldn't get you in trouble?

In one move, Josiah dodged a flailing limb, then wrapped an arm around her waist, lifting her off her brother. He swung Crimson up over his shoulder, pinning her there. "Run, Ethan, while I have her and she can't move."

Laughing, Ethan rolled away from them and jogged several feet away where he knelt and began assembling snowballs.

"Cheater!" Crimson squirmed, trying in vain to dislodge herself.

"You want to wrestle with someone, woman; you wrestle with me." Josiah tightened his grip, enjoying the feel of her in his arms. "Besides, that wasn't a fair fight, and you know it."

"Oh yeah?" Crimson panted, still trying to get free. "You think you're man enough to take me?"

She'd meant the comeback in complete innocence and humor, Josiah knew that, yet he'd had to take a firm grip on the raging inferno she always lit inside him. After a long moment, he allowed her to slide to her feet. He gazed down at her, heat sparking in his blue eyes. "Careful now; words like that could be taken as invitation. And I'm weak enough to fall for them."

Crimson chuckled lightly. "You're not weak. Not at all."

"With you, I am. I'm trying to be what you need me to be—patient, honorable. But, especially at times like these, it's difficult."

"I'm sor—" A wet snowball to the face cut her off. In disbelief, they turned to see the boys had drawn battle lines. Crimson and Josiah on one side, the boys on the other. "Oh, he's dead now," Crimson grumbled as she sank to her feet to gather more snow.

"We need to move; we're sitting ducks out here. C'mon!" Josiah pulled her back to her feet, and they ran towards one of the large trees. "We'll need to take shelter here, regroup, then go on the attack."

"I'm all for storming the keep." Crimson glared in the boys' direction, who were now talking smack at them.

"We'll make a few snowballs, just so we have some ammo, then we'll go get 'em."

"Deal." She touched knuckles with him, then they got to work.

What took place next would go down in the ranch history books as the Most Epic of Epic Snow Battles. Crimson and Josiah were so greatly out-numbered, there shouldn't have been much of a battle at all. But Josiah was a force to be reckoned with. With their plan firmly in place, the two began to move. They came at the boys from two different directions; snowballs whizzed through the air, most missing their intended targets.

Josiah flung the snow missiles with precision, trying to get them off balance, and rattle them. Several times, he caught snowballs aimed at him and flung them back. Eventually the boys had run out of ammo and quickly gave ground, running in every direction to escape his aim.

Crimson was a little stealthier. She'd held back and waited for the boys to be distracted before making her move. Josiah was busy throwing what-ever ammo he could get his hands on; Crimson snuck closer and began stomping the snowballs the boys had stored for use. And what she wasn't stomping into wet mush, she'd steal and use against them.

Eventually Billy called them all in for dinner. The Most Epic of Epic Snow Battles was over. Of course, both sides declared themselves the vic-tors.

Josiah stayed late at the big house that night. Close to eleven-thirty he whispered in Crimson's ear, "I'm gonna go. You staying here tonight?"

"Yeah," Crimson sighed. "I probably better."

"Make sure you lock up, and I'll see you in the morning, Little Red." He kissed her lightly, letting his mouth linger over hers for the briefest of moments.

"I love you, Josiah; thanks for making this Christmas beautiful."

"Thanks for being mine." He kissed her again before stepping out into the night.

Chapter 12
Old Demons

The snow lasted until the end of January. By that time, I was fairly over my delight in it. Now, I was just craving sunshine and warmth and thought a lot about the beach house that Gracie's parents owned in North Carolina. I missed the summers we spent there. Two weeks, each summer, except the last one when everything had ended. I missed the beach, the heat, the ocean waves. Josiah took me swimming a few times and that was nice, but it wasn't the same as the ocean. After our swim, he'd take me out to dinner. Those times made the winter blues a little more bearable.

I hadn't had much time to think any more about Lance and whether he was the man in Mom's ripped photo. Josiah kept me busy, whether with work on the ranch, or just hanging out and doing things with him, or those special, unexpected times he'd take me out, into town, swimming, or just dinner. Several times we went hiking, and even fishing. He told me he was planning a camping trip as soon as the weather warmed enough that we wouldn't freeze our butts off.

Josiah had me practice riding more; I was now comfortable enough to catch and saddle one of the ranch horses myself; but still, horseback riding wasn't really my thing. He agreed it wasn't his "thing" either, but it was still a good skill to know. Josiah also taught me how to work on my car, which was running great. He showed me how to check and add air to the tires, how to change a flat. I learned to check the oil and add oil when it was low. I wondered at his intent in coaching me in all these things. And again, when

I asked him the reason, he simply said they were good skills to know. And really, I had no argument against it. As my own life had cruelly schooled, you never knew what was around the corner. Life had a way of throwing you the unexpected.

One Friday afternoon, Josiah told me to get dressed, something nice—he was taking me into Boise for dinner. Giddy in excitement at the thought of going out to a fancy restaurant, at least fancier than the little diner in Salmon, I dressed with care that night. Or at least I tried to. Currently I was standing in front of my wardrobe, wishing Grace were here. She'd know exactly how to dress me. Biting my lip, trying to come up with something perfect, I browsed what was available. It was still cold outside, sometimes bitterly cold. And what if we did some walking around? I wanted to look beautiful but not freeze to death in the process. After fifteen minutes, I gave up and just called Gracie. "I need your help." I whined as soon as she answered.

"Yes, you should sleep with him," she responded.

"Oh *my gosh*!" I made a disgusted noise. "What is the matter with you?"

"That's not what you're calling about?"

"No! Yeesh! Perverted much?"

Gracie sighed. "What can I do for you then?"

"He's taking me out. He said to dress up."

"And you can't figure out how to dress that lovely little body for him."

"Sort of."

"Okay, lemme think. Go to your closet..." It boggled the mind how well she knew the status of my clothing, what had I to choose from, what she'd have to work with. But eventually she put the perfect outfit together for me—a dark blue ombre sweater dress, form-fitting and cut to just above the knee. It had cut-out shoulders and a boat neck. She paired it with my black leather boots and jacket and silver-threaded grey scarf. Gracie was a genius. I looked amazing. Thanking her, I quickly got off the phone.

Josiah was waiting for me when I came down the stairs. Everyone was. I heard his slow intake of breath and tried to keep the grin off my face. He told Billy we'd be back late, and not to wait up. Billy asked if he should lock up, or if I'd be staying elsewhere. Heat stained my cheeks and before I could respond, Josiah said, "Go ahead and lock up, Crimson'll take the bed; I'm fine on the couch."

Billy gave him an exasperated look before turning to me, "Will you need anything from the house?"

"I...I think I've got what I need. Thanks." From somewhere towards the back of the room, I heard a quiet cough that I knew, just *knew* came from Mike. Josiah must have known, too, because his dark eyes flashed a hard look in that direction before settling on me again. I kissed Billy on the cheek and said goodnight to Ethan before Josiah led me out the door.

He'd cleaned his car. Not that it was normally dirty or anything, but I could see the inside had been vacuumed, the outside washed and waxed. He'd hung a tropical smelling air freshener somewhere inside as well—coconut and pineapple floated on the breeze as he opened my door for me, then helped me inside. The drive was a comfortable, silent one. Music played softly in the background, as he kept one hand on the wheel, one hand holding mine. Occasionally, he'd lift said hand, kissing the back before putting it down again.

He drove us to the Cottonwood Grille, a beautiful seafood establishment that sat alongside the Boise River. A fire blazed in a large, indoor rock fireplace. Cheery lights were strung inside, giving it a romantic atmosphere. Josiah must have called ahead for reservations, because we didn't wait more than five minutes. The maître de led us to a table near the center of the room, with a nice view of the river and the fireplace. Josiah pulled out my chair for me, then helped me with my jacket. After we were seated, I took a minute or two to look him over. To really study him. His head was bare tonight. No beanie. He wore blue jeans, clean, no stains or tears, and a pair of black leather cowboy boots. He wore a tie. Deep grey, over a dark blue button-up shirt. I noticed all this as he removed his own jacket. And watched the way the fabric pulled and stretched with his movements. The way it emphasized his muscled form. In short, he was beautiful.

⊢✳⊣✳⊢

Josiah

Crimson was breathtaking. He couldn't keep his eyes off her. He tried not to stare, tried to keep the heat out of his eyes, so she wouldn't interpret his gaze as purely sexual in nature. But he couldn't help it. He was attracted to her, and all his animal instincts were firing. She was female to his male. And there was no denying that he wanted her. And in the way of any good alpha male, he was fully aware of the stares of the other men in the room, the way their eyes roved over her, the way they heated up, the way they desired her. He bristled in warning, just a quick, hard, flashing gaze that he shot around the room. Just enough of a look that said they could look but not touch.

The waitress came to take their drink order. Josiah had a hard time paying any attention to her, had a hard time taking his eyes off Crimson. His blue eyes ran over the golden skin of her exposed shoulder. He couldn't get enough of those shoulders. Her hair, the way it lay silky and smooth against her. Around those mouthwatering shoulders. He wanted to touch her. Needed to. Vaguely he made some reply to the waitress for lemon water. He caught the small grin that teased Crimson's lips and felt a surge of heat; his pulse sped up before he was able to settle it down again. "You are so beautiful." He uttered the words before he could even process what he was doing. Like he'd *had* to say them. Had to get them out.

Her brown eyes warmed as she returned his look. "Thank you; I was just thinking the same thing about you." She indicated his tie. "I've never seen this look on you—I like it. Then again, I like you in the scruff just as much."

Josiah shook his head in a slow movement. "You have the attention of the whole room—*you* are beautiful. Breathtakingly so."

"Thank you."

The waitress—Ginny was her name—brought their water and asked if they wanted an appetizer. Crimson shrugged, seemingly content to let him decide. Looking over the menu he ordered the coconut shrimp, knowing her love of seafood and all things tropical. For a while now, Josiah had wanted to take her some place nice, to wine and dine her. Well, not so much the wine part, but...he'd wanted to treat her like a lady, like she was cherished, and held high value for him. As this was not something he normally did, and in fact had never done before; he'd really had no idea where to go. Certainly nothing in Salmon would be appropriate. So, he'd researched and found the Cottonwood Grille. Looking at her now, seeing her glow, he knew he'd made the right decision.

Dinner was soon served, and their conversation never seemed to lack. He saw something flash in Crimson's eye as she took a bite of her shrimp. Her soft brown eyes had been taking him in, had lingered where his dragon tattoo peaked above the collar of his shirt. He shot her a curious look, "What?"

"What?" she tried to play the innocent.

"I saw that look; you have something on your mind. What is it?"

"Well..." she fidgeted with her glass, playing with the beads of water than ran down the sides. "I was thinking about...about...ink."

"Ink."

"Yeah, you know...ink."

"As in a tattoo."

"Yeah; what would you think...if I got one?"

Josiah knew she had a deep fear of needles; she'd shared that knowledge with him a few weeks back. They'd been lying together on his bed; he on his stomach; she on her side next to him. Her nimble fingers had traced over his dragon, caressing the skin. She loved that tattoo. Crimson had asked him if it had hurt and then she'd gone on to tell him how she was deathly afraid of needles. That even just to get blood drawn she'd have to lie down, or she'd pass out. Josiah looked at her closely now, his eyes taking her in and enjoying every inch of her, "I think it'd be crazy sexy. But, why...what made you decide you wanted to get one?"

Crimson blushed again, deeper this time. She looked down, not meeting his eyes. Josiah reached across the table, took her hand in his. He rubbed his thumb across her knuckles, then across her palm. "Crimson." His voice rumbled gentle and smooth. "Why?"

Crimson Sage

Josiah's large, worked roughened hands held mine. I watched in fascination as he smoothed the surface of my skin with his. "Why do you want to get a tattoo, Crimson?"

Looking up at him, I was caught. But how to explain my reasoning? Clearing my throat, which suddenly felt all raspy and dry, I shrugged lightly and shook my head. I wasn't sure why it was hard for me to tell him. It wasn't that big of a deal. Yet the words were still difficult to come by. Finally, I whispered, "You really think it would be sexy?"

"Absolutely. But you don't have to do that for me. You don't. You're perfect right now, just the way you are. Perfect."

I blew out a quick breath. "I'm not doing it *for* you. But, maybe in a way, because of you." Josiah shook his head, his blue eyes seemingly trying to read my mind, to understand. Grinning, I inhaled, then said, "You make me feel strong. I feel strong when I'm with you. Like I can face...*anything*. As long as you're there."

"So, this is about fear, then?"

"In part. More it's about not letting fear control me." I chuckled dryly, "I *hate* needles—I'm terrified of them. But I want to face my fear. And you give me the strength to do that."

"You *are* strong." His blue eyes were soft as they searched mine. "You don't get that from me."

"But I'm not." He didn't understand, and I needed him to. "It's you. You've taught me so much. You taught me how to survive. How to live. How to drive a stick. How to ride a horse. I couldn't have done those things without you."

Gently he squeezed my hand. "*You* did those things. You took those actions. And you're a lot stronger than you think."

"Maybe." I shrugged and sighed. His gaze left mine briefly to skate along my shoulders, lingering there for a moment. "I don't know…"

"I know."

"But I only feel strong when you're with me."

"Crimson…" he shook his head, his thumb still rubbing circles on my palm. "I'm not anything. Just a guy who survived. A guy who goes on each day. Living. A guy who…loves you."

His words had me blinking tears from my eyes. "Don't you see? That *is* what gives me strength." I stopped and took a deep breath as a thought suddenly occurred to me. "Do you not want me to do this?"

"I want you to do it for you. Not for me. I'm not worth it."

I shook my head at him this time. "I disagree. You *are* worth it. To me. And I am doing this for me."

"So long as we have that straight, we'll get you some ink." A calculating look entered his eyes as he suddenly chuckled, a low, sexy edge to the sound. "My girl's getting a tattoo—you're one tough chick."

"I'm *your* tough chick."

"Never doubt it."

Ginny returned, asking if we wanted dessert. Winking at me, Josiah told her we'd just take the check, as he had a surprise in mind. And now I'm wondering just what we're doing.

We stood, preparing to leave. Josiah came around the table to help me with my jacket, placing a kiss on my shoulder as he pulled the material up. He made a low sound deep in his throat as warm arms slid around my waist, under the jacket, pulling me against his chest. Slowly, he lowered his mouth to mine. Light, brushing movements, a tender claiming. Someone cleared their throat just off to the left, and I grinned as Josiah growled low in warning. Reluctantly, he raised his head, and I saw a woman standing there. She had to be about Billy's age, with pale blond hair, just a little darker than mine, laced with grey. I smiled, unsure just what she wanted. Were we in her way or was she about to scold us for being so public in our affectionate display.

"Excuse me." Her gaze flashed to Josiah before coming back to me. The look in her eyes was unsettling. It was a searching gaze. "I'm sorry, this is going to sound forward, and I don't mean to be. It's just…you look so much like my son, when he was your age. So much like him; it's uncanny."

My heart clenched, then began pounding in my chest. My throat suddenly felt dry, and I found it hard to swallow. At first, I couldn't figure why her words were bothering me as much as they were. "He had that same shade of blond hair. Same brown, almost golden eyes. He even had a mole, similar to yours, in that exact same place."

I just stared at her. My head couldn't form thoughts; my mouth couldn't form words. "He died. About five years ago, I guess. You just remind me so much of him—it stopped my heart for a minute is all. We'd tried to raise him right, but he—well he was always a wild one, I guess. Always flirting with danger. It caught up with him; he ran with the wrong crowd. He was killed, shot. Still don't know who did it. I miss him." She seemed to be rambling a little now. I still couldn't seem to find my voice; a tremble had started, and I was trying to bring it under control, to simply breathe. Her eyes just moved over my face, my hair, my mole.

"Excuse me, ma'am? Are you from around here?" Josiah asked. He kept his arm firmly around me, no doubt feeling me shake, just holding me tightly to him.

"We, my sister and I live here now. My husband died four years ago. Just couldn't take the loss. Lance was our only child. After he, my husband, passed I moved down from near Salmon. You ever heard of Salmon? It's little. Just a tiny dot on the map. Not much to draw folks up there. Unless you're the fishing sort."

"We're from Salmon, ma'am." Josiah nodded, then pulled me after him, intending to lead me away.

"You're from Salmon?" She looked at me expectantly. "Maybe I know your folks?"

My mouth trembled as I managed to rasp, "My parents were Theresa and Dean Smyth."

"I didn't know any Smyth's...there was Theresa Newell; Terri, we called her."

"My mother." I whispered again, desperately trying to keep the tremor from my voice.

"You don't say. She and Lance were great friends. Well, Lance always had a crush on her. Most everyone did then. But she'd only had eyes for Jon. He was Lance's best friend. They were tight, the three of them. And then your momma, she moved away. Just up and left. Jon and Lance were so heartbroken. Billy, your granddaddy, was too. Couldn't ever figure out what had happened."

By now my brain was firing on all pistons. I knew what had happened. Had pieced everything together. Lance had raped my mom. Lance was my biological father. I stared at the woman before me, wanting to scream at her, tell her what her son had done, but the words wouldn't come. My throat was entirely closed up.

"We're sorry for your loss, ma'am." Josiah knew, somehow sensing what was thrashing around inside me, then. The turmoil, the rage, and the pain. Without another word, he pulled me out the doors. Blindly, I let him lead me, not even noticing the brisk, cold wind that blew. I was shivering, but not from cold. He unlocked the passenger door and opened it, turning me to face him. Gathering me into his arms, he became a shelter in the storm of my emotions, simply holding me close. Holding me together. "Breathe, Crimson. Just breathe." He rubbed soothing circles into my back.

I sniffed, blinking my eyes. "She...he's..."

"I know." He squeezed me tighter. "I know."

Through trembling lips I whispered, "There are so many things I wanted to say…"

His hands continued their soothing paths over my back. "What good would it have done? She's already shattered. Would you do that to her? Hurt her more? He's dead. There is nothing that can be done, now."

"It hurts," I whispered against his neck, breathing him in. That calming, yet intoxicating scent that was all Josiah.

"I know it does." He kissed my temple, then my forehead. "But you're strong. So strong. This will not defeat you."

"No," I exhaled a cleansing breath. "It won't. But it does hurt. *So* much."

"I know it does." He breathed. "I wish I could take it from you. I wish I could take all the pain away." My head rested against his chest, and I listened to the soothing sound of his heart. After a few minutes he pulled back, then silently helped me into his car. After it was started, he got the heater going, and I shivered, unsure if I was cold, or still experiencing a trauma response. He took my hand in his. "This changes nothing. Not about your mom, not about you. You're still perfect. Still strong. Still amazing. This was an old demon, and you fought him and won."

Liking the idea that I'd battled a demon and won, I offered a tiny smile. The news about Lance—learning that about him, about Mom, about me—it didn't crush me. I *was* strong. Because Josiah was strong. I rolled my head to the side and looked at him. I loved him. He gave me strength, and I loved him. "You said you had a surprise for me. Do I still get it?"

"You still want it?" He looked over as he stopped at a red light, and I nodded. "All right, then. Hold on." When the light turned green, Josiah quickly flipped a U-turn, heading in the opposite direction. We drove in silence for about ten minutes before pulling up to the curb at a cute little coffee house. Outdoor seating was available, though they seemed pretty full. Each comfortable grouping had a tall burner giving off heat to those brave enough to endure the chilly night air. Patio lights twinkled from where they were hung, giving off a soft, almost dreamy glow.

"It's not much, but I remembered this café is known for having the best hot chocolate and espresso in the state. I thought we'd get some."

I smiled. "It's perfect; thank you." We placed our orders, then found a single seat available as we waited. Thankfully, it was near one of those lovely burners. Josiah pulled me onto his lap, drawing me closer to him, his arms holding me tightly. "Are you okay?"

"I am." I sighed, snuggling deeper into his warmth. "More than I thought I'd be. Thank you."

We sat and Josiah rubbed a distracting thumb along my thigh as we waited. Once they called our number, we'd decided that as lovely as the outdoor area was, we wanted to get home. As we walked back to his car, hand in hand, he leaned over and kissed my temple, lingering for the briefest moment. "You're perfect, Crimson. Just perfect."

Chapter 13
Fault Line

Crimson Sage

I debated whether to tell Billy what I'd learned. Josiah thought I should, to at the least, give this story some closure. So, I told him. And granted, we didn't have a confession, or proof that might have stood up in court, but in my mind, I knew it to be true. And Billy had agreed; he'd suspected Lance, especially as he saw me grow up. He mentioned a blood test. It would confirm if my DNA matched Lance's. But Josiah and I agreed there was no point in it. We'd only cause further pain and suffering to his mother—and she was damaged enough. I was a legal adult now, so there was no need to prove it for custody or child-support purposes. And besides, he was dead. Nothing could be gained from reopening these wounds. And there was nothing he or they had that I wanted. My mom had already given me the best gift possible—life.

Putting this trauma to rest somehow had me breathing easier, feeling more at peace. I couldn't quite put my finger on exactly why, but I was grateful all the same. We also decided not to tell Ethan. At least not right now. Maybe when he was a little older and it wouldn't confuse him, bringing unrest, difficult questions, and even more difficult answers. We were both doing so well and I didn't want to disrupt our progress, so I simply reveled in our successes and the weight lifted from my shoulders.

Spring was coming, and promise seemed to shine on the horizon in endless possibilities. I got a part-time job at a local coffee shop, the Java Shack. Just a few hours a week, no more than twenty. But it got me out of the house and allowed me to earn some income that wasn't dependent upon Billy, which made me feel good. One day about three weeks after I started, as I was on my way home—I'd just left town, when suddenly my car gave a sharp jerk to the right. Gripping the wheel tightly, I maneuvered to the side of the road and stopped. My heart pounded in my chest, as I sat still, just trying to calm its racing. Finally, on wobbly legs, I got out to look. My right front tire was flat. Heaving a deep sigh, I thanked the Almighty that Josiah had insisted on teaching me how to change a flat.

Gritting my teeth and silently griping at the need, I popped the trunk and began assembling the necessary items. I worked for about five minutes getting things set up when I heard a vehicle coming. It slowed, and I looked up, my eyes colliding with Mike's. The grin on his face wasn't friendly. And he wasn't alone. Two others were with him—a guy, maybe a little older than me and a girl with dark brown hair. Mike sat in the passenger seat; the girl sat between him and the driver. He rolled the window down. "Looks like you need help."

"No, I'm good." I tried to sound confident, but my heart was in my throat.

"I don't mind." His eyes looked me over, making my skin crawl.

"Josiah's on his way and should be here shortly." I hoped he bought my explanation and left me alone. "Thanks though."

Mike offered a knowing look, then scratched his chin. "Suit yourself."

Like a deer before a predator, I stayed immobile until they'd slowly driven away, Mike watching me in the mirror until they were out of sight. Once they were gone, I scrambled into my car as fast as I could. Slamming the door, I locked it, swallowing my fear and dialed Josiah. Which is what I should have done to begin with, but I figured he'd taught me how to do this for a reason. When he answered, I gasped, "I need you."

"What's wrong?" The tone of his voice brought warmth. There was safety there, and I was desperate for it, for him.

"I got a flat; I was getting ready to change it when Mike came by and offered to help. I told him you were on your way to do it." My voice trembled and shame threatened to overcome me. What did I have to be ashamed about? Still, it was there, coursing hand in hand with my fear.

"I'm leaving now." His engine revved as he took off. "Stay in your car; keep the door locked. Where are you?"

"A-about five miles outside Salmon proper. I can see the old windmill off to my right."

"I'm staying on the phone with you. Was Mike by himself?"

"No; he was with another guy and a girl. The guy looked about your age. I didn't recognize him. The girl was between them. She was younger, my age maybe. She had dark brown hair."

"What were they driving?"

"An older pickup. It was black with black rims."

"Sounds like Mace. They come back? You see anything?"

I looked in the mirrors and around me but saw nothing but empty road. "No; nothing."

"I'm almost there." Josiah arrived a couple minutes later, and I stepped from the car and into his arms. "You're shaking." He held me tightly. "Are you okay?"

"Yeah; just keyed up and glad you're here."

"I'll always be here. Let's get this changed and get you home."

It only took us—well more him than me, but I did help—about twenty minutes to get it changed. Then Josiah followed me home. He thought we ought to say something about it to Billy, but I asked if Mike had broken any rules. Josiah replied in the negative. "Then there's no need to say anything. All he did was offer to help."

His jaw tightened. "That's not what he was offering, and you know it."

"But that's what he *said*. And he has witnesses." I shrugged and blew out a breath. "There's no point in his knowing he got to me, right?"

Josiah scratched his scalp in an irritated manner. "I don't trust him."

"I don't either." I kissed his cheek, trying to soothe him. "I'll be careful. Promise."

"You did the right thing in calling me." He held me loosely within his arms, his fingers hooked in my belt loops. "I'm going to be keeping a closer eye on you for a while."

"What does that mean?" I kissed his chest, nuzzling along, enjoying his scent.

"It means I'll be following you to work and back."

Raising my head, I frowned. "I hardly think that's necessary."

"Humor me in this." His fingers released my belt loops as his hands settled heavily on my hips.

"Oh, all right," I grumbled reluctantly.

"Good; now come here." Josiah pulled me flush to him, the look in his eyes had my pulse picking up. My breath caught as his hands moved up my back, across my shoulders, cupping my throat, turning my face up to meet his. Slowly, he rubbed his thumb across my bottom lip, then leaned in to taste it. What this man could do with a kiss—I could spend forever just doing this.

Josiah was true to his word. For three weeks he followed me to and from work. When nothing else had happened, he began to relax his vigil. But he made sure I called or texted to let him know where I was and when I was leaving.

I knew he wasn't being a control freak, was just concerned for my safety, so I didn't get upset by his stance. To make up for his actions, Josiah insisted on taking me swimming several more times. Then we'd either go get our milkshake or he'd take me out to the diner. I'd tried to assure him it wasn't necessary, that I understood, but he wouldn't be persuaded.

On one such occasion, a woman I'd never seen before was paying Josiah an inordinate amount of attention. She had a sultry sort of look; bright green eyes framed in thick lashes with her silky mink brown chin-length hair. On her neck, just below her right ear I saw a butterfly tattooed in shades of green and black. Her ears were pierced multiple times and her clothes seemed rather street-savvy to me. She looked like someone Josiah might know; someone more his type, someone completely different from me.

As our waitress, Betz, led us to our table, the green-eyes girl had done a double-take, her gaze lighting up in pleased recognition. Those same eyes took my measure. Somehow, I got the impression she found me lacking. Her seeming dismissal left a quivery feeling in my gut as old insecurities came to life. If Josiah noticed her, he gave no indication. We sat down and looked the menu over, more out of habit than anything else. We pretty much always got the same thing when we came here.

Feeling eyes on me, I looked up and found the green-eyed girl was staring at me. She glanced at Josiah and back again, clearly trying to figure me out. Josiah noticed my gaze and looked in her direction. After a brief glance at her he turned back to me and asked if anything looked good. "I think I'll stick with the guacamole burger," I replied a little absently.

"Yeah, me too. It's pretty good."

"Do you know her?" I blurted, fighting to keep any hint of discomfort from my voice.

"Who?"

My eyebrow rose. "The girl with the green butterfly tattoo who can't take her eyes off you."

"She's been around, though not for a while."

"So, you do know her?" My heart thudded in my chest.

"We went to the same school." He shrugged, clearly dismissing her. "And it's a small town."

Betz returned with our milkshakes. No sooner had she walked away, and the green-eyed girl made her way to our table. Her gaze was focused solely on Josiah. She reminded me of a cat, the way she moved; I could almost imagine the sound of her purring. Josiah took note of the look on my face, and something flashed in his blue eyes as his jaw clenched.

"*Hello*, Josiah." She'd reached our table. "Long time...no see." Finger-nails painted a deep, shimmering green color lightly trailed along Josiah's forearm. He moved his arm away from her touch, reaching for my hand, keeping his eyes on mine.

"Charlene." His tone and attitude weren't what I'd call welcoming, but the impression I was getting was that he and Charlene were very well acquainted. Why hadn't he been more open with me?

"What've you been up to?" she asked, cocking her hip against the side of our booth.

"Charlene," his eyes were still on me, an almost pleading look in them. "I'd like you to meet my girlfriend, Crimson. Crimson, this is Charlene."

"Girlfriend?" she chuckled, her green eyes flicking to mine and away, "I didn't think you did girlfriends, Josiah."

"Things change."

She chuckled again, a disbelieving note in her voice. "*Have* you changed, really?"

Josiah broke eye contact with me, for the first time looking her right in the eye. "I've changed." His tone was definitive and dismissive. Final.

"I see..." Her eyes flashed in my direction, speculation in them now. "Well, I guess I'll see you around then." Silently I let out a breath I hadn't even been aware I was holding as she walked away.

"You alright?" Josiah asked, his thumb rubbing comfortingly over the back of my hand.

"Yeah." But I wasn't alright. My gut told me she was intimately familiar with my boyfriend, and I wanted to be sick.

"Don't let her get to you." He gently squeezed my hand. "She likes to stir the pot—she lives for it. If she knows she got to you, it'll just egg her on."

"*Who* is she again?" My voice shook as tears pricked my eyes.

"She's nobody." The tone of his voice held a measure of disgust. "Nobody you need to worry about and nobody I care about."

I blinked, trying to dislodge the tears. "What did she mean about, 'you don't do girlfriends'?"

He waited for me to meet his gaze, then he squeezed my hands again. "It means you're special. And important. And mean everything to me."

Betz came then with our orders, and I tried to let it go. To release my anxiety and not let it get to me, not let *her* get to me, but I couldn't help but wonder...just who was Charlene? And how well did Josiah really know her?

We finished our meal and headed home. Conversation, after Charlene walked away, had been stilted and not as easy as it usually was between us. I told Josiah I was tired and had a headache, that I wasn't feeling up for coming over tonight. His deep blue eyes frowned a little in concern; he placed a gentle kiss on my forehead and said goodnight. I hadn't been lying. By the time we'd reached the ranch house, my head was fairly pounding. I told Billy and Ethan goodnight and headed up to my room.

A hot shower sounded good, so I ran the water, letting it heat up. Somewhere in the back of my mind, I knew what I was doing. Feeding my insecurity. And I knew that most likely this was still leftover grief over the loss of my parents. Still, I couldn't seem to help myself. I knew I should trust him, that Josiah wouldn't lie to me, I *knew* this and yet still, it festered. I undressed and stepped under the steaming spray. Something wasn't sitting right about all this. Charlene knew him well enough to make the claim she was shocked he had a girlfriend. That alone told me Josiah *did* know her. And most likely knew her well.

Of course he'd had other relationships before me. Of course he had. Had *they* dated? I could understand that. She seemed more his type—more so than me. She'd have known how to handle Mike. I bet she wouldn't have needed to call Josiah. But if they had dated, *why* hadn't he just said that? Did he think I wouldn't understand? Suddenly a thought struck, sending cold shivers down my spine. *What if he still had feelings for her, and just didn't know how to say it?* Maybe, when they'd split up, he'd thought he'd never see her again. And maybe seeing her tonight brought those feelings back?

Once dry, I pulled on my pajamas, then started to brush my hair. Thinking like this was going to make me vomit; I needed a distraction. Just then my cellphone rang. Hesitantly I picked it up, assuming it would be Josiah. It was Gracie. Relieved, I answered it, "Hey, Beautiful."

"Hey, Beautiful, yourself. How are ya?"

"I'm good." I nodded at the phone, trying to sound like it.

"That's weird—you don't sound good."

Having zero desire to discuss my fears with Gracie, I quickly deflected, just playing it cool. "No; I am. Just have a headache is all. How're you?"

"I'm *good*. Great, in fact. Super, even."

"You don't say." I chuckled. "What's going on?"

"What are you doing in August?"

"Hmmm, not sure. I'll have to check my massive schedule and see if I'm open then. Are you planning another visit?"

"Um, no. Well, maybe. At some point, but not right now."

Her meandering had me laughing. "Okay; that makes so much sense."

"I'm not coming out there because I need *you* to come here…And. Help. Me. Get married!"

"*What*?" I screeched, my voice hitting notes only a pubescent young boy might hit. "You're engaged? *Oh my gosh*! Tanner proposed!! Whoohoo! Congratulations! I'm so happy for you."

"Well, I'm glad you're excited." She sounded smug now. "I need a maid-of-honor, and you're it."

"Yay! Have you picked out colors yet? August what?"

"Last Friday in August. And I'm doing coral and nautical blue."

"Nice. Yeah, I'll be there. Of course I will."

"Awesome, because I couldn't do this without you. "

"When did Tanner propose? And, how'd he do it?"

"Sometimes he just surprises the crap out of me. And this was one of those times. He took me out to dinner last night to make up for a fight we'd had last week. He did the champagne and everything…."

"Wait," I cut her off. "You guys had *champagne?* You're only twenty; he's twenty-one, but still."

"Fine, it was only sparkling cider; don't ruin this for me. He toasted me and apologized for not being perfect and as I drained my glass, I saw the ring. He cried, Crimson. When he asked me to marry him—Tanner cried. I love him so much."

"What did your parents say? They're okay with this? You're a little young...are you sure this is what you want?"

"I know it's crazy. I know it is, but I'm crazy about *him*. We've been together since sixth grade. There's never been anyone else for either of us. He's my other half. I love him. And Mom and Dad love him to death; he's basically a part of the family already."

"I knew they loved him. Tell him I said congratulations. I love you guys."

"Thanks, I gotta go. Love you, too."

Josiah

Dang Charlene anyway. What was she doing back in Salmon? Josiah thought he'd seen the last of her four years ago.

Charlene—tough, street-wise, and manipulative—she was from a chapter of his life that Josiah was determined to keep shut. He was a different man now, no longer haunted by those demons, and he didn't want any of that ugliness touching Crimson.

Crimson was like a clear mountain stream and Charlene was the muck and mud of a stagnant mill pond.

Josiah could tell Charlene had rattled Crimson. He could see the worry and the uncertainty on Crimson's face. The doubt. He'd told her the truth: Charlene was nobody to him—Crimson was everything. He wanted Crimson to trust him. He could feel her emotional withdrawal last night. He felt it physically. Maybe she just needed time; time to realize and remember that he'd never hurt her. That he'd always take care of her, keep her safe.

If time was what Crimson needed, if that was all he could give her, then he'd step back and allow her to work through this. He'd be patient and wait.

Crimson Sage

Gracie's phone call and her impending nuptials were sufficient to take my mind off thoughts of Charlene and what she might still mean to Josiah. By the next morning, I was waiting for him outside the barn, seated on one of his wooden chairs when he came down from the loft. "Hey," he looked me over, almost hesitant. "How's the head?"

"Better." Last night, after much self-reflection, I'd decided to simply trust him, trust in us.

Josiah leaned down and kissed the top of my head. Then, as I stood, he stepped back, stretching as he did. I took a moment to appreciate the view he offered, warmth curling in my middle. "I'm just going to ride the fence line today, make notes of any work that needs doing. I probably won't need you...go ahead and take it easy, okay? I should be back before you head to work."

My heart skipped a beat, then clenched in my chest. Josiah had never told me I wasn't needed. Even when he was more than capable of completing whatever job he'd lined up for us; he'd always wanted me along, wanted me with him. That sick, scared feeling came back with a fury. Trying to staunch the panic clawing its way up my throat, I analyzed what he'd said. Searching for clues in his words or eyes. The look in them seemed off, a little distant. Cooler somehow.

I swallowed. "Okay; if that's what you want." I waited for him to make some quip about always needing me, something about being worried about me. Instead, Josiah gave me a weak grin and brushed his lips lightly across my temple, before heading for the front of the barn.

Somehow, I made it back to the house, not really aware of where I was going or what I was doing. My mind kept dragging up all my fears. Putting them on display. Torturing me. Alone in my room, I lay back on the bed and wiped tears from my eyes. Maybe Josiah thought I needed space. Maybe he thought this was what *I* wanted. But, if that was the case, why not say so? Especially when I asked him if that was what *he* wanted.

What if he's trying to get some distance between us—so he can break up with me? What if he felt I was too clingy? Too needy? Was he just tired of dealing with all my emotional baggage? I'd tried to keep him away; I'd tried. He was the one who'd refused to let me be. He was the one who'd insisted. But was that what he was doing—trying to find a way to break up with me? I imagined it would be rather awkward for him, considering Billy and all. These thoughts just kept playing through my head, nothing making sense. Feeling as though I was coming out of my skin, and fighting back nausea, I decided to get ready for work now.

My job at the Java Shack was ideal; Tina, my manager, whom I adored and loved working for, tended to schedule me for the busier shifts, which made the day go faster. Though I intended to clock in early, knowing she wouldn't mind, I still had a few hours until my shift began, so decided to do some shopping, hoping some retail therapy would help.

Several times on the drive into town, my lips trembled, and I'd had to blink back tears. I hadn't told Josiah I was leaving and wondered if he'd even notice I was gone. Parking along the curb in front of the library, I checked my reflection, removing any evidence of tears, then headed inside. An hour later I left, having found four books I'd been wanting to read. As I closed the lid on my trunk, my phone buzzed again. Huffing a breath, I glanced at it. Josiah. Again. I'd ignored his first two texts. I can't even say why exactly. He just wasn't something I was ready to deal with right then. Biting my lip, I decided to park near the Java Shack, then do some window shopping. There were a few boutique-type stores along the main street in Salmon that I'd never checked out before. Soon I was heading off on foot, sunglasses on, just trying to enjoy the sunshine. I ended up getting a pedicure from Liza's

Nails, then went to Cuties Clothing and Shoes. I browsed there for another hour, trying on several shirts and shorts before making my purchase.

My phone rang while I'd been in the dressing room—Josiah again. Entirely a coward, shooting his 'I was strong' statement down, I sent him to voicemail. Not wanting to hear the distance in his voice. Didn't want to get into an argument, afraid that might be the catalyst he used to end us. Figuring I'd call him back later, maybe when I was home, I put my phone in my pocket, then headed to work.

Josiah

Crimson wasn't answering her phone. Josiah ended the call, then dialed again. Still nothing. He'd already tried texting her with no success. Checking the time, he saw she still had a couple hours yet before her shift started at the Shack. He'd intended to be back at the ranch before she left. Needing to see her, kiss her, reassure himself they were all right. That she still loved him, still wanted him, still believed in him.

Being without her today had driven him insane. His ride had been useless. He hadn't seen anything and knew he'd have to ride it again tomorrow. He'd take Crimson with him then.

He'd thought to just check in with her, say hello, let her know he was thinking of her, so he'd texted. Twice. When that had produced zero response, he'd called, needing to hear her voice. When she didn't answer right away, he didn't immediately worry. Maybe she was simply in the shower. Had set the phone down and hadn't checked it yet. But when she didn't call or text back, when five minutes turned to ten, then fifteen, then thirty, the feeling that something wasn't right started to nag at him.

That feeling only grew, gnawing at him, leaving him raw. He tried her several more times. Still nothing. Turning his horse back toward the ranch, Josiah kicked him into a gallop. He told himself to be calm. Crimson was fine. After glancing around the house and yard and seeing no sign of her, he unsaddled the gelding and fed and stabled him. Then he headed up to the loft. She wasn't there either. He grabbed his keys and headed for the big house. Mike was seated on the couch watching some basketball game; a couple of the other ranch boys were sprawled around the floor watching with him. Josiah went to the office. Billy told him Crimson had left for work already, that she wanted to do a little shopping, and that she'd seemed fine.

The strain and stress of not seeing her, not having her beside him had reached a boiling point. Josiah nodded stiffly and left. He needed to see her—now. He knew he wouldn't settle until he'd made certain she was all right. Gritting his teeth, he headed out the door.

Crimson Sage

I clocked in a little before the after-work rush hit. I'd been there maybe twenty-five minutes when Tina asked if Josiah and I had been in a fight.

Confused, I looked at her. "No; why?"

"Cuz that boy just pulled in and he looks like thunder." Her gaze was focused on the parking lot. Even furious the man was so beautiful it hurt. He ripped the door open, sending the bell over it ringing loudly, his blue eyes, fierce and angry, met mine and stayed there. Josiah stood in the doorway a long moment, just breathing. Unclenching his jaw, he jerked his chin to a corner table where he took a seat. His eyes were still on me, looking more feral than I'd ever seen him before, making my heart pound in my chest.

"Go talk to him." Tina muttered, nudging me in his direction. "He looks fit to erupt."

Hesitating, I tried to decide if running was even an option. Knowing I most likely wouldn't make it far, I told myself to stop being a wimp. Buying myself time, I slowly took off my apron, hanging it on my hook behind the register. Then I swallowed my fear and headed his way. His blue eyes were slowly traveling over me, making it difficult to breathe. Waiting for him to look up, I stopped about a foot away from his table. His eyes were now guarded, his gaze lowered.

After a lengthy moment, his gaze holding on the table, I finally sat across from him. My heart was in my throat, and the room seemed to spin ever so slightly, the silence only making it worse. "Hey." My voice came out all sorts of raspy, giving away my nerves. Not that he couldn't read them on me anyhow. His eyes now held mine, threatening to steal what little breath I had left. "What's up?"

It took him a full minute to respond, his jaw working. "You were gone."

"You knew I had work." I completely ignored the fact that I'd left early and hadn't communicated with him all afternoon.

His nostrils flared. "I tried to call. You never answered."

I shrugged, beginning to feel the heat of guilt. "I thought you'd know where I was."

He stabbed me with a look. "When you didn't answer the phone, I got worried."

"I'm sorry. I didn't think you'd…I didn't mean to worry you."

Josiah stood, taking my hand in his, gently pulling me to my feet. "Come outside with me." Something in the tone of his voice had warmth curling in my middle.

Tina shot Josiah a look. "She needs to clock back in, in ten."

"She'll be here." He pulled me outside and around the corner from prying eyes. Suddenly I found myself pressed up against the brick wall and Josiah was kissing me for all he was worth. I could taste the anger and the fear on his lips. Felt the anxiety and relief in his touch. He was shaking; I was shaking. His mouth left mine briefly to roam my neck. His fingers gripped my back, dragging me closer. My arms were tight around his neck, caught up in the emotion, the fever, as I kissed him back. Letting him taste my worries and fears about him.

Just as suddenly as he'd started, Josiah pulled back. Possessive eyes roved over my swollen mouth as we panted, trying to control our breathing. After a minute, he laid his forehead on mine. "I was worried, that's all. Just worried."

"I'm sorry." I kissed his chest, sorry for so many things, but unable to voice them right then.

He seemed to understand, because he kissed my temple, lingering there for a moment. "I'm sorry for being angry."

I blew out my breath. "I'm sorry for not texting back." I breathed in, then out. "I need to get back inside; I still have two hours left."

"I know." Josiah kissed me once more, lightly, and sighed as he let me step away from him, then followed me inside. "I'll take a coffee. Black."

"To go?" I moved behind the counter.

"No." Though, he was angled in my direction, Josiah was looking at Tina. "I won't interfere. Just...humor me. I'll order a pastry as well, then I'll order again in a little while."

"No trouble." She warned.

"None." Josiah turned to me, held my gaze a moment, then made his way back to the corner table.

The rest of my shift seemed to fly by and yet drag at the same time. I'd tried ignoring his presence, not because I was mad, but because I'd felt his regard as a physical touch, bringing such a longing. My mouth still recalled his kiss from earlier and I wanted more.

About fifteen minutes before closing, I was cleaning the glass at the front of the counter, when the bell above the door rang. Glancing over my shoulder, I felt my heart trip. The man was a few years older than me, with dark brown eyes and thick, curly brown hair that fell across his forehead. He combed it back with deft fingers as he moved aside for the woman with him. Charlene. Her green eyes found Josiah instantly; she tossed me a look, before beelining to him. Josiah hadn't even acknowledged her. No, his eyes were on her companion, whose gaze was on me.

A grin tugged at the stranger's lips as he shot a glance toward Josiah's corner, before refocusing on me. At their entrance, I'd quickly stepped back behind the counter. He approached me now, carefully looking me over. Then his brown eyes strayed to the menu board behind me. "Welcome to the Java Shack—how may I help you?" My eyes kept wanting to stray to Charlene; it took effort to keep them focused on my customer.

He grinned again, leaning one arm on the counter, his back was to Josiah. "What do you recommend?"

"Me?" I needed to get my mind back on coffee and not what was taking place in that corner.

"I've never been in before; I'd know, cuz I'd have remembered you. So yeah, what do you like?" He flashed another grin as he traced a heart on the countertop with his ring finger. Charlene laughed out loud as she took a seat across from Josiah. At the sound of her voice, my gaze had darted over, unable to help myself. And though she flirted, trying her best to get his attention, Josiah's blue eyes were focused on me, before shifting to the man at my counter. Something darker, more feral entered his gaze now.

"The black and white mocha is good." I said. "It's our special for the day."

"Oh yeah?" he chuckled like I was being cute. "You like it?"

"It's good." I shrugged, suddenly wanting this evening to be over with. "I'll take one."

"Anything for your girlfriend?" He glanced back in her direction, then turned back to me. "She's not my girlfriend. Just someone I know."

"She seems to know a lot of people." I grumbled. "Hot or iced?"

"Hot." His voice had gone low. "Definitely hot."

Mentally, I rolled my eyes. "Size?"

He grinned and ran teeth over his lower lip. "Large."

"That'll be four dollars and fifty cents, please." He gave me a five-dollar bill and said to keep the change. As I turned to make his drink, my eyes rolled for real this time. "Hey there; Sage, is it?" Glancing back, I caught him checking out my backside, lingering on my butt. *Pig.* Shaking my head in exasperation, I turned away. "Well, Sage—pretty name, pretty girl—my name's Rick."

"Rick...that kinda rhymes with something..." Hearing Josiah's voice much closer, hearing *that* tone in it had me spinning around again. Josiah stood at the counter, his blue eyes hard on the stranger.

Tina came out from the back room then, like she'd been monitoring the situation the whole time. "*No* trouble."

I finished with Rick's coffee and brought it to the counter. "Here you go."

"Aren't you going to write my name on it?" Rick asked. Josiah muttered something under his breath, and before I could respond, Tina took the cup from my hands and handed it to Rick. "We're closing now. Take your coffee if you still want it."

Rick chuckled darkly as Charlene stepped up, slipping an arm around him. "I'm starting to think no one here likes me," he told her with a mock whisper. She looked me over and whispered back, "I got that same reaction; I'm not taking it personal, though."

With one last lingering look at me, Rick sighed theatrically, then took his drink, sipping it loudly as they left. I breathed a sigh of relief, especially as Josiah swore under his breath. Tina shook her head. "When did she get back in town?"

Ignoring the question, Josiah stared after them until their taillights were gone. He shook his head, then reached behind the counter, grabbing the spray bottle and a rag. Without a word, he began wiping down the chairs and tables. After that he overturned the chairs onto the tables so the floor could be swept. Tina huffed under breath, then headed back to the office to finish her duties. Shrugging, I got the rest of the counter cleaned and prepped for the next day. Ten minutes later, Tina was locking up, and Josiah was walking me to my car. His silence was beginning to weigh on me. "Are you okay?" I unlocked the driver's door, then tossed my purse on the seat, before turning back to him.

Josiah stared at me for a moment in silence, then stepped closer, crowding me against the car. His fingers trailed over my shoulder, up my neck, along my jaw, then around to weave into the hair at the back of my neck. Tugging gently, he pulled my mouth up to his. It was slow, deep, and gentle. Not the fierce, desperate, almost angry kiss from before. He made love to me now. Soft, tender love. He tasted and touched. Teased and savored. Was provocative and deliberate. Trembling and out of breath, my head felt like it was spinning. Slowly he ended the kiss, lightly pulling at my lower lip as he leaned back.

Gripping the car frame, I was having a hard time coming up with any sort of cognitive thought. "Unless you want to finish this here, in this parking lot, you'd better get in and get that car started." His voice rumbled deliciously, and I nodded dully and then slid onto the seat and put the key in the ignition. But when I turned it, nothing happened. No click. No nothing. "Pop the hood; will you?" Josiah moved around to the front of the car. "You been having any problems with it?"

"No, none."

Josiah tried several things with no luck. The car remained dead. "I need my tools. I'll give you a ride home, then bring you back for your shift tomorrow. While you're at work I'll find out what's wrong with it."

Nodding, I grabbed my purse and the bag from the trunk, then locked up. We drove home in silence, Josiah holding my hand the whole way. As he pulled into the driveway, he gave my fingers a gentle squeeze. "Should I drop you at the house?" Looking at him, I tried to find the words. To tell him I was still scared he wanted to break up with me. That I didn't know how I would survive if that happened. That I desperately loved him. That I hated the distance between us. That I didn't want to be alone tonight and needed to stay with him. He must have read me pretty accurately, because he lifted my hand, kissing the back. "Or you could just stay with me tonight..."

I simply nodded, my throat too constricted to attempt speaking.

Chapter 14
Cruel Intent

C*rimson Sage*

Josiah drove me to work the following day for my afternoon shift. The busy afterschool rush was going strong, keeping my mind off last night. Josiah had been different last night. More intense. Such an intense control to his actions and intentions. I shivered just thinking about it, about him. After showering to freshen up, Josiah and I had settled together on the couch. Not his bed, the couch. He'd wrapped us in a blanket, then had tucked my head under his chin and for the longest time, had simply held me. Deeply contented just to be in his arms, I'd found myself relaxing, sinking into his warmth. Until he'd taken my hand, grazing each knuckle with his mouth, then turning it over, he'd kissed my palm, lightly nipping the skin there. When he'd pulled a finger into his mouth, teasing with tongue and teeth, my heart had jumped, my pulse had started pounding in my chest.

Then, he'd lifted my face up to his. Josiah's mouth was this magical place where the world just fell away. It was only him and only me. Just his touch. His scent. His taste. Just the sound of our hearts beating. Our pulses throbbing. Everything he did had been slow. Measured. Intentional. As if he'd been determined to remove any thoughts about earlier. So deliberate. He must have known his own limits, refusing to be rushed, to lose control, holding himself to a tight, strict line that he refused to cross.

When he'd felt me tremble, heard the yearning in my voice, he'd lifted his mouth from mine. Hands gently but firmly gripping, he'd held me again, held my arms down so I could no longer reach him. I'd wanted his mouth on mine, on me. I'd wanted *him*. And he'd held back. Logically, in the back of my mind and in my heart, I'd known he'd done it for me, because of what I'd shared with him. Because he respected me. But right then, in the hazy heat he'd created, I'd been a live wire. Burning and frustrated. So, he'd held me tight, and it wasn't until I'd finally relaxed and had fallen asleep that he'd released me.

Wistful, I shifted my gaze from the window to the two high school girls, seniors I was certain, who were standing at the glass pane looking out into the parking lot, staring at Josiah. I didn't blame them—he was a site for sore eyes—no doubt about it. I'd been watching him for a while now as he worked on my car. Right now, he was bent under the hood, backside facing in this general direction. And, *dang*. Reaching around to his back pocket, he pulled a rag out to wipe his hands. Once satisfied they were clean, he lowered the hood, then put his tools back in his car. He pulled his shirt off, trading it for a cleaner one, then headed for the front door. Swallowing, I watched him move, enjoying the spectacle.

One of the high school girls, the one with the bright purple tips in her light blond hair, fluffed her shoulder-length mass and waited for him as he came inside. Josiah's eyes sought mine and stayed there; a small, playful grin on his lips, like maybe he'd been thinking about last night, too. Just as he passed the girls, the eager one said, "Hi, Josiah" in a breathy hopeful voice. He gave a miniscule lift of his chin at her, but kept walking, never taking his eyes off mine. When he reached the counter, he leaned over, gently grasping the back of my neck, and pulled me close for a light, lingering kiss. He smelled of man, and confidence, and deliciousness. One of the girls sighed audibly, "Oh, *swoon*." I didn't disagree.

"Your car is fixed." He pulled back and grinned, heat in those blue orbs.

Blushing, I grinned back. "Thanks; what was wrong with it, and what do I owe you?"

"Had some loose wires is all." His traveled over my face before settling on my mouth as his voice took on a low, gravely rumble. "And I'll think of something."

His response had me blushing again. *Honestly, this man.* "Can I get you a coffee or anything?"

He checked the clock on the wall. "Nah, I gotta run. See you in an hour?"

"Definitely. Thanks again."

At the door, he stopped, turning back. "You wanna swim later?"

"Yeah, that sounds good."

"How about I grab your suit and meet you at the pool?"

He'd moved back to me, so I reached in my pocket. "Here, take my key. My coral suit is hanging in my shower."

"I'll see you there." And maybe this was the reason he'd come back because he'd kissed me again before leaving.

After my shift, I decided to run into Savemore to pick up a couple things I needed before meeting Josiah at the pool. When I came out, Charlene was leaning against the side of my car, causing my heart to trip in my chest.

"Hi." She grinned as I approached, smacking her gum in loud pops.

Stopping a couple feet from her, I waited. After a couple moments of silence, in which she seemed to study me, I finally said, "Excuse me, I need to get going; I'm meeting someone."

"Meeting Josiah?" She guessed.

"What if I am?" I absolutely did *not* want to deal with her right now. Not while I was still so emotionally raw.

"I just thought I should warn you about him. You seem like such a nice girl; I'd really hate for you to get messed up with his brand of trouble." Sincerity dripped from her voice.

I didn't buy her concerned act for a moment. "You seemed pretty interested in getting messed up with him last night."

"That's because I understand Josiah. He understands me. I'm not in danger of thinking he might love me. With us, we know it's just sex. Good, hot, *hard* sex." She grinned. "*You* look like you're in danger of falling in love with him."

Despite not buying her concern, her words were making me sick to my stomach. "You need to leave. Now." My gut clenched painfully at the thought of the two of them together.

She chuckled, obviously adept at reading me.

"Move." I shifted past her, getting my key in the lock. Charlene refused to budge, still leaning against the door, preventing me from opening it.

"You think he *loves* you?" She snorted. "Oh, *please.* He's playing you, Sage. Josiah doesn't do girlfriends. He does sex. The hard and heavy, make-you-scream kind. The kind a good girl like you would faint over. Don't believe me? Here, take a look." She shoved her cellphone in my face. "Here's your proof." Seemingly of their own volition, certainly against my conscious will and intention, my eyes focused on the image on the screen.

Swallowing back bile, tears pricked my eyes, as I turned away. But the damage was done. That image was forever seared onto my brain. She was right. It was proof. Irrefutable proof. They were both naked and having sex in the backseat of a car. The image was so raw, so wild, so gut-wrenching and heart-breaking. Pain and jealousy flashed through me. I couldn't get the image of her nails as they clawed his back, and the dragon tattoo out of my mind. Or the animalistic look on his face. What was worse was the look of pure ecstasy on Charlene's.

Shoving her hard to the side, I quickly opened the door to my car and got in, instantly locking it. I tried to still the shaking, tried to control the nausea. Charlene looked at me through the glass. "Just walk away, Sage. He's no good for you. Turn him loose and walk away."

Starting my car, I drove off, tires screeching, unsure which direction I was even going. Eventually I pulled over and stopped. A small voice told me I needed to give him the chance to explain, to tell me what I'd seen wasn't what it had looked like. I argued that the image could have been from years ago. It was hard to tell. They looked the same. I couldn't see any differences. I'm not sure how long I sat there on the side of the road, but eventually I became aware of where I was. I'd pulled off on a side street across from the library. My phone rang then. It was Josiah. I looked at the clock and noted that I'd been off work for forty-five minutes already.

I knew I needed to talk with him, to see his face, see the answer. So, I texted, "Running late, be right there." I took several deep breaths, then restarted the car and headed to the pool. Josiah was waiting, leaning against his car. Even in stillness I could see that animal way about him. Could imagine the way he'd move when... And I had to stop thinking about it before I threw up. I parked a row behind him, and sat for a moment, just watching him. Trying to get myself under control. Josiah's grin slipped off his face at the look he now saw on mine. Setting my coral swimsuit on his hood, he made his way to me.

At his approach, I looked down, suddenly feeling like a coward. Josiah tried the car door, but I hadn't unlocked it yet. "Crimson, what happened? What's wrong? Open the door."

Wiping my eyes, I took a deep breath, then stepped out. He instantly reached for me, but I jerked back out of his reach. He froze a moment before dropping his hands slowly to his sides. "What's going on?"

"Tell me about Charlene." My voice trembled and I hated it.

"What about her?" Dangerous was the tone of his voice now.

"How did you know her?"

"I told you." He spoke slow, calm. "It's a small town; we went to school together."

My lips trembled; I knew he knew her better than that. Mentally, I begged him not to lie. "Is that all? Just from school? You guys never hooked up, you never slept with her?"

"Where is this coming from?" His face tightened, anger clearly building.

"Just answer the stupid question, Josiah!"

"No; I never slept with her." His eyes were hard now. "We got drunk and smoked some weed together, but that was it. And that was a long time ago."

"Liar!" I screamed. "I saw you! I saw you with her. How can you stand there and tell me you never had sex with her? I saw the proof!"

Josiah stumbled half a step backward. The look on his face registered shock and disbelief. "What do you mean you saw *proof*? What are you talking about? What proof?"

"I notice you're not denying it now, huh?"

He pinched his brow, then reached in his pocket to pull my key out. He held it up, then lay it on the hood. "I told you I wasn't a virgin. You knew that. I told you I'd had sex before; you said that didn't bother you."

"Oh, so now, because you *lied* to me, this is *my* fault?" My palm slapped over my chest, feeling like it was caving in.

"I'm *not* lying to you." His deep blue eyes were like ice now.

"You are!" How much damage could my heart take before it just stopped? Tears welled. "You had sex with Charlene and now you're telling me you didn't. If that isn't lying, then I don't know what is!"

"Again; I'm NOT lying."

"I can't believe you." My heart shattered in my chest, making it difficult to speak. "I trusted you." Backing away, I reached for my key, then opened the car door.

"Crimson, wait! Please." He reached for my arm, but I shook him off.

"Don't touch me." I shook my head. "Don't ever touch me again. She showed me the picture of you together. Having sex. I can't believe you."

He seemed sincerely shocked and a part of me longed to trust him. "Charlene showed you a picture? Of me? Having sex with her?"

"*Yes*, Josiah. You and her having sex. In the backseat of a car."

"That wasn't me. It wasn't. I've *never* had sex with her."

There was no mistaking what I'd seen. And there was no going back now. "I can't believe you're still lying to me about this. I came here, hoping you'd be honest with me, but you just won't. I can understand if you were embarrassed, or ashamed, but I can't stand liars. I don't want to see you anymore. I'm leaving."

Josiah was in a state of shock; I could see that in his eyes—he just stared at me, like he couldn't comprehend what I'd just said to him. Ignoring the paleness of his normally tanned complexion, I used his shock to my advantage. Not waiting for him to recover, I quickly got into my car and drove off. He must have thought I meant I was simply heading back to the house and that he'd have time to figure things out. Like maybe he just needed to let me cool off and calm down some. I'm certain he never considered that I might have intended to head back to Virginia—I think he'd have put up a harder fight if he'd known. I called Gracie on the way home, asking if I could come stay for a while. She said of course but wanted to know what was wrong. Through tears, I explained that Josiah had lied to me, and it was big. And that I couldn't see him right now, not ever again.

Billy and Ethan were a little harder to convince, but in the end it didn't matter. I was twenty and legally able to make up my own mind. I didn't tell them what happened—I couldn't—it was too shameful, too painful. I just told them I needed to get away for a while.

Josiah tried calling several times that night. He even came to the house, but Billy wouldn't disturb me. I'd be flying out of Boise at eleven in the morning and arriving in Virginia by seven that night. Gracie said we were going to the beach house—since we didn't get to go last summer, it was the least she could do. "You need sun, sand, and surf. And clam chowder." That sounded amazing, so I called Tina and let her know I was leaving. I apologized, explaining I hated leaving her in a lurch, but I had to get away, and I understood if she was mad at me. Tina, wonderful woman that she is, had simply said I was a great employee and to keep her posted; that she'd try to hold my job for me, and that she hoped things worked out.

Billy and Ethan drove me to the airport. Billy hugged me tightly and said not to stay away too long. Ethan held back tears and said I'd better be coming back and this was not permanent, he wouldn't allow it. I somehow managed not to cry on the flight. But when I saw Grace, the floodgates opened, and everything came out. Gracie let me vent as she drove back to her house. She just listened in supportive silence, and I so appreciated it. I wasn't ready for constructive reasoning yet—I was still much too raw.

Josiah

Josiah sat in numb silence on his couch. Hollow. He felt as if he'd been gutted and didn't know how he was still breathing. He was pretty sure it wasn't possible to live when everything you are had been removed and you were nothing more than an empty shell.

She was gone.

Crimson was gone. He couldn't fathom it. Couldn't wrap his mind around the truth of it. *She couldn't be gone.* She'd been here. With him. She'd been his. He needed her. Didn't she know that?

Billy had told him Crimson had left, that he'd taken her to the airport. It was the first time Billy had ever raised his voice at Josiah, the first time he'd yelled at him, wanting to know what the heck had happened. Josiah didn't know. He couldn't make sense of the last forty-eight hours. Couldn't understand the things Crimson had said to him.

Charlene. She'd done something. She must have. She'd told Crimson something, done something to hurt her. And now Crimson was gone. He'd lost her.

Ethan came to see him next. He'd wanted to know what had happened. Josiah told him the same things he'd told Billy. Ethan said Crimson was with Grace in North Carolina and that he'd try and find out, from Grace and Sage, exactly what had happened.

He told Josiah that he believed him, trusted him, and that he'd help him get things figured out.

Now, instead of the utter darkness Josiah had been facing, he saw the smallest glimmer of hope, a slight little ray of sunshine hinted on the horizon.

Crimson Sage

The first night back in Virginia was nice, yet difficult. I'd missed Gracie's parents, Matt and Shelli. They'd always made me feel welcome. But this was the first time I'd been back since my parents died. The next morning Gracie and I drove to a local florist, where I bought some roses for Mom's and Dad's grave, then she drove me to Shenandoah Memorial Park where they were buried. Seeing their headstones was so hard, so incredibly painful. I cried and cried, wanting to be able to talk to my dad about this thing with Josiah. To get his advice and cry on his shoulder. I wanted to tell my mom about him and what had happened and explain how much I still loved him. How much it all hurt. How much I wanted him to apologize and explain what I'd seen and somehow make it all better. And then the painful realization that I'd never be able to talk with her or dad again, that they were just gone, reduced to a memory.

By the time we made it back to Gracie's house I was spent. Feeling as if I could sleep a year straight, I let the exhaustion take me. Gracie woke me for dinner. We didn't stay up too late as we planned to drive out about mid-morning, just the two of us. It's a five-hour drive to Nags Head in North Carolina, but the scenery was beautiful, making the drive enjoyable rather than boring.

Grace's parents had purchased the beach house years ago when one of her father's co-workers went through a nasty divorce. The sale of the house was part of the stipulations and Mr. Keller had seized the opportunity. It wasn't one of those big, luxurious ones you see in travel brochures, but it was charming all the same. Matt and Shelli had named it Shell Cottage when Gracie was just a toddler, and they'd been coming for summer visits ever since. The cottage was painted a pale ocean blue and had white old-fashioned shutters. It was a two-story cottage, if you didn't count the ground level which housed the carport, a storage shed and an outdoor shower for rinsing the sand away before heading inside. The front of the cottage boasted a wide front porch with steps that led right to the sand and surf. The bedrooms were all located on the top floor and the master bedroom had its own private balcony. The cottage sat at the end of the street and sand dunes ran right up to it.

I'd like to say that the ocean was right off the porch, but one of those fancy, expensive houses had been built about thirty yards in front of it about ten years ago. The Kellers didn't mind though; they could still see the ocean and the beach was the same distance away, just the view was slightly obstructed. As it was early May, the temperatures weren't hot yet, and there were periods of heavy rain. But as we drove into town, we noticed an inordinate number of motorcycles milling around. We discovered when we stopped for groceries that there was a bike show and seafood bake going on right now. Gracie thought this was exciting, but at the sight of all those leather-clad, tattooed bikers, I couldn't help but think of Josiah.

We ate at the cottage the first night and lit a fire in the fireplace. It was nice; cozy and relaxing. We could hear the waves as they crashed on the shore, always a comforting sound, as we made hot chocolate, sat on the couch, and talked. Not about the elephant in the room; no not that. Josiah was not brought up. And for that I was thankful. I knew Gracie would eventually get around to asking what exactly had happened. Most likely she hadn't been able to glean too much from my emotional breakdown the other night, and I knew she'd want to know more. But for now, we just talked about her life—what she was doing, how her work was going, how her parents were. We talked about Tanner and the wedding plans. We talked about Ethan and Billy and the ranch, but not about my reason for being here.

Traditionally, Gracie and I woke early on our first morning here and walk the beach, waiting on the sunrise, and looking for shells. But the following morning, a thick fog had rolled in. We still took our walk, though it wasn't what we'd been hoping for. The fog stuck around for a couple days, pressing against the windows like some peeping tom. We were starting to feel housebound. And I wondered how long she'd hold out before she sat me down for that talk I knew was looming. On the third morning, blessedly, the fog cleared. "Finally!" Gracie announced. "Let's head to Freaky Pete's before he thinks we've died...." Grace stopped mid-sentence, her face turning red and pained. "Sage, I'm so sorry. I wasn't thinking. I've been trying to be so casual and not say anything. I just didn't think."

I waved off her apology, knowing she hadn't meant anything by it. "Don't worry about it; I'm fine. Promise. Let's go get coffee and breakfast." Relieved, she wrapped her arms around me. From the storage shed, we retrieved two beachcomber bikes. As per usual, I took the powder blue one and Gracie the white one. Each bike had a basket mounted on the front. Freaky Pete's Coffee Shack was located about two miles up the Old Oregon Inlet Road. We'd been coming here for years, so Pete and his wife of forty years, Carol, knew us well. Pete looked somewhat like a modern-day pirate, just minus the eye patch and peg leg. He was tall with bushy red hair and a thick beard to match. Tattoos covering his arms, a testament to the rough life he'd lived in his youth. Pete looked tough, but we knew him as a sweet, gentle cinnamon roll of a father-figure. Carol was a warm, motherly sort of woman who was a bakery goddess; magic flowed from her hands and became decadent little pastries, rolls, breads, and doughnuts. Together, they ran Freaky Pete's Coffee and Bistro with their three sons.

Several patrons were already in line that morning and Pete was busy behind his counter, slinging out the drinks. He looked up, a smile on his tanned face for the new arrivals. The smile only became bigger as he saw who it was. "Gracie! Sage! My two favorite girls; where've you been?" He came around the counter to wrap us in a big bear hug before stepping back to look us over. His brow pinched and he shook his head. "Ah, I'm detecting sadness... Are you well?"

"It's been a hard year, Pete, but we're hanging in there." Gracie explained, saving me.

Pete hugged us again quickly, then asked what we'd like. "It's on the house; no arguments. We've missed you two. The boys'll be glad you're back."

Since Pete and Carol only had sons, they'd always said they'd be adopting us one day. And when we were in Nags Head, they basically did. Carol always had a special way of making us feel at home when we came to visit. Secretly, I think they hoped maybe we'd marry one of their sons who were all tall and strapping like their dad, but it'd have been like marrying a brother for Grace and me. Cam was the oldest at twenty-six now, then there was Fynn who was twenty-three, and Rafe, the baby, was twenty-one. As kids we'd all played together for those glorious weeks each summer. It was the boys who had taught us to surf and swim. All three were big and manly. Though, Cam and Rafe took more after Carol in coloring, having her dark brown curly hair and grey eyes. Fynn looked like a slightly smaller version of Pete. I swear each year we came they seemed bigger, more menacing. It had always been difficult to get a date with them around, as they took big brother tendencies to the extreme.

When our coffees were ready, Carol came out for her own hug, then handed us a paper bag with several treats inside. We thanked them as we left, promising to be back soon, before heading off to the pier to enjoy our breakfast. Pete said he'd let the boys know we were back in town—they'd find us soon enough.

We were standing side by side, slowly eating and drinking our way through our food and beverages from Pete's, just watching the fisherman as they tried to get one on the line, when suddenly we were grabbed from behind. My screech quickly turned into laughter as I recognized Fynn's arms around me. "Gotcha!" he exclaimed as he kissed my cheek.

"Fynn!" I laughed as he picked me up and spun me around.

Cam stood by shaking his head like the responsible older brother he was as Rafe soundly kissed Grace. "I'm practically a married woman, Rafe! Yeesh!" she laughed, holding up her left hand to show off her ring.

"I don't see him here." Rafe shrugged, looking around us.

"Yeah, you be lucky he's not," she shot back.

"Tanner finally worked up the nerve, huh?" Cam asked over my head as he pulled me in for a quick hug. Fynn still had an arm slung across my shoulders, so the hug was awkward, but somehow, he managed.

"Yeah; he did." She blushed happily.

Fynn looked me over, "You getting shorter, Sage?"

"No." I snorted. My height, or lack thereof, was often a topic of conversation with these three. Just because they were virtual giants, they felt they had to look down on everyone else. I mean, they *did* look down on everyone because they were so blasted tall.

"I think you are." He gave a sad little shake of head.

"I am not." My elbow hit his hip. "You're just big."

"Fynn's right; you do seem shorter." Rafe stepped closer, placing his hand on my head, leveling an imaginary line to the center of his chest.

I punched him in the shoulder and rolled my eyes. *Honestly.* "You guys off work?" I asked. In addition to working with their parents, Cam, Fynn, and Rafe had their own business, running the Three Boys Fishing Service where they sold their catch to the local restaurants.

"Nah, just taking a break." Cam said. I'd figured as much as they still had a fishy odor around them. "Dad called to say you guys were finally back."

"Let's do a bonfire tonight. We'll bring the 'dogs," Rafe suggested. Everyone agreed and soon they were heading back to work with a promise to see us later.

Grace and I finished our breakfast, then headed back to the house, deciding to spend the rest of the day soaking up the sun on the beach. While Grace was in the bathroom changing, I took a minute to check my phone. Ethan had texted, saying he missed me. Billy had, too. They weren't the only ones, though. Josiah had been texting daily, several times a day since I'd left, begging me to call. My heart clenched sharply as I read today's message. I wanted him so much. Wanted everything to be fixed between us. Grace returned and I swallowed back tears she pretended not to see. Sighing, I grabbed my towel and a book, and we headed out the door.

Hours later, the fire snapped and popped as the smoke drifted lazily around us, the sound of the surf a relaxing backdrop for the evening. Sundown brought an evening chill, so I huddled deeper into my sweatshirt, digging my toes into the sand. Fynn saw me shiver and slid closer, wrapping an arm around my shoulders, bringing me into his warmth. We were in a half-circle around the fire. Fynn to my right, with Grace to my left, and Rafe to her left. Cam sat to Fynn's right, angled so he could get a better look at Grace and me.

"Grace filled us in, Sage." Cam spoke across the flames; his voice was gentle. "Mom and Dad are heartbroken for you and The Kid. How're you holding up?"

Swallowing past the lump in my throat, I nodded. "We're good."

"We had no idea." Fynn squeezed me a little tighter, tucking my head under his chin. "We need to stay in touch better. Can't have stuff like this happening."

"You couldn't have done anything, Fynn," I mumbled against his chest.

"Still." Cam jabbed a stick into the fire, shooting sparks upward. "We should've known, should've been there for you."

"S'all right." I offered a thankful smile. "You're here now."

"We'll always be here, Sage." Rafe reached around Grace, mussing my hair. "For instance, what's the story with your wolf?"

That had me sitting up. "My...wolf?" I darted a look at Grace who met my gaze squarely with brows raised as if to say, *you had to know this was coming, now spill.*

"Yeah; you know," Fynn grumbled. "The dude who broke your heart. *That* wolf."

I snorted. "Who said he's a wolf?"

"She did," they said in unison, pointing at Grace.

"I see." I gave my *best friend* a disgusted look. "Well, since Grace has opened her big mouth, let her tell you."

"We're asking you." Cam replied as he added another log to the flames.

I huffed a frustrated breath and shot Grace another dirty look.

She shrugged, uncaring. "I'm just worried about you, Sage. And I've got to say it—it just doesn't sound like something Josiah would do. That boy *loves* you. Scary loves you."

I shifted the sand with my feet, pain scratching inside my chest again. "I saw the picture, Grace. And he lied about it."

"Is it possible it was a fake?" Grace asked. "I mean, people can do just about anything with their phones and cameras these days."

"Why would she fake something like that?" I snorted, crushing the surge of hope that flashed up inside me.

"Oh, I don't know..." Grace elbowed me in the side. "Look where you are and where you are not. You left your man without a fight. She has an open field now."

Was it possible that was all it was? Had I overreacted and Josiah was innocent? He'd been adamant that he'd never slept with her. But I couldn't get the image of him, his back, her nails raking across his skin, the look on her face, out of my mind. I swallowed, shaking my head, and shrugged. "I don't know; I guess it's possible..."

"What'd he have to say about it?" Cam asked, poking at the fire again.

I sighed. "Said he hadn't slept with her and that he wasn't lying."

"Has he lied to you before?" Fynn craned his head around to give me a considering look.

"No, not that I know of," I admitted, looking down at the sand as I moved my toes through it.

"Guys, Josiah worships her. I've never seen anything like it. I'll admit, I was prepared to dislike him. And at first, I didn't trust him—I mean, he makes you boys look tame. But after seeing him with Sage, there was just no denying that that boy is madly, deeply, *insanely* in love with her."

Squaring my shoulders, I said, "Well, it's not like I can do anything about it from here. And it's not something I want to discuss over the phone. It needs to be face to face. I guess I'll have to talk with him when I go back."

"You are going back, then?" Gracie asked.

"Yeah," I nodded. "If only to gather my things; I've got to go back at least for that. And if he still wants to talk and explain, I guess maybe I can give him a chance."

"Not everyone leaves or lies, Sage." Gracie quietly spoke. "You've got to learn to trust. Josiah would die for you. Literally. Doesn't that give him something?"

I didn't know what to say to Grace. I hated to think maybe I'd let my own fears play a role in my reaction. But in all honesty, I had to consider the possibility. I did find it hard to trust. And I knew I'd felt unworthy of Josiah. Like he had so much more to offer than I did. Regardless, there was nothing I could do from where I was currently. I'd be back in Idaho, at least temporarily, in another seven days. I'd see what happened then.

"Sage," Rafe looked to me. "Has he tried to be in touch since you've been here?"

"Every single day." Grace replied before I could. I rolled my eyes, then nodded. It was true, he had. I guess that had to count for something.

"You want us to talk to him, set him straight?" Fynn asked with a little too much enthusiasm.

I snorted. "Definitely not; in fact, it's best he doesn't even know about you guys. I don't think he'd understand our friendship, and he'd be highly irritated if he did." I snorted again, trying to imagine how Josiah would react to me sitting here with the guys.

Fynn placed a tender kiss at my temple. "Hey, we gotta work tomorrow night, but we have Friday off, and Smokey's is having their crab bake and dance out on the pier. How about you two join us; we'll be your bodyguards, and we'll have us some fun. Just like old times." We all quickly agreed on the plan; to meet up at Smokey's on Friday.

Josiah

Josiah was furious. He was beyond furious—he was murderous and then some. If it weren't for the fact that Red was seated beside him, and a table stood solidly between him and Charlene, he'd have his hands wrapped around her lying throat.

He'd finally been able to piece together what had happened. Charlene admitted to doctoring the picture she'd shown Crimson. And once Josiah had seen it, he couldn't blame Crimson for her fears and accusations. The picture looked real. Charlene had used three separate photos and overlapped, edited, and photo-shopped the images to create the one she'd shown to Crimson.

When asked her reasoning, Charlene said she'd just been having fun. Josiah had to lock himself in his chair to keep from launching himself at her. Red asked if he wanted to press charges. Josiah shook his head no—he simply never wanted to see her again. Ever.

Now that he had evidence of his innocence he needed to be in touch with Crimson. Needed to see her, to hold her, to show her it wasn't real; that it was a fake.

Chapter 15
Stormy Weather

Grace and I left the beach house a little after five on Friday night. We'd dressed up even though Smokey's wasn't really that kind of establishment; any reason to dress up worked for us. Grace wore a deep red sundress with matching wedge sandals. Her hair was pulled up into a sleek bun—she looked amazing—svelte and almost exotic. I opted for a deep blue maxiskirt with a white crop top that was open at the back. It covered everything, but if I lifted my arms or a breeze blew it showed at least an inch or more of my torso. The skirt had slits up to the thigh on both legs. Seeing as we'd be with the brothers tonight, we'd decided to go ahead and have fun—they'd make sure we were safe, and no one messed with us.

Smokey's was located on one of the main piers in Nags Head. Family owned and operated for the last seventy years, they served seafood and all manner of delicacies, offering a fun and family-oriented atmosphere. On Friday nights, local bands could book their outdoor area for concerts. Patio lights were strung up along the old-fashioned light posts and several sturdy wooden tables were set up around the outdoor dining area—Cam found us a table towards the back. The moon hung full and heavy tonight as the clouds played tag with it across the sky. A local band played, sounding like a combination of soul and a bluesy rock, drawing a few brave couples onto the dance floor.

As Grace and I weren't twenty-one yet, we opted for the virgin version of drinks, first trying a pina colada, then having a tropical iced tea. Grace kept checking her cell phone through dinner, and as she caught my eye, she quickly typed something in response and said, "Tanner keeps checking in with me; I told him I was out with three hot guys." We all laughed at that.

"Poor Tanner," I chuckled. "He's got his hands full with you."

She chuckled. "It would be way more fun if he hadn't already met these guys, then he'd *really* be worried. As it is, he said to give them a kiss from him."

Suddenly Grace's phone chimed again. She quickly sent a reply, a blush staining her cheeks. Moments later, Fynn's cell phone chirped. "Oh my gosh; you, too, Fynn?" I rolled my eyes.

"Hey, the two hottest girls I know are taken, so I need to keep playing the field. There's a waitress here I've had my eye on tonight."

"Wow, you move fast. Should I help you make her jealous?" I grinned, trying to ignore the implication that Josiah and I were still together.

"*Yes*," Fynn stood, taking my hand as he led me to the dance floor. He turned so my back was to the restaurant, then pulled me close as we started to sway. One hand strayed slowly, dangerously down my back. Against my ear, he whispered, "She's working tonight so make it good; I want her jealous enough to start a fight." He moved us back and forth to the music and I told myself to relax and enjoy the moment. Fynn was a great dancer, a strong lead. He was attractive and smelled amazing. Several of the other women here had been looking him over enviously. But I couldn't help but think that somehow this was wrong. I missed Josiah. I missed his arms around me. I wanted him to hold me. I wanted him period. And I guess there was my answer, I *did* need to talk with him, let him explain. See if I *was* wrong.

As if he knew where my mind was at, Fynn pulled me even closer, tucking my head against his chest. "Don't think about him, Sage. Think about this. Right now. This moment. This movement. This song." He gently kissed my forehead and sighed deeply. "Who knows; maybe if you can forget about him, you'll notice me, and I won't need the waitress."

Silently, I rolled my eyes and chuckled at his antics under my breath. "Just close your eyes, Sage, and be here, with me."

I did as he suggested, or at least I made the attempt. Not that I was planning to fall for Fynn but could at least try to enjoy my time with him and not be so miserable. Hopefully his waitress was paying close attention. The band started a new song, an appealing cover of an older Michael McDonald hit, *I Keep Forgettin*. We swayed and the wind shifted suddenly, and I caught a scent that reminded me so strongly of Josiah it caused me to shiver with longing. My heart skipped a beat, and my pulse pounded deeply, as I ached for him. He was so potent in my thoughts, I could have sworn I heard him say my name. Squeezing my eyes against the pain, trying to ward off the tears, I inhaled, not wanting to cry tonight; not here.

Josiah

Josiah breathed deeply, slowly, taking in the cool, wet, salty tang of the ocean air, trying to calm himself.

He stood in the shadows for a moment and watched as Crimson slow-danced with one of the three brothers. He watched as the man's hands traveled slowly down her back, coming dangerously low before veering off to her waist.

Grace said the three tall men, brothers all, were like family and not to worry—they were in on the surprise of his presence here tonight. But, as Josiah watched the woman he loved being held so intimately by the tall good-looking seaman, he felt the wolf, the animal inside him stir.

Josiah's deep blue eyes focused on Crimson and like a predator, he moved forward, stepping into the open.

Crimson Sage

Fynn suddenly stiffened and muttered, "What's this fool's problem?" He stopped moving, tightening his grip on me, keeping me against him. "You need something, Mister?" My head snapped up at the anger and challenge I heard in his voice. Fynn's face was hard set, but his eyes weren't on me. No, his cold gaze was on something behind me.

"Crimson," said the beautiful voice that had been haunting me. "Please, can we talk?"

Wrenching away from Fynn, I spun around, my heart threatening to escape my chest. "Josiah," I breathed, shocked. My eyes drank him in. Noticing everything about him, from his close-cropped dark ginger hair, the dark stubble that caressed his jaw and framed his mouth. The piercings in his ears and eyebrow. The tattoos. The way his black shirt hugged his frame, his deep blue eyes that were right on me. *He was here.* What was he doing here? "What are you doing here?" I whispered in disbelief.

"We need to talk." His voice was gentle, yet firm at the same time.

I shook my head trying to understand, to comprehend what my eyes were seeing. Josiah was *here*. Right here. But, how? When? Fynn's arm wrapped around my waist, pulling me back against him. My elbow nudged him. *What was his problem?*

Cam and Rafe joined us. "What's the problem, Fynn? This guy bothering you?" Rafe asked. No. No, no, no, this was *not* good.

"Don't know yet. He seems to want something with Sage." Fynn replied. Cam stepped between Josiah and us, his hands up and out in a calming and controlled manner. "Easy mister, this gal's taken. How about you just move on."

Josiah never even acknowledged them. His deep blue eyes were on me. "Tell them to let you go, Crimson. You need to come with me. Now."

"She's not going anywhere with you, buddy. You just move on," Rafe said. Josiah took a step towards me and Rafe and Cam immediately closed ranks making a solid block in front of me. Rafe put his hand against Josiah's chest. "Back off, mister." Rafe growled at him.

"Crimson." Josiah's voice had taken on a deeper timbre. Wilder. Savage. "Tell them to move."

I was finally able to snap out of my shock. "Guys," I swallowed, trying to get my heart under control and out of my throat. "It's all right." Again, I pulled away from Fynn, this time moving around Cam and Rafe until I was in front of Josiah.

His dark blue eyes had tracked my progress. His jaw unclenched and he breathed, "You're beautiful." He trembled and an echo shuddered through me. "Walk with me?" He held his hand out and I could see he was holding on by a thread. Fearing at any moment he might snap, I knew I needed to get him out of here; away from the boys, away from people that could get hurt.

Slowly I placed my hand in his as I met his gaze, and felt my legs weaken when his warm grip enveloped mine. He led me past the tables, the silent, curious stares of the other patrons, and down to the beach.

At the sand, I hesitated, pulling back—I wasn't wearing the right kind of shoes for beach walking. Josiah studied me, his eyes traveling my length, taking in the shoes I was wearing, lingering there for a moment. Suddenly he jerked me to him, his mouth finding mine. He was ravenous; his mouth moved over mine like a man starved, his hands clinging, held me close, pulled me closer. He was gentle, though. Careful with me.

The next thing I knew, I was in his arms, and he was carrying me, never breaking contact with my mouth. When his mouth finally left mine, I blinked and looked around. We were several hundred feet away from the pier and Smokey's. My gaze found Grace, Cam, Rafe, and Fynn as they followed at a safe distance, making sure I was okay. Josiah briefly glanced over his shoulder, snorted, then ignored them. Finding a piece of driftwood, he stopped and sat, just holding me. After several moments of measured silence, he leaned forward, inhaling my scent there. Against my throat, he finally spoke. "I nearly died when you left, Crimson." His tone indicated strain, frustrated emotion.

"I'm sorry; I just had to get away...after what I saw, after what had happened, I had to..."

Josiah's arms tightened around me, cutting me off as he growled, "I need to show you something." He scrolled through a couple pictures on his phone, then held it up so I could see it better. It took me a moment to realize exactly what I was seeing on the screen.

Nausea threatened as I took in the three pictures he showed me. The first was Josiah, passed out and alone in the back seat of a car. He wasn't wearing a shirt, just jeans; his arms were flung out in an odd formation that looked uncomfortable. The second was a picture of Charlene having sex with some guy in the backseat of a car—I remembered that look on her face and pain trembled in my chest again. The third was the picture she'd shown me, the one where she said she and Josiah had hooked up. The pain peaked, then I noticed something was off about the pictures. Something similar about them, too. The pain began to recede.

Shaking my head I looked up. "I don't... I don't understand."

He kissed my temple. "She *lied*, Crimson. She superimposed the images. The first one I showed you was from a party about four years ago. I'd passed out in that car. Red found me and can vouch that I was clothed and alone. The second was hers; she had a friend take it. It was completely staged. I told you she was a liar and would mess with you."

Tears welled in my eyes. "Why would she do that?" What was the matter with her?

"Because she gets off on it and she enjoys it. She's a narcissistic lying witch. And she knew I'd never given her the time of day despite how often she threw herself at me. I never lied to you, Crimson. *She did*. I'm not a virgin and I don't pretend to be. But I did not sleep with her."

"Have you ever done anything with her?" My voice wobbled, emotion still coursing through me.

He snorted in seeming disgust. "Charlene threw herself at me and every guy around every chance she got." Josiah blew out a breath. "She *has* kissed me, and I *have* seen her naked. Not by choice, though; it's hard to miss when she literally strips in front of me."

Relief, followed by shame, flooded through me as I realized the truth in what he was telling and showing me. Realized he'd been telling the truth the whole time. Now, I was heartbroken for an entirely different reason. Self-disgust curled in my gut, as tears pooled in my eyes and spilled over. "I, I...I'm sorry, Josiah." I whispered, sick to my stomach. "Sorry I believed her. I'm so sorry."

"No," he cut me off, arms tightening around me. "*I'm* sorry. It was a convincing picture, no doubt about it."

"I should have trusted you." Guilt left a bitter taste in my mouth. "How did you figure it out?"

"I tracked her down and threatened to beat the crap out of her if she didn't tell me what had happened." He didn't sound like he was joking.

"Josiah...you wouldn't have really done anything to her...?" I didn't think he would have, but I needed to hear it from him.

He snorted in derision. "Don't be too sure about that. She's lucky Red was there, and I didn't kill her. She *hurt* you. And she enjoyed it."

Wrapping my arms around his neck, I pulled myself closer, loving the deep, approving rumble that sounded through his chest. "I'm *so* sorry. Can you forgive me?"

"Of course, I forgive you. I *love* you, Crimson. And I'm not letting you go. *Ever.*"

I kissed him, then. Needing to show how truly sorry I was. Reveling in the feel of his mouth on mine again, savoring it, savoring him, I climbed further onto his lap. Straddling him, I wrapped my legs around him, enjoying the feeling of his warm, hard hands as they found my legs, my thighs. Soon we were both shuddering, desire pulsing strongly through us. Josiah groaned, then pulled back, pushing me away. "I said I forgave you, Crimson."

"Maybe I just can't forgive myself." I couldn't meet his eyes. "Maybe I need to make it up to you."

Josiah gently pulled my chin up and caught my gaze. "I nearly killed those three fools back there for simply being with you, knowing you had broken up with me. I understand fear and passion. I don't blame you. And you don't need to make anything up to me, especially not like this. It's over with; just let it go."

"How *did* you find me?" I wondered suddenly.

"Grace," he said. "She called to chew me out; I was able to explain what had happened and she helped set this up. She swears those three are in on it, that I had nothing to worry about, but...it was hard. Seeing his hands on you."

"*Grace* called you? When? When did you get here?"

"My flight arrived just after eleven this morning. After I got the rental car, I drove straight here. She told me what time and where to meet. I'm eternally grateful to her; I didn't think she even liked me."

I sighed and nuzzled closer, breathing in his scent. "She told me to give you a chance to explain. I'd planned to talk with you when I got back to Idaho."

"I know, but I couldn't wait." His arms tightened. "I had to see you. These last couple weeks have been hell."

"The guys were in on it as well?" I asked after several minutes of silence in which we simply held each other.

"Grace said they were." He grumbled, "Though *I* think they took their role a little too serious. There was no reason for his hands to be all over you."

His comment had me chuckling. "Fynn's hands weren't all over me, Josiah. We danced together. That's all. He's like a brother to me. Grace and I practically grew up with them."

"Don't kid yourself," he snorted. "If you were to ever give him the green light, he'd leap."

"Fynn?" I laughed. "No; definitely not. You're mistaken, I promise."

"Call them over." A challenge was in his voice.

"Josiah..." I pulled back to look at him.

His blue eyes left me to glance back at my friends. "Call them over."

"Will you be nice?" My grip on him tightened.

"I'm always nice." He kissed my nose.

"No fights." I tugged at his shirt. "Promise me."

"I promise not to start any fights."

My eyes narrowed. "That's not what I meant, and you know it. They mean a lot to me. I don't want them hurt."

"You think I'd hurt them?" He chuckled darkly. "There are three of them, Crimson. Just one of me."

"You mean to say you couldn't handle them?" I teased.

Josiah looked over his shoulder again. His blue eyes narrowing as he studied them for a brief moment. Then, under his breath as he turned back said, "I'd handle them; no problem."

I nodded. "That's what I figured. Please don't *hurt* them."

Josiah gazed boldly at me. His eyes traveled across my face, seeming to study each detail, before focusing on my mouth. His gaze held there for so long I began to anticipate his mouth on mine. Carefully, I licked my lips, waiting. Josiah flicked his gaze back up to meet mine, then. "I love you, Crimson. I won't hurt them." His mouth met mine. This kiss said so much. It said he'd missed me, that he loved me, that he needed me, that he forgave me.

Josiah's lips were warm as he moved them gently across mine, tasting and teasing. His whiskers scraped lightly against my skin, the abrasive nature more caress than not. His teeth nipped my jaw, moving down to my neck, where he growled against my skin.

"Seriously?" Grace called loudly, startling us both. "You guys *still* do this?" I pulled myself together as I shifted back from Josiah. He didn't release me, just loosened his grip so I could turn around to see Grace, Cam, Fynn, and Rafe joining us. "I take it you two have made up? Everything was explained?"

Josiah chuckled. "Everything has been explained, and we have made up, yes. Thank you, Grace." He looked at the guys, then. "And thanks to you as well. Grace tells me you were instrumental in tonight's events."

"Well, Josiah," Cam said as he approached, gaze firmly on his target. "If Gracie hadn't convinced us you really do love Sage, we wouldn't have let you get anywhere near her."

I groaned inwardly. Of course, Cam was going to take his role as big brother seriously. Josiah stiffened under me, then chuckled softly, darkly, and looked up at the three men. His blue eyes traveled over them before settling on Cam again. "Well, Cam, is it? If Grace hadn't convinced *me* that you were actually trying to help her get Crimson to talk with me...if I hadn't known *that*...it'd have taken *way* more than the three of you to stop me."

Silence spread between us as Josiah stared the brothers down. I took a slow, deep breath preparing to speak, when suddenly Rafe burst out laughing. "I like this guy. He's got guts." Rafe stepped forward offering a hand to Josiah.

Josiah stood, me still in his arms, letting me slide to my feet, and took Rafe's hand in his firm grip. I stayed glued to Josiah's side, mainly because he was still holding me tightly around the waist. Cam also stepped closer to shake Josiah's hand, and then Fynn stepped forward. Rather than reach out to shake hands, he reached for me, for my arm, attempting to pull me slightly away from Josiah. I think he just wanted a hug and to be sure that I was all right. His brown eyes assessed the reaction from Josiah who muttered low under his breath.

"Fynn." Cam warned his brother. Rafe and Cam stepped closer, ready to step in should the need arise.

"It's good; I'm just testing the waters," Fynn replied, never taking his eyes off Josiah. I'd stepped back, pressing further into Josiah's chest, more to stand as a block between the two than anything else. I was very fond of Fynn and didn't want to see him get hurt. Though why he thought it'd be a good idea to poke the wolf was beyond me. My eyes tried to convey to him that he needed to stop, but Fynn stayed focused on Josiah.

He reached for me again and this time Josiah planted a hand in his chest. The warning was clear. "While I'm thankful to you for your...help...this evening, I'm going to thank you for keeping your hands off my girl." Josiah's voice was level, controlled and yet so chock-full of meaning, that I expected fists to start flying.

"You sure about that?" Fynn taunted. "Maybe Sage has changed her mind."

"So sure, that if you touch her again, you won't be good for much for quite some time."

"Fynn," I said quietly. "Stop, please. I don't want to see anyone get hurt."

"*You* got hurt. Maybe *I* don't like seeing you hurt. In fact, I hate it." Anger began to bleed through his voice, as he finally shifted his focus to me. The look in his eye was one I'd never seen before. Longing, fear, desire, and pain. The idea that he was this emotionally involved, that he cared this much was shocking. I wasn't sure what to say. "It was a misunderstanding, Fynn." I shrugged. "I was lied to, but not by Josiah."

"Do you love him?" he asked. "Really love him?"

"I really do." I assured. "Very much."

"All right." He nodded, face closed off, before switching his gaze to Josiah. "Consider this a warning: Sage comes back here again because she got hurt from something in your world and I'll do everything within my power to see she stays here. With me. We clear?"

"Crystal." Josiah held his hand out to Fynn, who took it and gave him a firm grip. I breathed a silent sigh of relief as things seemed to be calming down. Josiah tightened his fingers along my stomach before releasing me. He placed a kiss on my forehead, then Rafe claimed his attention for a moment.

Grace stepped close, and I hugged her. "Thank you so much."

"What are best friends for?" She hugged me back, squeezing tightly. "I could see how miserable you were, and the Kid texted, telling me all he'd been able to find out. He said Josiah was chomping at the bit and desperate to get to you. So, I helped them get all this planned. You're not mad?"

"*So* not mad. I'm relieved and happy. Ethan was in on this, too?"

"Yeah." She chuckled quietly. "He's very protective of you and Josiah."

"And our boys?" I nodded towards Cam, Fynn, and Rafe.

"Oh, yes." She nudged my shoulder. "Though Fynn kind of threw me there at the end."

"Same." Fynn caught my eye, then, and with a glance at Josiah, came over. "You all right?" he nudged my shoulder with his.

"Yeah," I sighed. "I am." Grace squeezed my arm as she made her way to Rafe, Cam, and Josiah.

"I meant what I said, you know." Fynn looked down at me. "Give me one chance, Sage, and I'll never let you go."

"Fynn...I don't know what to say. You know I love you, but...." I shook my head helplessly, unsure as to how to continue.

"Yeah, I know, but only as your brother. Guess I played that card a little too close. I just thought I'd always have time." I didn't know how to respond. I'd always thought the three brothers were attractive, and I'd definitely had a crush on them when I was still in high school; but they'd never treated me with anything other than sibling-like affection. Fynn's declaration just caught me completely off-guard. I saw a light flicker in his eyes, then he grinned, nudging my shoulder again. "Hey, no worries. I love you just the same as I always have and always will. Just know that if things don't work out with your wolf, I'm here." He held his arms out, a friendly offering on his face. I glanced at Josiah, who nodded with a wry grin, before stepping into Fynn's arms.

He hugged me tightly, gently, brotherly with maybe a bit of emotion thrown in for good measure. I didn't linger in his embrace, knowing how Josiah would take it. Just long enough for Fynn to know that I appreciated him.

Josiah wrapped an arm around me, placing a kiss at my temple when I returned to him. "I love you," he breathed into my hair.

Chapter 16
We Belong

Crimson Sage

The beach house was quiet now. The distant crashing surf, the wind, and our breath, the only noise around us. I estimated the time somewhere near two in the morning. The moon spilled into the room Josiah and I were sharing. Tanner and Sawyer showed up just after midnight when we got back to the beach house. Thankfully, Sawyer treated me like an old friend and not like an old flame. I didn't know how much more Josiah could take. Gracie told us to take her parents' room at the back of the house, figuring we'd want some privacy. She and Tanner took the spare bedroom and Sawyer took the loft. The brothers went home before we left the beach, but not before we'd promised to come by Pete's in the morning so Josiah could be properly introduced.

Josiah and I weren't sleeping. We lay together in silence, fully clothed and fully awake. The balcony door was open, spilling fresh air into the room. The rest of the house was silent and it was almost like we were the only two people in the world. He shifted behind me, tightening the arm wrapped around me and across my stomach, dragging me closer. His breath danced along my shoulder, then his whiskers, then his lips. Josiah skimmed his mouth along my skin making me shudder. Slowly he moved up to my ear and breathed me in. "I missed this, missed you. I *hated* being separated from you, Crimson—it was hell. Never again," he breathed against my overheated skin.

Turning over, my eyes searched his, noting the pain there and the relief, the love. Leaning towards him, I nuzzled his mouth with mine. "I'm sorry I hurt you."

"I'm sorry you were hurt, sorry you were scared," he said against my lips. He kissed me then, slowly, deeply. Taking his time. My hands wrapped around his neck pulling myself closer, needing to be closer to him. Josiah's hands framed my face, slid down my neck, my shoulders. Trailed heat down my ribs to my hips, my thigh, where he wrapped his big, work-hardened hands, tugging me closer. Suddenly he rolled and I was above him looking down, enjoying the way the moon played across his features, the way it highlighted his skin. My breath caught in my throat as he gripped my hips, my thighs and held me to him. Time almost seemed to stand still in that moment.

Josiah leaned up and claimed my mouth again as if he couldn't get enough. His hands traveled my body, igniting, yet calming me at the same time. In a haze of desire, I leaned back, leisurely reaching for the bottom hem of my shirt. Slowly, I began to lift, pulling it upward, until Josiah seized my wrists, holding them tightly in his grip. "No; *no*, Little Red. I'm not doing this with you; we're not going there."

"I want to." I whispered, desire evident in my voice. "I want you."

"No," he growled, heat flashing in his eyes.

"Please, Josiah." I begged. "Please."

"Crimson Sage," he groaned out as he shook his head. "I love you. And, because I love you, I'm stopping this right now, right here. Physically you may be feeling this, needing this." I nodded, desperation building. "But I also know your reasons for waiting and we're *going* to wait. I'm going to honor that. I'm going to honor *you*." He was speaking calmly, firmly, trying to reason with me, with himself.

Physical frustration was so potent, so heady and intense, tears pricked my eyes as I growled, impatient. "But you *want* this; I can tell you do. Please, Josiah...." I wanted this. *Needed* him so bad.

He chuckled, a panicked, almost pained sound and took a firmer grip on me. "You have *no idea* how much I want this, but Crimson, *I want you more.* I almost lost you a week ago; I'm not taking that risk again." Josiah rolled me over again, this time he was over me, holding me down, holding my wrists so I was unable to move, unable to entice him further than I already had. I trembled and shuddered as my eyes beseeched him, and my mouth begged him, but Josiah wouldn't budge. Being firmly resolved, he lay down beside me and folded me in his arms, lacing my fingers with his, turning my back to him, holding me until the trembling stopped, until my breath was under control. And then he held me for the rest of the night while I slept. Keeping me safe, protecting me, even from myself.

When I finally woke the next morning and met Josiah's dark blue gaze, embarrassment washed over me like a tidal wave. I quickly ducked my head. He pulled my face up and waited for me to open my eyes. "Don't hide from me, please," he whispered against my cheek.

Sighing, I shook my head and met his gaze, just wanting to pull the covers over my head and never emerge. "I'm...not sure what came over me last night. I'm sorry, sorry I put you through that."

He chuckled darkly as he lowered his head to meet my gaze. "*I'm* not. At all. My *only* regret is not being able to give you what you wanted, not being in the right...position."

I snorted. "Uh, I'm not sure what you had in mind, but our *positions* were just fine for what I was after."

His hand slid to my hip, resting heavily there, gripping firmly. "Well, if we're just talking good old-fashioned steamy sex, then yeah, we were right on target, but you see, Little Red," he took my chin now, holding it still for him. "I don't just want to have sex with you—I mean I do—I really, *really* do, but before we get to that part, I need to make love to you several times first. I need you to know that what we're doing is not just sex, but something so much more."

"Oh," I blushed. "Okay..."

"You see, there's a difference," he leaned forward as he kissed my nose. "I've had sex before and it never meant anything, because I didn't really love those girls. We just...used each other's bodies." Josiah shifted, looking down into my eyes. I watched as the blue in his eyes turned to liquid. "I love *you* and I want to make sure that *you* know that no matter what kind of sex we have, no matter how hot and heavy, no matter how much I intend to drive you crazy...I'll be making love to you the whole time. We won't just be having sex; we'll be making love. That's a promise."

His comment about hot and heavy sex affected me in two ways. One, it made my blood boil in anticipation, and the other made me think of the comments that Charlene had made about Josiah. I took a deep breath, then exhaled. "Charlene said when you'd had sex it was hard, hot, and heavy..."

Josiah's blue eyes narrowed in anger. "Again, she was lying. She has no idea; at least, she has no first-hand experience. She's speculating at best."

"So, you're not hot and heavy when...you know...?"

He chuckled darkly as he leaned down to tease my mouth. "You'll have to be the judge of that and let me know."

"Which is what I was trying to learn last night." My exasperation might have shown through then.

"Yes, but last night you weren't my wife. And no matter how hot and heavy things get between us now, you won't learn about that side of me until we're married. But I do promise to do all that I can to make it a highly memorable and enjoyable experience for you when the time comes."

I sucked in a ragged breath and shivered. "You promise?"

"I unequivocally guarantee it."

"Oh..."

"We belong together, Crimson," he kissed me again, just lightly before pulling back and rolling out of bed. "Now, if I remember correctly, we have somewhere to be this morning. Some big guy named Pete, who I hear sired those three I met last night, wants to threaten me, and serve us breakfast, so we need to get going." His eyes ghosted over me as he inhaled. "You're far too tempting for my peace of mind right now so I'm going to take a shower. I'll be locking the door, and you should have plenty of hot water when I'm done, as my shower will be ice cold." I was still laughing when I heard the water turn on.

An hour later, we were heading to Pete's. Tanner had his Jeep with him, so Grace and Sawyer rode with him. I went with Josiah in his rental car. Pete's was typically busy, but we weren't in any rush. We stood in line and just enjoyed the morning and each other's company. "I say we spend the day on the beach, do a little swimming, and then BBQ tonight. Who's in?" Grace asked as we were getting closer to the counter and Pete. He'd spotted us as we arrived and gave a friendly wave, though his dark brown eyes were all over Josiah, sizing him up. Josiah took it all in stride and didn't let it bother him. He lifted our entwined hands to his mouth and kissed my knuckles.

"Good morning, Pete," I smiled as we finally reached the counter.

Pete smiled his big smile and returned the greeting. "What can I get you this morning?" We placed our orders for the coffees and some of Carol's pastries as well. Tanner found us a table outside where we sat to wait. We didn't wait long however, as both Pete and Carol soon approached with our order. She was whispering something up to him, her manner seemed firm and commanding. Pete grinned and shook his head, even as his gaze was zeroed in on Josiah.

We stood as they reached us and waited for Pete to disperse the drinks. Finally, Pete's eyes turned to Josiah once more. "Pete, Carol," I had an arm around Josiah. "This is Josiah. Josiah, meet Pete and Carol."

Carol gave me a hug, then, after a moment's hesitation, reached for Josiah as well. Pete shook Josiah's hand but continued to eye him carefully. "We heard a lot about you last night. Seemed to think you were man enough to take on my boys and then some."

I groaned inwardly at the challenge I heard in Pete's voice, but Josiah seemed unfazed. He chuckled. "Well, if they, or anyone else was foolish enough to get between me and my girl, they'd have to learn the hard way."

"Big man, huh?" Pete asked.

"When I need to be."

"Big enough to take me on?" Narrowed brown eyes met cool blue ones. Panic at the route the conversation was going, had me gasping, "Pete."

"You or anyone else. It doesn't matter to me. Nothing is coming between Crimson and me again." Josiah stated, holding Pete's gaze.

Pete studied him quietly for a moment, then a slow smile spread across his face. "And that's the way it should be." Pete pulled me close and kissed the top of my head. "She's like a daughter to us, a daughter we never had. So, don't be too harsh on us for worrying about her."

"We're good. I appreciate you looking out for her." Josiah shook Pete's hand again, then Pete excused himself to get back inside. He said the boys would find us later and to have a great time. Carol kissed my cheek before following him.

"That went well." Grace smiled.

"Could've been way worse," Tanner agreed. "Pete took *me* around the back and lectured me long and hard about the hazards of messing with his girl." Tanner leaned over to kiss Gracie on the cheek. I smiled as she blushed happily. My eyes closed briefly as I sank back into my chair and sipped my coffee, just enjoying the moment. Josiah tugged a lock of my hair, and when I met his gaze the look in his eye said we were all right. After breakfast we cleaned up our table and decided to walk along the storefronts. I asked Josiah how long he was staying for, and he smiled. "As long as you're here; I'll be here."

"I guess we're leaving in five days, then." I tightened my arm around him.

"Five days in paradise with you? I'll take it."

Josiah

Waking up with Crimson beside him had been heaven. Absolute heaven, especially after the hell he'd endured these last couple of weeks when she'd been gone. Josiah watched as she slept, memorizing her all over again. The way the morning light kissed her hair, her skin, her lips. He enjoyed her breaths, happy to hear the slow, peaceful whisper as she breathed in and out.

He listened to the sound of her heart as it beat in her chest and thought it was one of the most beautiful sounds he'd ever heard—aside from her saying she loved him.

This was right. *She* was right. And essential. He was never going to let her go, not ever again.

Crimson Sage

We hung out in town, stopping in different stores to look around; I ended up getting Ethan and the rest of the Ranch boys a T-shirt and Billy a new ball cap. Tanner, Sawyer, and Gracie headed back to the house and told us they'd meet us there. When we got back to the beach house, Sawyer was sitting on the porch steps; he waved at us as we pulled up. We carried our bags up the steps and to our room. I didn't see Grace or Tanner anywhere. The door to the spare room was closed so I assumed they'd wanted some privacy, and Sawyer had probably escaped the house to give it to them.

"You and Sawyer were an item." Josiah noted as he closed the door to our room. He hadn't asked a question, had simply made a statement.

I nodded. "Before I moved to Idaho we'd gone on a couple dates."

"Just a couple?"

"Yes." I hoped he wasn't concerned, but as Josiah sat beside me on the bed, said, "You have nothing to worry about. At all."

"I'm not worried." He took my hand in his, smoothing his thumb across my palm. "I just noticed the way he watches you is all. Like I noticed Fynn last night."

"You're very observant." I nudged his shoulder with mine. "I never even knew Fynn had liked me."

He raised our joined hands, kissing my knuckles. "They look at you the way I do." His mouth continued to my wrist in light, tender touches.

As he inhaled the scent there, offering a low sound of approval, I sighed. "No one affects me the way you do."

Josiah nipped the skin at my wrist. "Good."

The silky, golden-brown sand of the beaches at Nags Head caressed my feet as Josiah and I strolled along the shoreline. He held my hand as we walked; occasionally a wave came up high enough to wrap around our ankles. Thankfully the weather scored us some warm temperatures—despite the fact it was still spring, today was going to top out just under ninety degrees.

"Josiah," I took a deep breath, needing to tell him something, explain something to him. He looked over and waited. "I...know it wasn't fair to you, what I did. Accusing you and believing her. I know that wasn't fair and it wasn't right."

"I told you; I've already forgiven you."

"I know you have. I just... I can't get it out of my head. *I* can't get past it." I allowed silence to settle for a minute while I tried to gather my thoughts.

Josiah lifted our enjoined hands up to his mouth and ran his lips gently across my knuckles, something I noticed he seemed to enjoy doing. "Tell me about it; tell me what happened, what she did."

I took a deep breath, then told him everything. How she was waiting for me by my car, how she told me, in detail, all that she'd done with him. How I'd never be able to measure up to his standard. And how I'd already been feeling that way, like somehow I didn't fit in his world. Josiah listened silently as I spoke, just accepting what I had to say, letting me get it off my chest, all the way up until I said that last part. The part where I didn't feel like I fit in. "Wait." He stopped our forward momentum, pulling me to a stop. "Hold up. What do you mean you don't think you *fit* in my world?"

I shrugged. "Because I'm such a wimp...afraid of life...and you...well, you're not. I've never seen anyone as strong as you. Never. I'm always afraid I'll let you down. And I have; I did." I inhaled. My breath shuddering. "Because I was weak, and afraid, you got hurt. My fears hurt *you*..."

Josiah cupped my face, lifting it so I had to look at him. "Shut *up*," he whispered, then kissed my lips lightly. "Just stop. You *are* strong. You're one of the strongest people I know. The bravest. You didn't have my life growing up, you didn't have to learn to be strong and fight back. And yet, when the pain came, *you held on*. For Ethan. You had the chance, had the choice to end all the pain, yet you chose to face it, to fight it. That *is* strength. That *is* bravery. Crimson...for crying out loud, woman—I couldn't be more proud of you."

"But I hurt you, Josiah." Tears filled my eyes, and I had to blink to clear my vision.

He shook his head. "I won't deny that what happened hurt, but you were hurt, too. Instead of dwelling on past mistakes that we cannot go back and change, let's look at our future and learn from it. Deal?"

"Deal," I whispered against his lips. We walked on then and he held me close. I felt better, relieved even. I still didn't quite have the confidence in myself that he seemed to have, but I felt better than I had in weeks.

The day was getting warmer as the sun continued to climb in the sky, and eventually we stripped down to our suits and went into the water. As Josiah and I waded in up to our thighs, he turned and looked at me. "You know what?" he chuckled. "This is my first time at the beach."

"*What?* You've never been to the ocean before?"

"Nope. Always wanted to go but never had. It's not like Idaho is close to the beach or anything."

I smiled. "So, how are you liking it?"

"I'm still taking it all in. It didn't register that I was coming to the beach, or that I'd see the ocean, at first. My sole focus was on you. *Is* on you."

I laughed lightly. "But...?"

"But I do like it. It's beautiful. I can see why you love it as much as you do." Josiah pulled me closer, and we held each other close, letting the water soothe us, the sun warm us.

Josiah

Crimson was insane. Nuts. *Not strong?* She didn't *fit* into his world? What was she even talking about? She was one of the strongest, most courageous people he knew. Josiah marveled at her own self-doubt as he watched her frolic in the salty waves.

It was his happy photo come to life. Crimson had been used to a warm, comfortable environment. One filled with family and love, devotion and acceptance. It's easy to be a good person, a strong person when things were going well, when everything was perfect and nice.

Josiah knew from experience that people tended to show their true selves—the side they kept hidden from view—when times were tough. Crimson, despite everything life had thrown at her, chose to fight on. Even if it had been just for Ethan. Still, she'd thought about someone else first, put them before herself.

And she thought she was weak, that she wasn't strong. A weak person wouldn't have cared. A weak person would have let go and sought the easy way out.

No, Crimson was strong. Beautiful, strong, and his.

Crimson Sage

The next three days were full of sunshine, and Josiah and I spent nearly every minute of them on the beach. We'd walk, then wade in, then nap as we dried off, then take more walks, go hiking, find tide pools and seashells. At night we had bonfires before heading in for bed. Tanner and Sawyer left yesterday needing to get back for work. Cam, Fynn, and Rafe came by nearly every afternoon just to hang out and talk. Josiah teased that they were checking up on him, making sure I was happy. I just laughed, but a part of me wondered if he might be right. On two separate occasions the boys asked Josiah if he wanted to go out on the fishing boat with them. Being a guy who enjoyed a challenge, he took them up on the offer. Josiah seemed to like it; he liked the water and blessedly was not affected by seasickness. Cam, Fynn, and Rafe were impressed with him and said if he ever needed a job, they'd hire him. Josiah thanked them and said he'd see.

On our last night in Nags Head, we decided to go back to Smokey's for dinner. Pete and Carol and the boys joined us, and it was a nice evening. Another local band, Stormy Weather, was playing and this time Josiah danced with me. Their beat was good, a little bluesy, a little southern rock. We danced several dances; Josiah was a great dancer. He even let the boys cut in a few times, and twice I saw him dance with Grace.

I hated goodbyes; and somehow because Mom and Dad were gone, Pete and Carol seemed like surrogate parents now more than ever. Saying goodbye to them tomorrow would be hard. I tried not to think about it and just enjoyed the evening. Josiah and I returned to our seats, and my pulse was pounding, but it was a good feeling. Grace and Cam had just returned to our table when Cam announced, "I like this band." He wasn't wrong and we all agreed. We'd have to let management know they should have them back. I settled back in my seat, angling to snuggle into Josiah's shoulders. He gently kissed my brow, letting his mouth linger there for a moment. I sighed in contentment and closed my eyes.

"What the..." Josiah's voice trailing off into silence had me opening my eyes. He was staring away from our table and into the crowd. Following his gaze, I noticed the five people standing a few feet from our table. Their eyes were on me. I sat up a little straighter, wondering what they were doing when suddenly they held up signs. Five in all. Each one had a word on it. I focused on the words, trying to comprehend. *Crimson—will—you—marry—me?*

As everything clicked into place and realization began to settle in, Josiah was suddenly kneeling before me, a ring in his palm. His blue eyes seemed darker than normal, almost smoky. And they were full of emotion. "I already got permission from Ethan and Billy. I even talked with the boys, and Pete and Carol, and Grace. So, what do you say, Crimson? Will you do me the extreme honor of being my wife?"

I blinked to rid my eyes of the misty moisture that suddenly plagued me. "You're serious?" I asked, needing clarification. "You really want to marry me?"

"I really do."

"Then, yes. Yes, Josiah!" He didn't wait a second longer. That ring was on my finger, and I was in his arms, his mouth on mine. He lifted me and dimly I was aware of the clapping and cheering going on around us. Happy wasn't a strong enough word for what I was feeling right now. It was more than euphoric. I couldn't put it into words. He set me down, breaking the kiss, then lifted my hand to his mouth, kissing that ring on my finger. I stared at it, appreciating its beauty. He'd gone non-traditional, picking a deep red stone, set in antique gold, giving it a vintage look that I couldn't help but admire.

"It's a garnet." He spoke against the shell of my ear as his arms went around me. "As soon as I saw it, I knew I wanted it for you. Do you like it?"

"I love it," I breathed. "It's beautiful."

"*You're* beautiful." He kissed my jaw. "And I need you in my life. Permanently."

"You have me, now and forever." I couldn't seem to help the smile on my face, like it was now a permanent fixture. As we were swarmed with our friends and the strangers around us, offering their congratulations, I just couldn't seem to stop smiling. I'd never seen Josiah smile so much either. He was lighthearted and happy. He even took it in stride when the boys came up to offer their congratulations and Fynn lifted me for a quick, hard kiss.

When I called Ethan to tell him the news, his only comment was, "Yes! I love it when a plan comes together." Laughing out loud, I told him we'd see him tomorrow.

The following morning we loaded up the rental car as we finished cleaning the beach house. Our only stop before leaving town was Freaky Pete's. Josiah promised them we'd be back soon, which made me happy. After topping off the gas, we were on the road. Our flight left at nine that night, so we had to be at the airport by seven. Matt and Shelli met us at the airport to give Gracie a ride home, and to say goodbye and congratulate us on our engagement. Gracie made them wait until Josiah and I were through airport security before allowing them to leave.

I ended up sleeping for most of the flight, but that was fine with Josiah; he said he liked to hold me, liked to watch me sleep. Billy didn't need to pick us up as Josiah had left his car in the long-term parking. As we drew closer to the ranch a thought suddenly occurred to me. "It'll be weird...a little...being engaged at the ranch but not yet married."

"I was thinking about that." He rubbed at his lower lip with a knuckle. "It's been nice having you to myself this last week. But I guess we'll need to do things differently here."

"Yeah... It was one thing to sleep over, occasionally, but I don't think I should move in or anything." I shot him a look, wondering about his thoughts on the subject. "Do you?"

He took my hand in his, giving it a gentle squeeze. "Don't get me wrong, I love having you there with me, and it's going to suck big time with you all the way up in your own room away from me, but I get that we need to set a good example for Ethan and the other boys."

"So...how...I mean, what's the next step in all this?"

His thumb traced slow patterns on my palm. "Let me ask you this: how soon would you like to get married?"

"I...don't know...how soon do you want to get married?" My mind was drawing a blank; I couldn't track my thoughts to know what I wanted in that regard.

"I asked you first." He grinned.

"Josiah!" I squeezed his hand sharply. "You can't put that all on me...."

"Okay." His blue eyes held a dare. "How's this weekend work for you?"

"*What?*" He can't be serious. Wait. *Is he?*

"Look," he raised our joined hands to his mouth and nipped me with his teeth. "Just a few days ago you were nearly in tears over...certain needs...and you did your darndest to entice me into your way of thinking and feeling, which was some kind of hell, let me tell you. And you were just saying it'll be weird sleeping in separate beds—this fixes everything."

"Are you being serious?" My face was red; I could feel the heat.

"Sure; why not?"

"You'd get married next week?" My heart pounded in my chest.

"I would." His tone sounded serious. It held a level of heat that sent shivers through me.

"Well, um, I'm not sure..." It was incredibly difficult to focus on his question when the desire he was sending kept interfering with my thoughts.

"*I've* been thinking about it. A lot. Just so you know—I really do *want* you."

The sincerity in his voice, and in his gaze made me chuckle weakly. *This man.* In the end we agreed to look at a calendar and come up with some dates tomorrow. For the time being I'd continue to stay in my room at the end of the hall. But we promised each other, plans would be made and soon.

Chapter 17
Illusion

*C*rimson Sage

It didn't take long to get back in the swing of things. Ethan and Billy were ecstatic with my return, claiming to have missed me 'so much'. Which I guess was probably true. They were two more people I had to add to my list of people I'd hurt. Both Ethan and Billy brushed my apology aside, saying they understood, and loved me too much to let it fester and bother them. They were glad I was home and that things were back to normal. And they were more than happy with the engagement news.

And maybe the focus would have been a little more intense on me had something else, something bigger not have happened. The first morning Josiah and I were back, we learned that, while we'd been gone Mike and Adam had run away. Both were just weeks shy of their eighteenth birthdays and graduating from the program. Billy told us about it over coffee. So far there were no leads as to where they'd gone, or who may have helped them. And the absolute precise manner in which they'd vanished made us believe they must have had help. Billy said they'd disappeared the day after Josiah left.

The room they'd shared had been searched and several very disturbing things had been discovered. Clothing belonging to Maggie Tyler, the girl who'd been attacked a few months back, had been found stuffed under a broken floorboard, along with a couple pieces of my clothing—a bra and a pair of panties. With those items was a list of names with phone numbers—Charlene's name had been on that list; it was determined the list was simply contacts for parties and drugs. They'd also found several photos of me and a few other girls in the area. Maggie had been questioned again, to verify she'd been wearing the clothing at the time of her attack. She indicated the clothes were hers; but either couldn't or wouldn't say if she'd been wearing them at the time.

A measurable difference was felt in the atmosphere at the ranch with the departure of Adam and Mike. While there was certainly curiosity as to the whereabouts of the missing boys and their actions and activities, there was almost a united sigh of relief as well. And even stranger, was the difference between how Josiah and I handled the news. Relief was my primary feeling. No more having to be on guard around Mike or worry about Ethan. Josiah, on the other hand, seemed more tense. More on guard. He'd taken to escorting me into town again, even when I went to talk with Tina at the Java Shack about getting my job back. "How long will the surveillance continue?" I asked him as we left Burger King with our milkshakes.

"Just being careful," was his measured, almost vague response.

"You're worried," I pressed.

"I didn't like the idea of Mike being around you; I like the idea of him roaming around with no one to monitor him, especially after he had your clothes, even less." His eyes had taken on a stormy look.

Josiah was riding an edge, and I didn't know how to reach him, to calm him. I took his hand in mine, kissing the back of it, trying to reassure him. "You can't follow me everywhere. You have a job and tomorrow I begin work again."

Those stormy eyes landed on me, with heat riding the clouds in his gaze. "I won't interfere with your work, or mine. But I intend to keep an eye on you either way."

"Josiah...." I wasn't convincing him, was I?

"Crimson." Nope, there was no budge in him. He was set.

I sighed deeply. "I love you." Really, that was all I could do, just love him.

The heat in his eyes deepened. "I love you, too."

"October," I told him suddenly after a few minutes of silence while we enjoyed our shakes.

"October?" He raised his brow.

"How does October work? For a date?"

Josiah scratched his chin in exaggerated thoughtfulness. "Yeah...I guess that'd work all right. Nothing open sooner? Like this weekend, or tonight, huh?"

I chuckled. "I like the fall, all the colors and crispness."

"October it is." His voice deepened. "Gotta day to go with that month?"

"The fifth." I finished my drink.

"And why the fifth?" Tenderly, he tucked a strand of hair behind my ear, letting his fingers linger along my neck.

"My parents were married on the fifth of March..." I shrugged.

"The fifth it is." He nodded. "How about dresses? Do you know what you want? Or do you know what kind of wedding you want it to be?"

"I don't know what you'll think of this idea...but I was thinking of a retro, Fifties look..."

"That sounds perfect actually." His fingers were still caressing along my neck, inching around to the back of my skull. Threading into my hair, pulling me to him. Against my cheek, he said, "I guess we should get busy, then. Get invitations sent out." His lips moved from my ear to my jaw. "Where do you want to get married at?"

"The ranch seems the best place." A whispered croak was all I could manage through the desire he stirred in me.

"Agreed." His mouth found mine then and I didn't think about anything but him for some time.

Josiah

Pleased was too mild a word for the happiness and relief Josiah felt after Crimson said yes. Every emotion he'd felt for her was suddenly intensified. Her lemony scent clung to the very air he breathed. She was all he knew, needed, or wanted. And like a predator with a sure-kill in sight he closed in; his attention focused solely on her.

The news that Mike was missing fractured his euphoria. There was suddenly an unseen player on the field, and all of Josiah's warning bells were ringing simultaneously.

Not for a second did he think Mike just up and left. There was too much unfinished business between them. And he knew Mike would be back to test himself against Josiah. He'd be back to try and take Crimson from him. But Josiah was a wolf used to warfare, and he was ready.

Crimson Sage

Despite Josiah's concern over the missing boys and what they might be up to, time seemed to move steadily, peacefully forward. Summer arrived with warm weather and sunny, clear skies. Eventually he relaxed his self-imposed vigil when two months had gone by, and nothing had been seen of them. Charlene and the other names on the list found in Mike's room had been thoroughly questioned. Red was thinking that maybe they'd headed south, to California. Billy agreed, saying Mike had family there he might be trying to connect with. Red told us that the proper channels and authorities had been notified, that he'd done what could be done.

Billy had taken the departure of Mike and Adam hard; it was obvious he hated seeing any of his boys heading off in the wrong direction. I worried, seeing the failure he felt in his eyes, in the set of his shoulders. He'd tried steering Mike along the right path, but the boy'd been uncooperative at best. Defiantly biding his time at worst. Like me, Ethan was relieved at his absence, and as time continued, he finally opened up about how his arm had really been broken. It had been Mike, just like I'd feared. And as I'd suspected he'd threatened to hurt me if Ethan ever told anyone. My emotions were raging at the news, fierce, protective anger roared through me. Ethan was concerned I was mad at him, but I reassured him I wasn't, just that I was glad he'd told me and that he was okay.

My dress had been ordered—well, both dresses. My maid-of-honor dress for Gracie's wedding was a deep navy blue, floor-length, form-fitting, and strapless. Gracie was ecstatic with how it looked on me when I sent her a picture at my fitting. I'd been helping her make wedding favors and decorations, then shipping them to her. I liked the fact that even though we had so much space between us, I was still able to be involved.

My dress for my own wedding was my favorite. I wished I could have worn my mom's wedding dress, but they'd just gone to a justice of the peace for their vows and had a reception later. Mom said she'd never minded not having a real wedding; that she'd had all she ever wanted. But I'd found some pictures she'd cut out of a magazine years ago and pressed into the back of her Bible. I'd kept them, at the time, not having any thoughts about wedding-type plans. The pictures had been Mom's, so they were special to me. But later, as I began to think about my own wedding, those pictures came to mind. I dug them out and began building my idea from there. It was the closest thing I could come up with to wearing my mother's dress.

I found the one I'd wanted online at a consignment-type store and ordered it. Its color was candlelight, a sort of soft cream, more gold than ivory. I ordered a matching lace veil and a deep burgundy slip. Josiah would be in slate grey, with a black vest, and a bow tie and suspenders also in the deep burgundy color. Gracie would be my only attendant; her dress was a medium grey color with red accents. Josiah asked Ethan to be his best man. Ethan was more than proud of that honor. Tina said her sister-in-law was a photographer and she'd ask her to do our pictures. Everything seemed to be coming along. Josiah and I agreed that even though we were getting married in October, we still wanted to have an ice cream and milkshake bar at the reception. There were five more weeks until I had to leave for Gracie's wedding and Josiah and Ethan would be going with me. I'd already shipped the dress to her, so that was one less thing to worry over.

And despite the planning that was taking place for two weddings within a couple months of each other, I found I was calm. Life was good. I felt good. I was happy and at peace. At times I'd get sad thinking about how much I wished Mom and Dad were here and a part of all this. I'd get a little teary-eyed, but then I'd focus on all the good in my life. And I'd think that if Mom and Dad hadn't died, I'd never have moved to Idaho, never would have met Josiah, wouldn't even be planning my own wedding right now. It wasn't that I wished for things to be different, so much as I was trying to just accept things as they were and not worry over details that I was unable to control. Would I trade Josiah to have my parents back? I couldn't say that I would. It would be an impossible decision to make. It was one I was thankful I didn't *have* to make.

Another sore spot occurred one night about four weeks after I'd been back. The sore spot came in the form of a butterfly tattoo and green eyes. Josiah was supposed to meet me that night after work. It was our usual thing. He'd driven me into town for my shift and would be back later to pick me up; but he'd texted to say he was running late. Ethan had stopped him, all upset, saying he couldn't find Daisy. So, Josiah had helped him look around and now was running late to pick me up. He'd said to wait inside the Java Shack, but it was such a nice night that I decided to stretch my limits and wait for Josiah on one of the metal benches just outside the Shack doors. Tina was still inside counting the till; and I knew she had a shotgun that she kept handy, "just in case".

I'd been outside for maybe five minutes when I saw headlights and heard the rumble of a motor. A tall, dark truck pulled into the Shack parking lot. It stopped about thirty feet away from me in a pool of deep shadow. The passenger door opened, and I felt my jaw drop. Charlene slipped out, and glancing around carefully, made her way to me—sauntered was more like it. Her hips were swaying in confidence; her green eyes were bright and focused on me. As I watched her approach, with a little bit of resentment at her sexual appeal, my eyes flashed to her tattoo, and I decided right then and there that I was going to finally get mine done. Why? Because I wanted one, and I was tired of putting it off. And even though Josiah had told me I was brave, and he loved me just as I was, I suddenly wanted to do this. I was excited to tell him about it. Right now, Charlene was just an irritating distraction I wanted to squash like a mosquito.

"I have nothing to say to you, so just leave me alone." I stated as she got closer. Charlene glanced over her shoulder at the driver of the pickup and grinned. I couldn't see who she was looking at, the shadows were too dark, and the windows were tinted. "Oh honey, don't be like that." She stopped right in front of me, and my eyes flitted again over her butterfly tat, making me grin in anticipation. She wasn't leaving.

Deciding to ignore her, I pulled out my phone, hoping to see an update from Josiah, wanting to tell him my idea. Tina was keeping a close eye on us and even though I wasn't worried about Charlene at all, I knew that if I felt threatened, I could just go inside.

"Why'd you come back here?" Charlene asked, her voice suddenly low with a slight tremor in it. "You were gone and in the clear. *Why'd* you come back?"

"Sorry to spoil your plans, Charlene, but Josiah and I are together and there is nothing you can do to stop it. You *tried*. That won't work again, so just run along with your little boy-toy there and leave us be."

Irritation flashed across her face. "You're not safe here, Crimson. You need to leave. *Now.* Tonight."

I shook my head at her. "*What*? What the heck are you even saying?"

She leaned toward me, over me. "Listen to me you stupid girl; you are not *safe* here. Leave."

I snorted at that. Was she for real? "Oh, so you can move in and try for Josiah again? I don't think so."

"This isn't about Josiah or you. It's about hi..." The driver of the truck suddenly lay on the horn, blaring it loudly. Charlene jumped, and for the briefest moment the look on her face seemed fearful. Then she took a deep breath. "I tried. Don't say I didn't warn you." She'd barely climbed back into the truck before the driver peeled out, kicking up gravel and dust as they left.

My mind was trying to piece together what had just happened. Part of me was thinking about what kind of tattoo I planned to get, the other part wondered what Charlene's purpose had been in coming here. I didn't have long to ponder as Josiah soon pulled up. I waved at Tina, letting her know I was leaving, then climbed into the GT. One look at Josiah, and I knew he wasn't happy I'd been outside waiting for him. "Sorry," I rushed to explain as I buckled my seatbelt. "It was such a nice night, I thought it would be all right. And Tina was right there watching me the whole time. I was safe."

Josiah clenched and unclenched his jaw several times, then rotated his neck to relieve the tension I knew he was feeling. "I'd appreciate it if you'd take extra care to be careful, Crimson. Please."

"I am."

"Sitting outside, alone, in the dark is not being careful."

"Tina was right there. I was never out of her sight."

"Yeah, I know. She called to say Charlene was here harassing you again. Were you going to tell me about it?"

My heart plummeted at that news. Of course, he had Tina keeping him informed as to how I was doing. That was why he'd pulled up so quickly. "Yes."

"Yes? Yes, what? Yes, she was there, or yes, you were going to tell me?"

"Both. Charlene came by. We spoke. She made her threats, said I should've stayed gone, blah, blah, blah. I ignored her and told her to take a hike. I told her you were mine and I was ready to fight for you."

Josiah groaned and ran a hand over his face, chuckling dryly, "You told her you'd fight her?"

"Well, not in so many words, but I told her you were mine, we were together, and there was nothing she could do about it. It's essentially the same thing."

Josiah took my hand in his, lifting it to his lips. "I love you."

"I love you, too."

"Was that all she said?"

"Pretty much," I sighed, deciding not to mention that I almost felt like Charlene had been warning me. I wanted to be strong and brave, and most likely she was just messing with me, trying to shake me again. I didn't want to give her that satisfaction. And besides, I planned on getting ink done. That was brave, right? Charlene didn't matter. So, I quickly jumped to a safer subject. "Did you find Daisy?"

"No," he sighed, clearly bothered. "Not yet."

"That's odd; she's never been gone like this before."

"I know," Josiah responded as we pulled into the ranch driveway. "Ethan's pretty worried. We're going out at first light to ride around and see if we can't find her."

"What do you think could've happened to her?"

"It's hard to say. She could have run into coyotes, a cougar, or a snake. She might have fallen into a pit or something, broken a leg, got snagged going across a creek..."

"I'd like to come along."

"All right. You can be a part of the search. Do you want to drive or ride?"

"It doesn't matter; I can do either." We just needed to find her. Ethan didn't need this loss on top of everything else.

We left the ranch by six thirty the next morning. Cullen and Mitchell, who were both sixteen and had permits, drove the ranch truck, and Josiah, me, Ethan, Kelly, and Ryan rode horses. Billy, Jack, and Dean stayed behind at the ranch to continue to search around the house, and to make sure someone was there in case Daisy wandered in by herself.

For three days we searched, with no sign of her. Josiah and I checked with our closest neighbors. Nothing. Ethan was heartbroken. And I was heartbroken for him. We couldn't figure out what could have happened to her. Josiah thought it might be possible a cougar had carried her off—we discussed that possibility in private, away from Ethan, not wanting to traumatize him any more than he already was. I worried, knowing this heartache was too soon after the loss of our parents. Next month would be a year since they'd died. It was crazy to think how much time had gone by, how much had changed in our lives.

One week later, pounding on my bedroom door woke me up. Dazedly, I tried to blink the sleep from my eyes. "Sage!" I recognized Kelly's voice and jumped from bed, absently noting that the sun was just beginning to rise. Wrenching the door open, I saw tears in Kelly's eyes. "What happened?" I asked, my heart lodging painfully in my throat.

"It's Daisy," he gasped. "She's back, but she's hurt bad. Real bad."

Grabbing a light sweatshirt from my bed, I followed him to the kitchen. Ethan was seated on the floor, holding Daisy in his arms. The poor dog was trembling with fatigue and pain. She was covered in blood. I couldn't tell if it was all hers or not. "Kelly, go wake Josiah for me, please. Tell him I need him." Kelly nodded and ran out the back door, letting it slam behind him. I stared at Daisy for a moment, not sure what to do. Ethan held her, trying to calm and reassure her. *Water*, I thought suddenly. *She'll need water*. But was it safe to give her any? I just didn't know. What if she had internal damage and the water made it worse?

Josiah arrived then, out of breath. He stared at the dog for a moment, then caught my eye. I could see the questions there. The same questions I was sure were on my face. "Ethan, we're gonna need to get her to the vet. This is more than I can deal with. She's in a lot of pain and Doc Bean can help with that. I'll call now."

Doc Bean had been the area vet in Salmon for the last twenty years. I'd met him a couple times when he came out to the ranch for one reason or another. Josiah got him on the phone and Doc Bean said he'd open his clinic, and to bring Daisy right over. Kelly woke Billy up while Josiah was on the phone. We carefully got Daisy loaded into the bed of the truck. Ethan sat in the back and held her; I told Billy I'd keep him informed. Doc Bean was waiting when we got there. He had the equivalent of a dog-gurney ready for us. Ethan wanted to go back with her to the exam room. Doc let him; then after he got her tranquilized, had Ethan wait with us while he performed the exam and got her cleaned up.

An hour later Doc Bean came back out and wiped sweat from his brow. Ethan jumped to his feet, fear on his face. "How is she?"

"She's weak. She's malnourished and dehydrated. Looks as if she's possibly been beaten; a couple ribs are broken and her back right leg is as well. Do you know what happened to her?"

Ethan was crying, his grey eyes were swimming in tears. I pulled him close. Josiah shook his head in silent anger. "Daisy went missing about ten days ago. We'd searched the entire ranch, riding out on horseback even to try and find her."

"How *did* you end up finding her? Where was she?" Doc asked.

Ethan lifted his head from my shoulder and wiped his eyes. "I couldn't sleep this morning. I got up, like I've been doing every morning since she was gone and went to the back porch to look for her. This morning, she was there, crawling towards the steps, trying to get to me."

Doc Bean nodded his head and chewed his lip a little. "I'd like to keep her overnight, just for observation. Her dehydration is extreme. I'll keep her under sedation for a few more hours so I can keep the IV connected."

"Can I stay here with her for a while?" Ethan asked. I turned to Josiah and Doc Bean. Doc nodded his head.

"We'll go get breakfast from Tom's." Josiah said. "What would you like?"

"Can I have a coffee?" Ethan asked, blinking sleepy, tear-stained eyes.

I sighed, then nodded. "What else?" I asked. "You need more than coffee."

"Cinnamon roll pancakes?" he asked hopefully.

"Okay." Josiah nodded. "Doc? Anything for you?"

"That sounds good actually." He reached for his wallet.

"Nah, it's on us." I smiled, grateful. "How do you take your coffee?"

"Black is great, thanks."

Josiah and I were gone for maybe an hour and a half by the time we'd ordered our breakfast, eaten, then ordered the to-go meals for Ethan and Doc. Out of earshot of Ethan, we discussed all the possibilities of what might have happened over our meal. He thought it was obvious someone had taken her, but it didn't make sense to me why someone might have done that. What would their purpose have been? And did she escape, or was she let go?

When we got back to the vet, we asked Doc if there was anything he could tell us from what he'd found on her that might give us some clues. He'd said there wasn't much; some gravel in the wounds, things like that, but nothing concrete. I'd let Billy know, and he said Red wanted to talk with us when we got back.

It didn't take Ethan long to eat; the poor kid had been starving, I'm sure. The appetite that had gone missing was suddenly back with Daisy's return. It also didn't take him long to ask if he could stay the night here at the clinic with her. Doc Bean explained it wouldn't be a good idea, but so long as she continued improving, we could pick her up tomorrow. Ethan gave the doctor his cell number so they could be in touch throughout the day, and the doctor promised to keep him updated, but cautioned he might not be able to respond immediately, especially if other calls came in. Then, we made Ethan say goodbye and drove home.

Back at the house, I told Ethan to shower, then take a nap, the kid was beat. Sleepily, he'd hugged me, his breath shuddering with his emotion, then slowly climbed the stairs. We found Billy in his office doing paperwork. The house had been quiet; he said Bentley had taken the other boys out fishing on one of the ranch creeks. After filling Billy in on what had happened at the Doc's, he told us he'd followed the bloody trail Daisy had left all the way to the road. Seemed it had ended about thirty yards from the driveway.

Obviously, someone had taken her. Taken her and abused her. Then brought her back to let us know they'd done it. The question was who. My instincts screamed Mike. To me, it seemed like something he'd do. Billy didn't seem to think it was—whether it was denial, or not, he was reluctant to consider the possibility. Billy reasoned, Mike hadn't been seen or heard from since he ran away. And what could have been his reasons? Like me, Josiah thought it was easily something Mike might have done, but again, why?

Josiah

When Daisy went missing Josiah began to worry. Something wasn't right; he could feel it. It was too odd. Too coincidental. Especially with Mike gone and Charlene back in town again.

Josiah took to following Crimson to work again. He'd get up and walk the perimeter of the house and the yard during the night, listening for anything out of the ordinary.

He was determined to keep Crimson safe despite the malice he felt lurking in the shadows. Something was building. Something mean and angry. And it was getting closer.

Crimson Sage

A week later, we were no closer to finding any answers. But Daisy had been brought home with no complications. Doc cautioned to keep her quiet and calm. No letting her jump or climb things yet. So, as a special treat, Billy had allowed the younger boys to camp out on the living room floor until Daisy was healed enough to climb the stairs to Ethan's room.

Work continued as usual, and I'd begun saving money for the wedding. I'd already bought the airline tickets for Ethan, Josiah, and me to fly back to North Carolina. And Josiah had a nice shirt and tie set aside for the occasion as well. Tina tried to give me extra hours as I needed or wanted them, but it was hard in a small town. She assured me things would get busier as the fair drew closer. Either way I was happy.

There'd been no further problems with Charlene, or with Daisy, who had healed nicely. There'd been no sign of Mike either. Summer continued at a leisurely pace: Warm, sunny days, starry nights, and bonfires. And I finally told Josiah my idea for my tattoo. We were sitting around his firepit, enjoying the crackling flames and the drone of frogs in the background. He angled his chair toward me, those blue eyes boring deep into mine. Twice he started to speak, then stopped, before finally saying, "I thought maybe you'd changed your mind about it. Why?"

"Because." I traced patterns onto the wooden arm rest with a finger. Why was he being so serious about this? I knew he wasn't opposed to ink.

"Because?" He drew the question out.

"Because I want one." Truly, I did and needed him to understand that.

He studied me a moment longer, letting his eyes move along my shoulder. "You really want a tattoo?"

"Yeah," I nodded. "I really do."

"Okay." His eyes softened. "But don't do this for me. Do this for you."

"I am doing this for me." I grinned, excitement building. "But I want you to like it, too. You're not...you're not disappointed, are you?"

Josiah stood, then pulled me to my feet. "No, Little Red." His arms slid around me. "I'm not disappointed. At all." His arms tightened as he kissed my forehead. "I love you. You know that, right?"

"Yeah," I whispered, my eyes closing, enjoying the feel of his lips on me. "Yeah, I do."

"Good." He nuzzled along my ear, inhaling deeply, gravelly. "Now, when do you want to do this?"

My eyes popped open. "As soon as possible. Before I chicken out again. Which I'm determined not to do. So soon. Please."

He chuckled, then kissed me soundly. "Let me give Jason a call and see when he can get you in."

Four days later, I was sitting in Jason's padded tattoo chair, trying to be calm, taking slow deep breaths, just focusing on the warmth in Josiah's hand as he held mine. When we'd arrived, the friendly, pierced, tattooed lady behind the counter had offered a smile. I was equal parts anxiety and excitement. "So..." I joked. "If I start crying like a little girl..., will you all laugh at me?"

She looked at me and blinked. "Yeah, we will. There's no crying allowed. We even have a sign." She pointed to something behind me. Sure enough, right above the door we'd just walked through was a sign that read, "Absolutely NO crying permitted, by order of Management."

"Well, okay then." I chuckled nervously. "No crying. I got this."

Josiah snorted under his breath as he pulled me close and kissed my temple. "I'm here. I've got you. You can do this."

Hopefully my excitement and confidence would carry me through. After filling out the needed paperwork, and paying for the work to be done, I was led over to Jason's table where he was preparing my tattoo image. When Josiah and I had been in North Carolina, we'd drawn a heart in the sand with our initials inside it and I'd taken a picture of it. From that image, I'd sketched my idea. It would go on the back of my left shoulder, closest to my heart.

"All right." Jason leaned closer. "You ready?"

Exhaling, I nodded. Jason reached for his tattoo machine, turned it on, then dipped the needle in the ink. Then he touched the needle to my skin and began. Josiah held my hand, and I gripped it as if my life depended on it. And it hurt. The tattoo. It really did. But not as bad as I thought it would.

All said and done, it took a little over two hours to complete. Both Jason and Josiah were pleased with how it turned out. And before Jason applied the ointment and bandage to protect it, he handed me a mirror. Other than the fact that my skin was red and a little swollen, my tattoo looked awesome. I breathed a sigh of relief. Jason had done a brilliant job of incorporating the blues, grays, and whites of the ocean surf as it splashed up, forming a border around the heart with our initials in it on the golden sand. He'd added waving tufts of golden-brown sea grass and had captured the sunrise in stunning colors. Pinks, corals, purples, and yellows filled the skyline. I'd wanted a sunrise, not a sunset, a beginning, not an ending. Jason had nailed it.

A sense of accomplishment flooded me, and I couldn't have been happier. Six days later, however, my heart hit the floor as I stepped from my shower, and noticed my tattoo seemed to be peeling away. Panicking, I quickly called Josiah.

"What's up, Little Red?" He sounded sleepy.

"I think something's wrong with my tattoo. It's peeling!" His silence made my panic grow. "Did you hear me?"

"Yeah." He sounded off, maybe unsure? Definitely shocked. "Are you sure?"

"Yes!" I tried to calm myself. "I'm staring right at it. It's peeling."

"Crimson," his voice held a hint of, *oh, no*. And my heart clenched. "Did you tell Jason you wanted a *permanent* tattoo?"

"What?" I gasped, now starting to feel lightheaded. "What do you mean permanent?"

"Permanent. As in, it won't peel away after a while."

"No, I didn't tell him that!" This is *not* happening! "I didn't know I had to. You mean all that work, all that pain will have to be re-done? I don't...I just...I'm...."

Josiah was suddenly laughing. Wait. Why is he *laughing?* "Crimson," he gasped, still chuckling. "Sweetie...relax. I'm just messing with you. The peeling is normal." He chuckled again. "It's your body healing, that's all." I let my silence speak for itself. "Ah, c'mon." He cajoled. "Don't be mad."

"Jerkface."

"Sorry," he chuckled again, then sighed. "That was too good to pass up. I love you."

"You're still a jerkface." I grumbled, knowing I'd probably laugh about it later. "And I love you, too."

Chapter 18
Malice

*C*rimson Sage

Three weeks later, my tattoo had healed beautifully, and I was thoroughly pleased with it. Josiah, Ethan, and I were headed to North Carolina for Gracie's wedding and everything seemed to be going well. Both Josiah and I had a week off work for the event, and the ranch seemed to have settled into a peaceful state. The boys had all adjusted to the recent disappearances of Mike and Adam. And none of them needed summer school—I'd take that as a win. Daisy was fully healed and back to her old self. Billy was keeping her with him while we were gone. And to top it off, Charlene seemed to have moved out of the Salmon area. At least, neither Josiah nor I had seen her in several weeks.

God seemed to have smiled down on Gracie because the day of her wedding dawned bright and clear. Pete had even closed the coffee shop for the event so he and his family could be there. Everything went off without a hitch. Gracie was beautiful, radiant. And as I watched her dad walk her down the aisle toward her future, I had to blink back tears. Tears of happiness and sadness. I loved Gracie and was so happy for her. And Tanner obviously worshipped the ground she walked on. But I couldn't help but think of my own mom and dad. They would have been here with me. They *should* have been here with me.

Josiah caught my eye then, almost like he knew what I might have been thinking, like he knew I might be feeling some mixed emotions. He smiled and the look in his dark blue eyes gave me a surge of heat, of love. I was okay.

Josiah would make sure I was all right. With just a smile he could banish whatever fears and pain I was experiencing. I smiled back, swallowing my sadness. Taking a deep breath, I focused on the vows being spoken. Focused on the radiant happiness on Gracie's face. The way Tanner couldn't keep his eyes off her, the way he followed her every movement, hung on her every word. I felt the passion in his voice as he made his promises to her, heard the love and devotion in his words. And I couldn't be happier for my best friend.

Our trip to North Carolina only lasted four days this time. We'd arrived two days before the wedding and left the day after. And as much as Ethan enjoyed being at the beach, he was anxious to get back to Daisy. I'd tried to reassure him that all was well and there was nothing to worry about, but Ethan responded like a first-time mom away from her newborn. Josiah and I teased him a little about it, but he took it all in stride.

We arrived back in Salmon a week before the fair started and Ethan was over the moon excited with all the cowboys in town. He happily watched all their fancy rigs as they rolled in. Billy made plans to take the ranch boys to the rodeo, and we all looked forward to the experience.

The comradery as of late felt very much like a family. A great big, mixed and blended family.

That thought hit me. That word. *Family*. It had been so long since I'd felt the closeness of a family. That sense of belonging, of having one's own people. And now, here, I had a huge one, full of love and laughter. Everything in my life had changed, and some changes were painful, but those changes brought about some of my biggest blessings and deepest happiness. And as I thought about Josiah, and our upcoming wedding, I realized just how big and wonderful this particular blessing was. Our future was bright. Our path was clear. The only thing on the horizon was love.

Back at work, as I was preparing a vanilla chai latte for a visiting cowboy, Tina slid a note to me, bumping my hip with hers. After handing the drink to him, he winked as he walked away, spurs jangling merrily, with a "Thanks, ma'am." I had a moment then, so read the note. "Parking lot" was all it said. Blushing, I assumed it was Josiah and quickly looked for him. Nope, wasn't Josiah. Charlene stood next to a sleek white Corvette, just staring at the Shack.

Her presence was a dark cloud over my bright sunshiny day. And things had been going so well. Ugh, why was she back here again? What did she want with me? Was she here to make weird comments and threats again? I almost called Josiah but decided not to. He'd warned me she would mess with me if she could. Well, I wouldn't give her the satisfaction. If she came inside, I'd serve her same as any other customer. Tina, I knew, would have my back.

And if she was still here when it was time to clock out, well, I could always call Josiah, then. Though, I was hesitant to alert him. He'd finally begun to relax and was letting me drive myself to and from work again. If her presence back here ruined that, I'd…well, I don't know what I'd do. But it would be something. Mentally, I laughed at me trying to be all tough as I filled two more orders. The bell over the door rang indicating yet another customer. Tina had said things picked up around Rodeo time, and she was right. Business was booming. I didn't mind though; it kept me busy.

My back was to the counter as I searched the various flavors of syrups, looking for sugar-free caramel. "Nice ink. Who's J and C?" asked a male voice from behind me. Glancing over my shoulder, I saw the vanilla chai cowboy from earlier was back again. He nodded at the tattoo on my shoulder.

"It's for Josiah and Crimson," I said, turning back around.

"Oh yeah?" he asked. "And who're they?"

"I'm Crimson," I replied.

"And I'm Josiah." Came the voice to my back. "Any more questions?"

I whipped around to see Josiah standing at the counter. His deep blue eyes were focused on the cowboy, who was in turn looking Josiah over. "Well, all right then." The cowboy rubbed at his jaw and shot me a glance. "You have a great day, ma'am." He tipped his hat at us then walked out.

I blinked, then turned to Josiah. "That was weird."

"Irritating is more like." Josiah grumbled, his gaze still on the cowboy who was now climbing into his rig.

Wanting to distract him from his irritation, I leaned on the counter and asked, "What's up?"

Josiah's gaze returned to me, the corner of his mouth lifting into a wolfish grin as his blue eyes traveled over my face and lower before flicking back up to meet mine. "Just wanted to see your face. Maybe steal a kiss or two."

I grinned, happy to see him, happy he was here. "Hmmm...you don't say..."

"When's your break?" Such intent in that simple question.

"Five minutes." My voice came out way too breathy, but it was all I could manage.

"I'll wait," he promised.

Less than five minutes later, we were sitting in Josiah's car, holding hands, and sipping the milkshakes he'd brought us. "Tina called." He took a sip as he gently squeezed my fingers. "Did she bother you in any way?"

I didn't need to ask who he meant. "Figures." I should have known Tina would let him know about Charlene.

"For what it's worth," his thumb rubbed against my palm. "I was already in town and on my way to see you when she called."

I sighed. "No, she never even came inside."

He finished his drink and turned in my direction. "You're off at four, right?"

"Yep." Nodding, I finished my own drink, swallowing down the last bit of cold, creamy chocolate goodness.

"I'll wait for you at the house." Josiah got out of his car, then walked around to open my door. "Then, after you're ready, we'll meet everyone at the rodeo."

I wrapped my arms around his middle, hugging him close as I buried my face against his chest. "Can't wait." Josiah kissed me, hands framing my face, mouth lingering over mine before letting me go. But not before making me promise to let him know if Charlene showed up again. Agreeing, I quickly returned to finish my shift.

Josiah

Josiah got back to the ranch just before Billy, Bentley, and the boys headed off to the fair. The big blue bus was parked in front of the house, the engine running.

"We'll see you in an hour or so," Josiah called to Billy as they pulled away. He couldn't help the smile that tugged at his lips. The boys' excitement was infectious, and he found it uplifting. Moving about the ranch, he completed his afternoon duties, thoughts on Crimson and the way her mouth had felt under his. Their wedding couldn't come soon enough. He wanted that woman. Wanted and needed her something fierce. Checking his watch, he saw she should be off work and heading home now. He had time, so he ran up and showered, before dressing for the rodeo. As he was headed down to wait for Crimson at the big house, his phone buzzed. He answered without looking at the display.

"Josiah?" The voice sounded stressed, or excited maybe.

"Yeah?" He paused on his way to the house.

"Hey, this is Simmons down the road; you got some horses out man."

"*Dangit*;" That's just what he needed. "Where at?"

"Western field—they're heading down the back road."

"All right." Crap. "Thanks; I'll get on it." Josiah quickly shot off a text to Crimson, letting her know he was running late, then jumped in the ranch truck, hoping to get them corralled without issue. It took him over thirty minutes to gather them and get them situated. He was surprised, by the time he was done, that he hadn't heard from Crimson. Locking the gate behind himself, he shot her a text letting her know he'd be there soon.

When ten minutes had passed and still no response, Josiah began to feel a tickling sensation at the base of his skull. Something was off. Suddenly, he felt an overwhelming need to get back to the house. It was imperative. Heart in his throat, he raced home, dust flying behind him.

Crimson Sage

Josiah's text said horses were out and he was running late, so utilizing that time, I showered and dressed, eager for him to see my new outfit. The red gingham blouse with short denim skirt paired well with my cowboy boots and the cute straw cowboy hat I'd picked up in town. After making sure I looked nice, I decided to wait in the barn, not wanting to get too sweaty before we left. Moving along the aisle, I scratched the horses' noses, murmuring softly to them as I went. Footsteps sounded outside; he was back. "I'm in here, babe," I called as I made my way to the front of the barn. Almost there, the door wrenched open, blinding me in the sudden bright sunshine. Blinking, I took in the large shadow standing in the doorway.

"Just where I always wanted you," said a voice that shot ice down my spine.

With a hand to my face, Mike shoved me backward further into the interior of the barn. Trembling, I stumbled but managed to stay on my feet. My heart raced as he moved closer and two others followed, closing the door behind them. "Get out," I whispered, though I'd tried making my voice hard.

Mike chuckled darkly. "Crimson, you and I are finally going to spend some quality time together."

"Josiah's on his way." I pulled my phone out, intending to show them, hoping to scare them into leaving. The hard hand slapping across my face caught me off guard, knocking the phone from my grip as I stumbled to the side. The horses moved restlessly in their stalls and my mouth tasted like copper. I tried not to panic, but fear had me by a choke hold.

"Hurry it up, Mike." Grumbled one of the other men as he loomed closer. "He ain't going to be gone that long." His leering eyes made my stomach turn. With a trembling hand, I faced the three of them and wiped the blood from my mouth.

Josiah

At the sight of the unfamiliar white corvette parked near the barn, Josiah slammed the truck to a stop as he leaped out. His eyes darted around. *Where were they?* "Crimson!" he yelled, his breath heaving out of him. A scream shattered the air, coming from the barn, and Josiah saw red.

Hurtling in that direction, he nearly ripped the door from its hinges as he flung it open. A tiny part of his mind cautioned this could be a trap, but he was too far past furious to care. Crimson was held down as Mike knelt between her legs. She struggled against him, trying to kick. Two men, strangers, helped to hold her as she bucked against them.

The first man never saw Josiah coming. Never saw the boot that landed to the side of his head knocking him out cold, never felt the one to his ribs for good measure. The second man, alerted to the commotion, spun, lunging upward, swiping for Josiah with a knife. Josiah stepped inside the swing, trapping the arm with the weapon against his body as he heaved upward, hearing the satisfying crunch as the elbow broke. The man screamed and the knife went flying, but Josiah wasn't finished. From the corner of his eye, he saw Mike and Crimson rolling, but his focus was on eliminating the target in front of him.

The man snarled as he cradled his broken arm against his body and lunged for Josiah again, trying to drive him back and off balance. Josiah brought a knee up into the man's face, then slammed his fist into his solar plexus, dropping him to the ground. There Josiah kicked him with enough force to snap the man's leg and end the fight. Two down.

Spinning, he froze as his eyes darted around trying to make sense of what he was seeing. Crimson sat hunched on the ground, shaking. Her clothes were torn and all askew. Blood was smeared across her cheek. Her neck. Her forearms and hands. In her grip she held tightly to an equally bloody knife. Several feet away, Mike lay on his back, unmoving, eyes wide open, staring at nothing. His neck and shirt were coated with blood from the wound in his throat. His pants were unzipped, bunched some, but not pulled down, though his disgusting intent was obvious.

Josiah moved to him, placed two fingers against his throat, feeling for a pulse. Nothing. *Good.* Turning, he carefully approached Crimson, keeping his movements slow and even so as not to startle her. As he neared, she tensed, her grip on the knife tightening. "Little Red," he said softly. "Baby, it's me." Josiah slowly lowered himself to her eye level. "Let me help, Crimson." A tremor flitted across her face, and she trembled again. "Can you put the knife down, Baby?" His heart was breaking. "*Please?*" He needed to hold her, needed her to know she was okay, but she wouldn't look at him. Her gaze had shifted to Mike. "He's gone." Josiah told her, keeping his voice level. "Dead."

"Good."

Crimson Sage

Good. I didn't know where to look. I wasn't even sure what I was seeing. Then my gaze snagged, landing on the knife in my hands. Josiah wanted me to put it down. Could I? Mike was dead. He couldn't hurt me anymore. His blood was all over the knife, covering the blade and hilt. My hands. I didn't want his blood on my hands. Drop the knife, Crimson. Open your hands and drop it. *Drop it!* My fingers flinched as I forced my hands open, almost shoving the knife away. My breath labored in lungs that struggled to find a rhythm, but I heard Josiah's sigh of relief. Moving carefully, he pulled the knife away, out of my reach.

Suddenly, one of the other men groaned and I flinched back from Josiah, my eyes darting towards the sound. "I need to take care of them." He kept his voice low, calm. "I'm not leaving, though. I'm right here. Just sit tight, okay?"

I nodded as the tremors grew in intensity and wrapped my arms tighter around myself. Josiah moved out of sight quickly then. I heard a solid thud, another, a groan, silence, then the sound of dragging. I don't know how long he was gone. My mind was fragmented. Images, sounds. I could separate the sound of my own breathing. I knew that sound. Josiah was back then, kneeling in front of me, bringing a trace of cool night air and woodsmoke. "May I touch you, Crimson? I need to get you out of here."

"Yes," I whispered as I shook.

"Can you tell me where you hurt?" Josiah moved carefully closer. "Are you injured anywhere?"

I jerked my chin in the negative. "He...he didn't...I wasn't." I shook my head again. "I'm not hurt."

I couldn't decipher the look in his eye at my statement but caught his stuttered intake of breath as he carefully looked me over. Then, still moving slow, like I was a frightened, wild animal, Josiah removed his flannel and wrapped it around my shoulders. "I'm going to lift you now. Tell me if anything hurts, okay?" Gently, so gently, he gathered me into his arms and lifted. Holding me as if I were made of glass and might shatter, he carried me to one of the chairs near his firepit. There, a fire was already blazing warmly. He must have lit it when he dragged those men out. He'd smelled of smoke when he came back...and though I felt the heat from the flames, I couldn't seem to stop shaking. Like I was fevered. Josiah shifted slightly, tenderly pulling me closer, deeper into his embrace. "I've got you. I've got you, Crimson." He repeated that line over and over, a mantra for my tattered heart.

We sat there for what seemed forever, waiting. For the police to arrive, for me to stop shaking, I didn't know, but still Josiah held me. "You survived, Crimson. Again. You're strong. So strong, Baby. You'll survive this as well. I'll be here to help you."

I tried to nod my head, to agree with him, but the trembling was too much. I didn't have the strength. Josiah adjusted his grip, holding me tighter. "Shower," I whimpered; I wanted to be clean, wanted the blood off. "I'm so cold."

"I know you are, Babe, and I'm sorry, but you're going to need to hold on a little longer. We can't contaminate any evidence. The police will be here soon."

In the distance, and fast approaching, were the sirens. Soon, flashing lights lit up the yard. Suddenly, we were surrounded by a cacophony of noises, voices telling Josiah he'd need to let me go. Telling me I needed to let go of him. But I couldn't. If he let go, if I let go, there'd be no putting me back together again. I needed him like I needed air in my lungs, so I clung to him, burying my face against his chest. He was my strength. I wouldn't survive this without him. One of the medics was trying to pry my arms away, to reason with me, saying they needed to assess me and make sure I was all right, but I just held on tighter.

A strange noise suddenly pierced the night, sharp and high pitched, and shattering. It took a little while to register the noise was coming from me—*I* was shattering. Josiah held me closer, rocking me in his embrace. "Sh, sh, shhhhh...Crimson. It's okay; I'm right here. You're safe." He turned to those closest to us. "Just give her some room! Give her some space. Please."

"She's gonna need a sedative," the medic told his partner, who agreed. Moments later, he turned back with a syringe in hand. As the medic pulled my arm away, Josiah held me closer, trying to reassure me. "It's okay, Crimson. They're just trying to help." His mouth was at my ear, his voice trying to soothe. "You're so strong, you can do this. You're the strongest person I know. I love you, Crimson. Do you hear me? *I love you.*"

There. Josiah spoke the only words that could get through to me. He loved me. I was strong, and I would survive, and he loved me. I barely registered the tiny prick in my arm, but soon began to feel warm. My head felt heavy, and I blinked, trying to stay awake. The last thing I remembered was Josiah's mouth tenderly touching mine before everything went dark.

Chapter 19
Sunrise

Josiah

Josiah couldn't get the images out of his head. Couldn't silence the sound of her terrified scream; his ears rang with it.

When he'd stepped inside the barn, when he'd seen Crimson on the floor, Mike hunched over her. When he'd seen the blood on her face, the fear in her eyes, he'd lost it. He had no clear memory of his actions or intent, other than to get to Crimson, to save her. He remembered the first man dropping. Remembered the sound of bone breaking. He remembered the knife flying to the side.

By the time he'd turned back to Crimson and Mike, whatever had happened between them was done. Mike had been lying on his back, blood soaking the ground around him from the wound in his throat. Crimson was seated several feet from him, that knife in hand.

He'd had to swallow the bile, the horror, the rage that wanted to consume him. Emotions rioted, nearly crippling him. But no. Crimson needed him. Needed him now, and he had to be strong for her. The helplessness at watching her go through this, and being entirely unable to help, unable to take it away, was excruciating.

His eyes trailed over her sleeping form as he listened to the heart monitor, taking in the bruised torn lip with one tiny, neat stitch in it. He continued downward, knowing she was bruised along her collarbone and rib cage. Her thighs, wrist, and ankles. And found a new emotion surging through him. Gratitude. He was so *thankful* he'd made it back in time.

Thankful Mike had been stopped before he could do anything. He was simply thankful.

Billy always kept his Bible with him, carrying it everywhere. Josiah thought about that worn, leather-bound book. About what it represented. *Who* it represented. Faith, belief of this nature was not something that came easy to Josiah. And yet, he felt a stirring in his breast. A seeking. A reverence. Such profound gratitude. Bowing his head, letting it rest on the bed beside Crimson, he gently took her hand in his, and prayed. Simply, with heartfelt emotion, he expressed his gratitude, thanking God for His mercy and protection.

Crimson Sage

Bright lights stunned my eyes when I blinked them open. It took me far too long for comfort to recall what had happened and where I was. Leaning forward, I moved to sit up, but a blinding pain in my side had me groaning and slumping back.

Suddenly, Josiah was leaning over me. "Crimson? Hey, Baby. Don't move; okay? Just hold still."

"My head..." I croaked, the pounding in my skull now making itself known. The more alert I became, the more pain I discovered. Everything hurt. Tears pricked my eyes, and I bit back a whimper.

"I know, Baby." He threaded our fingers together. "I know... I'm sorry. The doctors say you have a mild concussion and several bruised ribs. You should try to hold still as much as possible."

"How...how long have I been here?" That was the most confusing thing. I remembered bits and pieces, but how *long* ago those events happened was bothering me most.

Josiah carefully lifted my hand, brushing his lips across the back of it. Then he smoothed a thumb along my jaw. "Do you remember what happened?"

Emotion surged, blurring my vision, but I managed a tiny nod. "Mike is dead."

Josiah's gaze stayed glued to mine. "Yes."

I swallowed, trying to keep my breathing calm. "The others?"

Josiah ground his jaw, before speaking in a measured tone. "Once they came to, they were taken into custody and have been booked into the county jail." He inhaled, held it, then let it slowly out, as if he was struggling. "This was all last night. You've been here not quite a day." No doubt at the confused look on my face as I tried to piece the timeframe together, he gently squeezed my hand. "The medics gave you a mild sedative last night. You were...understandably upset. Red called Billy and he and Ethan came down here. They left a couple hours ago, but should be back soon. I think you'll be able to go home today."

"When?" I whispered, hating the thought of what seeing me like this might do to them.

He shrugged. "The doctor still needs to do his eval, and Red needs your statement. Then, if there're no complications, I think you'll be released."

I nodded, then cleared my throat, before looking for something to drink. Seemingly anticipating my need, Josiah handed the water cup to me. Cool water slid down my parched throat and as I swallowed, felt a burning, pulling sensation there. My hand moved automatically tracing the bandage there.

"It's just a scratch, not deep. No stitches." Josiah reassured, even as he clenched his jaw, anguish clearly evident in his eyes. He kissed the tips of my fingers. "I wish I could take all this away. Make it better somehow. I wish there was something I could say, something I could do. Crimson...I hate this, hate being so useless!"

I smiled, trying to be brave, feeling the tug at my lip as I did. "You're not useless."

"I feel pretty useless...." Violence laced his words, and I knew it was not directed at me.

"You saved me." This time, I squeezed his hand, needing him to know this truth. "Again."

He bowed his head as he groaned, "I was almost too late."

I brushed fingers through his hair, trying to comfort us both. "No, you were right on time—just when I needed you, you were there."

Josiah shook his head, clearly not seeing things as I saw them. "I wasn't. Not in time—you were hurt."

All this time Josiah had been my strength, my rock. It hurt me to see him like this. To see him this broken. "You told me you loved me. Remember?"

He captured my hand, bringing it to his face as he kissed my palm. "Of course."

Tears threatened again. "I needed that, needed to hear that. Those words...Josiah, those words mean *everything* to me. You mean everything to me."

"I love you, Crimson Sage Smyth." He rose, leaned over, and tenderly touched his lips to mine. "I love you."

The doctor came about forty minutes later, ascertaining whether I wanted Josiah in the room or not for my evaluation, and of course I did. All in all, that took about thirty-five minutes. Once done, he said he'd be back to discharge me as soon as the paperwork was ready. Not quite ten minutes later, Red showed up to take my statement. Josiah held my hand as I recounted what I recalled, his thumb brushing back and forth, soothing. Red was patient, gently asking each question to get the clearest picture to present to the prosecuting attorney.

When he was done, Red thanked me. "You're a brave one, you know that, right?" I simply nodded, not feeling very brave. He gently patted my shoulder on his way out. "I'll send Billy and Ethan in; they're waiting." Ethan's eyes were red and swollen and Billy didn't look a whole lot better. Ethan nearly lunged for me, but Josiah cautioned him to slow down on account of my injuries. But bruised ribs or not, I reached for my brother, holding him close.

"I was so scared, Sage. So scared." His voice trembled as he tucked his head against my neck, clearly fighting tears, not wanting to cry in front of me.

"I'm okay, Kid." I kissed the top of his head. "I'm okay. Josiah made it in time. And Mike won't be bothering us anymore. I promise."

Ethan sniffed and shuddered before pulling away. Nodding, he swallowed as he backed up. Billy took my hand as he gently placed a kiss on my forehead. "You gave me a terrible scare...." He cleared his throat and shook his head, then patted my hand before he inhaled, then let it go.

We were, all of us, still in a state of shock. From experience, I knew time was what we needed. Healing. And time. Mike was no longer a threat, and that truth alone had me breathing easier. Still, a hospital, with all its disinfected atmosphere, was not a comfortable place to be, and I just wanted to go home. I wanted to shower and wash the grime and memory away.

Not too long after, the nurse brought my discharge papers and pain meds. Once I had them signed, I was able to gather my things. Not that I had much. My clothing and shoes had been taken as evidence. Billy had brought a pair of sweats and a T-shirt for me along with a pair of flip-flops.

As we pulled into the ranch yard and the barn came into view, I suddenly tensed. My heart began to pound, and my breath kept catching in my throat. Josiah felt the tension in my frame where I leaned against him in the backseat. His arms around me tightened carefully. "It's all right. You're safe." I nodded, knowing this, but couldn't help the fear that trembled through me. "Hey, how about you stay with me tonight?" Josiah whispered against my ear.

"Please." I somehow managed past the hard lump in my throat.

I was slow getting out of the car, my ribs protesting profusely. But as I stood, the ranch yard was suddenly filled with happy, anxious faces—all the boys wanting to see me. Josiah and I reassured them I was okay, just a little sore and tired. But I was strong and would heal. Josiah also told Billy I was staying with him tonight. Billy nodded in understanding. Ethan looked at me, carefully checking to make certain I was all right and not just trying to be brave. Pulling him close for a hug, I told him I'd see him tomorrow.

Taking my hand, Josiah led me to his loft. He matched his pace to my shuffling steps, as I took several slow shallow breaths, trying to keep the pain, the memories at bay. Josiah unlocked the door to his loft and held it for me. "Are you able to shower on your own?"

I chuckled, blushing. "I think I can manage it, and don't make me laugh."

"Holler if you need anything; I'll be right here. I know you're about ready for pain meds; I can see it in your eyes."

I nodded before carefully hobbling into the bathroom, closing the door behind me. Staying the night here as much as I had, I'd started keeping some of my clothes here just in case I ever needed them. And as I cautiously stepped into Josiah's shower, knowing I had clean clothes to wear once I was done, I was fervently thankful.

Dinner was pretty much ready by the time I left the bathroom. After my shower, I'd stood in front of Josiah's mirror, getting a first glimpse of my body since...since the attack. I could find nothing beautiful about it. With trembling lips, I'd closed my eyes against my reflection and simply breathed. Fighting for calm. There was no way to hide what had been done and I couldn't help but wonder what Josiah might think. How he'd react. Would he be repulsed? Would he be too afraid to touch me? To kiss me? I inhaled once more, holding it until my ribs ached, then slowly let it back out. Josiah was waiting; I needed to go.

The aroma of grilled cheese and tomato soup had my stomach rumbling in need as I stepped from the bathroom. Josiah'd lit candles and opened the big bay window to allow the cool evening breeze to flow in. We ate in silence, just taking our time, each seemingly lost in our own heads. After dinner, we moved to the couch and without a word, Josiah picked up his comb and began working through the tangles in my hair.

After several minutes of silence, he tenderly traced the shell of my ear and kissed my temple. "Penny for your thoughts?"

I tried to smile, but it felt a little wobbly. "I was going to ask you the same; you've been quiet tonight."

Josiah moved to sit beside me and turned his head to study me. His eyes searched mine thoroughly, carefully. Then after a lengthy moment, he stood and reached for me. Careful of my tender ribs, he pulled me to my feet, then lifted and carried me into the bathroom. He flicked on the lights, then stood me in front of the mirror. We stared at my reflection for a moment, the bright light doing nothing to hide the kaleidoscope of colors on my skin. Bending, he inhaled against the back of my head, then brushed my hair aside as he kissed the side of my neck. Turning me to face him, he kissed over each bruise and laceration on my face. He kissed the ones on my shoulders, my collarbone. My arms and wrists.

Lifting the hem of my shirt to expose my abdomen, he paused as I tensed. The bruises were especially bad here. Echoes of Mike's fist hitting me sounded and I clenched my eyes against the sight. But it was too late. I'd seen and so had Josiah. Large fingerprint marks marred the surface of my skin. Both along my ribs and along my collarbone. Ugly marks from an ugly man. I tried to keep the trembling at bay but was unable to control the tears.

Josiah slid his arms around me, careful not to cause pain. "Crimson, *stop*; I see that look in your eyes." He kissed my forehead. "*You* are perfect. Beautiful. Brave. Mike may have marked your body, but those marks will fade in time. If I had the power, I'd take them away. In a heartbeat, I'd do it." He embraced me then, wrapping his arms around me. Simply held me until the trembling subsided. When it did, he shifted, turning me to face him. Then, looking me in the eye, he kissed each and every visible mark on my body. And with each press of his lips, he softly rubbed his thumb over the wound and said, "You are beautiful. His marks will fade—and he was not the last one to touch you—*I was*. And I've covered these marks with my own hands. Hands that love you, Crimson; hands that will protect you. And these hands will never hurt you."

His words were a healing balm. One, I'd desperately needed. His words and actions helped me reject the idea I was somehow damaged goods. His touch made a lie of the notion Josiah might no longer want me. And I was able to see a glimpse of the woman he claimed me to be. He sparked my courage. He filled me with light, with hope, with acceptance, with love. I felt a little like a snake as it sheds its skin, sloughing off the old and dead to reveal the new. Inhaling slowly, deeply, I held my breath for as long as I could before the pain became too much. What he'd said allowed me to release the dread and shame I felt over how I looked and what had happened. With those words, I shed it like the cold dead skin of memory that it was now.

We settled back on the couch, and after a few minutes of silence, Josiah breathed into my hair. "I'm sure you have internal bruising that I can't reach with my hands, so let my words touch them—don't let Mike hurt you any more than he already has. Don't give him that power. Don't be afraid to face this ranch, or the barn. Don't let him steal your peace and joy away."

Leaning into his embrace as much as my ribs allowed, I buried my face in his chest, listening to his heartbeat, letting it soothe me. I'd come so far this last year with everything that had happened, and now, I'd be lying if I said I was fine. I knew there'd be moments when I'd question whether I'd survive this, too. But Josiah would be here. Strong. And capable.

And now, here, in the peaceful silence of his loft, Josiah was once again calling me back from the edge, keeping me safe. He faced my fears beside me and helped me conquer them. He took what was ugly in my life and somehow made it beautiful. Made me feel beautiful. Made me feel complete and whole. I wasn't sure how he managed it, but Josiah had that gift. His words gave me the will to live, not just to survive, but to really live.

Gently he cupped my face, bringing my mouth up to his. Carefully, so he wouldn't hurt me, he kissed my bruised lips, letting his linger over mine.

"I *love* you, Crimson," he breathed into me, igniting me, and fanning the flames between us, bringing me to life. I'd been so lost before, but Josiah had found me.

Epilogue

Ethan was adjusting his dark red bowtie again. He shrugged his shoulders, shifting his feet, uncomfortable in his suit, uncomfortable in front of the crowd of guests. He just had to be patient for a little while longer, then he could move. Grace glanced to her left. Josiah seemed uncomfortable as well. Though, he was impatient for a completely different reason. She couldn't help but grin at their antics. Josiah was waiting for his bride, needing to see her. That much was evident by the look on his face. Grace wondered if he'd cry when she appeared. Music played softly in the background—The Dixie Cups and *Chapel of Love*. Sage had wanted a Fifties-themed wedding. And that's what she'd gotten.

The Ranch yard had been transformed in preparation for the ceremony; chairs were set up, and deep red and gray bows adorned the aisle. She heard Josiah take a deep breath, hold it, then slowly let it out, trying to settle his nerves. The song would be ending soon and that would be Sage's cue to walk down the aisle to her future husband. Josiah had asked Ethan to be his best man and a few moments ago he'd walked Grace down the aisle, and they'd taken their places as Josiah and Sage's only attendants. Now they were waiting for Billy to bring Sage out the back door.

They'd stuck to tradition, Josiah and Sage, to not see each other before the vows. The song finished playing; a moment's pause and then the familiar Bridal Chorus began. Everyone stood and faced the back of the house.

The door opened and Billy stepped out—he looked good in a tux—Grace was impressed.

Sage was beautiful. Radiant. Her dress was a close replica of one she'd found from a magazine clipping her mother had saved for a wedding she'd never had. The dress was candlelight, with lace sleeves over a sweetheart bodice. It had a full skirt that stopped just at Sage's calves. She carried red roses. Her veil was short, just coming to her waist as was custom for the period. Grace couldn't help the tears that welled, thinking of Sage's parents, and all that Sage had overcome to be here today. Grace knew Terri would have been so proud of her daughter.

Just then, Grace heard a long, trembling breath being sucked in, then suddenly choked off. Yes, those were indeed tears streaming down the man's face. Josiah. The tough guy. The feral wolf. Was crying.

Honestly, Grace didn't think there was a dry eye in the house as Billy gave his granddaughter away in marriage—something he'd never been able to do with his only daughter, Terri. And as she stood there and watched her best friend say her vows, she couldn't help but think just how right the world was.

"I now pronounce you husband and wife—you may kiss your bride," the pastor stated a few minutes later. Josiah took another deep breath, then lifted Sage's veil. Tenderly he cupped her face, his thumb lightly grazing her lip. Grace watched as he leaned down and kissed Sage. She was sure Josiah had meant to keep the kiss chaste, they were in front of the pastor, after all. But kissing was a thing with them, a weakness, and suddenly he was dragging her against him; their mouths moving urgently together.

"Oh crap." Grace hoped they'd pull it together and remember they had an audience. But did they? No, they didn't. She tapped Josiah on the shoulder. "Hello? We're all still here. Watching you." When that only produced a growling response, Grace tried another tactic. "Sage? Sweetie? You're ruining your makeup. Come on you two; come up for air already."

Still nothing. No stopping. Drastic measures and all that. "I'm going to eat your cake, Sage. I swear I am." This time Sage pulled back a little.

Oxygen must have begun to filter through their brains, allowing them to become aware of the loud catcalls and snickering from their audience. Sage hid her head against Josiah's chest. Grace chuckled at their expense. "Oh no, no more of that. Come on; I'm hungry, and we all want cake. Besides, in about three hours, you can do that and more to your little heart's content."

That, more than anything, seemed to have snagged Josiah's attention. Squaring his shoulders, he dutifully led Sage back down the aisle to thunderous applause and a bright and happy future. Though, everyone present would swear, he seemed to be counting the seconds until they could finally be alone.

The End

If you enjoyed this book, would you PLEASE do me the honor of leaving a review? Reviews mean so much to authors. Especially Indie authors. In advance, let me simply thank you.

Read on for a sneak peek at book two in the Beauty from Ashes series, featuring Cam, Fynn, and Rafe from book one.

In Matters of the Heart – Fynn's Story

✳ *This is rough draft, so yes, you MAY find errors, and yes, this may change from the final piece. Still, I hope you enjoy this glimpse into Fynn's story.*
Chapter ONE

Fynn was convinced God hated him. Either that, or He had a wicked sense of humor. How else might one explain losing the girl he'd been certain he was in love with just last year, watching her walk down the aisle and everything. And now, here he was in full Viking costume, complete with faux fur, woad paint, and battle ax—in the middle of July, he might add—standing with hands braced on the bed rail of his truck, feet spread shoulder-width apart, while being patted down by local law enforcement.

"He's clean." The officer finished his search and stepped back.

"Can I put my hands down now?" Fynn shot a dark look over his shoulder at the sergeant in charge. Who also just happened to be his ex-best friend from high school. At one point, he and Dirk had been practically brothers and joined at the hip. That all went to hell when Fynn had discovered Ellen, Dirk's little sister, had grown up. And then, six months after that, Dirk had found the two of them together. Hence the *ex* in that relationship. Oh, nothing had happened between Fynn and Ellen, just some heated kisses, but Dirk had blown a casket and flipped his literal top. Needless to say, the relationship between Fynn and Ellen hadn't lasted long after that explosion. She'd gone away to med-school and they'd lost touch.

Fynn shot Dirk another dark look. He'd really like Ellen. Maybe even more than he had Sage. He'd tried to keep the line of communication open, but she'd resisted, hating the tension, anger, and hurt that continued boiling over the affair.

"We've got probable cause, search the truck." Dirk sneered, no doubt enjoying every aspect of this.

"Dispatch said the perp was wearing red, like a fireman." One of the officers replied.

"The perp had an ax. *He* has an ax. Search the truck." Dirk moved closer, taking Fynn's right hand in his, placing a cuff on that wrist. "Don't give me a reason to take you down, Carson. Cooperate, and this will probably be over with soon."

"Finally living out your wildest fantasies, huh?" Fynn grit his teeth in irritation as the other cuff was placed, then he was walked to the patrol car so the search could be conducted.

"What kind of sick freak, are you, Carson?" Dirk looked him over, contempt written clearly in his tone and on his face. "What statement are you trying to make here?"

"It's called a costume, idiot. You know, for a costume party?"

"In *July?*"

"Hey, I didn't make the event, I was just attending. An accident at Twelve and Admiral had me running late, so I cut over to Croatan, and now here I am."

"Landers," the officer that had patted him down called. "Dispatch says the perp was spotted going north on Twelve. This ain't our guy. Let's go."

Fynn chuckled darkly, curled his lip, and winked at Dirk. "Now that smarts, doesn't it?"

Dirk spun Fynn around to get at the handcuffs. Leaning in, he growled, "Stay away from my sister."

"Ellen isn't even in Nags Head."

"Yeah, you just go on believing that if you know what's good for you." The cuffs came off, and Dirk pushed Fynn away as he backed up. With one last angry look at Fynn, the officers piled back into their patrol cars and sped away.

Fynn stared after them, absentmindedly rubbing at his wrists. He climbed back in his truck and sat there for a minute, wondering. What had Dirk meant by his last statement? Shaking his head, he restarted the truck and headed north again, hoping he wasn't too late for the costume party. Though he had to admit, he wasn't that interested in going any longer, to be honest. Darn Dirk anyway. Always ruining his fun. If Fynn didn't know better, he'd think Dirk quite literally kept an eye out for him just to cause problems. *Jerk.*

All for what? Because he'd caught his baby sister and Fynn locking lips? So what. She'd been eighteen. Wasn't like she was a kid or anything. And *man,* she'd been a good kisser. Even back then. When she'd been so young and inexperienced. They both had been. Fynn sighed. That was a long time ago. Water under the bridge, as they say.

Shifting mental gears, he thought about the woman he was going to see tonight...what was her name again? Jenna? Tina? Laura? Something with an 'uh' at the end. *Crap.* He was starting to sound like Rafe. What was he even doing? Going to a costume party in the middle of July? Really? In all fairness, she'd been cute and had come on to him. They'd literally bumped into each other as she was coming from his parents' coffee shop, Freaky Pete's. After the awkward apologies, she'd asked if he was local. He'd ended up walking with her along the boardwalk as they talked and ended up exchanging numbers. Then she'd invited him to the costume party she was hosting for her twenty-first birthday. He'd almost said, no. Twenty-one? Six years younger than his ripe old age of twenty seven. Or nearly twenty-seven. And truthfully, it wasn't that big an age gap. Though, he still somehow felt he was far older than she was. And yet, he'd allowed himself to be talked into going to this stupid party.

Why did he do things like this? Fynn shook his head, then took the next exit, turning the truck around and heading back home. Besides, this blue paint was really starting to itch. And tomorrow, he was scheduled to work at the coffee shop for the opening shift, then had Beach Watch for the afternoon. He was tired and getting too old for this stuff.

Chapter TWO

Ellen pulled on her scrubs, smoothing her hands over the plum-colored fabric, then pinned on her name tag. Looking in the mirror, she let her green eyes move over her reflection, giving herself a pep talk. *You've got this. You look good. Hair is...hair. It's...there and...covers your head. Just like it's supposed to.* She sighed as she ran a critical eye over it, trying not to note how she'd had the same style for the last six years. That is to say, she'd worn it in a ponytail. Nothing fancy. Just a simple ponytail. For six years. In all honesty, she hadn't had a lot of time for anything else, nor had she had the heart for it. She'd been on exactly three dates in that time. Three single dates. With three different men. No one held any attraction for her.

He had, though. She still thought of him. Wondered how he was. If he'd married and settled down by now. He probably had a couple of kids already. That thought brought both a smile and a heartache. She'd hoped once, long ago, to be that person for him. Sighing, turning from the mirror, she tucked her mahogany wisps back behind her ears, marveling yet again, despite how much hairspray she used to tame it, she still ended up with flyaways. *He'd* always liked her hair. Had said it was the first thing he'd noticed about her when he'd begun to notice her as a woman. The second thing had been her legs. He'd spent ample time that summer with his hands in her hair and all over her legs.

She'd always loved his hands. Loved the way he'd made her feel. Wanted. Safe. Like a woman. Like she was the *only* woman. Her heart gave another pang for what might have been. And she blinked the moisture from her eyes, then checked to make sure her mascara was still in place. Thinking of him had put some color in her cheeks, lightening the scattering of freckles there. He'd always said they'd reminded him of a galaxy. His own personal galaxy. He'd trace them, making up names for various groupings he swore were there as he traced them with his finger.

Ellen pulled herself from her reminiscing and checked the time. She needed to get going; she didn't want to be late her first day at work. She'd debated long and hard about taking this job. It was a cut in pay, for sure, but it brought her home and her mother wasn't getting any younger. Last year's pulmonary issues aside, Ellen wanted to be close to her. To help her and keep an eye on her. It'd been hard on her mom since their father passed two years ago. So, despite the continued strained relations with Dirk, Ellen had applied for the opening and moved home.

Dirk. He'd ruined everything. Why, even after all this time, could he still not see that? Still not see how fully he'd broken his own sister's heart. Regardless, Mom needed her. Blinking, then squaring her shoulders, Ellen jerked her chin in affirmation, then grabbed her purse and headed out the door.

Four days later, and some eight plus hours into her ten-hour shift, Sandi found Ellen behind the nurses' station doing paperwork. Sandi, Ellen guessed, was in her later forties and had been the one to hire Ellen. She was an open book with a blond pixie cut and light blue-grey eyes. Sandi was on the shorter side stature-wise but made up for it with her big personality. "Oh, good, you're free." Sandi huffed as she rushed up, glancing over her shoulder. "Hurry before anyone gets in there and claims him." She fanned her face with the clipboard in hand. "He's. A. *Looker!*"

Ellen chuckled. "You're a married woman, Sandi. I'll tell Sam on you." She'd talked about her twenty-year marriage to her high school sweetheart Sam nearly every day since Ellen had met her.

"Not for me, silly. *You.*" Sandi pulled her to her feet, trying to shove her down the hall to the waiting patient. "You're young, attractive, and single, and I saw no ring on *his* finger."

Ellen sighed inwardly. Why was every woman over the age of forty she came in contact with determined to see her married off. Even back at her old job, they were like this. Despite their best efforts, nothing ever came of it. Ellen sighed again, then rolled her eyes as she pulled the curtain open. And felt her heart clean stop in her chest. Why did life have to be this way?

Author's Note, Part Two

F or God has not given us a spirit of fear, but of power, and of love, and of a sound mind.

2 Timothy 1:7 NKJV

Dear Reader, you beautiful, beautiful soul,

Life (and our eternal enemy) can sure throw some tough hits. I know; I've been there and have walked those paths. As shared earlier, I was an abused child. It was my mother who abused me. Physically, mentally, and verbally. At nine years old, as I prayed to God to make her stop, I couldn't figure out *why* He didn't. Why He seemed silent. Distant. Uncaring. That abuse continued for close to five years, until finally it had reached such an extreme, that the courts had to remove me and my siblings from her custody. My dad then received custody of us and began taking us to church. At nine years old, I couldn't see what God was doing and how He was working in my life. But *He* knew what He was doing.

If God had stopped the abuse, no doubt I would have remained in my mother's custody. And she'd wanted NOTHING to do with God. She took me to seances and made me pray to a mother-father god. She encouraged me to be sexually deviant and exposed me to all sorts of sexually depraved things. I don't share this for you to despise my mother. She, herself, had been an abused child, by her own mother, and in far crueler ways than I had experienced. And she wasn't given the relief that I received with my dad. More important than all of that, I share this so that you might have hope in dark circumstances. So that your faith may be strengthened.

With God's grace, I was able to forgive her. Truly forgive her. And I loved her deeply and miss her to this day.

So, claim that Scripture above. Imbed it in your consciousness and remind yourself of it daily. God loves you, and He is ALWAYS working to bring you closer to Him.

Acknowledgements

Where do I begin? I think the best place is with a *heartfelt* thank you, to you, The Reader. Without you, I couldn't do what I do. So, thank you for walking this journey with me, and for reading my books and hopefully falling in love with these characters.

I want to thank my Beta Readers. Your insight is SO incredibly helpful, and I appreciate you more than you can possibly know. So, thank you to, Amanda, Mary, Cortney, Kym, and Dawn, you ladies are fabulously outstanding and your insight is invaluable.

Thank you to Kristin Vayden for your mad editing skills, for loving these characters, and this story. Thank you for always helping me to see it from a different angle, and for guiding me to make it so much better.

Again, Jena Brignola, you've taken thoughts in my head and somehow, magically, you've made them reality. Your cover skills are insane. Thank you.

To, Rachel, at Closed Door Romance, thank you for your excellent skills in the marketing department. You do SUCH a wonderful job pulling scenes and quotes. It blows my mind how you highlight those moments so succinctly. Thank you.

Now, to my family. To my husband and best friend, William, thank you. To my sons, Aaron and Andrew, thank you. To my daughter Lindsay and my bonus son, Hunter, thank you. I couldn't life without you all. You are essential to me, never doubt it.

And finally, to my Lord and Savior, Jesus Christ, truly, Lord, I can do nothing apart from You. You make this all possible. Thank You for the gifts You've given me, and Lord, let me always use them to Your glory. Amen.

About the Author

A child of divorce and abuse, E. L. Irwin found escape in reading and writing. She's a self-described romantic-rebel who wears her heart on her sleeve and tends to shoot from the hip on subjects that matter. E.L. lives in the Pacific Northwest on a small farm with her husband, children, and four dogs. When not reading or writing romance, E.L. enjoys riding horses, going for drives, tattoos, antique shopping, starry nights, the smell and sound of rain, a deep red wine, a smooth whisk(e)y, camping, bonfires, and hanging out with her horses, cows, chickens, ducks, and goats.

NEWSLETTER SIGNUP:

S can the code to signup for my monthly newsletter and receive first-hand knowledge of upcoming projects, release news, and giveaways. When you sign up, you'll receive the prequel chapters for Out of the Blue, book 1 in the Blues Avenue series, where you get to meet Kate and Asher before they meet in the story.

www.ingramcontent.com/pod-product-compliance
Lightning Source LLC
Chambersburg PA
CBHW032351310726

48973CB00007B/1960